"And now," I said, "we[...] Stonehenge, and you're [...] on your next birthday."

"Remember the entry in the journal, Legion?" Foster said. "'I came to the place of the Hunters, and it was a place I knew of old, and there was no hive, but a Pit built by men of the Two Worlds . . .'"

I glanced at the screen. "Here's another big number for you. That object on the screen is at an altitude—give or take a few percent—of thirty thousand miles." A pattern of dots flashed across the screen, faded, flashed again. . . . Foster watched the screen, saying nothing.

"I don't like that thing blinking at us," I said. I looked at the big red button beside the screen. Without waiting to think it over, I jabbed at it. On the screen, the red blip separated, a smaller blip moving off at right angles to the main mass.

"It looks like I've launched a bomb from the ship overhead," I said in a strained voice.

The climb back up the tunnel took three hours, and every foot of the way I was listening to a refrain in my head: This may be it; this may be it; this may be . . .

I crawled out of the tunnel mouth, then grabbed Foster's arm and pointed overhead. "What's that?"

Foster looked up. A brilliant point of blue light, brighter than a star, grew perceptibly as we watched. "That's no bomb," he said. "It's coming down slowly . . . like a—"

We watched as the vessel settled into place dead center on the ancient ring of stones. A slit of yellow light appeared on the side of the hull, then it widened to a square. A ladder extended itself, dropping down to touch the ground.

"If somebody with tentacles starts down that ladder," I said, in an unnaturally shrill voice, "I'm getting out of here."

"No one will emerge," Foster said quietly. "I think we'll find, Legion, that this ship of space is at our disposal."

—from *A Trace of Memory*

LEGIONS OF
SPACE

KEITH LAUMER

edited & compiled by
ERIC FLINT

preface by
JOEL ROSENBERG

LEGIONS OF SPACE

Copyright © 2004 to Baen Books.

A Trace of Memory was first published as a serialized story in *Amazing* magazine (July–September 1962) and then reissued as a novel by Berkley in 1963. *Planet Run*, coauthored with Gordon R. Dickson, was first published in 1967 by Doubleday. "The Choice" was first published in *Analog* in July, 1969. "Three Blind Mice" was first published in *The Many Worlds of Science Fiction* (Ben Bova, ed.), E.P. Dutton, 1971. "Mind Out of Time" was first published as "The Mind Out of Time" in *The Farthest Reaches* (Joseph Elder, ed.), Trident 1968. "Message to an Alien" was first published in *Analog* in June, 1970.

A Baen Books Original

Baen Publishing Enterprises
P.O. Box 1403
Riverdale, NY 10471
www.baen.com

ISBN: 0-7434-8855-5

Cover art by Jeff Easley

First printing, October 2004

Distributed by Simon & Schuster
1230 Avenue of the Americas
New York, NY 10020

Production by Windhaven Press, Auburn, NH (www.windhaven.com)
Printed in the United States of America

CONTENTS

Preface

by Joel Rosenberg

During a time when some major writer first makes his—or, rarely, her—splash in SF, like some star flaring suddenly into a nova, there's an understandable tendency to let your eyes get dazzled by that, and not quite see the other stars that burn, stably if not nearly so visibly, year after year.

Or, to try analogy instead of metaphor—the field is created not just by the work of the master, but by the journeyman, as well.

Like, say, Keith Laumer, one of the great journeyman writers of the field, although that's sometimes hard to remember. The Retief stories have made such a strong impact and provided so many good catch-phrases ("I thought the nuances were the best part" is my own favorite) that it's sometimes easy to forget the other stories, and when people think of other Laumer stories, all too often, they're thinking of the Bolo stories, and stopping there.

Which is a shame. Those less well-known stories are a whole lot of fun, in fact, and well worth the bother. Sure; looking back in time, the early sixties are much more marked by *Stranger in a Strange Land*, *The Man in the High Castle*, *Glory Road* and *Dune* than *A Trace of Memory*—but that's not the point; the workmanlike Laumer story is still a fun ride more than forty years later.

You'll see some of the same things over and over again, and frankly, some of them can be annoying— like the always-similar tough-guy talk, which does wear pretty thin on early twenty-first-century ears. But more, you'll see the details—Laumer was always obsessed with the details of how things are done, whether it's climbing a wall, or escaping from being entombed. And if Heinlein had his Competent Man, and Poul Anderson his Man Who Counts, Laumer has his Guy Who Gets Things Done, and it's always fun to watch that theme get played out, over and over again, in all sorts of different variations.

Like these stories.

Oh, they're not without flaws. There's a few things just plain wrong with *A Trace of Memory*, for example. It's really just too much story for a 66,000-word novel, for one, and, geez, having a character "My Name is Legion," when it turns out that, well, that's just the character's name? There's a few more flaws that I'm sure are there, but can't quite name.

Flaws and all, and it's classic Laumer: a character who, once started, just won't give up, even when he's not always sure what it is that he's refusing to give up, and it's about time it got back into print for a whole new generation or two who missed it the first time.

Without giving anything away, I think that I know the old joke that Laumer was working from in writing "The Choice"—and it's not a bad joke. Just light, although there's some echoes of the minor characters in the Retief stories, who just can't think things through.

"Three Blind Mice," "Mind Out of Time," and "Message to an Alien" are all worth reading, as classic Laumer—and if you think that the latter story doesn't have some implications for modern politics, think again. Please think again.

The real gem, though, in this collection is *Planet Run*, written with Gordy Dickson. It's hard to say enough good about this one; it's got both Laumer's and Gordy's strengths, but blended so seamlessly that it's just about impossible to say who wrote what. I would have thought that the Kipling reference was Gordy's, but I have it on the best authority that bringing it in was Laumer's idea; Gordy and I discussed the story over lunch one day.

When people write the history of science fiction, they understandably tend to focus on the novas and supernovas of the field—Heinlein, Doc Smith, Niven & Pournelle, Varley, Gibson, and Vinge. And that's understandable.

For me, there's lots to be learned and a lot of fun to be had from going back and spending an afternoon with an accomplished journeyman writer like Keith Laumer, and I'm glad I did.

You'll be glad, too. Enjoy.

—Joel Rosenberg

A TRACE OF MEMORY

Prologue

He awoke and lay for a moment looking up at a low ceiling, dimly visible in a faint red glow, feeling the hard mat under his back. He turned his head, saw a wall and a panel on which a red indicator light glared.

He swung his legs over the side of the narrow couch and sat up. The room was small, grey-painted, unadorned. Pain throbbed in his forearm. He shook back the loose sleeve of the strange purple garment, saw a pattern of tiny punctures in the skin. He recognized the mark of a feeding Hunter . . . Who would have dared?

A dark shape on the floor caught his eye. He slid from the couch, knelt by the still body of a man in a purple tunic stained black with blood. Gently he rolled the body onto its back.

Ammaerln!

He seized the limp wrist. There was a faint pulse. He rose—and saw a second body and, near the door, two more. Quickly, he went to each . . .

All three were dead, hideously slashed. Only Ammaerln still breathed, faintly.

He went to the door, shouted into the darkness. The ranged shelves of a library gave back a brief echo. He turned back to the grey-walled room, noticed a recording monitor against a wall. He fitted the neurodes to the dying man's temples. But for this gesture of recording Ammaerln's life's memories, there was nothing he could do. He must get him to a therapist—and quickly.

He crossed the library, found a great echoing hall beyond. This was not the Sapphire Palace beside the Shallow Sea. The lines were unmistakable: he was aboard a ship, a far-voyager. Why? How? He stood uncertain. The silence was absolute.

He crossed the Great Hall and entered the observation lounge. Here lay another dead man, by his uniform a member of the crew. He touched a knob and the great screens glowed blue. A giant crescent swam into focus, locked; soft blue against the black of space. Beyond it a smaller companion hung, gray-blotched, airless. What worlds were these?

An hour later he had ranged the vast ship from end to end. In all, seven corpses, cruelly slashed, peopled the silent vessel. In the control sector the communicator lights glowed, but to his call there was no answer from the strange world below.

He turned to the recording room. Ammaerln still breathed weakly. The memory recording had been completed; all that the dying man remembered of his long life was imprinted now in the silver cylinder. It remained only to color-code the trace.

His eyes were caught by a small cylinder project-
ing from the aperture at the side of the high couch
where he had awakened—his own memory trace! So
he himself had undergone the Change. He took the
color-banded cylinder, thrust it into a pocket—then
whirled at a sound. A nest of Hunters, swarming globes
of pale light, clustered at the door. Then they were on
him. They pressed close, humming in their eagerness.
Without the proper weapon he was helpless.

He caught up the limp body of Ammaerln. With the
Hunters trailing in a luminous stream he ran with his
burden to the shuttle-boat bay.

Three shuttles lay in their cradles. He groped to a
switch, his head swimming with the sulfurous reek of
the Hunters; light flooded the bay, driving them back.
He entered the lifeboat, placed the dying man on a
cushioned couch.

It had been long since he had manned the controls
of a ship, but he had not forgotten.

Ammaerln was dead when the lifeboat reached the
planetary surface. The vessel settled gently and the lock
cycled. He looked out at a vista of ragged forest.

This was no civilized world. Only the landing ring
and the clearing around it showed the presence of man.

There was a hollow in the earth by a square marker
block at the eastern perimeter of the clearing. He
hoisted the body of Ammaerln to his back and moved
heavily down the access ladder. Working bare-handed,
he deepened the hollow, placed the body in it, scraped
earth over it. Then he rose and turned back toward
the shuttle boat.

Forty feet away, a dozen men, squat, bearded,
wrapped in the shaggy hides of beasts, stood between
him and the access ladder. The tallest among them
shouted, raised a bronze sword threateningly. Behind

these, others clustered at the ladder. Motionless he watched as one scrambled up, reached the top, disappeared into the boat. In a moment the savage reappeared at the opening and hurled down handfuls of small bright objects. Shouting, others clambered up to share the loot. The first man again vanished within the boat. Before the foremost of the others had gained the entry, the port closed, shutting off a terrified cry from within.

Men dropped from the ladder as it swung up. The boat rose slowly, angling toward the west, dwindling. The savages shrank back, awed.

The man watched until the tiny blue light was lost against the sky.

Chapter One

The ad read: *Soldier of fortune seeks companion in arms to share unusual adventure. Foster, Box 19, Mayport.*

I crumpled the newspaper and tossed it in the general direction of the wire basket beside the park bench, pushed back a slightly frayed cuff, and took a look at my bare wrist. It was just habit; the watch was in a hock shop in Tupelo, Mississippi. It didn't matter. I didn't have to know what time it was.

Across the park most of the store windows were dark along the side street. There were no people in sight; they were all home now, having dinner. As I watched, the lights blinked off in the drug store with the bottles of colored water in the window; that left the candy and cigar emporium at the end of the line. I fidgeted on the hard bench and felt for a cigarette I didn't have.

I wished the old boy back of the counter would call it a day and go home. As soon as it was dark enough, I was going to rob his store.

I wasn't a full-time stick-up artist. Maybe that's why that nervous feeling was playing around under my rib cage. There was really nothing to it. The wooden door with the hardware counter lock that would open almost as easily without a key as with one; the sardine-can metal box with the day's receipts in it. I'd be on my way to the depot with fare to Miami in my pocket ten minutes after I cracked the door. I'd learned a lot harder tricks than petty larceny back when I had a big future ahead with Army Intelligence. That was a long time ago, and I'd had a lot of breaks since then—none good.

I got up and took another turn around the park. It was a warm evening, and the mosquitoes were out. I caught a whiff of frying hamburger from the Elite Café down the street. It reminded me that I hadn't eaten lately. There were lights on at the Commercial Hotel and one in the ticket office at the station. The local police force was still sitting on a stool at the Rexall talking to the counter girl. I could see the .38 revolver hanging down in a worn leather holster at his hip. All of a sudden, I was in a hurry to get it over with.

I took another look at the lights. All the stores were dark now. There was nothing to wait for. I crossed the street, sauntered past the cigar store. There were dusty boxes of stogies in the window and piles of homemade fudge stacked on plates with paper doilies under them. Behind them, the interior of the store looked grim and dead. I looked around, then turned down the side street toward the back door—

A black sedan eased around the corner and pulled in to the curb. A face leaned over to look at me through lenses like the bottoms of Tabasco bottles. The hot evening air stirred, and I felt my damp shirt cold against my back.

"Looking for anything in particular, Mister?" the cop said.

I just looked at him.

"Passing through town, are you?" he asked.

For some reason I shook my head.

"I've got a job here," I said. "I'm going to work—for Mr. Foster."

"What Mr. Foster?" The cop's voice was wheezy, but relentless; a voice used to asking questions.

I remembered the ad—something about an adventure; Foster, Box 19. The cop was still staring at me.

"Box nineteen," I said.

He looked me over some more, then reached across and opened the door. "Better come on down to the station house with me, Mister," he said.

At Police Headquarters, the cop motioned me to a chair, sat down behind a desk, and pulled a phone to him. He dialed slowly, then swiveled his back to me to talk. There was an odor of leather and unwashed bedding. I sat and listened to a radio in the distance wailing a sad song.

It was half an hour before I heard a car pull up outside. The man who came through the door was wearing a light suit that was neither new nor freshly pressed, but had that look of perfect fit and taste that only the most expensive tailoring can achieve. He moved in a relaxed way, but gave an impression of power held in reserve. At first glance I thought he was in his middle thirties, but when he looked my way I saw the fine lines around the blue eyes. I got to my feet. He came over to me.

"I'm Foster," he said, and held out his hand. I shook it.

"My name is Legion," I said.

The desk sergeant spoke up. "This fellow says he come here to Mayport to see you, Mr. Foster."

Foster looked at me steadily. "That's right, Sergeant. This gentleman is considering a proposition I've made."

"Well, I didn't know, Mr. Foster," the cop said.

"I quite understand, Sergeant," Foster said. "We all feel better, knowing you're on the job."

"Well, you know," the cop said.

"We may as well be on our way then," Foster said. "If you're ready, Mr. Legion."

"Sure, I'm ready," I said. Mr. Foster said goodnight to the cop and we went out. On the pavement in front of the building I stopped.

"Thanks, Mr. Foster," I said. "I'll comb myself out of your hair now."

Foster had his hand on the door of a deceptively modest-looking cabriolet. I could smell the solid leather upholstery from where I stood.

"Why not come along to my place, Legion," he said. "We might at least discuss my proposition."

I shook my head. "I'm not the man for the job, Mr. Foster," I said. "If you'd like to advance me a couple of bucks, I'll get myself a bite to eat and fade right out of your life."

"What makes you so sure you're not interested?"

"Your ad said something about adventure. I've had my adventures. Now I'm just looking for a hole to crawl into."

"I don't believe you, Legion." Foster smiled at me, a slow, calm smile. "I think your adventures have hardly begun."

I thought about it. If I went along, I'd at least get a meal—and maybe even a bed for the night. It was better than curling up under a tree.

"Well," I said, "a remark like that demands time for an explanation." I got into the car and sank back in a seat that seemed to fit me the way Foster's jacket fit him.

"I hope you won't mind if I drive fast," Foster said. "I want to be home before dark." We started up and wheeled away from the curb like a torpedo sliding out of the launching tube.

I got out of the car in the drive at Foster's house, and looked around at the wide clipped lawn, the flower beds that were vivid even by moonlight, the line of tall poplars and the big white house.

"I wish I hadn't come," I said. "This kind of place reminds me of all the things I haven't gotten out of life."

"Your life's still ahead of you," Foster said. He opened the slab of mahogany that was the front door, and I followed him inside. At the end of a short hall he flipped a switch that flooded the room before us with soft light. I stared at an expanse of pale grey carpet about the size of a tennis court, on which rested glowing Danish teak furniture upholstered in rich colors. The walls were a rough-textured grey; here and there were expensively framed abstractions. The air was cool with the heavy coolness of air conditioning. Foster crossed to a bar that looked modest in the setting, in spite of being bigger than those in most of the places I'd seen lately.

"Would you care for a drink?" he said.

I looked down at my limp, stained suit and grimy cuffs.

"Look, Mr. Foster," I said. "I just realized something. If you've got a stable, I'll go sleep in it—"

Foster laughed. "Come on; I'll show you the bath."

❖   ❖   ❖

I came downstairs, clean, showered, and wearing a set of Foster's clothes. I found him sitting, sipping a drink and listening to music.

"The *Liebestod*," I said. "A little gloomy, isn't it?"

"I read something else into it," Foster said. "Sit down and have a bite to eat and a drink."

I sat in one of the big soft chairs and tried not to let my hand shake as I reached for one of the sandwiches piled on the coffee table.

"Tell me something, Mr. Legion," Foster said. "Why did you come here, mention my name—if you didn't intend to see me?"

I shook my head. "It just worked out that way."

"Tell me something about yourself," Foster said.

"It's not much of a story."

"Still, I'd like to hear it."

"Well, I was born, grew up, went to school—"

"What school?"

"University of Illinois."

"What was your major?"

"Music."

Foster looked at me, frowning slightly.

"It's the truth," I said. "I wanted to be a conductor. The army had other ideas. I was in my last year when the draft got me. They discovered I had what they considered an aptitude for intelligence work. I didn't mind it. I had a pretty good time for a couple of years."

"Go on," Foster said. Well, I'd had a bath and a good meal. I owed him something. If he wanted to hear my troubles, why not tell him?

"I was putting on a demonstration. A defective timer set off a charge of H-E fifty seconds early on a one-minute setting. A student was killed; I got off easy with a busted eardrum and a pound or two of gravel embedded in my back. When I got out of the

hospital, the army felt real bad about letting me go—
but they did. My terminal leave pay gave me a big
weekend in San Francisco and set me up in business
as a private investigator.

"I had enough left over after the bankruptcy proceedings a few months later to get me to Las Vegas.
I lost what was left and took a job with a casino
operator named Gonino.

"I stayed with Gonino for nearly a year. Then one
night a visiting bank clerk lost his head and shot him
eight times with a .22 target pistol. I left town the same
night.

"After that I sold used cars for a couple of months
in Memphis; then I made like a life guard at Daytona;
baited hooks on a thirty-foot tuna boat out of Key West;
all the odd jobs with low pay and no future. I spent
a couple of years in Cuba; all I got out of that was
two bullet scars on the left leg, and a prominent
position on a CIA blacklist.

"After that things got tough. A man in my trade can't
really hope to succeed in a big way without the little
blue card in the plastic cover to back his play. I was
headed south for the winter, and I picked Mayport to
run out of money."

I stood up. "I sure enjoyed the bath, Mr. Foster, and
the meal, too—I'd like real well to get into that bed
upstairs and have a night's sleep just to make it complete; but I'm not interested in the job." I turned away
and started across the room.

"Legion," Foster said. I turned. A beer bottle was
hanging in the air in front of my face. I put a hand
up fast and the bottle slapped my palm.

"Not bad set of reflexes for a man whose adventures
are all behind him," Foster said.

I tossed the bottle aside. "If I'd missed, that would
have knocked my teeth out," I said angrily.

"You didn't miss—even though you're weaving a little from the beer. And a man who can feel a pint or so of beer isn't an alcoholic—so you're clean on that score."

"I didn't say I was ready for the rummy ward," I said. "I'm just not interested in your proposition—whatever it is."

"Legion," Foster said, "maybe you have the idea I put that ad in the paper last week on a whim. The fact is, I've been running it—in one form or another—for over eight years."

I looked at him and waited.

"Not only locally—I've run it in the big-city papers, and in some of the national weekly and monthly publications. All together, I've had perhaps fifty responses."

Foster smiled wryly. "About three quarters of them were from women who thought I wanted a playmate. Several more were from men with the same idea. The few others were hopelessly unsuitable."

"That's surprising," I said. "I'd have thought you'd have brought half the nuts in the country out of the woodwork by now."

Foster looked at me, not smiling. I realized suddenly that behind the urbane façade there was a hint of tension, a trace of worry in the level blue eyes.

"I'd like very much to interest you in what I have to say, Legion. I think you lack only one thing—confidence in yourself."

I laughed shortly. "What are the qualifications you think I have? I'm a jack-of-no-trades—"

"Legion, you're a man of considerable intelligence and more than a little culture; you've traveled widely and know how to handle yourself in difficult situations—or you wouldn't have survived. I'm sure your training includes techniques of entry and fact-gathering not known to the average man; and perhaps most important, although you're an honest man, you're capable of breaking the law—when necessary."

"So that's it," I said.

"No, I'm not forming a mob, Legion. As I said in the ad—this is an unusual adventure. It may—probably will—involve infringing various statutes and regulations of one sort or another. After you know the full story I'll leave you to judge whether it's justifiable."

If Foster was trying to arouse my curiosity, he was succeeding. He was dead serious about whatever it was he was planning. It sounded like something no one with good sense would want to get involved in—but on the other hand, Foster didn't look like the sort of man to do anything foolish . . .

"Why don't you tell me what this is all about?" I said. "Why would a man with all this—" I waved a hand at the luxurious room—"want to pick a hobo like me out of the gutter and talk him into taking a job?"

"Your ego has taken a severe beating, Legion—that's obvious. I think you're afraid that I'll expect too much of you—or that I'll be shocked by some disclosure you may make. Perhaps if you'd forget yourself and your problems for the moment, we could reach an understanding—"

"Yeah," I said. "Just forget my problems . . ."

"Chiefly money problems, of course. Most of the problems of this society involve the abstraction of values that money represents."

"Okay," I said. "I've got my problems, you've got yours. Let's leave it at that."

"You feel that because I have material comfort, my problems must of necessity be trivial ones," Foster said. "Tell me, Mr. Legion: have you ever known a man who suffered from amnesia?"

✧　　　✧　　　✧

Foster crossed the room to a small writing desk, took something from a drawer, then looked at me.

"I'd like you to examine this," he said.

I went over and took the object from his hand. It was a small book, with a cover of drab-colored plastic, unornamented except for an embossed design of two concentric rings. I opened the cover. The pages were as thin as tissue, but opaque, and covered with extremely fine writing in strange foreign characters. The last dozen pages were in English. I had to hold the book close to my eyes to read the minute script:

January 19, 1710. Having come nigh to calamity with the near lofs of the key, I will henceforth keep this journal in the English tongue . . .

"If this is an explanation of something, it's too subtle for me," I said.

"Legion, how old would you say I am?"

"That's a hard one," I said. "When I first saw you I would have said the late thirties, maybe. Now, frankly, you look closer to fifty."

"I can show you proof," Foster said, "that I spent the better part of a year in a military hospital in France. I awakened in a ward, bandaged to the eyes, and with no memories whatever of my life before that day. According to the records made at the time, I appeared to be about thirty years of age."

"Well," I said, "amnesia's not so unusual among war casualties, and you seem to have done pretty well since."

Foster shook his head impatiently. "There's nothing difficult about acquiring material wealth in this society, though the effort kept me well occupied for a number of years—and diverted my thoughts from the question of my past life. The time came, however, when I had the leisure to pursue the matter. The clues I had were meager enough; the notebook I've shown you was found near me, and I had a ring on my finger." Foster held out his hand. On the middle finger was a massive signet, engraved with the same design of concentric circles I had seen on the cover of the notebook.

"I was badly burned; my clothing was charred. Oddly enough, the notebook was quite unharmed, though it was found among burned debris. It's made of very tough stuff."

"What did you find out?"

"In a word—nothing. No military unit claimed me. I spoke English, from which it was deduced that I was English or American—"

"They couldn't tell which, from your accent?"

"Apparently not; it appears I spoke a sort of hybrid dialect."

"Maybe you're lucky. I'd be happy to forget my first thirty years."

"I spent a considerable sum of money in my attempts to discover my past," Foster went on. "And several years of time. In the end I gave it up. And it wasn't until then that I found the first faint inkling."

"So you did find something," I said.

"Nothing I hadn't had all along. The notebook."

"I'd have thought you would have read that before you did anything else," I said. "Don't tell me you put it in the bureau drawer and forgot it."

"I read it, of course—what I could read of it. Only a relatively small section is in English. The rest is a cipher. And what I read seemed meaningless—quite unrelated to me. You've glanced through it; it's no more than a journal, irregularly kept, and so cryptic as to be little better than a code itself. And of course the dates; they range from the early eighteenth century through the early twentieth."

"A sort of family record, maybe," I said. "Carried

on generation after generation. Didn't it mention any
names, or places?"

"Look at it again, Legion," Foster said. "See if you
notice anything odd—other than what we've already
discussed."

I thumbed through the book again. It was no more
than an inch thick, but it was heavy—surprisingly heavy.
There were a lot of pages—I shuffled through hundreds of closely written sheets, and yet the book was
less than half used. I read bits here and there:

*"May 4, 1746. The Voyage was not a Succefs. I must
forsake this avenue of Enquiry . . ."*

*"October 23, 1790. Builded the weft Barrier a cubit
higher. Now the fires burn every night. Is there no limit
to their infernal perfiftence?"*

*"January 19, 1831. I have great hopes for the Phila-
delphia enterprise. My greatest foe is impatience. All
preparations for the Change are made, yet I confefs
I am uneasy . . ."*

"There are plenty of oddities," I said. "Aside from
the entries themselves. This is supposed to be old—
but the quality of the paper and binding beats anything
I've seen. And that handwriting is pretty fancy for a
quill pen—"

"There's a stylus clipped to the spine of the book,"
Foster said. "It was written with that."

I looked, pulled out a slim pen, then looked at
Foster. "Speaking of odd," I said. "A genuine antique
early colonial ball-point pen doesn't turn up every
day—"

"Suspend your judgment until you've seen it all,"
Foster said.

"And two hundred years on one refill—that's not
bad." I riffled through the pages, then I tossed the
book onto the table. "Who's kidding who, Foster?" I
said.

"The book was described in detail in the official record, of which I have copies. They mention the paper and binding, the stylus, even quote some of the entries. The authorities worked over it pretty closely, trying to identify me. They reached the same conclusion as you—that it was the work of a crackpot; but they saw the same book you're looking at now."

"So what? So it was faked up some time during the war—what does that prove? I'm ready to concede it's forty years old—"

"You don't understand, Legion," Foster said. "I told you I woke up in a military hospital in France. But it was an AEF hospital and the year was 1918."

Chapter Two

I glanced sideways at Foster. He didn't look like a nut . . .

"All I've got to say it," I said, "you're a hell of a spry-looking ninety."

"You find my appearance strangely youthful. What would be your reaction if I told you that I've aged greatly in the past few months? That a year ago I could have passed as no older than thirty without the slightest difficulty—"

"I don't think I'd believe you," I said. "And I'm sorry, Mr. Foster; but I don't believe the bit about the 1918 hospital either. How can I? It's—"

"I know. Fantastic. But let's go back a moment to the book itself. Look closely at the paper; it's been examined by experts. They're baffled by it. Attempts to analyze it chemically failed—they were unable to take a sample. It's impervious to solvents—"

"They couldn't get a sample?" I said. "Why not just tear off the corner of one of the sheets?"

"Try it," Foster said.

I picked up the book and plucked at the edge of one of the blank sheets, then pinched harder and pulled. The paper held. I got a better grip and pulled again. It was like fine, tough leather, except that it didn't even stretch.

"It's tough, all right," I said. I took out my pocket knife and opened it and worked on the edge of the paper. Nothing. I went over to the bureau and put the paper flat against the top and sawed at it, putting my weight on the knife. I raised the knife and brought it down hard. I didn't so much as mark the sheet. I put the knife away.

"That's some paper, Mr. Foster," I said.

"Try to tear the binding," Foster said. "Put a match to it. Shoot at it if you like. Nothing will make an impression on that material. Now, you're a logical man, Legion. Is there something here outside ordinary experience or is there not?"

I sat down, feeling for a cigarette I still didn't have.

"What does it prove?" I said.

"Only that the book is not a simple fraud. You're facing something which can't be dismissed as fancy. The book exists. That is our basic point of departure."

"Where do we go from there?"

"There is a second factor to be considered," Foster went on. "At some time in the past I seem to have made an enemy. Someone, or something, is systematically hunting me."

I tried a laugh, but it felt out of place. "Why not sit still and let it catch up with you? Maybe it could tell you what the whole thing is about."

Foster shook his head. "It started almost thirty years ago," he said. "I was driving south from Albany,

New York, at night. It was a long straight stretch of road, no houses. I noticed lights following me. Not headlights—something that bobbed along, off in the fields along the road. But they kept pace, gradually moving alongside. Then they closed in ahead, keeping out of range of my headlights. I stopped the car. I wasn't seriously alarmed, just curious. I wanted a better look, so I switched on my spotlight and played it on the lights. They disappeared as the light touched them. After half a dozen were gone, the rest began closing in. I kept picking them off. There was a sound, too, a sort of high-pitched humming. I caught a whiff of sulphur then, and suddenly I was afraid—deathly afraid. I caught the last one in the beam no more than ten feet from the car. I can't describe the horror of the moment—"

"It sounds pretty weird," I said. "But what was there to be afraid of? It must have been some kind of heat lightning."

"There is always the pat explanation," Foster said. "But no explanation can rationalize the instinctive dread I felt. I started up the car and drove on—right through the night and the next day. I sensed that I must put distance between myself and whatever it was I had met. I bought a home in California and tried to put the incident out of my mind—with limited success. Then it happened again."

"The same thing? Lights?"

"It was more sophisticated the next time. It started with interference—static—on my radio. Then it affected the wiring in the house. All the lights began to glow weakly, even though they were switched off. I could feel it—feel it in my bones—moving closer, hemming me in. I tried the car; it wouldn't start. Fortunately, I kept a few horses at that time. I mounted and rode into town—and at a fair gallop, you may be sure. I saw

.

the lights, but outdistanced them. I caught a train and kept going."

"I don't see—"

"It happened again; four times in all. I thought perhaps I had succeeded in eluding it at last. I was mistaken. I have had definite indications that my time here is drawing to a close. I would have been gone before now, but there were certain arrangements to be made."

"Look," I said. "This is all wrong. You need a psychiatrist, not an ex-tough guy. Delusions of persecution—"

"It seemed obvious that the explanation was to be found somewhere in my past life," Foster went on. "I turned to the notebook, my only link. I copied it out, including the encrypted portion. I had photostatic enlargements made of the initial section—the part written in unfamiliar characters. None of the experts who have examined the script have been able to identify it.

"I necessarily, therefore, concentrated my attention on the last section—the only part written in English. I was immediately struck by a curious fact I had ignored before. The writer made references to an Enemy, a mysterious 'they,' against which defensive measures had to be taken."

"Maybe that's where you got the idea," I said. "When you first read the book—"

"The writer of the log," Foster said, "was dogged by the same nemesis that now follows me."

"It doesn't make any sense," I said.

"For the moment," Foster said, "stop looking for logic in the situation. Look for a pattern instead."

"There's a pattern, all right," I said.

"The next thing that struck me," Foster went on, "was a reference to a loss of memory—a second point of some familiarity to me. The writer expresses frustration at the inability to remember certain facts which would have been useful to him in his pursuit."

"What kind of pursuit?"

"Some sort of scientific project, as nearly as I can gather. The journal bristles with tantalizing references to matters that are never explained."

"And you think the man that wrote it had amnesia?"

"Not exactly amnesia, perhaps," Foster said. "But there were things he was unable to remember."

"If that's amnesia, we've all got it," I said. "Nobody's got a perfect memory."

"But these were matters of importance; not the kinds of thing that simply slip one's mind."

"I can see how you'd want to believe the book had something to do with your past, Mr. Foster," I said. "It must be a hard thing, not knowing your own life story. But you're on the wrong track. Maybe the book is a story you started to write—in code, so nobody would accidentally read the stuff and kid you about it."

"Legion, what was it you planned to do when you got to Miami?"

The question caught me a little off-guard. "Well, I don't know," I hedged. "I wanted to get south, where it's warm. I used to know a few people—"

"In other words, nothing," Foster said. "Legion, I'll pay you well to stay with me and see this thing through."

I shook my head. "Not me, Mr. Foster. The whole thing sounds—well, the kindest word I can think of is 'nutty.'"

"Legion," Foster said, "do you really believe I'm insane?"

"Let's just say this all seems a little screwy to me, Mr. Foster."

"I'm not asking you just to work for me," Foster said. "I'm asking for your help."

"You might as well look for your fortune in tea leaves," I said, irritated. "There's nothing in what you've told me."

"There's more, Legion. Much more. I've recently made an important discovery. When I know you're with me, I'll tell you. You know enough now to accept the fact that this isn't entirely a figment of my imagination."

"I don't know anything," I said. "So far it's all talk."

"If you're concerned about payment—"

"No, damn it," I barked. "Where are the papers you keep talking about? I ought to have my head examined for sitting here humoring you. I've got troubles enough—" I stopped talking and rubbed my hands over my scalp. "I'm sorry, Mr. Foster," I said. "I guess what's really griping me is that you've got everything I think I want—and you're not content with it. It bothers me to see you off chasing fairies. If a man with his health and plenty of money can't enjoy life, what the hell is there for anybody?"

Foster looked at me thoughtfully. "Legion, if you could have anything in life you wanted, what would you ask for?"

"Anything? I've wanted a lot of different things. Once I wanted to be a hero. Later, I wanted to be smart, know all the answers. Then I had the idea that a chance to do an honest job, one that needed doing, was the big thing. I never found that job. I never got smart either, or figured out how to tell a hero from a coward, without a program."

"In other words," Foster said, "you were looking for an abstraction to believe in—in this case, Justice. But you won't find justice in nature. It's a thing that only man expects or acknowledges."

"There are some good things in life; I'd like to get a piece of them."

"Don't lose your capacity for dreaming, in the process."

"Dreams?" I said. "Oh, I've got those. I want an island somewhere in the sun, where I can spend my time fishing and watching the sea."

"You're speaking cynically—but you're still attempting to concretize an abstraction," Foster said. "But no matter—materialism is simply another form of idealism."

I looked at Foster. "But I know I'll never have those things—or that Justice you were talking about, either. Once you really know you'll never make it . . ."

"Perhaps unattainability is an essential element of any dream," Foster said. "But hold onto your dream, whatever it is—don't ever give it up."

"So much for philosophy," I said. "Where is it getting us?"

"You'd like to see the papers," Foster said. He fished a key ring from an inner pocket. "If you don't mind going out to the car," he said, "and perhaps getting your hands dirty, there's a strong-box welded to the frame. I keep photostats of everything there, along with my passport, emergency funds and so on. I've learned to be ready to travel on very short notice. Lift the floorboards; you'll see the box."

"It's not all that urgent," I said. "I'll take a look in the morning—after I've caught up on some sleep. But don't get the wrong idea—it's just my knot-headed curiosity."

"Very well," Foster said. He lay back, sighed. "I'm tired, Legion," he said. "My mind is tired."

"Yeah," I said, "so is mine—not to mention other portions of my anatomy."

"Get some sleep," Foster said. "We'll talk again in the morning."

❖   ❖   ❖

I pushed back the light blanket and slid out of bed. Underfoot, the rug was as thick and soft as a working girl's mink. I went across to the closet and pushed the button that made the door slide aside. My old clothes were still lying on the floor where I had left them, but I had the clean ones Foster had lent me. He wouldn't mind if I borrowed them for a while longer—it would be cheaper for him in the long run. Foster was as looney as a six-day bike racer, but there was no point in my waiting around to tell him so.

The borrowed outfit didn't include a coat. I thought of putting my old jacket on but it was warm outside and a grey pin-stripe with grease spots wouldn't help the picture any. I transferred my personal belongings from the grimy clothes on the floor, and eased the door open.

Downstairs, the curtains were drawn in the living room. I could vaguely make out the outline of the bar. It wouldn't hurt to take along a bite to eat. I groped my way behind the bar, felt along the shelves, found a stack of small cans that rattled softly. Nuts, probably. I reached to put a can on the bar and it clattered against something I couldn't see. I swore silently, felt over the obstruction. It was bulky, with the cold smoothness of metal, and there were small projections with sharp corners. It felt for all the world like—

I leaned over it and squinted. With the faint gleam of moonlight from a chink in the heavy curtains falling just so, I could almost make out the shape; I crouched a little lower, and caught the glint of light along the perforated jacket of a .30 caliber machine gun. My eye followed the barrel, made out the darker square of the entrance hall, and the tiny reflection of light off the polished brass doorknob at the far end.

I stepped back, flattened against the wall, with a

hollow feeling inside. If I had tried to walk through that door . . .

Foster was crazy enough for two ordinary nuts. My eyes flicked around the room. I had to get out quickly before he jumped out and said *Boo!* and I died of heart failure. The windows, maybe. I came around the end of the bar, got down and crawled under the barrel of the gun and over to the heavy drapes, pushing them aside. Pale light glowed beyond the glass. Not the soft light of the moon, but a milky, churning glow that reminded me of the phosphorescence of sea water . . .

I dropped the curtain, ducked back under the gun into the hall, and pushed through a swinging door into the kitchen. There was a faint glow from the luminous handle of the refrigerator. I yanked it open, spilling light on the floor, and looked around. Plenty of gleaming white fixtures—but no door out. There was a window, almost obscured by leaves. I eased it open and almost broke my fist on a wrought-iron trellis.

Back in the hall, I tried two more doors, both locked. A third opened, and I found myself looking down the cellar stairs. They were steep and dark as cellar stairs always seem to be, but they might be the way out. I felt for a light switch, flipped it on. A weak illumination showed me a patch of damp-looking floor at the foot of the steps. It still wasn't inviting, but I went down.

There was an oil furnace in the center of the room, with dusty duct-work spidering out across the ceiling; some heavy packing cases of rough wood were stacked along one wall, and at the far side of the room, there was a boarded-up coal bin—but no cellar door.

I turned to go back up. Then I heard a sound and froze. Somewhere a cockroach scuttled briefly. Then I heard the sound again, a faint grinding of stone against stone. I peered through the cob-webbed shadows, my mouth suddenly dry. There was nothing.

The thing for me to do was to get up the stairs fast, batter the iron trellis out of the kitchen window, and run like hell. The trouble was, I had to move to do it, and the sound of my own steps was so loud it was paralyzing. Compared to this, the shock of stumbling over the gun was just a mild kick, like finding a whistle in your Cracker-jacks. Ordinarily I didn't believe in things that went bump in the night, but this time I was hearing the bumps myself, and all I could think about was Edgar Allen Poe and his cheery tales about people who got themselves buried before they were thoroughly dead.

There was another sound, then a sharp snap, and I saw light spring up from a crack that opened across the floor in the shadowy corner. That was enough for me. I jumped for the stairs, took them three at a time, and banged through the kitchen door. I grabbed up a chair, swung it around and slammed it against the trellis. It bounced back and cracked me across the mouth. I dropped it, tasting blood. Maybe that was what I needed. The panic faded before a stronger emotion—anger. I turned and barged along the dark hall to the living room—and lights suddenly went on. I whirled and saw Foster standing in the hall doorway, fully dressed.

"OK, Foster!" I yelled. "Just show me the way out of here."

Foster held my eyes, his face tense. "Calm yourself, Mr. Legion," he said softly. "What's happened here?"

"Get over there to that gun," I snapped, nodding toward the .30 caliber on the bar. "Disarm it, and then get the front door open. I'm leaving."

Foster's eyes flicked over the clothes I was wearing.

"So I see," he said. He looked me in the face again. "What is it that's frightened you, Legion?"

"Don't act so innocent," I said. "Or am I supposed to get the idea the brownies set up that booby trap while you were asleep?"

His eyes went to the gun and his expression tightened. "It's mine," he said. "It's an automatic arrangement. Something's activated it—and without sounding my alarm. You haven't been outside, have you?"

"How could I—"

"This is important, Legion," Foster rapped. "It would take more than the sight of a machine gun to panic you. What have you seen?"

"I was looking for a back door," I said. "I went down to the cellar. I didn't like it down there so I came back up."

"What did you see in the cellar?" Foster's face looked strained, colorless.

"It looked like . . ." I hesitated. "There was a crack in the floor, noises, lights . . ."

"The floor," Foster said. "Certainly. That's the weak point." He seemed to be talking to himself.

I jerked a thumb over my shoulder. "Something funny going on outside your windows, too."

Foster looked toward the heavy hangings. "Listen carefully, Legion," he said. "We are in grave danger— both of us. It's fortunate you arose when you did. This house, as you must have guessed by now, is something of a fortress. At this moment, it is under attack. The walls are protected by some rather formidable defenses. I can't say as much for the cellar floor; it's merely three feet of ferro-concrete. We'll have to go now—very swiftly, and very quietly."

"OK—show me," I said. Foster turned and went back along the hall to one of the locked doors where he pressed something. The door opened and I followed him inside a small room. He crossed to a blank wall, pressed against it. A panel slid aside—and Foster jumped back.

"God's wounds!" he gasped. He threw himself at the wall and the panel closed. I stood stock still; from somewhere there was a smell like sulphur.

"What the hell goes on?" I said. My voice cracked, as it always does when I'm scared.

"That odor," Foster said. "Quickly—the other way!"

I stepped back and Foster pushed past me and ran along the hall, with me at his heels. I didn't look back to see what was at my own heels. Foster took the stairs three at a time, pulled up short on the landing. He went to his knees, shoved back an Isfahan rug as supple as sable, and gripped a steel ring set in the floor. He looked at me, his face white.

"Invoke thy gods," he said hoarsely, and heaved at the ring. A section of floor swung up, showing the first step of a flight leading down into a black hole. Foster didn't hesitate; he dropped his feet in, scrambled down. I followed. The stairs went down about ten feet, ending on a stone floor. There was the sound of a latch turning, and we stepped out into a larger room. I saw moonlight through a row of high windows, and smelled the fragrance of fresh night air.

"We're in the garage," Foster whispered. "Go around to the other side of the car and get in—quietly." I touched the smooth flank of the rakish cabriolet, felt my way around it, and eased the door open. I slipped into the seat and closed the door gently. Beside me, Foster touched a button and a green light glowed on the dash.

"Ready?" he said.

"Sure."

The starter whined half a turn and the engine caught. Without waiting, Foster gunned it, let in the clutch. The car leaped for the closed doors, and I ducked, and then saw the doors snap aside as the low-slung car roared out into the night. We took the first turn in the drive at forty, and rounded onto the highway at sixty, tires screaming. I took a look back and caught a glimpse of the house, its stately façade white in the moonlight—and then we were out of sight over a rise.

"What's it all about?" I called over the rush of air. The needle touched ninety, kept going.

"Later," Foster barked. I didn't feel like arguing. I watched in the mirror for a few minutes, wondering where all the cops were tonight. Then I settled down in the padded seat and watched the speedometer eat up the miles.

Chapter Three

It was nearly four-thirty and a tentative grey streak showed through the palm fronds to the east before I broke the silence.

"By the way," I said. "What was the routine with the steel shutters, and the bullet-proof glass in the kitchen, and the handy home-model machine gun covering the front door? Mice bad around the place, are they?"

"Those things were necessary—and more."

"Now that the short hairs along my spine have relaxed," I said, "the whole thing looks pretty silly. We've run far enough now to be able to stop and turn around and stick our tongues out."

"Not yet—not for a long while yet."

"Why don't we just go back home," I went on, "and—"

"No!" Foster said sharply. "I want your word on that,

Legion. No matter what—don't ever go near that house again."

"It'll be daylight soon," I said. "We'll feel pretty asinine about this little trip after the sun comes up, but don't worry, I won't tell anybody—"

"We've got to keep moving," Foster said. "At the next town, I'll telephone for seats on a flight out of Miami."

"Hold on," I said. "You're raving. What about your house? We didn't even stick around long enough to make sure the TV was turned off. And what about passports, and money, and luggage? And what makes you think I'm going with you?"

"I've kept myself in readiness for this emergency," Foster said. "There are disposition instructions for the house on file with a legal firm in Jacksonville. There is nothing to connect me with my former life, once I've changed my name and disappeared. As for the rest— we can buy luggage in the morning. My passport is in the car; perhaps we'd better go first to Puerto Rico, until we can arrange for one for you."

"Look," I said. "I got spooked in the dark, that's all. Why not just admit we made fools of ourselves?"

Foster shook his head. "The inherent inertia of the human mind," he said. "How it fights to resist new ideas."

"The kind of new ideas you're talking about could get both of us locked up in the chuckle ward," I said.

"Legion," Foster said, "I think you'd better write down what I'm going to tell you. It's important— vitally important. I won't waste time with preliminaries. The notebook I showed you—it's in my jacket. You must read the English portion of it. Afterwards, what I'm about to say may make more sense."

"I hope you don't feel your last will and testament coming on, Mr. Foster," I said. "Not before you tell

me what that was we were both so eager to get away
from."

"I'll be frank with you," Foster said flatly. "I don't
know."

Foster wheeled into the dark drive of a silent service station, eased to a stop, set the brake and slumped
back in the seat.

"Do you mind driving for a while, Legion?" he said.
"I'm not feeling very well."

"Sure I'll drive," I said. I opened the door and got
out and went around to his side. Foster sat limply, eyes
closed, his face drawn and strained. He looked older
than he had last night—years older. The night's exper-
iences hadn't taken anything off my age, either.

Foster opened his eyes, looked at me blankly. He
seemed to gather himself with an effort. "I'm sorry,"
he said. "I'm not myself."

He moved over and I got in the driver's seat. "If
you're sick," I said, "we'd better find a doctor."

"No, it's all right," he said blurrily. "Just keep
going . . ."

"We're a hundred and fifty miles from Mayport
now," I said.

Foster turned to me, started to say something—and
slumped in a dead faint. I grabbed for his pulse; it was
strong and steady. I rolled up an eyelid and a dilated
pupil stared sightlessly. He was all right—I hoped. But
the thing to do was get him in bed and call a doctor.
We were at the edge of a small town. I let the brake
off and drove slowly into town, swung around a corner and pulled up in front of the sagging marquee of
a run-down hotel. Foster stirred as I cut the engine.

"Foster," I said, "I'm going to get you into a bed.
Can you walk?" He groaned softly and opened his
eyes. They were glassy. I got out and got him to the

sidewalk. He was still half out. I walked him into the dingy lobby and over to a reception counter where a dim bulb burned. I dinged the bell. It was a minute before an old man shuffled out from where he'd been sleeping. He yawned, eyed me suspiciously, looked at Foster.

"We don't want no drunks here," he said. "Respectable house."

"My friend is sick," I said. "Give me a double with bath. And call a doctor."

"What's he got?" the old man said. "Ain't contagious, is it?"

"That's what I want a doctor to tell me."

"I can't get the doc 'fore in the morning. And we got no private bathrooms."

I signed the register. We rode the open-cage elevator to the fourth floor, went along a gloomy hall to a door painted a peeling brown. It didn't look inviting; the room inside wasn't much better. There was a lot of flowered wallpaper and an old-fashioned wash-stand and two wide beds. I stretched Foster out on one. He lay relaxed, a serene expression on his face—the kind undertakers try for but never quite seem to manage. I sat down on the other bed and pulled off my shoes. It was my turn to have a tired mind. I lay on the bed and let it sink down like a grey stone into still water.

I awoke from a dream in which I had just discovered the answer to the riddle of life. I tried to hold onto it, but it slipped away; it always does.

Grey daylight was filtering through the dusty windows. Foster lay slackly on the broad sagging bed, a ceiling lamp with a faded fringed shade casting a sickly yellow light over him. It didn't make things any cheerier; I flipped it off.

Foster was lying on his back, arms spread wide,

breathing heavily. Maybe it was only exhaustion, and he didn't need a doctor after all. He'd probably wake up in a little while, raring to go.

As for me, I was feeling hungry again. I'd have to have a buck or so for sandwiches. I went over to the bed and called Foster's name. He didn't move. If he was sleeping that soundly, maybe I wouldn't bother him . . .

I eased his wallet out of his coat pocket, took it to the window and checked it. It was fat. I took a ten, put the wallet on the table. I remembered Foster had said something about money in the car. I had the keys in my pocket. I got my shoes on and let myself out quietly. Foster hadn't moved.

Down on the street I waited for a couple of yokels who were looking over Foster's car to move on, then slid into the seat, leaned over, and got the floor boards up. The strong box was set into the channel of the frame. I scraped the road dirt off the lock and opened it with a key from Foster's key ring, took out the contents. There was a bundle of stiffish papers, a passport, some maps—marked up—and a wad of currency that made my mouth go dry. I riffled through it: fifty grand if it was a buck.

I stuffed the papers, money, and passport back in the box and locked it, and climbed out onto the sidewalk. A few doors down the street there was a dirty window lettered MAE'S EAT. I went in, ordered hamburgers and coffee to go, and sat at the counter with Foster's keys in front of me, thinking about the car that went with them. The passport only needed a little work on the picture to get me wherever I wanted to go, and the money would buy me my choice of islands. Foster would have a nice long nap, and then take the train home. With his dough, he'd hardly miss what I took.

The counterman put a paper bag in front of me and

I paid him and went out. I stood by the car, jingling the keys on my palm and thinking. I could be in Miami in an hour, and I knew where to go for the passport job. Foster was a nice guy and I liked him—but I'd never have a break like this again. I reached for the car door and a voice said, "Paper, mister?"

I jumped and looked around. A dirty-faced kid was looking at me. "Sure," I said. I gave him a single and took the paper, flipped it open. A Mayport dateline caught my eye:

POLICE RAID HIDEOUT

A surprise raid by local police led to the discovery here today of a secret gangland fortress. Chief Chesters of the Mayport Police stated that the raid came as an aftermath of the arrival in the city yesterday of a notorious northern gang member. A number of firearms, including army-type machine guns, were seized in the raid on a house 9 miles from Mayport on the Fernandina road. The raid was said by Chief Chesters to be the culmination of a lengthy investigation.

C.R. Foster, 50, owner of the property, is missing and feared dead. Police are seeking the ex-convict who visited the house last night. It is feared that Foster may have been the victim of a gangland murder.

I banged through the door to the darkened room and stopped short. In the gloom I could see Foster sitting on the edge of the bed, looking my way.

"Look at this," I yelped, flapping the paper in his face. "Now the cops are dragging the state for me— and on a murder rap at that! Get on the phone and get this thing straightened out—if you can. You and your little green men! The cops think they've stumbled on Al Capone's arsenal. You'll have fun explaining that one . . ."

Foster looked at me interestedly. He smiled.

"What's funny about it, Foster?" I yelled. "Your dough may buy you out, but what about me?"

"Forgive me for asking," Foster said pleasantly, "but—who are you?"

There are times when I'm slow on the uptake, but this wasn't one of them. The implications of what Foster had said hit me hard enough to make my knees go weak.

"Oh, no, Mr. Foster," I said. "You can't lose your memory again—not right now, not with the police looking for me. You're my alibi; you're the one that has to explain all the business about the guns and the ad in the paper. I just came to see about a job, remember?"

My voice was getting a little shrill. Foster sat looking at me, wearing an expression between a frown and a smile, like a credit manager turning down an application.

He shook his head slightly. "My name is not Foster."

"Look," I said. "Your name was Foster yesterday—that's all I care about. You're the one that owns the house the cops are all upset about. And you're the corpse I'm supposed to have knocked off. You've got to go to the cops with me—right now—and tell them I'm just an innocent bystander."

I went to the window and raised the shades to let some light into the room, turned back to Foster.

"I'll explain to the cops about you thinking the little men were after you—" I stopped talking and stared at Foster. For a wild moment I thought I'd made a mistake—that I'd wandered into the wrong room. I knew Foster's face, all right; the light was bright enough now to see clearly; but the man I was talking to couldn't have been a day over twenty years old.

I went close to him, staring hard. There were the same cool blue eyes, but the lines around them were gone. The black hair grew lower and thicker than I remembered it, and the skin was clear.

I sat down hard on my bed. *"Mama mia,"* I said.

"¿Que es la dificultad?" Foster said.

"Shut up," I moaned. "I'm confused enough in one language." I was trying hard to think but I couldn't seem to get started. A few minutes earlier I'd had the world by the tail—just before it turned around and bit me. Cold sweat popped out on my forehead when I thought about how close I had come to driving off in Foster's car; every cop in the state would be looking for it by now—and if they found me in it, the jury wouldn't be out ten minutes reaching a verdict of guilty.

Then another thought hit me—the kind that brings you bolt upright with your teeth clenched and your heart hammering. It wouldn't be long before the local hick cops would notice the car out front. They'd come in after me, and I'd tell them it belonged to Foster. They'd take a look at him and say, "Nuts, the bird we want is fifty years old, and where did you hide the body?"

I got up and started pacing. Foster had already told me there was nothing to connect him with his house in Mayport; the locals there had seen enough of him to know he was pushing middle age, at least. I could kick and scream and tell them this twenty-year-old kid was Foster, but I'd never make it stick. There was no way to prove my story; they'd figure Foster was dead and that I'd killed him—and anybody who thinks you need a *corpus* to prove murder better read his Perry Mason again.

I glanced out of the window and did a double take. Two cops were standing by Foster's car. One of them went around to the back and got out a pad and took down the license number, then said something over his shoulder and started across the street. The second cop planted himself by the car, his eye on the front of the hotel.

I whirled on Foster. "Get your shoes on," I croaked. "Let's get the hell out of here."

We went down the stairs quietly and found a back door opening on an alley. Nobody saw us go.

An hour later, I sagged in a grimy coach seat and studied Foster, sitting across from me—a middle-aged nut with the face of a young kid and a mind like a blank slate. I had no choice but to drag him with me; my only chance was to stick close and hope he got back enough of his memory to get me off the hook.

It was time for me to be figuring my next move. I thought about the fifty thousand dollars I had left behind in the car, and groaned. Foster looked concerned.

"Are you in pain?" he said.

"And how I'm in pain," I said. "Before I met you I was a homeless bum, broke and hungry. Now I can add a couple more items: the cops are after me, and I've got a mental case to nursemaid."

"What law have you broken?" Foster said.

"None," I barked. "As a crook, I'm a washout. I've planned three larcenies in the last twelve hours, and flunked out on all of them. And now I'm wanted for murder."

"Whom did you kill?" Foster inquired courteously.

I leaned across so I could snarl in his face: "You!"

Then, "Get this through your head, Foster. The only crime I'm guilty of is stupidity. I listened to your crazy story; because of you I'm in a mess I'll never get straightened out." I leaned back. "And then there's the question of old men that take a nap and wake up in their late teens; we'll go into that later, after I've had my nervous breakdown."

"I'm sorry if I've been the cause of difficulty," Foster said. "I wish that I could recall the things you've spoken of. Is there anything I can do to assist you now?"

"And you were the one who wanted help," I said. "There is one thing; let me have the money you've got on you; we'll need it."

Foster got out his wallet—after I told him where it was—and handed it to me. I looked through it; there was nothing in it with a photo or fingerprints. When Foster said he had arranged matters so that he could disappear without a trace, he hadn't been kidding.

"We'll go to Miami," I said. "I know a place in the Cuban section where we can lie low, cheap. Maybe if we wait a while, you'll start remembering things."

"Yes," Foster said. "That would be pleasant."

"You haven't forgotten how to talk, at least," I said. "I wonder what else you can do. Do you remember how you made all that money?"

"I can remember nothing of your economic system," Foster said. He looked around. "This is a very primitive world, in many respects," he said. "It should not be difficult to amass wealth here."

"I never had much luck at it," I said. "I haven't even been able to amass the price of a meal."

"Food is exchanged for money?" Foster asked.

"Everything is exchanged for money," I said. "Including most of the human virtues."

"This is a strange world," Foster said. "It will take me a long while to become accustomed to it."

"Yeah, me, too," I said. "Maybe things would be better on Mars."

Foster nodded. "Perhaps," he said. "Perhaps we should go there."

I groaned, then caught myself. "No, I'm not in pain," I said. "But don't take me so literally, Foster."

We rode along in silence for a while.

"Say, Foster," I said. "Have you still got that notebook of yours?"

Foster tried several pockets, came up with the book. He looked at it, turned it over, frowning.

"You remember it?" I said, watching him.

He shook his head slowly, then ran his finger around the circles embossed on the cover.

"This pattern," he said. "It signifies . . ."

"Go on, Foster," I said. "Signifies what?"

"I'm sorry," he said. "I don't remember."

I took the book and sat looking at it. I didn't really see it, though. I was seeing my future. When Foster didn't turn up, they'd naturally assume he was dead. I'd been with him just before his disappearance. It wasn't hard to see why they'd want to talk to me— and my having vanished too wouldn't help any. My picture would blossom out in post offices all over the country; and even if they didn't catch me right away, the murder charge would always be there, hanging over me.

It wouldn't do any good to turn myself in and tell them the whole story; they wouldn't believe me, and I wouldn't blame them. I didn't really believe it myself, and I'd lived through it. But then, maybe I was just imagining that Foster looked younger. After all, a good night's rest—

I looked at Foster, and almost groaned again. Twenty was stretching it; eighteen was more like it. I was willing to swear he'd never shaved in his life.

"Foster," I said. "It's got to be in this book; who you are, where you came from—it's the only hope I've got."

"I suggest we read it, then," Foster said.

"A bright idea," I said. "Why didn't I think of that?" I thumbed through the book to the section in English and read for an hour. Starting with the entry dated January 19, 1710, the writer had scribbled a few lines every few months. He seemed to be some kind of pioneer in the Virginia Colony. He complained about prices, and the Indians, and the ignorance of the other settlers and every now and then threw in a remark about the Enemy. He often took long trips, and when he got home, he complained about those, too.

"It's a funny thing, Foster," I said. "This is supposed to have been written over a period of a couple of hundred years, but it's all in the same hand. That's kind of odd, isn't it?"

"Why should a man's handwriting change?" Foster said.

"Well, it might get a little shaky there toward the last, don't you agree?"

"Why is that?"

"I'll spell it out, Foster," I said. "Most people don't live that long. A hundred years is stretching it, to say nothing of two."

"This must be a very violent world, then," Foster said.

"Skip it," I said. "You talk like you're just visiting. By the way, do you remember how to write?"

Foster looked thoughtful. "Yes," he said. "I can write."

I handed him the book and the stylus. "Try it," I said. Foster opened to a blank page, wrote, and handed the book back to me.

"Always and always and always," I read.

I looked at Foster. "What does that mean?" I looked

at the words again, then quickly flipped to the pages
written in English. I was no expert on penmanship, but
this came up and cracked me right in the eye.

The book was written in Foster's hand.

"It doesn't make sense," I was saying for the forti-
eth time. Foster nodded sympathetic agreement.

"Why would you write out this junk yourself, and
then spend all that time and money trying to have it
deciphered? You said experts worked over it and
couldn't break it. But," I went on, "you must have
known you wrote it; you knew your own handwriting.
But on the other hand, you had amnesia before; you
had the idea you might have told something about
yourself in the book . . ."

I sighed, leaned back and tossed the book over to
Foster. "Here, you read a while," I said. "I'm arguing
with myself and I can't tell who's winning."

Foster looked the book over carefully.

"This is odd," he said.

"What's odd?"

"The book is made of khaff. It is a permanent
material—and yet it shows damage."

I sat perfectly still and waited.

"Here on the back cover," Foster said. "A scuffed
area. Since this is khaff, it cannot be an actual scar.
It must have been placed there."

I grabbed the book and looked. There was a faint
mark across the back cover, as though the book had
been scraped on something sharp. I remembered how
much luck I had had with a knife. The mark had been
put here, disguised as a casual nick in the finish. It
had to mean something.

"How do you know what the material is?" I asked.

Foster looked surprised. "In the same way that I
know the window is of glass," he said. "I simply know."

"Speaking of glass," I said. "Wait till I get my hands on a microscope. Then maybe we'll begin to get some answers."

Chapter Four

The two-hundred pound señorita with the wart on her upper lip put a pot of black Cuban coffee and a pitcher of salted milk down beside the two chipped cups, leered at me in a way that might have been appealing thirty years before, and waddled back to the kitchen. I poured a cup, gulped half of it, and shuddered. In the street outside the café a guitar cried *Estrellita*.

"Okay, Foster," I said. "Here's what I've got: The first half of the book is in pot-hooks—I can't read that. But this middle section: the part coded in regular letters—it's actually encrypted English. It's a sort of résumé of what happened." I picked up the sheets of paper on which I had transcribed my deciphering of the coded section of the book, using the key that had been micro-engraved in the fake scratch on the back cover.

I read:

> For the first time, I am afraid. My attempt to construct the communicator called down the Hunters upon me. I made such a shield as I could contrive, and sought their nesting place.
>
> I came there and it was in that place that I knew of old, and it was no hive, but a pit in the ground, built by men of the Two

Worlds. And I would have come into it, but the Hunters swarmed in their multitudes. I fought them and killed many, but at last I fled away. I came to the western shore, and there I hired bold sailors and a poor craft, and set forth.

In forty-nine days we came to shore in this wilderness, and there were men as from the dawn of time, and I fought them, and when they had learned fear, I lived among them in peace, and the Hunters have not found this place. Now it may be that my saga ends here, but I will do what I am able.

The Change may soon come upon me; I must prepare for the stranger who will come after me. All that he must know is in these pages. And say I to him:

Have patience, for the time of this race draws close. Venture not again on the Eastern continent, but wait, for soon the Northern sailors must come in numbers into this wilderness. Seek out their cleverest metal-workers, and when it may be, devise a shield, and only then return to the pit of the Hunters. It lies in the plain, 50/10,000 parts of the girth of this(?) to the west of the Great Chalk Face, and 1470 parts north from the median line, as I reckon. The stones mark it well with the sign of the Two Worlds.

I looked across at Foster. "It goes on then with a blow-by-blow account of dealings with aborigines. He was trying to get them civilized in a hurry. They figured he was a god and he set them to work building roads and cutting stone and learning mathematics and so on. He was doing all he could to set things up so this stranger who was to follow him would know the score, and carry on the good work."

Foster's eyes were on my face. "What is the nature of the Change he speaks of?"

"He never says—but I suppose he's talking about death," I said. "I don't know where the stranger is supposed to come from."

"Listen to me, Legion," Foster said. There was a hint of the old anxious look in his eyes. "I think I know what the Change was. I think he knew he would forget—"

"You've got amnesia on the brain, old buddy," I said.

"—and the stranger is—himself. A man without a memory."

I sat frowning at Foster. "Yeah, maybe," I said. "Go on."

"And he says that all that the stranger needs to know is there—in the book."

"Not in the part I decoded," I said. "He describes how they're coming along with the road-building job, and how the new mine panned out—but there's nothing about what the Hunters are, or what had gone on before he tangled with them the first time."

"It must be there, Legion; but in the first section, the part written in alien symbols."

"Maybe," I said. "But why the hell didn't he give us a key to that part?"

"I think he assumed that the stranger—himself—would remember the old writing," Foster said. "How could he know that it would be forgotten with the rest?"

"Your guess is as good as any," I said. "Maybe better; you know how it feels to lose your memory."

"But we've learned a few things," Foster said. "The pit of the Hunters—we have the location."

"If you call this 'ten thousand parts to the west of chalk face' a location," I said.

"We know more than that," Foster said. "He mentions a plain; and it must lie on a continent to the east—"

"If you assume that he sailed from Europe to America, then the continent to the east would be Europe," I said. "But maybe he went from Africa to South America, or—"

"The mention of Northern sailors—that suggests the Vikings—"

"You seem to know a little history, Foster," I said. "You've got a lot of odd facts tucked away."

"We need maps," Foster said. "We'll look for a plain near the sea—"

"Not necessarily."

"—and with a formation called a chalk face to the east."

"What's this 'median line' business?" I said. "And the bit about ten thousand parts of something?"

"I don't know. But we must have maps."

"I bought some this afternoon," I said. "I also got a dime-story globe. I figured we might need them. Let's get out of this and back to the room, where we can spread out. I know it's a grim prospect, but . . ." I got to my feet, dropped some coins on the oilcloth-covered table, and led the way out.

It was a short half block to the flea trap we called home. We kept out of it as much as we could, holding our long daily conferences across the street at the Novedades. The roaches scurried as we passed up the dark stairway to our not much brighter room. I crossed to the bureau and opened a drawer.

"The globe," Foster said, taking it in his hands. "I wonder if perhaps he meant a ten-thousandth part of the circumference of the earth?"

"What would he know about—"

"Disregard the anachronistic aspect of it," Foster said. "The man who wrote the book knew many things. We'll have to start with some assumptions. Let's make the obvious ones; that we're looking for a plain on the west coast of Europe, lying—" He pulled a chair up to the scabrous table and riffled through to one of my scribbled sheets: "50/10,000s of the circumference of the earth—that would be about 125 miles—west of a chalk formation, and 3675 miles north of a median line . . ."

"Maybe," I said, "he means the Equator."

"Certainly. Why not? That would mean our plain lies on a line through—" he studied the small globe "—Warsaw, and south of Amsterdam."

"But this part about a rock outcropping," I said. "How do we find out if there's any conspicuous chalk formation around there?"

"We can consult a geology text. There may be a library in this neighborhood."

"The only chalk deposits I ever heard about," I said, "are the White cliffs of Dover."

"White cliffs . . ."

We both reached for the globe at once.

"One hundred twenty-five miles west of the chalk cliffs," said Foster. He ran a finger over the globe. "North of London, but south of Birmingham. That puts us reasonably near the sea—"

"Where's the atlas?" I said. I rummaged, came up with a cheap tourists' edition, flipped the pages.

"Here's England," I said. "Now we look for a plain."

Foster put a finger on the map. "Here," he said. "A large plain—called Salisbury."

"Large is right," I said. "It would take years to find a stone cairn on that. We're getting excited about nothing. We're looking for a hole in the ground, hundreds of years old—if this lousy notebook means anything—

maybe marked with a few stones—in the middle of miles of plain. And it's all guesswork anyway . . ." I took the atlas, turned the page.

"I don't know what I expected to get out of decoding those pages," I said. "But I was hoping for more than this."

"I think we should try, Legion," Foster said. "We can go there, search over the ground. It would be costly, but not impossible. We can start by gathering capital—"

"Wait a minute, Foster," I said. I was staring at a larger-scale map showing southern England. Suddenly my heart was thudding. I put a finger on a tiny dot in the center of Salisbury Plain.

"Six, two and even," I said. "There's your Pit of the Hunters . . ."

Foster leaned over, read the fine print.

"Stonehenge."

I read from the encyclopedia page:

—this great stone structure, lying on the Plain of Salisbury, Wiltshire, England, is preeminent among megalithic monuments of the ancient world. Within a circular ditch 300' in diameter, stones up to 22' in height are arranged in concentric circles. The central altar stone, over 16' long, is approached from the northeast by a broad roadway called the Avenue—

"It's not an altar," said Foster.

"How do you know?"

"Because—" Foster frowned. "I know, that's all."

"The journal said the stones were arranged in the sign of the Two Worlds," I said. "That means the concentric circles, I suppose; the same thing that's stamped on the cover of the notebook."

"And the ring." Foster said.

"Let me read the rest: *A great sarsen stone stands*

upright in the Avenue; the axis through the two stones, when erected, pointed directly to the rising of the sun on Midsummer Day. Calculations based on this observation indicate a date of approximately 1600 B.C.

Foster took the book and I sat on the window sill and looked out at a big Florida moon over the ragged line of roofs with a skinny royal palm sticking up in silhouette. It didn't look much like the postcard views of Miami. I lit a cigarette and thought about a man who long ago had crossed the North Atlantic in a dragon boat to be a god among the Indians. I wondered where he came from, and what it was he was looking for, and what kept him going in spite of the hell that showed in the spare lines of the journal he kept. If, I reminded myself, he had ever existed . . .

Foster was poring over the book. "Look," I said. "Let's get back to earth. We have things to think about, plans to make. The fairy tales can wait until later."

"What do you suggest?" Foster said. "That we forget the things you've told me, and the things we've read here, discard the journal, and abandon the attempt to find the answers?"

"No," I said. "I'm no sorehead. Sure, there's some things here that somebody ought to look into—some day. But right now what I want is the cops off my neck. And I've been thinking. I'll dictate a letter; you write it—your lawyers know your handwriting. Tell them you were on the thin edge of a nervous breakdown—that's why all the artillery around your house—and you made up your mind suddenly to get away from it all. Tell them you don't want to be bothered, that's why you're traveling incognito, and that the northern mobster that came to see you was just stupid, not a killer. That ought to at least cool off the cops—"

Foster looked thoughtful. "That's an excellent suggestion," he said. "Then we need merely to arrange for passage to England, and proceed with the investigation."

"You don't get the idea," I said. "You can arrange things by mail so we get our hands on that dough of yours—"

"Any such attempt would merely bring the police down on us," Foster said. "You've already pointed out the unwisdom of attempting to pass myself off as—myself."

"There ought to be a way . . ." I said.

"We have only one avenue of inquiry," Foster said. "We have no choice but to explore it. We'll take passage on a ship to England—"

"What'll we use for money—and papers? It would cost hundreds. Unless—" I added, "—we worked our way. But that's no good. We'd still need passports—plus union cards and seamen's tickets."

"Your friend," Foster said. "The one who prepares passports. Can't he produce the other papers as well?"

"Yeah," I said. "I guess so. But it will cost us."

"I'm sure we can find a way to pay," Foster said. "Will you see him—early in the morning?"

I looked around the blowsy room. Hot night air stirred a geranium wilting in a tin can on the window sill. An odor of bad cooking and worse plumbing floated up from the street.

"At least," I said, "it would mean getting out of here."

Chapter Five

It was almost sundown when Foster and I pushed through the door to the saloon bar at the Ancient Sinner and found a corner table. I watched Foster spread out his maps and papers. Behind us there was a murmur of conversation and the thump of darts against a board.

"When are you going to give up and admit we're wasting our time?" I said. "Two weeks of tramping over the same ground, and we end up in the same place."

"We've hardly begun our investigation," Foster said mildly.

"You keep saying that," I said. "But if there ever was anything in that rock-pile, it's long gone. The archaeologists have been digging over the site for years, and they haven't come up with anything."

"They don't know what to look for," Foster said. "They were searching for indications of religious significance, human sacrifice—that sort of thing."

"We don't know what we're looking for either," I said. "Unless you think maybe we'll meet the Hunters hiding under a loose stone."

"You say that sardonically," Foster said. "But I don't consider it impossible."

"I know," I said. "You've convinced yourself that the Hunters were after us back at Mayport when we ran off like a pair of idiots."

"From what you've told me of the circumstances—" Foster began.

"I know; you don't consider it impossible. That's the trouble with you; you don't consider anything impossible. It would make life a lot easier for me if you'd let me rule out a few items—like leprechauns who hang out at Stonehenge."

Foster looked at me, half-smiling. It had only been a few weeks since he woke up from a nap looking like a senior class president who hadn't made up his mind whether to be a preacher or a movie star, but he had already lost that mild, innocent air. He learned fast, and day by day I had seen his old personality reemerge and—in spite of my attempts to hold onto the ascendancy—dominate our partnership.

"It's a failing of your culture," Foster said, "that hypothesis becomes dogma almost overnight. You're too close to your Neolithic, when the blind acceptance of tribal lore had survival value. Having learned to evoke the fire god from sticks, by rote, you tend to extend the principle to all 'established facts.'"

"Here's an established fact for you," I said. "We've got fifteen pounds left—that's about forty dollars. It's time we figure out where to go from here, before somebody starts checking up on those phony papers of ours."

Foster shook his head. "I'm not satisfied that we've exhausted the possibilities here. I've been studying the geometric relationships between the various structures; I have some ideas I want to check. I think it might be a good idea to go out at night, when we can work without the usual crowd of tourists observing every move."

I groaned. "My dogs are killing me," I said. "Let's hope you'll come up with something better—or at least different."

"We'll have a bite to eat here, and wait until dark to start out," Foster said.

The publican brought us plates of cold meat and potato salad. I worked on a thin but durable slice of ham and thought about all the people, somewhere, who were sitting down now to gracious meals in the glitter of crystal and silver. I'd had too many greasy French fries in too many cheap dives the last few years. I could feel them all now, burning in my stomach. I was getting farther from my island all the time—and it was nobody's fault but mine.

"The Ancient Sinner," I said. "That's me."

Foster looked up. "Curious names these old pubs

have," he said. "I suppose in some cases the origins are lost in antiquity."

"Why don't they think up something cheery," I said. "Like 'The Paradise Bar and Grill' or 'The Happy Hour Café'. Did you notice the sign hanging outside?"

"No."

"A picture of a skeleton. He's holding one hand up like a Yankee evangelist prophesying doom. You can see it through the window there."

Foster turned and looked out at the weathered sign creaking in the evening wind. He looked at it for a long time. When he turned back, there was a strange look around his eyes.

"What's the matter—?" I started.

Foster ignored me, waved to the proprietor, a short fat country man. He came over to the table, wiping his hands on his apron.

"A very interesting old building," Foster said. "We've been admiring it. When was it built?"

"Well, sir," the publican said, "this here house is many a hundred year old. It were built by the monks, they say, from the monastery what used to stand nearby here. It were tore down by the King's men, Henry, that was, what time he drove the papists out."

"That would be Henry the Eighth, I suppose?"

"Aye, it would that. And this house is all that were spared, it being the brewing-house, as the king said were a worthwhile institution, and he laid on a tithe, that two kegs of stout was to be laid by for the king's use each brewing time."

"Very interesting," Foster said. "Is the custom still continued?"

The publican shook his head. "It were ended in my granfer's time, it being that the Queen were a teetotaler."

"How did it acquire the curious name—'The Ancient Sinner?' "

"The tale is," the publican said, "that one day a lay brother of the order were digging about yonder on the plain by the great stones, in search of the Druid's treasure, albeit the Abbot had forbid him to go nigh the heathen ground, and he come on the bones of a man, and being of a kindly turn, he had the thought to give them Christian burial. Now, knowing the Abbott would nae permit it, he set to work to dig a grave by moonlight in holy ground, under the monastery walls. But the Abbott, being wakeful, were abroad and come on the brother a-digging, and when he asked the why of it, the lay brother having visions of penances to burden him for many a day, he ups and tells the Abbott it were a ale cellar he were about digging, and the Abbott, not being without wisdom, clapped him on the back, and went on his way. And so it was the ale-house got built, and blessed by the Abbott, and with it the bones that was laid away under the floor beneath the ale-casks."

"So the ancient sinner is buried under the floor?"

"Aye, so the tale goes, though I've not dug for him myself. But the house has been knowed by the name these four hundred years."

"Where was it you said the lay brother was digging?"

"On the plain, yonder, by the Druid's stones, what they call Stonehenge," the publican said. He picked up the empty glasses. "What about another, gentlemen?"

"Certainly," Foster said. He sat quietly across from me, his features composed—but I could see there was tension under the surface calm.

"What's this all about?" I asked softly. "When did you get so interested in local history?"

"Later," Foster murmured. "Keep looking bored."

"That'll be easy," I said. The publican came back and placed heavy glass mugs before us.

"You were telling us about the lay brother's finding

the bones," Foster said. "You say they were buried in Stonehenge?"

The publican cleared his throat, glanced sideways at Foster.

"The gentlemen wouldna be from the University now, I suppose?" he said.

"Let's just say," Foster said easily, smiling, "that we have a great interest in these bits of lore—an interest supported by modest funds, of course."

The publican made a show of wiping at the rings on the table top.

"A costly business, I wager," he said. "Digging about in odd places and all. Now, knowing where to dig; that's important, I'll be bound."

"Very important," Foster said. "Worth five pounds, easily."

" 'Twere my granfer told me of the spot; took me out by moonlight, he did, and showed me where his granfer had showed him. Told me it were a fine great secret, the likes of which a simple man could well take pride in."

"And an additional five pounds as a token of my personal esteem," Foster said.

The publican eyed me. "Well, a secret as was handed down father to son . . ."

"And, of course, my associate wishes to express his esteem, too," Foster said. "Another five pounds worth."

"That's all the esteem the budget will bear, Mr. Foster," I said. I got out the fifteen pounds and passed the money across to him. "I hope you haven't forgotten those people back home who wanted to talk to us," I said. "They'll be getting in touch with us any time now, I'll bet."

Foster rolled up the bills and held them in his hand. "That's true, Mr. Legion," he said. "Perhaps we shouldn't take the time . . ."

"But being it's for the advancement of science," the publican said, "I'm willing to make the sacrifice."

"We'll want to go out tonight," Foster said. "We have a very tight schedule."

The landlord dickered with Foster for another five minutes before he agreed to guide us to the spot where the skeleton had been found.

When he left, I began. "Now tell me."

"Look at the signboard again," Foster said. I looked. The skull smiled, holding up a hand.

"I see it," I said. "But it doesn't explain why you handed over our last buck—"

"Look at the hand. Look at the ring on the finger."

I looked again. A heavy ring was painted on the bony index finger, with a pattern of concentric circles.

It was a duplicate of the one on Foster's finger.

The publican pulled the battered Morris Minor to the side of the highway and set the brake.

"This is as close as we best take the machine," he said. We got out, looked across the rolling plain where the megaliths of Stonehenge loomed against the last glow of sunset.

The publican rummaged in the boot, produced a ragged blanket and two long four-cell flashlights, gave one to Foster and the other to me. "Do nae use the electric torches until I tell ye," he said, "lest the whole country see there's folks abroad here." We watched as he draped the blanket over a barbed wire fence, clambered over, and started across the barren field. Foster and I followed, not talking.

The plain was deserted. A few lonely lights showed on a distant slope. It was a dark night with no moon. I could hardly see the ground ahead. A car moved along a distant road, its headlights bobbing.

We moved past the outer ring of stones, skirting fallen slabs twenty feet long.

"We'll break our necks," I said. "Let's have one of the flashlights."

"Not yet," Foster whispered.

Our guide paused; we came up to him.

"It were a mortal long time since I were last here-abouts," he said. "I best take me bearings off the Friar's Heel . . ."

"What's that?"

"Yon great stone, standing alone in the Avenue." We squinted; it was barely visible as a dark shape against the sky.

"The bones were buried there?" Foster asked.

"Nay, all by theirself, they was. Now it were twenty paces, granfer said, him being fifteen stone and long in the leg . . ." The publican muttered to himself, pacing off distances.

"What's to keep him from just pointing to a spot after a while," I said to Foster, "and saying 'This is it'?"

"We'll wait and see," Foster said.

"They were a hollow, as it were, in the earth," the publican said, "with a bit of stone by it. I reckon it were fifty paces from here—" he pointed, "—yonder."

"I don't see anything," I said.

"Let's take a closer look." Foster started off and I followed, the publican trailing behind. I made out a dim shape, with a deep depression in the earth before it.

"This could be the spot," Foster said. "Old graves often sink—" Suddenly he grabbed my arm. "Look . . . !"

The surface of the ground before us seemed to tremble, then heave. Foster snapped on his flashlight. The earth at the bottom of the hollow rose, cracked open. A boiling mass of luminescence churned, and a globe of light separated itself, rose, bumbling along the face of the weathered stone.

"Saints preserve us," the publican said in a choked voice. Foster and I stood, rooted to the spot, watching. The lone globe rose higher—and abruptly shot straight toward us. Foster threw up an arm and ducked. The ball of light veered, struck him a glancing blow, darted off a few yards, hovered. In an instant, the air was alive with the spheres, boiling up from the ground, and hurtling toward us, buzzing like a hive of yellow-jackets. Foster's flashlight lanced out toward the swarm.

"Use your light, Legion!" he shouted hoarsely. I was still standing, frozen. The globes rushed straight at Foster, ignoring me. Behind me, I heard the publican turn and run. I fumbled with the flashlight switch, snapped it on, swung the beam of white light on Foster. The globe at his head vanished as the light touched it. More globes swarmed to Foster—and popped like soap bubbles in the flashlight's glare—but more swarmed to take their places. Foster reeled, fighting at them. He swung the light—and I heard it smash against the stone behind him. In the instant darkness, the globes clustered thick around his head.

"Foster," I yelled, "run!"

He got no more than five yards before he staggered, went to his knees. "Cover," he croaked. He fell on his face. I rushed the mass of darting globes, took up a stance straddling his body. A sulfurous reek hung around me. I coughed, concentrated on beaming the light around Foster's head. No more were rising from the crack in the earth now. A suffocating cloud pressed around both of us, but it was Foster they went for. I thought of the slab; if I could get my back to it, I might have a chance. I stooped, got a grip on Foster's coat, and started back, dragging him. The lights boiled around me. I swept the beam of light and kept going until my back slammed against the stone. I crouched against it. Now they could only come from the front.

I glanced at the cleft the lights had come from. It looked big enough to get Foster into. That would give him some protection. I tumbled him over the edge, then flattened my back against the slab and settled down to fight in earnest.

I worked in a pattern, sweeping vertically, then horizontally. The globes ignored me, drove toward the cleft, fighting to get at Foster, and I swept them away as they came. The cloud around me was smaller now, the attack less ravenous. I picked out individual globes, snuffed them out. The hum became ragged, faltered. Then there were only a few globes around me, milling wildly, disorganized. The last half dozen fled, bumbling away across the plain.

I slumped against the rock, sweat running down into my eyes, my lungs burning with the sulphur.

"Foster," I gasped. "Are you all right?"

He didn't answer. I flashed the light onto the cleft. It showed me damp clay, a few pebbles.

Foster was gone.

Chapter Six

I scrambled to the edge of the pit and played the light around inside. It shelved back at one side, and a dark mouth showed, sloping down into the earth— the hiding place from which the globes had swarmed.

Foster was wedged in the opening. I scrambled down beside him, tugged him back to the level ground. He was still breathing; that was something.

I wondered if the pub owner would come back, now that the lights were gone—or if he'd tell someone what had happened, bring out a search party. Somehow, I doubted it. He didn't seem like the type to ask for trouble with the ghosts of ancient sinners.

Foster groaned, opened his eyes. "Where are . . . they?" he muttered.

"Take it easy, Foster," I said. "You're OK now."

"Legion," Foster said. He tried to sit up. "The Hunters . . ."

"OK, call 'em Hunters if you want to. I haven't got a better name for them. I worked them over with the flashlights. They're gone."

"That means . . ."

"Let's not worry about what it means. Let's just get out of here."

"The Hunters—they burst out of the ground—from a cleft in the earth."

"That's right. You were halfway into the hole. I guess that's where they were hiding."

"The Pit of the Hunters," Foster said.

"If you say so," I said. "Lucky you didn't go down it."

"Legion, give me the flashlight."

"I feel something coming on that I'm not going to like," I said. I handed him the light and he flashed it into the tunnel mouth. I saw a polished roof of black glass arching four feet over the rubble-strewn bottom of the shaft. A stone, dislodged by my movement, clattered away down the 30 degree slope.

"Hell, that tunnel's man-made," I said, peering into it. "And I don't mean Neolithic man."

"Legion, we'll have to see what's down there," Foster said.

"We could come back later, with ropes and big insurance policies," I said.

"But we won't," said Foster. "We've found what we were looking for—"

"Sure," I said, "and it serves us right. Are you sure you feel good enough to make like Alice and the White Rabbit?"

"I'm sure. Let's go."

Foster thrust his legs into the opening, slid over the edge and disappeared. I followed him. I eased down a few feet, glanced back for a last look at the night sky, then lost my grip and slid. I hit bottom hard enough to knock the wind out of me, I got to my hands and knees on a level, gravel-strewn floor.

"What is this place?" I dug the flashlight out of the rubble, flashed it around. We were in a low-ceilinged room ten yards square. I saw smooth walls, the dark bulks of massive shapes that made me think of sarcophagi in Egyptian burial vaults—except that these threw back highlights from dials and levers.

"For a couple of guys who get shy in the company of cops," I said, "we've a talent for doing the wrong thing. This is some kind of Top Secret military installation."

"Impossible," Foster replied. "This couldn't be a modern structure, at the bottom of a rubble-filled shaft—"

"Let's get out of here fast," I said. "We've probably set off an alarm already."

As if in answer, a low chime cut across our talk. Pearly light sprang up on a square panel. I got to my feet, moved over to stare at it. Foster came to my side.

"What do you make of it?" he said.

"I'm no expert on stone-age relics," I said. "But if that's not a radar screen, I'll eat it."

I sat down in the single chair before the dusty control console, and watched a red blip creep across the screen. Foster stood behind me.

"We owe a debt to that ancient sinner," he said. "Who would have dreamed he'd lead us here?"

"Ancient sinner?" I said. "This place is as modern as next year's juke box."

"Look at the symbols on the machines," Foster said. "They're identical with those in the first section of the journal."

"All pot-hooks look alike to me," I said. "It's this screen that's got me worried. If I've got it doped out correctly, that blip is either a mighty slow airplane—or it's at one hell of an altitude."

"Modern aircraft operate at great heights," Foster said.

"Not at this height," I said. "Give me a few more minutes to study these scales . . ."

"There are a number of controls here," Foster said, "obviously intended to activate mechanisms—"

"Don't touch 'em," I said. "Unless you want to start World War III."

"I hardly think the results would be so drastic," Foster replied. "Surely this installation has a simple purpose—unconnected with modern wars—but very possibly connected with the mystery of the journal—and of my own past."

"The less we know about this, the better," I said. "At least, if we don't mess with anything, we can always claim we just stepped in here to get out of the rain—"

"You're forgetting the Hunters," said Foster.

"Some new anti-personnel gimmick."

"They came out of this shaft, Legion. It was opened by the pressure of the Hunters bursting out."

"Why did they pick that precise moment—just as we arrived?" I asked.

"I think they were aroused," said Foster. "I think they sensed the presence of their ancient foe."

I swung around to look at him.

"I see the way your thoughts are running," I said. "You're their Ancient Foe, now, huh? Just let me get this straight: that means that umpteen hundred years ago, you personally had a fight with the Hunters—here at Stonehenge. You killed a batch of them and ran. You hired some kind of Viking ship and crossed the Atlantic. Later on, you lost your memory, and started being a guy named Foster. A few weeks ago you lost it again. Is that the picture?"

"More or less."

"And now we're a couple of hundred feet under Stonehenge—after a brush with a crowd of luminous stinkbombs—and you're telling me you'll be nine hundred on your next birthday."

"Remember the entry in the journal, Legion? 'I came to the place of the Hunters, and it was a place I knew of old, and there was no hive, but a Pit built by men of the Two Worlds . . .'"

"Okay," I said. "So you're pushing a thousand."

I glanced at the screen, got out a scrap of paper, and scribbled a rapid calculation. "Here's another big number for you. That object on the screen is at an altitude—give or take a few percent—of thirty thousand miles."

I tossed the pencil aside, swung around to frown at Foster. "What are we mixed up in, Foster? Not that I really want to know. I'm ready to go to a nice clean jail now, and pay my debt to society—"

"Calm down, Legion," Foster said. "You're raving."

"OK," I said, turning back to the screen. "You're the boss. Do what you like. It's just my reflexes wanting to run. I've got no place to run to. At least with you I've always got the wild hope that maybe you're not completely nuts, and that somehow—"

I sat upright, eyes on the screen. "Look at this,

Foster," I snapped. A pattern of dots flashed across the screen, faded, flashed again . . .

"Some kind of IFF," I said. "A recognition signal. I wonder what we're supposed to do now."

Foster watched the screen, saying nothing.

"I don't like that thing blinking at us," I said. "It makes me feel conspicuous." I looked at the big red button beside the screen. "Maybe if I pushed that . . ." Without waiting to think it over, I jabbed at it.

A yellow light blinked on the control panel. On the screen, the pattern of dots vanished. The red blip separated, a smaller blip moving off at right angles to the main mass.

"I'm not sure you should have done that," Foster said.

"There *is* room for doubt," I said in a strained voice. "It looks like I've launched a bomb from the ship overhead."

The climb back up the tunnel took three hours, and every foot of the way I was listening to a refrain in my head: This may be it; this may be it; this may be . . .

I crawled out of the tunnel mouth and lay on my back, breathing hard. Foster groped his way out beside me.

"We'll have to get to the highway," I said, untying the ten-foot rope of ripped garments that had linked us during the climb. "There's a telephone at the pub; we'll notify the authorities . . ." I glanced up.

"Hold it!" I grabbed Foster's arm and pointed overhead. "What's that?"

Foster looked up. A brilliant point of blue light, brighter than a star, grew perceptibly as we watched.

"Maybe we won't get to notify anybody after all," I said. "I think that's our bomb—coming home to roost."

"That's illogical," Foster said. "The installation would hardly be arranged merely to destroy itself in so complex a manner."

"Let's get out of here," I yelled.

"It's approaching us very rapidly," Foster said. "The distance we could run in the next few minutes would be trivial by comparison with the killing radius of a modern bomb. We'll be safer sheltered in the cleft than in the open."

"We could slide down the tunnel," I said.

"And be buried?"

"You're right; I'd rather fry on the surface."

We crouched, watching the blue glare directly overhead, growing larger, brighter. I could see Foster's face by its light now.

"That's no bomb," Foster said. "It's not falling; it's coming down slowly . . . .like a—"

"Like a slowly falling bomb," I said. "And it's coming right down on top of us. Goodbye, Foster. I can't claim it's been fun knowing you, but it's been different. We'll feel the heat any second now. I hope it's fast."

The glaring disc was the size of the full moon now, unbearably bright. It lit the plain like a pale blue sun. There was no sound. As it dropped lower, the disc foreshortened and I could see a dark shape above it, dimly lit by the glare thrown back from the ground.

"The thing is the size of a ferry boat," I said.

"It's going to miss us," Foster said. "It will come to ground several hundred feet to the east of us."

We watched the slender shape float down with dreamlike slowness, now five hundred feet above, now three hundred, then hovering just above the giant stones.

"It's coming down smack on top of Stonehenge," I yelled.

We watched as the vessel settled into place dead

center on the ancient ring of stones. For a moment they were vividly silhouetted against the flood of blue radiance; then abruptly, the glare faded and died.

"Foster," I said. "Do you think it's barely possible—"

A slit of yellow light appeared on the side of the hull, then it widened to a square. A ladder extended itself, dropping down to touch the ground.

"If somebody with tentacles starts down that ladder," I said, in an unnaturally shrill voice, "I'm getting out of here."

"No one will emerge," Foster said quietly. "I think we'll find, Legion, that this ship of space is at our disposal."

"I'm not going aboard that thing," I said for the fifth time. "I'm not sure of much in this world, but I'm sure of that."

"Legion," Foster said, "this is no twentieth century military vessel. It obviously homed on the transmitter in the underground station, which appears to be directly under the old monument—which is several thousand years old—"

"And I'm supposed to believe the ship has been orbiting the earth for the last few thousand years, waiting for someone to push the red button? You call that logical?"

"Given permanent materials, such as those the notebook is made of, it's not impossible—or even difficult."

"We got out of the tunnel alive. Let's settle for that."

"We're on the verge of solving a mystery that goes back through the centuries," said Foster, "a mystery that I've pursued, if I understand the journal, through many lifetimes—"

"One thing about losing your memory: you don't

have any fixed ideas to get in the way of your theories."

Foster smiled grimly. "The trail has brought us here. We must follow it—wherever it leads."

I lay on the ground, staring up at the unbelievable shape across the field, the beckoning square of light. "This ship—or whatever it is," I said; "it drops down out of nowhere and opens its doors. And you want to walk right into the cozy interior."

"Listen!" Foster cut in.

I heard a low rumbling then, a sound that rolled ominously, like distant guns.

"More ships—" I started.

"Jet aircraft," Foster said. "From the bases in East Anglia probably. Of course, they'll have tracked our ship in—"

"That's all for me," I yelled, getting to my feet. "The secret's out—"

"Get down, Legion," Foster shouted. The engines were a blanketing roar now.

"What for? They—"

Two long lines of fire traced themselves across the sky, curving down—

I hit the dirt behind the stone in the same instant the rockets struck. The shock wave slammed at the earth like a monster thunderclap, and I saw the tunnel mouth collapse. I twisted, saw the red interior of the jet tailpipe as the fighter hurtled past, rolling into a climbing turn.

"They're crazy," I yelled. "Firing on—"

A second barrage blasted across my indignation. I hugged the muck and waited while nine salvoes shook the earth. Then the rumble died, reluctantly. The air reeked of high explosives.

"We'd have been dead now if we'd tried the tunnel," I gasped, spitting dirt. "It caved at the first rocket.

And if the ship was what you thought, Foster, they've destroyed something—"

The sentence died unnoticed. The dust was settling and through it the shape of the ship reared up, unchanged except that the square of light was gone. As I watched, the door opened again and the ladder ran out once more, invitingly.

"They'll try next time with nukes," I said. "That may be too much for the ship's defenses—and it will sure be too much for us—"

"Listen," Foster cut in. A deeper rumble was building in the distance.

"To the ship!" Foster called. He was up and running, and I hesitated just long enough to think about trying for the highway and being caught in the open—and then I was running, too. Ahead, Foster stumbled crossing the ground that had been ripped up by the rocket bursts, made it to the ladder, and went up it fast. The growl of the approaching bombers grew, a snarl of deadly hatred. I leaped a still-smoking stone fragment, took the ladder in two jumps, plunged into the yellow-lit interior. Behind me, the door smacked shut.

I was standing in a luxuriously fitted circular room. There was a pedestal in the center of the floor, from which a polished bar projected. The bones of a man lay beside it. While I stared, Foster sprang forward, seized the bar, and pulled. It slid back easily. The lights flickered and I had a moment of vertigo. Nothing else happened.

"Try it the other way," I yelled. "The bombs will fall any second—" I went for it, hand outstretched. Foster thrust in front of me. "Look!"

I stared at the glowing panel he was pointing to— a duplicate of the one in the underground chamber. It showed a curved white line, with a red point ascending from it.

"We're clear," Foster said. "We've made a successful take-off."

"But we can't be moving—there's no acceleration. There must be soundproofing—that's why we can't hear the bombers—"

"No soundproofing would help if we were at ground zero," Foster said. "This ship is the product of an advanced science. We've left the bombers far behind."

"Where are we going? Who's steering this thing?"

"It steers itself, I would judge," Foster said. "I don't know where we're going, but we're well on the way."

I looked at him in amazement. "You like this, don't you, Foster? You're having the time of your life."

"I can't deny that I'm delighted at this turn of events," Foster said. "Don't you see? This vessel is a launch, or lifeboat, under automatic control. And it's taking us to the mother ship."

"Okay, Foster," I said. I looked at the skeleton on the floor behind him. "But I hope we have better luck than the last passenger."

Chapter Seven

It was two hours later, and Foster and I stood silent before a ten-foot screen that had glowed into life when I touched a silver button beside it. It showed us a vast emptiness of bottomless black, set thick with coruscating points of polychrome brilliance that hurt to look at. And against that backdrop: a ship, vast beyond imagining, blotting out half the titanic vista with its bulk—

But dead.

Even from the distance of miles, I could sense it.

The great black torpedo shape, dull moonlight glinting along the unbelievable length of its sleek flank, drifted: a derelict. I wondered for how many centuries it had waited here—and for what?

"I feel," said Foster, "somehow—I'm coming home." I tried to say something, croaked, cleared my throat.

"If this is your jitney," I said, "I hope they didn't leave the meter ticking on you. We're broke."

"We're closing rapidly," said Foster. "Another ten minutes, I'd guess . . ."

"How do we go about heaving to, alongside? You didn't come across a book of instructions, did you?"

"I think I can predict that the approach will be automatic."

"This is your big moment, isn't it?" I said. "I've got to hand it to you, pal; you've won out by pluck, just like the Rover Boys."

The ship appeared to move smoothly closer, looming over us, fine golden lines of decorative filigree work visible now against the black. A tiny square of pale light appeared, grew into a huge bay door that swallowed us.

The screen went dark, there was a gentle jar, then motionlessness. The port opened, silently.

"We've arrived," Foster said. "Shall we step out and have a look?"

"I wouldn't think of going back without one," I said. I followed him out and stopped dead, gaping. I had expected an empty hold, bare metal walls. Instead, I found a vaulted cavern, shadowed, mysterious, rich with a thousand colors. There was a hint of strange perfume in the air, and I heard low music that muttered among stalagmite-like buttresses. There were pools, playing fountains, waterfalls, dim vistas stretching away, lit by slanting rays of muted sunlight.

"What kind of place is it?" I asked. "It's like a fairyland, or a dream."

"It's not an earthly scheme of decoration," Foster said, "but I find it strangely pleasing."

"Hey, look over there," I yelped suddenly, pointing. An empty-eyed skull stared past me from the shadows at the base of a column.

Foster went over to the skull, stood looking down at it. "There was a disaster here," he said. "That much is plain."

"It's creepy," I said. "Let's go back; I forgot to get film for my Brownie."

"The long-dead pose no threat," said Foster. He was kneeling, looking at the white bones. He picked up something, stared at it. "Look, Legion."

I went over. Foster held up a ring.

"We're onto something hot, pal," I said. "It's the twin to yours."

"I wonder . . . who he was."

I shook my head. "If we knew that—and who killed him—or what—"

"Let's go on. The answers must be here somewhere." Foster moved off toward a corridor that reminded me of a sunny avenue lined with chestnut trees—though there were no trees, and no sun. I followed, gaping.

For hours we wandered, looking, touching, not saying much but saturated in wonder, like kids in a toy factory. We came across another skeleton, lying among towering engines. Finally we paused in a giant storeroom stacked high with supplies.

"Have you stopped to think, Foster," I said, fingering a length of rose-violet cloth as thin as woven spider webs. "This boat's a treasure-house of salable items. Talk about the wealth of the Indies—"

"I seek only one thing here, my friend," Foster said; "my past."

"Sure," I said. "But just in case you don't find it,

you might consider the business angle. We can set up
a regular shuttle run, hauling stuff down—"

"You earthmen," sighed Foster. "For you every new
experience is immediately assessed in terms of its
merchandising possibilities. Well, I leave that to you."

"Okay, okay," I said. "You go on ahead and scout
around down that way, if you want—where the
technical-looking stuff is. I want to browse around
here for a while."

"As you wish."

"We'll meet at this end of the big hall we passed
back there. Okay?"

Foster nodded and went on. I turned to a bin filled
with what looked like unset emeralds the size of
walnuts. I picked up a handful, juggled them lovingly.

"Anyone for marbles?" I murmured to myself.

Hours later, I came along a corridor that was like
a path through a garden that was a forest, crossed a
ballroom like a meadow floored in fine-grained rust-
red wood and shaded by giant ferns, and went under
an arch into the hall where Foster sat at a long table
cut from yellow marble. A light the color of sunrise
gleamed through tall pseudo-windows.

I dumped an armful of books on the table. "Look
at these," I said. "All made from the same stuff as the
journal. And the pictures . . ."

I flipped open one of the books, a heavy folio-sized
volume, to a double-page spread in color showing a
group of bearded Arabs in dingy white djellabas staring toward the camera, a flock of thin goats in the
background. It looked like the kind of picture the
National Geographic runs, except that the quality of
the color and detail was equal to the best color
transparencies.

"I can't read the print," I said, "but I'm a whiz at
looking at pictures. Most of the books showed scenes

like I hope I never see in the flesh, but I found a few that were made on earth—God knows how long ago."

"Travel books, perhaps," Foster said.

"Travel books that you could sell to any university on earth for their next year's budget," I said, shuffling pages. "Take a look at this one."

Foster looked across at the panoramic shot of a procession of shaven-headed men in white sarongs, carrying a miniature golden boat on their shoulders, descending a long flight of white stone steps leading from a colonnade of heroic human figures with folded arms and painted faces. In the background, brick-red cliffs loomed up, baked in desert heat.

"That's the temple of Hat-Shepsut in its prime," I said. "Which makes this print close to four thousand years old. Here's another I recognize." I turned to a smaller, aerial view, showing a gigantic pyramid, its polished stone facing chipped in places and with a few panels missing from the lower levels, revealing the cruder structure of massive blocks beneath.

"That's one of the major pyramids, maybe Khufu's," I said. "It was already a couple thousand years old, and falling into disrepair. And look at this—" I opened another volume, showed Foster a vivid photograph of a great shaggy elephant with a pinkish trunk upraised between wide-curving yellow tusks.

"A mastodon," I said. "And there's a woolly rhino, and an ugly-looking critter that must be a saber-tooth. This book is *old* . . ."

"A lifetime of rummaging wouldn't exhaust the treasures aboard this ship," said Foster.

"How about bones? Did you find any more?"

Foster nodded. "There was a disaster of some sort. Perhaps disease. None of the bones was broken."

"I can't figure the one in the lifeboat," I said. "Why

was he wearing a necklace of bear's teeth?" I sat down across from Foster. "We've got plenty of mysteries to solve, all right, but there are some other items we'd better talk about. For instance: where's the kitchen? I'm getting hungry."

Foster handed me a black rod from among several that lay on the table. "I think this may be important," he said.

"What is it, a chop stick?"

"Touch it to your head, above the ear."

"What does it do—give you a massage?"

I pressed it to my temple . . .

I was in a grey-walled room, facing a towering surface of ribbed metal. I reached out, placed my hands over the proper perforations. The housings opened. For apparent malfunction in the quaternary field amplifiers, I knew, auto-inspection circuit override was necessary before activation—

I blinked, looked around at the yellow table, and piled books, the rod in my hand.

"I was in some kind of powerhouse," I said. "There was something wrong with—with . . ."

"The quaternary field amplifiers," Foster said.

"I seemed to be right there," I said. "I understood exactly what it was all about."

"These are technical manuals," Foster said. "They'll tell us everything we need to know about the ship."

"I was thinking about what I was getting ready to do," I said, "the way you do when you're starting into a job; I was trouble-shooting the quaternary whatzits— and I knew how . . . !"

Foster got to his feet and moved toward the doorway. "We'll have to start at one end of the library and work our way through," he said. "It will take us a while, but we'll get the facts we need. Then we can plan."

✧　　✧　　✧

Foster picked a handful of briefing rods from the racks in the comfortably furnished library and started in. The first thing we needed was a clue as to where to look for food and beds, or for operating instructions for the ship itself. I hoped we might find the equivalent of a library card-catalog; then we could put our hands on what we wanted in a hurry.

I went to the far end of the first rack and spotted a short row of red rods that stood out vividly among the black ones. I took one out, thought it over, decided it was unlikely that it was any more dangerous than the others, and put it against my temple . . .

As the bells rang, I applied neuro-vascular tension, suppressed cortical areas upsilon-zeta and iota, and stood by for—

I jerked the rod from my head, my ears still ringing with the shrill alarm. The effect of the rods was like reality itself, but intensified, all attention focused single-mindedly on the experience at hand. I thought of the entertainment potentialities of the idea. You could kill a tiger, ride an airplane down in flames, face the heavyweight champion—I wondered about the stronger sensations, like pain and fear. Would they seem as real as the impulse to check the whatchamacallits or tighten up your cortical thingamajigs?

I tried another rod.

At the sound of the apex-tone, I racked instruments, walked, not ran, to the nearest transfer-channel—

Another:

Having assumed duty as Alert Officer, I reported first to coordination Control via short-line, and confirmed rapport—

These were routine SOP's covering simple situations aboard ship. I skipped a few, tried again:

Needing a xivometer, I keyed instruction-complex One, followed with the code—

Three rods further along, I got this:

The situation falling outside my area of primary conditioning, I reported in corpo to Technical Briefing, Level Nine, Section Four, Sub-section Twelve, Preliminary. I recalled that it was now necessary to supply my activity code . . . my activity code . . . my activity code . . . (A sensation of disorientation grew; confused images flickered like vague background-noise; then a clear voice cut across the confusion:)

YOU HAVE SUFFERED PARTIAL PERSONALITY-FADE. DO NOT BE ALARMED. SELECT A GENERAL BACKGROUND ORIENTATION ROD FROM THE NEAREST EMERGENCY RACK. ITS LOCATION IS . . .

I was moving along the stacks, to pause in front of a niche where a U-shaped plastic strip was clamped to the wall. I removed it, fitted it to my head—(Then:) I was moving along the stacks, to pause in front of a niche—

I was leaning against the wall, my head humming. The red stick lay on the floor at my feet. That last bit had been potent: something about a general background briefing—

"Hey, Foster!" I called. "I think I've got something . . ."
He appeared from the stacks.

"As I see it," I said, "this background briefing should tell us all we need to know about the ship; then we can plan our next move more intelligently. We'll know what we're doing." I took the thing from the wall, just as I had seemed to do in the phantom scene the red rod had projected for me.

"These things make me dizzy," I said, handing it to Foster. "Anyway, you're the logical one to try it."

He took the plastic shape, went to the reclining seat at the near end of the library hall, and settled himself. "I have an idea this one will hit harder than the others," he said.

He fitted the clamp to his head and . . . instantly his eyes glazed; he slumped back, limp.

"Foster!" I yelled. I jumped forward, started to pull the plastic piece from his head, then hesitated. Maybe Foster's abrupt reaction was standard procedure—but I didn't like it much.

I went on reasoning with myself. After all, this was what the red rod had indicated as normal procedure in a given emergency. Foster was merely having his faded personality touched up. And his full-blown, three-dimensional personality was what we needed to give us the answers to a lot of the questions we'd been asking. Though the ship and everything in it had lain unused and silent for forgotten millennia, still the library should be good. The librarian was gone from his post for forgotten centuries, and Foster was lying unconscious, and I was thirty thousand miles from home—but I shouldn't let trifles like that worry me . . .

I got up and prowled the room. There wasn't much to look at except stacks and more stacks. The knowledge stored here was fantastic, both in magnitude and character. If I ever get home with a load of these rods . . .

I strolled through a door leading to another room. It was small, functional, dimly lit. The middle of the room was occupied by a large and elaborate divan with a cap-shaped fitting at one end. Other curious accoutrements were ranked along the walls. There wasn't much in them to thrill me. But bone-wise I had hit the jackpot.

Two skeletons lay near the door, in the final slump of death. Another lay beside the fancy couch. There was a long-bladed dagger beside it.

I squatted beside the two near the door and examined them closely. As far as I could tell, they were as human as I was. I wondered what kind of men they had been, what kind of world they had come from, that could build a ship like this and stock it as it was stocked.

The dagger that lay near the other bones was interesting: it seemed to be made of a transparent orange metal, and its hilt was stamped in a repeated pattern of the Two Worlds motif. It was the first clue as to what had taken place among these men when they last lived: not a complete clue, but a start.

I took a closer look at an apparatus like a dentist's chair parked against the wall. There were spidery-looking metal arms mounted above it, and a series of colored glass lenses. A row of dull silver cylinders was racked against the wall. Another projected from a socket at the side of the machine. I took it out and looked at it. It was a plain pewter-colored plastic, heavy and smooth. I felt pretty sure it was a close cousin to the chop-sticks stored in the library. I wondered what brand of information was recorded in it as I dropped it in my pocket.

I lit a cigarette and went out to where Foster lay. He was still in the same position as when I had left him. I sat down on the floor beside the couch to wait.

It was an hour before he stirred, heaved a sigh, and opened his eyes. He reached up, pulled off the plastic headpiece, dropped it on the floor.

"Are you okay?" I said. "Brother, I've been sweating . . ."

Foster looked at me, his eyes traveling up to my uncombed hair and down to my scuffed shoes. His eyes narrowed in a faint frown. Then he said something—in a language that seemed to be all Z's and Q's.

"Don't spring any surprises on me, Foster," I said hoarsely. "Talk American."

A look of surprise crossed his face. He stared into my eyes again, then glanced around the room.

"This is a ship's library," he said.

I heaved a sigh of relief. "You gave me a scare, Foster. I thought for a second your memory was wandering again."

Foster was watching my face as I spoke. "What was it all about?" I said. "What have you found out?"

"I know you," said Foster slowly. "Your name is Legion."

I nodded. I could feel myself getting tense again. "Sure, you know me. Just take it easy, pal. This is no time to lose your marbles." I put a hand on his shoulder. "You remember, we were—"

He shook my hand off. "That is not the custom in Vallon," he said coldly.

"Vallon?" I echoed. "What kind of routine is this, Foster? We were friends when we walked into this room an hour ago. We were hot on the trail of something, and I'm human enough to want to know how it turned out."

"Where are the others?"

"There's a couple of 'others' in the next room," I snapped. "But they've lost a lot of weight. I can find you several more, in the same condition. Outside of them there's only me—"

Foster looked at me as if I wasn't there. "I remember Vallon," he said. He put a hand to his head. "But I remember, too, a barbaric world, brutal and primitive. You were there. We traveled in a crude railcar, and then in a barge that wallowed in the sea. There were narrow, ugly rooms, evil odors, harsh noises."

"That's not a very flattering portrait of God's country," I said; "but I'm afraid I recognize it."

"The people were the worst," Foster said.

"Misshapen, diseased, with swollen abdomens and wasted skin and withered limbs."

"Some of the boys don't get out enough," I said.

"The Hunters! We fled from them, Legion, you and I. And I remember a landing-ring . . ." He paused. "Strange, it had lost its cap-stones and fallen into ruin."

"Us natives call it Stonehenge."

"The Hunters burst out of the earth. We fought them. But why should the Hunters seek me?"

"I was hoping you'd tell me," I said. "Do you know where this ship came from? And why?"

"This is a ship of the Two Worlds," he replied. "But I know nothing of how it came to be here."

"How about all that stuff in the journal? Maybe now you—"

"The journal!" Foster broke in. "Where is it!"

"In your coat pocket, I guess."

Foster felt through his jacket awkwardly, brought out the journal. He opened it.

I moved around to look over his shoulder. He had the book open to the first section, the part written in the curious alien characters that nobody had been able to decipher.

And he was reading it.

We sat at the library table of deep green, heavy, polished wood, the journal open at its center. For hours I had waited while Foster read. Now at last he leaned back in his chair, ran a hand through the youthful black hair, and sighed.

"My name," he said, "was Qulqlan. And this," he laid his hand upon the book, "is my story. This is one part of the past I was seeking. And I remember none of it . . ."

"Tell me what the journal says," I asked. "Read it to me."

Foster picked it up, riffled the pages. "It seems that I awoke once before, in a small room aboard this vessel. I was lying on a memo-couch, by which circumstance I knew that I had suffered a Change—"

"You mean you'd lost your memory?"

"And regained it—on the couch. My memory-trace had been re-impressed on my mind. I awoke knowing my identity, but not how I came to be aboard this vessel. The journal says that my last memory was of a building beside the Shallow Sea."

"Where's that?"

"On a far world—called Vallon."

"Yeah? And what next?"

"I looked around me and saw four men lying on the floor, slashed and bloody. One was alive. I gave him what emergency treatment I could, then searched the ship. I found three more men, dead; none living. Then the Hunters attacked, swarming to me—"

"Our friends the fire-balls?"

"Yes; they would have sucked the life from me— and I had no shield of light. I fled to the lifeboat, carrying the wounded man. I descended to the planet below; your earth. The man died there. I buried him in a shallow depression in the earth and marked the place with a stone."

"The ancient sinner," I said.

"Yes . . . I suppose it was his bones the lay brother found."

"And we found out last night that the depression was the result of dirt sifting into the ventilator shaft. But I guess you didn't know anything about the underground installation, way back then. Doesn't the journal say anything . . . ?"

"No, there is no mention made of it here." Foster shook his head. "How curious to read of the affairs of this stranger—and know he is myself."

"How about the Hunters? How did they get to earth?"

"They are insubstantial creatures," said Foster, "yet they can endure the vacuum of space. I can only surmise that they followed the lifeboat down."

"They were tailing you?"

"Yes; but I have no idea why they pursued me. They're harmless creatures in the natural state, used to seek out the rare fugitive from justice on Vallon. They can be attuned to the individual; thereafter, they follow him and mark him out for capture."

"Kind of like bloodhounds," I said. "Say, what were you: a big-time racketeer on Vallon?"

"The journal is frustratingly silent as to my Vallonian career," said Foster. "But this whole matter of the unexplained inter-galactic voyage and the evidences of violence aboard the ship make me wonder whether I, and perhaps my companions, were being exiled for crimes done in the Two Worlds."

"Wow! So they sicced the Hunters on you!" I said. "But why did they hang around at Stonehenge all this time?"

"There was a trickle of power feeding the screens," said Foster. "They need a source of electrical energy to live; until a hundred years ago it was the only one on the planet."

"How did they get down into the shaft without opening it up?"

"Given time, they pass easily through porous sub-, stances. But, of course, last night, when I came on them after their long fast, they simply burst through, in their haste."

"Okay. What happened next—after you buried the man?"

"The journal tells that I was set upon by natives, men who wore the hides of animals. One of their number entered the ship. He must have moved the drive lever. It lifted, leaving me marooned."

"So those were his bones we found in the boat," I mused, "the ones with the bear's-tooth necklace. I wonder why he didn't come into the ship."

"Undoubtedly he did. But remember the skeleton we found just inside the landing port? That must have been a fairly fresh and rather gory corpse at the time the savage stepped aboard. It probably seemed to him all too clear an indication of what lay in store for himself if he ventured further. In his terror he must have retreated to the boat to wait, and there starved to death.

"He was stranded in your world, and you were stranded in his."

"Yes," said Foster. "And then, it seems, I lived among the brute-men and came to be their king. I waited there by the landing ring through many years in the hope of rescue. Because I did not age as the natives did, I was worshipped as a god. I would have built a signaling device, but there were no pure metals, nothing I could use. I tried to teach them, but it was a work of centuries."

"I should think you could have set up a school, trained the smartest ones," I said.

"There was no lack of intelligent minds," Foster said. "It is plain that the savages were of the blood of the Two Worlds. This earth must have been seeded long ago by some ancient castaways."

"But how could you go on living—for hundreds of years? Are your people supermen that live forever?"

"The natural span of a human life is very great. Among your people, there is a wasting disease from which you all die young."

"That's no disease," I said. "You just naturally get old and die."

"The human mind is a magnificent instrument," Foster said, "not meant to wither quickly."

"I'll have to chew that one over," I said. "Why didn't you catch this disease?"

"All Vallonians are inoculated against it."

"I'd like a shot of that," I said. "But let's get back to you."

Foster turned the pages of the journal. "I ruled many peoples, under many names," he said. "I traveled in many lands, seeking for skilled metal-workers, glass-blowers, wise men. But always I returned to the landing-ring."

"It must have been tough," I said, "exiled on a strange world, living out your life in a wilderness, century after century . . ."

"My life was not without interest," Foster said. "I watched my savage people put aside their animal hides and learn the ways of civilization. I taught them how to build, and keep herds, and till the land. I built a great city, and I tried—foolishly—to teach their noble caste the code of chivalry of the Two Worlds. But although they sat at a round table like the great Ring-board at Okk-Hamiloth, they never really understood. And then they grew too wise, and wondered at their king, who never aged. I left them, and tried again to build a long-signaler. The Hunters sensed it, and swarmed to me. I drove them off with fires, and then I grew curious, and followed them back to their nest—"

"I know," I said. " '—and it was a place you knew of old: no hive but a Pit built by men.' "

"They overwhelmed me; I barely escaped with my life. Starvation had made the Hunters vicious. They would have drained my body of its life-energy."

"And if you'd known the transmitter was there—but you didn't. So you put an ocean between you and them."

"They found me even there. Each time I destroyed many of them, and fled. But always a few lived to breed and seek me out again."

"But your signaler—didn't it work?"

"No. It was a hopeless attempt. Only a highly developed technology could supply the raw materials. I could only teach what I knew, encourage the development of the sciences, and wait. And then I began to forget."

"Why?"

"A mind grows weary," Foster said. "It is the price of longevity. It must renew itself. Shock and privation hasten the Change. I had held it off for many centuries. Now I felt it coming on me.

"At home, on Vallon, a man would record his memory at such a time, store it electronically in a recording device, and, after the Change, use the memory-trace to restore, in his renewed body, his old recollections in toto. But, marooned as I was, my memories, once lost, were gone forever.

"I did what I could; I prepared a safe place, and wrote messages that I would find when I awoke—"

"When you woke up in the hotel, you were young again, overnight. How could it happen?"

"When the mind renews itself, erasing the scars of the years, the body, too, regenerates. The skin forgets its wrinkles, and the muscles their fatigue. They become again as they once were."

"When I first met you," I said, "you told me about waking up back in 1918, with no memory."

"Yours is a harsh world, Legion. I must have forgotten many times. Somewhere, some time, I lost the vital link, forgot my quest. When the Hunters came again, I fled, not understanding."

"You had a machine gun set up in the house at Mayport. What good was that against the Hunters?"

"None, I suppose," Foster replied. "But I didn't know. I only knew that I was—pursued."

"And by then you could have made a signaler," I said. "But you'd forgotten how—or even that you needed one."

"But in the end I found it—with your help, Legion. But still there is a mystery: What came to pass aboard this ship all those centuries ago? Why was I here? And what killed the others?"

"Look," I said. "Here's a theory: there was a mutiny, while you were in the machine having your memory fixed. You woke up and it was all over—and the crew was dead."

"That hypothesis will serve," said Foster. "But one day I must learn the truth of this matter."

"What I can't figure out is why somebody from Vallon didn't come after this ship. It was right here in orbit."

"Consider the immensity of space, Legion. This is one tiny world, among the stars."

"But there was a station here, fitted out for handling your ships. That sounds like it was a regular port of call. And the books with the pictures: they prove your people have been here off and one for thousands of years. Why would they stop coming?"

"There are such beacons on a thousand worlds," said Foster. "Think of it as a buoy marking a reef, a trailblaze in the wilderness. Ages could pass before a wanderer chanced this way again. The fact that the ventilator shaft at Stonehenge was choked with the debris of centuries when I first landed there shows how seldom this world was visited."

I thought about it. Bit by bit Foster was putting together the jig-saw pieces of his past. But he still had a long way to go before he had the big picture, frame and all. I had an idea:

"Say, you said you were in the memory machine. You

woke up there—and you'd just had your memory restored. Why not do the same thing again, now? That is, if your brain can take another pounding this soon."

"Yes," he said. He stood up abruptly. "There's just a chance. Come!"

I followed him out of the library into the room with the bones. He moved over to look down at them curiously.

"Quite a fracas," I said. "Three of 'em."

"This would be the room where I awakened," said Foster. "These are the men I saw dead."

"They're still dead," I said. "But what about the machine?"

Foster walked across to the fancy couch, leaned down beside it, then shook his head. "No," he said. "Of course it wouldn't be here . . ."

"What?"

"My memory-trace: the one that was used to restore my memory—that other time."

Suddenly I recalled the cylinder I had pocketed hours before. With a surprising flutter at my heart I held it up, like a kid in a classroom who knows he's got the right answer. "This it?"

Foster glanced at it briefly. "No, that's an empty—like those you see filed over there." He pointed to the rack of pewter-colored cylinders on the opposite wall. "They would be used for emergency recordings. Regular multi-life memory-traces would be key-coded with a pattern of colored lines."

"It figures," I said. "That would have been too easy. We have to do everything the hard way." I looked around. "It's a big bureau to look for a collar button under, but I guess we can try."

"It doesn't matter, really. When I return to Vallon, I'll recover my past. There are vaults where every citizen's trace is stored."

"But you had yours here with you."

"It could only have been a copy. The master trace is never removed from Okk-Hamiloth."

"I guess you'll be eager to get back there," I said. "That'll be quite a moment for you, getting back home after all these years. Speaking of years: were you able to figure out how long you were marooned down on earth?"

"I lost all record of dates long ago," said Foster. "I can only estimate the time."

"About how long?" I persisted.

"Since I descended from this ship, Legion," he said, "three thousand years have passed."

"I hate to see the team split up," I said. "You know, I was kind of getting used to being an apprentice nut. I'm going to miss you, Foster."

"Come with me to Vallon, Legion," he said.

We were standing in the observation lounge, looking out at the bright-lit surface of the earth thirty thousand miles away. Beyond it, the dead-white disk of the moon hung like a cardboard cut-out.

"Thanks anyway, buddy," I said. "I'd like to see those other worlds of yours but in the end I might regret it. It's no good giving an Eskimo a television set. I'd just sit around on Vallon pining for home: beat-up people, stinks, and all."

"You could return here some day."

"From what I understand about traveling in a ship like this," I said, "a couple of hundred years would pass before I got back, even if it only seemed like a few weeks en route. I want to live out my life here—with the kind of people I know, in the world I grew up in. It has its faults, but it's home."

"Then there is nothing I can do, Legion," Foster said, "to reward your loyalty and express my gratitude."

"Well, ah," I said. "There is a little something. Let me take the lifeboat, and stock it with a few goodies from the library, and some of those marbles from the storeroom, and a couple of the smaller mechanical gadgets. I think I know how to merchandise them in a way that'll leave the economy on an even keel—and incidentally set me up for life. As you said, I'm a materialist."

"As you wish," Foster said. "Take whatever you desire."

"One thing I'll have to do when I get back," I said, "is open the tunnel at Stonehenge enough to sneak a thermite bomb down it—if they haven't already found the beacon station."

"As I judge the temper of the local people," Foster said, "the secret is safe for at least three generations."

"I'll bring the boat down in a blind spot where radar won't pick it up," I said. "Our timing was good: in another few years, it wouldn't have been possible."

"And this ship would soon have been discovered," Foster said. "In spite of radar-negative screens."

I looked at the great smooth sphere hanging, haloed, against utter black. The Pacific Ocean threw back a brilliant image of the sun.

"I think I see an island down there that will fill the bill perfectly," I said. "And if it doesn't, there are a million more to choose from."

"You've changed, Legion," Foster said. "You sound like a man with a fair share of *joie de vivre*."

"I used to think I was a guy who never got the breaks," I said. "There's something about standing here looking at the world that makes that kind of thinking sound pretty dumb. There's everything down there a man needs to make his own breaks—even without a stock of trade goods."

"Every world has its rules of life," Foster said. "Some

more complex than others. To face your own reality—
that's the challenge."

"Me against the universe," I said. "With those odds,
even a loser can look good." I turned to Foster.
"We're in a ten-hour orbit," I said. "We'd better get
moving. I want to put the boat down in southern
South America. I know a place there where I can off-
load without answering too many questions."

"You have several hours before the most favorable
launch time," Foster said. "There's no hurry."

"Maybe not," I said. "But I've got a lot to do—" I
took a last look toward the majestic planet beyond the
viewscreen, "—and I'm eager to get started."

Chapter Eight

I sat on the terrace watching the sun go down into
the sea and thinking about Foster, somewhere out there
beyond the purple palaces on the far horizon, in the
ship that had waited for him for three thousand years,
heading home at last. It was strange to reflect that for
him, traveling near the speed of light, only a few days
had passed, while three years went by for me—three
fast years that I had made good use of.

The toughest part had been the first few months,
after I put the lifeboat down in a cañon in the desert
country south of a little town called Itzenca, in Peru.
I waited by the boat for a week, to be sure the vigi-
lantes weren't going to show up, full of helpful suggestions and embarrassing questions; then I hiked to
town, carrying a pack with a few carefully selected
items to start my new career. It took me two weeks
to work, lie, barter, and plead my way to the seaport

town of Callao and another week to line up passage home as a deck hand on a banana scow. I disappeared over the side at Tampa, and made it to Miami without attracting attention. As far as I could tell, the cops had already lost interest in me.

My old friend, the heavy-weight señorita, wasn't overjoyed to see me, but she put me up, and I started in on my plan to turn my souvenirs into money.

The items I had brought with me from the lifeboat were a pocketful of little grey dominoes that were actually movie film, and a small projector to go with them. I didn't offer them for sale, direct. I made arrangements with an old acquaintance in the business of making pictures with low costume budgets for private showings; I set up the apparatus and projected my films, and he copied them in 35 mm. I told him that I'd smuggled them in from East Germany. He didn't think much of Krauts, but he admitted you had to hand it to them technically; the special effects were absolutely top-notch. His favorite was the one I called the Mammoth Hunt.

I had twelve pictures altogether; with a little judicious cutting and a dubbed-in commentary, they made up into fast-moving twenty-minute short subjects. He got in touch with a friend in the distribution end in New York, and after a little cagey fencing over contract terms, we agreed on a deal that paid a hundred thousand for the twelve, with an option on another dozen at the same price.

Within a week after the pictures hit the neighborhood theatres around Bayonne, New Jersey, in a cautious tryout, I had offers up to half a million for my next consignment, no questions asked. I left my pal Mickey to handle the details on a percentage basis, and headed back for Itzenca.

The lifeboat was just as I'd left it; it would have been

all right for another fifty years, as far as the danger of anybody stumbling over it was concerned. I explained to the crew I brought out with me that it was a fake rocket ship, a prop I was using for a film I was making. I let them wander all over it and get their curiosity out of their systems. The consensus was that it wouldn't fool anybody; no tail fins, no ray guns, and the instrument panel was a joke; but they figured that it was my money, so they went to work setting up a system of camouflage nets (part of the plot, I told them) and offloading my cargo.

A year after my homecoming, I had my island—a square mile of perfect climate, fifteen miles off the Peruvian coast—and a house that was tailored to my every whim by a mind-reading architect who made a fortune on the job—and earned it. The uppermost floor—almost a tower—was a strong-room, and it was there that I had stored my stock in trade. I had sold off the best of the hundred or so films I had picked out before leaving Foster, but there were plenty of other items. The projector itself was the big prize. The self-contained power unit converted nuclear energy to light with 99 percent efficiency. It scanned the "films", one molecular layer at a time, and projected a continuous picture—no sixteen-frames-a-second flicker here. The color and sound were absolutely life-like—with the result that I'd had a few complaints from my distributor that the Technicolor was kind of washed-out.

The principles involved in the projector were new, and—in theory, at least—way over the heads of our local physicists. But the practical application was nothing much. I figured that, with the right contacts in scientific circles to help me introduce the system, I had a billion-dollar industry up my sleeve. I had already fed a few little gimmicks into the market; a tough paper, suitable for shirts and underwear; a chemical that bleached teeth white as the driven snow; an all-color pigment for artists. With the knowledge I had absorbed from all the briefing rods I had studied, I had the techniques of a hundred new industries at my fingertips—and I hadn't exhausted the possibilities yet.

I spent most of a year roaming the world, discovering all the things that a free hand with a dollar bill could do for a man. The next year I put in fixing up the island, buying paintings and rugs and silver for the house, and a concert grand piano. After the first big thrill of economic freedom had worn off, I still enjoyed my music.

For six months I had a full-time physical instructor giving me a twenty-four-hour-a-day routine of diet, sleep, and all the precision body-building my metabolism could stand. At the end of the course I was twice the man I'd ever been, the instructor was a physical wreck, and I was looking around for a new hobby.

Now, after three years, it was beginning to get me: boredom, the disease of the idle rich, that I had sworn would never touch me. But thinking about wealth and having it on your hands are two different things, and I was beginning to remember almost with nostalgia the tough old times when every day was an adventure, full of cops and missed meals and a thousand unappeased desires.

Not that I was really suffering. I was relaxed in a comfortable chair, after a day of surf fishing and a modest dinner of Chateaubriand. I was smoking a skinny cigar rolled by an expert from the world's finest leaf, and listening to the best music a thousand-dollar hi-fi could produce. And the view, though free, was worth a million dollars a minute. After a while I would stroll down to the boathouse, start up the

Rolls-powered launch, and tool over to the mainland, transfer to my Caddie convertible, and drive into town where a tall brunette from Stockholm was waiting for me to take her to the movies. My steady gal was a hard-working secretary for an electronics firm.

I finished up my stogie and leaned forward to drop it in a big silver ashtray, when something caught my eye out across the red-painted water. I sat squinting at it, then went inside and came out with a pair of 7x50 binoculars. I focused them and studied the dark speck that stood out clearly now against the gaudy sky. It was a heavy-looking power boat, heading dead toward my island.

I watched it come closer, swing off toward the hundred-foot concrete jetty I had built below the sea-wall, and ease alongside in a murmur of powerful engines. They died, and the boat sat in a sudden silence dwarfing the pier. I studied the bluish-grey hull, the inconspicuous flag aft. Two heavy deck guns were mounted on the foredeck, and there were four torpedoes slung in launching cradles. The hardware didn't make half as much impression on me as the ranks of helmeted men drawn up on deck.

I sat and watched. The men shuffled off onto the pier, formed up into two squads. I counted; forty-eight men, and a couple of officers. There was the faint sound of orders being barked, and the column stepped off, moving along the paved road that swung between the transplanted royal palms and hibiscus, right up to the wide drive that curved off to the house. They halted, did a left face, and stood at parade rest. The two officers, wearing class A's, and a tubby civilian with a briefcase came up the drive, trying to look as casual as possible under the circumstances. They paused at the foot of the broad flight of Tennessee marble steps leading up to my perch.

The leading officer, a brigadier general, no less, looked up at me.

"May we come up, sir?" he said.

I looked across at the silent ranks waiting at the foot of the drive.

"If the boys want a drink of water, Sarge," I said, "tell 'em to come on over."

"I am General Smale," the B.G. said. "This is Colonel Sanchez of the Peruvian Army—" he indicated the other military type "—and Mr. Pruffy of the American Embassy at Lima."

"Howdy, Mr. Pruffy," I said. "Howdy, Mr. Sanchez. Howdy—"

"This . . . ah . . . call is official in nature, Mr. Legion," the general said. "It's a matter of great importance, involving the security of your country."

"OK, General," I said. "Come on up. What's happened? You boys haven't started another war, have you?"

They filed up onto the terrace, hesitated, then shook hands, and sat down gingerly in the chairs. Pruffy held his briefcase in his lap.

"Put your sandwiches on the table, if you like, Mr. Pruffy," I said. He blinked, gripped the briefcase tighter. I offered my hand-tooled cigars around; Pruffy looked startled, Smale shook his head, and Sanchez took three.

"I'm here," the general said, "to ask you a few questions, Mr. Legion. Mr. Pruffy represents the Department of State in the matter, and Colonel Sanchez—"

"Don't tell me," I said. "He represents the Peruvian government, which is why I don't ask you what an armed American force is doing wandering around on Peruvian soil."

"Here," Pruffy put in. "I hardly think—"

"I believe you," I said. "What's it all about, Smale?"

"I'll come directly to the point," he said. "For some time, the investigative and security agencies of the US government have been building a file on what for lack of a better name has been called 'The Martians.'" Smale coughed apologetically.

"A little over three years ago," he went on, "an unidentified flying object—"

"You interested in flying saucers, General?" I said.

"By no means," he snapped. "The object appeared on a number of radar screens, descending from extreme altitude. It came to earth at . . ." he hesitated.

"Don't tell me you came all the way out here to tell me you can't tell me," I said.

"—A site in England," Smale said. "American aircraft were dispatched to investigate the object. Before they could make identification, it rose again, accelerated at tremendous speed, and was lost at an altitude of several hundred miles."

"I thought we had better radar than that," I said. "The satellite program—"

"No such specialized equipment was available," Smale said. "An intensive investigation turned up the fact that two strangers—possibly Americans—had visited the site only a few hours before the—ah—visitation."

I nodded. I was thinking about the close call I'd had when I went back to see about lobbing a bomb down the shaft to obliterate the beacon station. There were plainclothes men all over the place, like old maids at a movie star's funeral. It was just as well; they never found it. The rocket blasts had collapsed the tunnel, and apparently the whole underground installation was made of non-metallic substances that didn't show up in detecting equipment. I had an idea metal was passé where Foster came from.

"Some months later," Smale went on, "a series of

rather curious short films went on exhibition in the
United States. They showed scenes representing conditions on other planets, as well as ancient and prehis-
toric incidents here on earth. They were prefaced with
explanations that they merely represented the opinions
of science as to what was likely to be found on distant
worlds. They attracted wide interest, and with few
exceptions, scientists praised their verisimilitude."

"I admire a clever fake," I said. "With a topical
subject like space travel—"

"One item which was commented on as a surprising inaccuracy, in view of the technical excellence of
the other films," Smale said, "was the view of our
planet from space, showing the earth against the backdrop of stars. A study of the constellations by astrono-
mers quickly indicated a 'date' of approximately 7000
B.C. for the scene. Oddly, the north polar cap was
shown centered on Hudson's Bay. No south polar cap
was in evidence. The continent of Antarctica appeared
to be at a latitude of some 30, entirely free of ice."

I looked at him and waited.

"Now, studies made since that time indicate that
nine thousand years ago, the North Pole was indeed
centered on Hudson's Bay," Smale said. "And Antarctica
was in fact ice-free."

"That idea's been around a long time," I said. "There
was a theory—"

"Then there was the matter of the views of Mars,"
the general went on. "The aerial shots of the 'canals'
were regarded as very cleverly done." He turned to
Pruffy, who opened his briefcase and handed a couple
of photos across.

"This is a scene taken from the film," Smale said.
It was an 8x10 color shot, showing a row of mounds
drifted with pinkish dust, against a blue-black horizon.

Smale placed another photo beside the first. "This

one," he said, "was taken by automatic cameras in the successful Mars probe of last year."

I looked. The second shot was fuzzy, and the color was shifted badly toward the blue, but there was no mistaking the scene. The mounds were drifted a little deeper, and the angle was different, but they were the same mounds.

"In the meantime," Smale bored on relentlessly, "a number of novel products appeared on the market. Chemists and physicists alike were dumbfounded at the theoretical base implied by the techniques involved. One of the products—a type of pigment—embodied a completely new concept in crystallography."

"Progress," I said. "Why, when I was a boy—"

"It was an extremely tortuous trail we followed," Smale said. "But we found that all these curious observations making up the 'Martians' file had, in the end, only one factor in common. And that factor, Mr. Legion, was you."

Chapter Nine

It was a few minutes after sunrise, and Smale and I were back on the terrace toying with the remains of ham steaks and honeydew.

"That's one advantage of being in jail in your own house—the food's good," I commented.

"I can understand your feelings," Smale said. "Frankly, I didn't relish this assignment. But it's clear that there are matters here which require explanation. It was my hope that you'd see fit to cooperate voluntarily."

"Take your army and sail off into the sunrise,

General," I said. "Then maybe I'll be in a position to do something voluntary."

"Your patriotism alone—"

"My patriotism keeps telling me that where I come from, a citizen has certain legal rights," I said.

"This is a matter that transcends legal technicalities," Smale said. "I'll tell you quite frankly, the presence of the task force here only received *ex post facto* approval by the Peruvian government. They were faced with the *fait accompli*. I mention this only to indicate just how strongly the government feels in this matter."

"Seeing you hit the beach with a platoon of infantry was enough of a hint for me," I said. "You're lucky I didn't wipe you out with my disintegrator rays."

Smale choked on a bite of melon.

"Just kidding," I said. "But I haven't given you any trouble. Why the reinforcements?"

Smale stared at me. "What reinforcements?"

I pointed with a fork. He turned, gazed out to sea. A conning tower was breaking the surface, leaving a white wake behind. It rose higher, water streaming off the deck. A hatch popped open, and men poured out, lining up. Smale got to his feet, his napkin falling to the floor.

"Sergeant!" he yelled. I sat, open-mouth, as Smale jumped to the stair, went down it three steps at a time. I heard him bellowing, the shouts of men and the clatter of rifles being unstacked, feet pounding. I went to the marble banister and looked down. Pruffy was out on the lawn in purple pajamas, yelping questions. Colonel Sanchez was pulling at Smale's arm, also yelling. The Marines were forming up on the lawn.

"Let's watch those petunias, Sergeant," I yelled.

"Keep out of this, Legion," Smale shouted.

"Why should I be the only one not yelling," I yelled. "After all, I own the place."

Smale bounded back up the stairs. "You're my prime responsibility, Legion," he barked. "I'm getting you to a point of maximum security. Where's the cellar?"

"I keep it downstairs," I said. "What's this all about? Interservice rivalry? You afraid the sailors are going to steal the glory?"

"That's a nuclear-powered sub," Smale barked. "It belongs to the Russian Navy."

I stood there with my mouth open, looking at Smale without seeing him, and trying hard to think fast. I hadn't been too startled when the Marines showed up; I had gone over the legal aspects of my situation months before, with a platoon of high-priced legal talent; I knew that sooner or later somebody would come around to hit me for tax evasion, draft dodging, or overtime parking; but I was in the clear. The government might resent my knowing a lot of things it didn't, but no one could ever prove I'd swiped them from Uncle Sam. In the end, they'd have to let me go—and my account in a Swiss bank would last me, even if they managed to suppress any new developments from my fabulous lab. In a way, I was glad the showdown had come.

But I'd forgotten about the Russians. Naturally, they'd be interested, and their spies were at least as good as the intrepid agents of the US Secret Service. I should have realized that sooner or later, they'd pay a call—and the legal niceties wouldn't slow them down. They'd slap me into a brain laundry, and sweat every last secret out of me as casually as I'd squeeze a lemon.

The sub was fully surfaced now, and I was looking down the barrels of half a dozen five-inch rifles, any one of which could blast Smale's navy out of the water with one salvo. There were a couple of hundred men, I estimated, putting landing boats over the side and spilling into them. Down on the lawn, the sergeant was snapping orders, and the men were double-timing off to positions that must have been spotted in advance. It looked like the Russians weren't entirely unexpected. This was a game the big boys were playing, and I was just a pawn, caught in the middle. My rosy picture of me confounding the bureaucrats was fading fast. My island was about to become a battlefield, and whichever way it turned out, I'd be the loser. I had one slim possibility; to get lost in the shuffle.

Smale grabbed my arm. "Don't stand there, man!" he snapped. "Which way—"

"Sorry, General," I said, and slammed a hard right to his stomach. He folded, but still managed to lunge for me. I gave him a left to the jaw, and he dropped. I jumped over him, plunged through the French doors, and took the spiral glass stairway four at a time, whirled, and slammed the strong-room door behind me. The armored walls would stand anything short of a direct hit with a good-sized artillery shell, and the boys down below were unlikely to use any heavy stuff for fear of damaging the goods they'd been sent out to collect. I was safe for a little while.

Now I had to do some fast, accurate thinking. I couldn't carry much with me—when and if I made it off the island. A few briefing rods, maybe; what was left of the movies. But I had already audited most of the rods; I knew them as well as I know my tax bracket. One listen to a rod gave you a fast picture of the subject; two or three repeats engraved it on your brain. The only reason a man couldn't know everything was that too much, too fast, would overload the mind—and amnesia wiped the slate clean.

I didn't have time to use any more rods, and I couldn't carry anything. But just to walk off and leave it all . . .

I rummaged through odds and ends, stuffing small items into my pockets. I came across a dull silvery cylinder, three inches long, striped in black and gold—a memory trace. It reminded me of something . . .

That was an idea. I still had the U-shaped plastic headpiece that Foster had used to acquire a background knowledge of his old home. I had tried it once—for a moment. It had given me a headache in two seconds flat, just pressed against my temple. It had been lying here ever since. But maybe now was the time to try it again. Half the items I had here in my strong-room were mysteries, like the silver cylinder in my hand, but I knew exactly what the plastic headband could give me. It contained all anyone needed to know about Vallon and the Two Worlds, and all the marvels they possessed.

I glanced out the armor-glass window. Smale's Marines were trotting across the lawn; the Russians were fanning out along the water's edge. It looked like business all right. Still, it would take them a while to get warmed up—and more time still to decide to blast me out of my fort. It had taken an hour or so for Foster to soak up the briefing; maybe I wouldn't be much longer at it.

I tossed the cylinder aside, tried a couple of drawers, found the inconspicuous strip of plastic that encompassed a whole civilization. I carried it across to a chair, settled myself, then hesitated. This thing had been designed for an alien brain, not mine. Suppose it burnt out my wiring, left me here gibbering, for Smale or the Ruskis to work over?

But the alternative was to leave my island virtually empty-handed, settle for what I might in time manage to salvage from my account—if I could devise a way of withdrawing money without calling down the Gestapo . . .

No, I wouldn't go back to poverty without a struggle. What I could carry in my head would give me independence—even immunity from the greed of nations. I could barter my knowledge for my freedom.

There were plenty of things wrong with the picture, but it was the best I could do on short notice. Gingerly I fitted the U-shaped band to my head. There was a feeling of pressure, then a sensation like warm water rising about me. Panic tried to rise, faded. A voice seemed to reassure me. I was among friends, I was safe, all was well . . .

Chapter Ten

I lay in the dark, the memory of towers and trumpets and fountains of fire in my mind. I put up my hand, felt a coarse garment. Had I but dreamed . . . ? I stirred. Light blazed in a widening band above my face. Through narrowed eyes I saw a room, a mean chamber, dusty, littered with ill-assorted rubbish. In a wall there was a window. I went to it, stared out upon a green sward, a path that curved downward to a white strand. It was a strange scene, and yet—

A wave of vertigo swept over me, faded. I blinked, tried to remember.

I reached up, felt something clamped over my head. I pulled it off and it fell to the floor with a faint clatter: a broad-spectrum briefing device, of the type used to indoctrinate unidentified citizens who had undergone a Change unprepared . . .

Suddenly, like water pouring down a drain, the picture in my mind faded, left me standing in my old familiar junk room, with a humming in my head and a throb in my temples. I had been about to try the briefing gimmick, and had wondered if it would work. It had—with a vengeance. For a minute there I had stumbled around the room like a stranger, yearning for dear old Vallon. I could remember the feeling—but it was gone now. I was just me, in trouble as usual.

There were a lot of tantalizing ideas floating around in my mind, right at the edge of consciousness. Later I'd have to sit down and go over them carefully. Right now, I had my hands full. Two armies had me cornered, and all the guns belonged to the opposition. That part was okay; I didn't want to fight anybody. All I wanted out of this situation was me.

A rattle of gunfire outside brought me to the window in a jump. It was the same view as a few moments before, but it made more sense now. There was the still smoking wreckage of the PT boat, sunk in ten feet of water a few yards from the end of the jetty. Somebody must have tried to make a run for it. The Russian sub was nowhere in sight; probably it had landed the men and backed out of danger from any unexpected quarter. Two or three corpses lay in view, down by the water's edge. From where I stood I couldn't say whether they were good guys or villains.

There were more shots, coming from somewhere off to the left. It looked like the boys were fighting it out old style: hand to hand, with small arms. It figured; after all, what they wanted was me and all my clever ideas intact, not a smoking ruin.

I don't know whether it was my romantic streak or my cynical one that had made me drive the architect nuts putting secret passages in the walls of my chateau and tunnels under the lawn, but I was glad now I had them. There was a narrow door in the west wall of the strong-room that gave onto a tight spiral stair. From there I could take my choice: the boathouse, the edge of the woods behind the house, or the beach a hundred yards north of the jetty. All I had to do was—

The house trembled a split second ahead of a terrific blast that slammed me to the floor. I felt blood start from my nose. Head ringing, I scrambled to my feet, groped through the dust to my escape hatch. Somebody outside was getting impatient. It wouldn't do to have my fancy getaway route fall in before I had used it. I felt another shell hit the house: mortars, I guessed, or rockets. I must have slept through the preliminaries and wakened just in time for the main bout.

My fingers were on the sensitive pressure areas that worked the concealed door. I took a last glance around the room, where the dust was just settling from the last blast. My eyes fell on a plain pewter-colored cylinder lying where I had tossed it an hour before—but now I knew what it was. In one jump I was across the room and had grabbed it up. I remembered finding it aboard the lifeboat when I tidied up; it had lain concealed among the bones of the man with the beartooth necklace. He must have come across it, admired its pretty colors, and tucked it away in his fur pants. And now I, with my Vallonian memories banked in my mind, could appreciate just how precious an object it was. It was Foster's memory. It would be only a copy, undoubtedly; still, I couldn't leave it behind.

A blast heavier than the last one rocked the house; a big chunk of plaster fell. It was way past time to go. Snorting and coughing from the dust, I got back to the emergency door, went through it, and started down.

At the bottom I paused to think it over, and the earth jumped again. I fell back, saw the roof of the beach tunnel collapse. That left the woods and the boathouse. I didn't have much time to decide; the tunnels might go any second. Apparently my architect had economized on the tunnel shorings. But then, he hadn't figured on any major wars happening in the front yard.

The fight was going on, as near as I could judge, to the south of the house and behind it. Probably the woods were full of skirmishers, taking advantage of the cover. The best bet was the boathouse, direct. I'd have preferred to wait until dark, but the idea didn't seem practical under the circumstances. I took a deep breath and started into the tunnel. With a little luck I'd find my boat intact. I would have to pull out under the noses of the combatants, but maybe the element of surprise would give me a few hundred yards' start. I had enough horses to beat anything afloat to the mainland—if I could make a clean break.

The tunnel was dark but that didn't bother me. It ran dead straight to the boathouse. I came to the wooden slat door and stood for a moment, listening; everything was quiet. I eased it open and stepped on to the ramp inside the building. In the gloom polished mahogany and chrome-work threw back muted highlights. I circled, slipped the mooring rope, and was about to step into the cockpit when I heard the bolt of a rifle smack home. I whirled, threw myself flat. The deafening *bam!* of a .30 caliber fired at close quarters laid a pattern of fine ripples on the black water. I rolled, hit with a splash that drowned a second shot, and dove deep. Three strokes took me under the door, out into the green gloom of open water. I hugged the yellowish sand of the bottom, angled off to the right, and kept going.

I had to get out of my jacket, and somehow I managed it, almost without losing a stroke. And there were all the goodies I'd stashed away in the pockets, down to the bottom of the drink. I still had Foster's memory-trace; it was in my slacks and there wasn't time to get out of them nor to kick off my tennis shoes. Ten strokes, fifteen, twenty. I knew my limit: twenty-five good strokes on a full load of air; but I had dived in a hurry . . .

Twenty-five . . . and another . . . and one more. And up above a man was waiting, rifle aimed, for my head to break the surface.

Thirty strokes, and here I come, ready or not. I rolled on my back, got my face above the surface. I got half a gulp of fresh air before the shot slapped spray into my face and echoed off across the water. I sank like a stone, kicked off, and made another twenty-five yards before I had to come up. The rifleman was faster this time. The bullet crossed my shoulder like a hot iron, and I was under water again. My kick-work was weak now; the strength was draining from my arms fast. I had to have air—but I could almost feel the solid smack of a steel-jacketed bullet against my skull. I had to keep going. My chest was on fire and there was a whirling blackness all around me. I felt consciousness fading, but maybe just one more stroke . . .

As from a distance I observed the clumsy efforts of the swimmer, watched the flounderings of the poor, untrained creature . . .

It was apparent that an override of the autonomic system was required. With dispatch I activated cortical area omicron, re-routed the blood supply, drew an emergency oxygen source from stored fats, diverting the necessary energy to break the molecular bonds.

Now, with the body drawing on internal sources, ample for six hundred seconds at maximum demand, I stimulated areas upsilon and mu. I channeled full survival-level energy to the muscle complexes involved, increased power output to full skeletal tolerance, eliminated waste motion.

The body drove through the water with the fluid grace of a sea-denizen . . .

I floated on my back, breathing in great surges of cool air and blinking at the crimson sky. I had been under water, a few yards from shore, drowning. Then there was an awareness, like a voice, telling me what to do. From out of the mass of Vallonian knowledge I had acquired, I had drawn what I needed. And now I was here, half a mile from the beach, winded but intact. But there was no time now to wonder at miracles . . .

I raised my head and glanced toward the house. A column of smoke rose from a gaping cavity where the bedroom windows used to be. A man jumped up, darted across the lawn, fell. I heard a shot a few seconds later, floating lazily across the still sunset water. There was no visible activity at the water's edge; the rifleman was gone. He probably thought he'd finished me, especially if he had noticed blood in the water.

I thought about sharks. I hadn't heard of any in this neighborhood, but a little blood was just the thing to bait them in. I twisted, got a look at the throbbing burn across my left shoulder where the rifleman's bullet had grazed; it was nothing much, just a skin gouge. It didn't seem to be bleeding. If it had been, there wasn't much I could do about it. It was no time for worrying. I had to keep my mind on the problem of getting to the mainland. It was a fifteen-mile swim, but if the boys on shore could keep each other occupied, I ought to be able to make it. I thought again about pulling off my pants and shoes but decided against it; I'd be in awkward shape without them—if I made it.

I felt beat: as though I hadn't eaten all day—which wasn't too strange, because I hadn't. Well, at least I wouldn't get stomach cramps while circling the island. From there I'd strike out for shore. And the first thing

I would do when I got out of this would be to order the biggest, rarest steak in South America.

I took a last look toward the house. I could see fire inside it now. I guessed each side was rationalizing the destruction as denial to the enemy. It had been a nice place and I'd miss it. Some day somebody was going to pay for it.

Chapter Eleven

I sat at the kitchen table in Margareta's Lima apartment and gnawed the last few shreds off the stripped T-bone, while my girl poured me another cup of coffee.

"Now tell me about it," she said. "Why did they burn your house? And how did you succeed in getting here?"

"They got so interested in the fight, they lost their heads," I said. "That's the only explanation I can think of. I thought I'd be as safe as a two-dollar watch at a pickpockets' convention: I figured they'd go to some pains to avoid damaging me. I guessed wrong."

"But your own people . . ."

"Maybe they were right: they couldn't afford to let the Ruskis get me. Funny—if they'd just thought to write me a letter and ask for my co-operation . . ."

"But how did you get covered with mud? And the blood stains on your back?"

"I had a nice long swim: five hours' worth. Then another hour getting through a mangrove swamp. Lucky I had a moon. Then a three-hour hike . . . and here I am."

"I hope you're feeling better now that you've had something to eat. You looked terrible."

"Another block and I wouldn't have made it. I felt sucked dry. The scratch on my back is nothing, but maybe the shock . . . I don't know."

"Lie down now and sleep," said Margareta. "What do you want me to do?"

"Get me some clothes," I said. "A grey suit, white shirt, black tie and shoes. And go to my bank and draw some money, say five thousand. Oh yeah, see if there's anything in the papers. If you see anybody hanging around the lobby when you come back, don't come up; give me a call and I'll meet you."

She stood up. "This is really awful," she said. "Can't your embassy—"

"Didn't I mention it? A Mr. Pruffy, of the embassy, came along to hold Smale's hand . . . not to mention a Colonel Sanchez. I wouldn't be surprised if the local cops weren't in the act by now . . . unless they all think I'm dead. That impression won't last long after you show up with a nice fresh check on my account and spend part of it on a man's suit. I'll get some sleep and light out as soon as you get back."

"Where will you go?"

"I'll get to the airport and play it by ear. I don't think they've alerted everybody. It was a hush-hush deal, until it went sour; now they're still picking up the pieces."

"The bank won't be open for hours yet," said Margareta. "Go to sleep and don't worry. I'll take care of everything."

I made it to the bedroom and slid out on the big wide bed, and consciousness slipped away like a silk curtain falling.

I knew I wasn't alone as soon as I opened my eyes. I hadn't heard anything, but I could feel someone in the room. I sat up slowly, looked around.

He was sitting in the embroidered chair by the

window: an ordinary-looking fellow in a tan tropical suit, with an unlighted cigarette in his mouth and no particular expression on his face.

"Go ahead, light up," I said. "Don't mind me."

"Thanks," he said, in a thin voice. He took a lighter from an inner pocket, flipped it, held it to the cigarette.

I stood up. There was a blur of motion from my visitor, and the lighter was gone and a short-nosed revolver was in its place.

"You've got the wrong scoop, mister," I said. "I don't bite."

"I'd rather you wouldn't move suddenly, Mr. Legion," he said. He coughed, his eyes on mine. "My nerves aren't what they used to be." The gun was still on me.

"Which side are you working for?" I said. "And can I put my shoes on, or are you afraid I'll pull a gun out of my sock?"

He rested the pistol on his knee. "Get completely dressed, Mr. Legion."

"Sorry," I said. "No can do. No clothes."

He frowned slightly. "My jacket will be a little small for you," he said. "But I think you can manage."

I was sitting on the bed again. "I'm going to get out a cigarette," I said. "Try not to shoot me." I reached for a package on the table, lit up. His eyes stayed on mine.

"How come you didn't figure I was dead?" I asked, blowing smoke at him.

"We checked the house," he said. "No body."

"Why, you incompetent asses. You were supposed to think I drowned."

"That possibility was considered. But we made the routine checks anyway."

"Nice of you to let me sleep it out. How long have you been here?"

"Only a few minutes," he said. He glanced at his watch. "We'll have to be going in another fifteen."

"What do you want with me?" I said. "You blew up everything you were interested in."

"The Department wants to ask you a few questions."

"Look, I'm just a dumb guy," I whined. "I don't know nothing about all that stuff. I was just the guy that peddled it, see?"

He took a drag on his cigarette, squinted at me through the smoke. "You ran up an A average in college," he said, "including English."

"You boys really do your homework." I looked at the pistol. "I wonder if you'd really shoot me," I mused.

"I'll try to make the position clear," he said. "Just to avoid any unfortunate misunderstanding. My instructions are to bring you in, alive—if possible. If it appears that you may evade arrest . . . or fall into the wrong hands, I'll be forced to use the gun."

I pulled my shoes on, thinking it over. My best chance to make a break was now, while there was only one watchdog. But I had a feeling he was telling the truth about shooting me. I had already seen the boys in action at the house.

He got up. "Let's step into the living room, Mr. Legion." I moved past him through the door. In the living room the clock on the mantel said eleven. I'd been asleep for five or six hours. Margareta ought to be getting back any minute . . .

"Put this on," he said. I took the light jacket, wedged myself into it, looked at my reflection in the big rectangular mirror that occupied most of a wall above the low divan.

"It's not the real me," I said. "I usually—"

The telephone rang.

I looked at my watchdog. He shook his head. We stood and listened to it ring. After a while it stopped.

"We'd better be going now," he said. "Walk ahead of me, please. We'll take the elevator to the basement and leave by the service entrance—"

He stopped talking, eyes on the door. There was the rattle of a key. The gun came up.

"Hold it," I snapped. "It's the girl who owns the apartment." I moved to face him, my back to the door.

"That was foolish of you, Legion," he said. "Don't move again."

I watched the door in the big mirror on the opposite wall. The knob turned, the door swung in . . . and a thin brown man in white shirt and white pants slipped into the room. As he pushed the door back he transferred a small automatic to his left hand. My keeper threw a lever on the revolver that was aimed at my belt buckle.

"Stand absolutely still, Legion," he said. "If you have a chance, that's it." He moved aside slightly, looked past me to the newcomer. I watched in the mirror as the man in white behind me swiveled to keep both of us covered.

"This is a fail-safe weapon," said my first owner to the new man. "I think you know about them. We leaked the information to you. I'm holding the trigger back; if my hand relaxes, it fires, so I'd be a little careful about shooting, if I were you."

The thin man swallowed, a black leather bow tie bobbing against his Adam's apple. He didn't say anything. He was having to make some tough decisions. His instructions would be the same as my other friend's: to bring me in alive, if possible.

"Who does this bird represent?" I asked my man. I noticed my voice was pitched half an octave higher than usual.

"He's a Russian agent."

I looked in the mirror at the man again. "Nuts," I

said. "He looks like a waiter in a chili joint. He probably came up to take our order."

"You talk too much when you're nervous," said my keeper between his teeth. He held the gun on me steadily. I watched his trigger finger to see if it looked like relaxing.

"I'd say it's a stalemate," I said. "Let's take it once more from the top. Both of you go out and—"

"Shut up, Legion." My man licked his lips, glanced at my face. "I'm sorry. It looks as though—"

"You don't want to shoot me," I blurted out loudly. In the mirror I had seen the door, which was standing ajar, ease open an inch, two inches. "You'll spoil this nice coat . . ." I kept on talking: "And anyway it would be a big mistake, because everybody knows Russian agents are stubby men with wide cheekbones and tight hats—"

Silently Margareta slipped into the room, took two quick steps, and slammed a heavy handbag down on the slicked-back pompadour that went with the Adam's apple. The man in white stumbled and fired a round into the rug. The automatic dropped from his hand, and my pal in tan stepped to him and hit him hard on the back of the head with his pistol. He whirled toward me, hissed "Play it smart" just loud enough for me to hear, then turned to Margareta. He slipped the gun into his pocket, but I knew he could get it out again in a hurry.

"Very nicely done, Miss," he said. "I'll have this person removed from your apartment. Mr. Legion and I were just going."

Margareta looked at me. I thought over two or three remarks but none of them seemed to fit. I didn't intend to see her get hurt—or involved. Apparently my FBI type was willing to leave her out of it, if I went quietly. On the other hand, this was my last chance to get out of the net before it closed for good. My keeper was watching, waiting for me to try something, tip Margareta off . . .

"It's okay, honey," I said. "This is Mr. Smith . . . of our Embassy. We're old friends." I stepped past her, headed for the door. My hand was on the knob when I heard a solid thunk behind me. I whirled in time to clip the FBI on the jaw as he fell forward. Margareta looked at me, wide-eyed.

"That handbag packs a wallop," I said. "Nice work, Maggie." I knelt, pulled off the fellow's belt, and cinched his hands behind his back with it. Margareta got the idea, did the same for the other man, who was beginning to groan now.

"Who are these men?" she said. "What—"

"I'll tell you all about it later. Right now, I have to get to some people I know, get this story on the wires, out in the open. State'll be a little shy about gunning me down or locking me up without trial, if I give the show enough publicity."

I reached in my pocket, handed her the black-and-gold-marked cylinder. "Just to be on the safe side," I said, "mail this to me: John Jones—at Itzenca, general delivery."

"All right," said Margareta. "And I have your things." She stepped into the hall, came back with a shopping bag and a suit carton. She took a wad of bills from her handbag and handed it to me.

I went to her and put my arms around her. "Listen, honey: as soon as I leave, go to the bank and draw fifty grand. Get out of the country. They haven't got anything on you except that you beaned a couple of intruders in your apartment, but it'll be better if you disappear. Leave an address care of Poste Restante, Basel, Switzerland. I'll get in touch when I can."

She put up an argument but I made my point.

Twenty minutes later I was pushing through the big glass doors onto the sidewalk, clean-shaven, dressed to the teeth, with five grand on one hip and a .32 on the other. I'd had a good meal and a fair sleep, and against me the secret services of two or three countries didn't have a chance.

I got as far as the corner before they nailed me.

Chapter Twelve

"You have a great deal to lose," General Smale was saying, "and nothing to gain by your stubbornness. You're a young man, vigorous and, I'm sure, intelligent. You have a fortune of some million and a quarter dollars, which I assure you you'll be permitted to keep. As against that prospect, so long as you refuse to co-operate, we must regard you as no better than a traitorous criminal—and deal with you accordingly."

"What have you been feeding me?" I said. "My mouth tastes like somebody's old gym shoes and my arm's purple to the elbow. Don't you know it's illegal to administer drugs without a license?"

"The nation's security is at stake," snapped Smale.

"The funny thing is, it must not have worked, or you wouldn't be begging me to tell all. I thought that scopolamine or whatever you're using was the real goods."

"We've gotten nothing but gibberish," Smale said, "most of it in an incomprehensible language. Who the devil are you, Legion? Where do you come from?"

"You know everything," I said. "You told me yourself. I'm a guy named Legion, from Mount Sterling, Illinois, population one thousand eight hundred and ninety-two."

"I'm a humane man, Legion. But if necessary I'll beat it out of you."

"You?" I smiled, curling a lip. "You mean you'll call in a herd of plug-uglies: real crooks, to do the dirty work. My only crime is knowing something you politicians want, and you're willing to lie, cheat, steal, torture, and kill to get it. You know that and so do I; let's not kid each other. I know your measure as a man, Mr. General."

Smale had gone white. "I'm in a position to inflict agonies on you, you insolent rotter," he grated. "I've refrained from doing so. You might add that to your analysis of my character. I'm a soldier; I know my duty. I'm prepared to give my life; if need be, my honor. I'm even prepared to forego your good opinion—so long as I obtain for my government the information you're withholding."

"Turn me loose; then ask me in a nice way. As far as I know, I haven't got anything of military significance to tell you, but if I were treated as a free citizen I might be inclined to let you be the judge of that."

"Tell us now; then you'll go free."

"Sure," I said. "I invented a combination rocket ship and time machine. I traveled around the solar system and made a few short trips back into history. In my spare time I invented other gadgets. I'm planning to take out patents, so naturally I don't intend to spill any secrets. Can I go now?"

Smale got to his feet. "Until we can safely move you, you'll remain in this room. You're on the sixty-third floor of the Yordano Building. The windows are of unbreakable glass, in case you contemplate a particularly untidy suicide. Your person has been stripped of all potentially dangerous items, though I suppose you could still swallow your tongue and suffocate. The door is of heavy construction, and securely locked."

"I forgot to tell you," I said. "I mailed a letter to a friend, telling him all about you. The sheriff will be here with a posse any minute now, to spring me—"

"You mailed no letter," Smale said. "Unfortunately, we don't feel it would be advisable to allow any furniture to remain here which you might be foolish enough to dismantle for use as a weapon. It's rather a drab room to spend your future in, but until you decide to cooperate this will be your world."

I didn't say anything. I sat on the floor and watched him leave. I caught a glimpse of two uniformed men outside the door. No doubt they'd take turns looking through the peephole. I'd have solitude without privacy. I wondered if Margareta had managed to mail the cylinder.

I stretched out on the floor, which was padded with a nice thick rug, presumably so that I wouldn't beat my brains out against it just to spite them. I was way behind on my sleep: being interrogated while unconscious wasn't a very restful procedure. I wasn't too worried. In spite of what Smale said, they couldn't keep me here forever. Maybe Margareta had gotten clear and told the story to some newsmen; this kind of thing couldn't stay hidden forever. Or could it?

I thought about what Smale had said about my talking gibberish under the narcotics. That was an odd one . . .

Quite suddenly I got it. By means of the drugs they must have tapped a level where the Vallonian background briefing was stored: they'd been firing questions at a set of memories that didn't speak English. I grinned, then laughed out loud. Luck was still in the saddle with me.

The glass was in double panels, set in aluminum frames and sealed with a plastic strip. The space between the two panels of glass was evacuated of air, creating an insulating barrier against the heat of the sun. I ran a finger over the aluminum. It was dural: good tough stuff. If I had something to pry with, I might possibly lever the metal away from the glass far enough to take a crack at the edge, the weak point of armor-glass . . . if I had something to hit it with.

Smale had done a good job of stripping the room—and me. I had my shirt and pants and shoes, but no tie or belt. I still had my wallet—empty, a pack of cigarettes with two wilted weeds in it, and a box of matches. Smale had missed a bet: I might set fire to my hair and burn to the ground. I might also stuff a sock down my throat and strangle, or hang myself with a shoe lace—but I wasn't going to.

I looked at the window some more. The door was too tough to tackle, and the heavies outside were probably hoping for an excuse to work me over. They wouldn't expect me to go after the glass; after all, I was still sixty-three stories up. What would I do if I did make it to the window sill? But we could worry about that later, after I had smelled the fresh air.

My forefinger found an irregularity in the smooth metal: a short groove. I looked closer, saw a screw head set flush with the aluminum surface. Maybe if the frame was bolted together—

No such luck; the screw I had found was the only one. What was it for? Maybe if I removed it I'd find out. But I'd wait until dark to try it. Smale hadn't left a light fixture in the room. After sundown I'd be able to work unobserved.

A couple of hours went by and no one came to disturb my solitude, not even to feed me. Maybe they planned to starve me out; or maybe they weren't used to being jailers and had forgotten the animals had to be fed.

I had a short scrap of metal I'd worked loose from my wallet. It was mild steel, flimsy stuff, only about an inch long, but I was hoping the screw might not be set too tight. Aluminum threads strip pretty easily, so it probably wasn't cinched up too hard.

There was no point in theorizing. It was dark now; I'd give it a try. I went to the window, fitted the edge of metal into the slotted screw-head, and twisted. It turned, just like that. I backed it off ten turns, twenty; it was a thick bolt with fine threads. It came free and air whooshed into the hole. The screw apparently sealed the panel after the air was evacuated.

I thought it over. If I could fill the space between the panels with water and let it freeze . . . quite a trick in the tropics. I might as well plan to fill it with gin and set it on fire.

I was going in circles. Every idea I had started with 'if.' I needed something I could manage with the material at hand: cloth, a box of matches, a few bits of paper.

I got out a cigarette, lit up, and while the match was burning examined the hole from which I'd removed the plug. It was about three-sixteenths of an inch in diameter and an inch deep, and there was a hole near the bottom communicating with the air space between the glass panels. It was an old-fashioned method of manufacture but it seemed to have worked all right: the air was pumped out and the hole sealed with the screw. It had at any rate the advantage of being easy to service if the panel leaked. Now, with some way of pumping air *in*, I could blow out the panels . . .

There was no pump on the premises but I did have some chemicals: the match heads. They were old style too, like a lot of things in Peru: the strike-once-and-throw-away kind.

I sat on the floor and started to work, chipping the

heads off the matchsticks, collecting the dry, purplish material on a scrap of paper. Thirty-eight matches gave me a respectable sample. I packed it together, rolled it in the paper, and crimped the ends. Then I tucked the makeshift firecracker into the hole the screw had come from.

Using the metal scrap I scraped at the threads of the screw, burring them. Then I started it in the hole, half a dozen turns, until it came up against the match heads.

The shoes Margareta had bought me were the latest thing in Lima styles, with thin soles, pointed toes, and built-up leather heels: Bad on the feet, but just the thing to pound with. I thought about trying to work loose a piece of rug to shield my face, but decided against it. I'd have to stand aside and take my chances.

I took the shoe by the toe and hefted it: the flexible sole gave it a good action, like a well-made sap. There were still a couple of 'ifs' in the equation, but a healthy crack on the screw ought to drive it against the packed match-heads hard enough to detonate them, and the expanding gasses from the explosion ought to exert enough pressure against the glass panels to break them. I'd know in a second.

I flattened myself against the wall, brought the shoe up, and laid it on the screw-head with everything I had . . .

There was a deafening boom, a blast of hot air, and a chemical stink, then a gust of cool night wind—and I was on the sill, my back to the street six hundred feet below, my fingers groping for a hold on the ledge above the window. I found a grip, pulled up, reached higher, got my feet on the muntin strip, paused to rest for three seconds, reached again . . .

I pulled my feet above the window level and heard shouts in the room below:

"—fool killed himself!"

"Get a light in here!"

I clung, breathing deep, and murmured thanks to the architect who had stressed a strong horizontal element in his façade and arranged the strip windows in bays set twelve inches from the face of the structure. Now, if the boys below would keep their eyes on the street long enough for me to get on the roof—

I looked up, to get an idea how far I'd have to go— and gripped the ledge convulsively as the whole building leaned out, tilting me back . . .

Cold sweat ran into my eyes. I squeezed the stone until my knuckles creaked and held on. I laid my cheek against the rough plaster, listening to my heart thump. Adrenalin and high hopes had gotten me this far . . . and now it had all drained out and left me, a frail ground-loving animal, flattened against the cruel face of a tower, like a fly on a ceiling, with nothing between me and the unyielding concrete below but the feeble grip of fingers and toes. I started to yell for help, and the words stuck in my dry throat. I breathed in shallow gasps, feeling my muscles tightening, until I hung, rigid as a board, afraid even to roll my eyeballs for fear of dislodging myself. I closed my eyes, felt my hands going numb, and tried again to yell: only a thin croak emerged.

A minute earlier I had had only one worry: that they'd look up and see me. Now my worst fear was that they wouldn't.

This was the end. I'd been close before, but not like this. My fingers could take the strain for maybe another minute, maybe even two; then I'd let go, and the wind would whip at me for a few timeless seconds, before I hit . . .

I had had a lot of big ideas but in the cosmic scheme I was a gnat on a windshield. I thought I'd learned something, was a jump ahead of most guys, and could play the meaningless game with a certain flair. But my fancy philosophies were words written in smoke when they came up against the raw power of blind instinct. My conscious mind had an I.Q. of 148, but the idiot subconscious that had frozen me here hadn't learned anything since the first ape that had owned it rode out a storm in a tree-top and lived to be my ancestor . . . I heard a sound and it was me, whimpering. I was a poor weakling, out of his element, bleating for mercy.

Down inside of me something didn't like the picture. A small defiance flickered, found a foothold, burned brighter. I would die . . . but that would solve a lot of problems. And if I had to die, at least I could die trying.

My mind moved in to take over from my body. It was the body that was wasting my last strength on a precarious illusion of safety, numbing my senses, paralyzing me. It was a tyranny I wouldn't accept. I needed a cool head and a steady hand and an unimpaired sense of balance; and if the imbecile body wouldn't cooperate the mind would take it by the scruff of the neck and force it. I'd been feeding this hulk for thirty-odd years; now it would do what I told it. First: loosen the grip—

Yes! If it killed me: bend those fingers! Sure, I might fall—all the way—and splatter when I hit, but did this lousy slab of meat expect to live forever? I had news for it: time was short, any way you figured.

I was standing a little looser now, my hands resting flat, my legs taking the load. I had a good wide ledge to stand on: nearly a foot, and in a minute I was going to reach up and get a new hold and lift one foot at a time . . . and if I slipped, at least I'd have done it my way.

I let go, and the building leaned out, and to hell with it . . .

I felt for the next ledge, gripped it, pulled up, found a toe-hold.

Sure, I was dead. It was a long way to the top, and there was a fancy cornice I'd never get over, but when the moment came and I started the long ride down I'd thumb my nose at the old hag, Instinct, who hadn't been as tough as she thought she was . . .

I was under the cornice now, hanging on for a breather, and listening to the hooting and hollering from the window far below. A couple of heads had popped out and taken a look, but it was dark up where I was and all the attention was centered down where the crowd had gathered and lights were playing, looking for a mess. Pretty soon now they'd begin to get the drift—so I'd better be going.

I looked up at the overhang . . . and felt the old urge to clutch and hang on. So I leaned outward a little further, just to show me who was boss. It was a long reach, and I'd have to risk it all on one lunge because, if I missed, there wasn't any net, and my fingers knew it. I heard my nails rasp on the plaster. I grated my teeth together and unhooked one hand: it was like a claw carved from wood. I took a half-breath, bent my knees slightly; they were as responsive as a couple of bumper-jacks bolted on to the hip. Tough; but it was now or never . . .

I let go with both hands and stretched, leaning back . . .

My wooden hands bumped the edge, scrabbled, hooked on, as my legs swung free, and I was hanging like an old-time sailor strung up by the thumbs. A wind off the roof whipped at my face and now I was a tissue-paper doll, fluttering in the breeze.

I had to pull now, pull hard, heave myself up and over the edge, but I was tired, too tired. My crepe paper arms with the wooden hands seemed to belong to someone else, someone who'd been dead a long time . . .

But the someone was me: death was an old story, one that I wrote myself. This was something that had happened before, long ago, and the palindrome of life was finished where it started, and a dark curtain was falling . . .

Then from the darkness a voice was speaking in a strange language: a confusion of strange thought symbols, but through them an ever more insistent call:

. . . *dilate the secondary vascular complex, shunt full conductivity to the upsilon neuro-channel. Now, stripping oxygen ions from fatty cell masses, pour in electrochemical energy to the sinews* . . .

With a smooth surge of power I pulled myself up, fell forward, rolled onto my back, and lay on the flat roof, the beautiful flat roof, still warm from the day's sun.

I was here, looking at the stars, safe; and later on when I had more time I'd stop to think about it. But now I had to move, before they had time to organize themselves, cordon off the building, and start a floor-by-floor search.

Staggering from the exertion of the long climb I got to my feet, went to the shed housing the entry to the service stair. The door was locked. I didn't waste any time kicking at it; I got a leg up and stood on the doorknob. Two jumps and it snapped off. I pushed the stub of the shaft through and tickled the back edge of the locking tongue, eased it out. The door opened.

A short flight of steps led down to a storeroom. There were dusty boards, dried-up paint cans, odd tools. I picked up a five-foot length of two-by-four and a hammer with one claw missing, and stepped out into the hall. The street was a long way down and I didn't feel like wasting time with stairs. I found the elevator, pushed the button, stood in front of it whistling. A fat man in a drab suit came along, looked at me distastefully, thought about telling me that the workmen used the freight elevator, then changed his mind and said nothing.

The elevator arrived. I stepped in jauntily. The fat man followed me, pushed the button for the foyer. I smiled and nodded, went on whistling.

We stopped and the doors opened. I waited for the fat man to leave, then glanced out, tightening my grip on the hammer, and followed. I could see the lights in the street out front and in the distance there was the wail of a siren, but nobody in the lobby looked my way. I headed across toward the side exit, dumped the board at the door, tucked the hammer in the waist band of my pants, and stepped out onto the pavement. There were a lot of people hurrying past but this was Lima: they didn't waste a glance on a barefooted carpenter.

I moved off, not hurrying. There was a lot of rough country between me and Itzenca, the little town near which the life boat was hidden in a cañon, but I aimed to cover it in a week. Some time between now and tomorrow I'd have to figure out a way to equip myself with a few necessities, but I wasn't worried. A man who had successfully taken up human-fly work in middle life wouldn't have any trouble stealing a pair of boots.

Foster had shoved off for home three years ago, local time, although to him, aboard the ship, only a few weeks might have passed. My lifeboat was a midge compared to the mother ship he rode, but it had plenty of speed. Once aboard the lugger . . . and maybe I could put a little space between me and the big boys I was up against now.

I had used the best camouflage I knew of on the boat. The near-savage native bearers who had done my

unloading and carried my Vallonian treasures across the
desert to the nearest railhead were not the gossipy type.
If General Smale's boys had heard about the boat, they
hadn't mentioned it. And if they had: well, I'd solve
that one when I got to it. There were still quite a few
'ifs' in the equation, but my arithmetic was getting
better all the time.

Chapter Thirteen

I took the precaution of sneaking up on the lifeboat
in the dead of night, but I could have saved myself a
crawl. Except for the fact that the camouflage nets had
rotted away to shreds, the ship was just as I had left
it, doors sealed. Why Smale's team hadn't found it, I
didn't know; I'd think that one over when I was well
away from Earth.

It had been a long tough trip from Lima to the
cañon, but I had made it without interference. I had
swapped my platinum finger ring for a beat-up .38
pistol, but I hadn't had to use it. In a shabby bar in
one of the villages I passed through I had heard a
battered radio sputtering news; there was no mention
of the assault on the island, or of my escape. It seemed
that all parties were willing to cover it up and pretend
it hadn't happened.

I went into the post office at Itzenca and picked up
the parcel Margareta had mailed me with Foster's
memory-trace in it. While I was checking to see
whether Uncle Sam's minions had intercepted the
package and substituted a carrot, I felt something
rubbing against my shin. I glanced down and saw a grey
and white cat, reasonably clean and obviously hungry.

I didn't know whether I'd ploughed through a field of wild catnip the night before or if it was my way with a finger behind the furry ears, but Kitty followed me out of Itzenca and right into the bush. She kept pace with me, leading most of the time, as far as the space boat, and was the first one aboard.

I didn't waste time with formalities. I had once audited a briefing rod on the boat's operation—not that I had ever expected to use the information for a take-off. Once aboard, I hit the controls and cut a swathe through the atmosphere that must have sent fingers jumping for panic buttons from Washington to Moscow.

I didn't know how many weeks or months of unsullied leisure stretched ahead of me now. There would be time and to spare for exploring the boat, working out a daily routine, chewing over the details of both my memories, and laying plans for my arrival on Foster's world, Vallon. But first I wanted to catch a show that was making a one-night stand for me only: the awe-inspiring spectacle of the retreating earth.

I dropped into a seat opposite the screen and flipped into view the big luminous ball of wool that was my home planet. I'd been hoping to get a last look at my island, but I couldn't see it. The whole sphere was blanketed in cloud: a thin worn blanket in places but still intact. But the moon was a sight! An undipped Edam cheese with the markings of Roquefort. For a quarter of an hour I watched it grow until it filled my screen. It was too close for comfort. I dumped the tabby out of my lap and adjusted a dial. The dead world swept past, and I had a brief glimpse of burst bubbles of craters that became the eyes and mouth and pock marks of a face on a head that swung away from me in disdain and then the sibling planets dwindled and were gone forever.

The lifeboat was completely equipped, and I found comfortable quarters. An ample food supply was available by the touch of a panel on the table in the screen-room. That was a trick my predecessor with the dental jewelry hadn't discovered, I guessed. During the courses of my first journey earthward and on my visits to the boat for saleable playthings while she lay in dry-dock, I had discovered most of the available amenities aboard. Now I luxuriated in a steaming bath of recycled water, sponged down with disposable towels packed in scented alcohol, fed the cat and myself, and lay down to sleep for about two weeks.

By the third week I was reasonably refreshed and rested. The scars from my recent brushes with what passed as the law were healed. I had gotten over regretting the toys I'd left behind on my island and the money in my banks in Lima and Switzerland, and even Margareta. I was headed for a new world; there was no point in dragging along old attachments.

The cat was a godsend, I began to realize. I named her Itzenca, after the village where she adopted me, and I talked to her by the hour. I always had felt that there was a subtle difference between talking to some-body else and talking to yourself. The latter gets a little tedious after the first few days but you can keep the other up indefinitely. So Itz got talked to plenty as we rode to the stars.

"Say, Itz," said I, "where would you like your sand box situated? Right there in front of the TV screen? There's not much traffic there, since we cleared the solar system. You'd have the place all to yourself.

No, said Itzenca by a flirt of her tail. And she walked over behind a crate that had never been unloaded on earth.

I pulled out a box of junk and slid the sand box in its place. Itzenca promptly lost interest and instead jumped up on the junk box which fell off the bench and scattered small objects of khaff and metal in all directions.

"Come back here, blast you," I said, "and help me pick up this stuff."

Itz bounded after a dull-gleaming silver object that was still rolling. I was there almost as quick as she was and grabbed up the cylinder. Suddenly the horsing around was over. This thing was somebody's memory.

I dropped onto a bench to examine it, my Vallonian-inspired pulse pounding. "Where the heck did this come from, cat?" I said.

Itz jumped up into my lap and nosed the cylinder. I was trying to hark back to those days three years before when I had loaded the lifeboat with all the loot it would carry, for the trip back to earth.

"Listen, Itz, we've got to do some tall remembering. Let's see: there was a whole rack of blanks in the memory-recharging section of the room where we found the three skeletons. Yeah, now I remember: I pulled this one out of the recorder set, which means it had been used, but not yet color-coded. I showed it to Foster when he was hunting his own trace. He didn't realize I'd pulled it out of the machine and he thought it was an empty. But I'll bet you somebody had his mind taped, and then left in a hurry, before the trace could be color-coded and filed.

"On the other hand, maybe it's a blank that had just been inserted when somebody broke up the playhouse . . . But wasn't there something Foster said . . . about when he woke up, way back when, with a pile of fresh corpses around him? He gave somebody emergency treatment and to a Vallonian that would include a complete memory-transcription . . . Do you realize what I've got here in my hand, Itz?"

She looked up at me inquiringly.

"This is what's left of the guy that Foster buried: his pal, Ammaerln, I think he called him. What's inside this cylinder used to be tucked away in the skull of the ancient sinner. The guy's not so dead after all. I'll bet his family will pay plenty for this trace, and be grateful besides. That'll be an ace in the hole in case I get too hungry on Vallon."

I got up and crossed the apartment; Itz followed me out to my sleeping couch. I dropped the trace in a drawer beside Foster's own memory.

"Wonder how Foster's making out without his past, Itz? He claimed the one I've got here would only be a copy of the original stored at Okk-Hamiloth, but my briefing didn't say anything about copying memories. He must be somebody pretty important to rate that service."

Suddenly my eyes were riveted to the markings on Foster's trace lying in the drawer. "'Sblood! The royal colors!" I sat down on the bed with a lurch. "Itzenca, old gal, it looks like we'll be entering Vallonian society from the top. We've been consorting with a member of the Vallonian nobility!"

During the days that followed, I tried again and again to raise Foster on the communicator . . . without result. I wondered how I'd find him among the millions on the planet. My best bet would be to get settled down in the Vallonian environment, then start making a few inquiries.

I would play it casually: act the part of a Vallonian who had merely been traveling for a few hundred years—which wasn't unheard of—and play my cards close to my gravy stains until I learned what the score was. With my Vallonian briefing I ought to be able to carry it off. The Vallonians might not like illegal immigrants any better than they did back home, so I'd keep my interesting foreign background to myself.

I would need a new name. I thought over several possibilities and selected "Drgon." It was as good a Vallonian jawbreaker as any.

I canvassed the emergency wardrobe that was standard equipment on Far-Voyager lifeboats. There was everything from fur-lined parka-type suits for outings on worlds like Pluto to sheer silk one-man-air-conditioner balloon over-alls for stepping out on Venus. In amongst them was a selection of dresses reminiscent of ancient Greece. They had been the sharp style of Vallon when Foster left home. They looked comfortable. I picked one in a sober color, then got busy with the cutting and seaming unit to fit it to my frame. I didn't plan to attract unnecessary attention with ill-fitting garments when I crossed my first Vallonians.

Itzenca watched with interest. "What the heck am I going to do with you on Vallon?" I asked her. "The only cat on the planet. You may have to put up with an iggrfn for a boyfriend," I said, searching my Vallonian memory. "They're about the nearest thing to you in size and shape . . . but they're kind of objectionable, personality wise."

I finished off my new duds, then dug through the handicrafts gear and picked out a sheet of khaffite, a copper-like Vallonian alloy that was supposed to have almost the durability of khaff without being so hard to work. There were appropriate tools in the little workshop for shaping it and adding decoration.

"Don't worry," I said to Itz. "You won't go ashore shabbily clad either. You'll be a knockout in this item." I parked her on the workbench and sat down to my tools. I clipped out an inch-wide strip of the khaffite, shaped it in a circle, and fitted it with a slip-out catch. After a leisurely meal I spent what passed for an evening etching "Itzenca" on the new collar with plenty of curlicues. Then I fitted it on her; she didn't seem to mind a bit.

"There. All set to wow those Vallonians like they've never been wowed." Itzenca purred.

We strolled into the observation lounge. Strange bright-hued star systems glowed far away. "We'll be stepping out with our memories any night now," I said.

The proximity alarms were ringing. I watched the screen with its image of a great green world rimmed on one edge with glaring white from the distant giant sun, on the other flooded with a cool glow reflected from the blue outer planet. The trip was almost over and my confidence was beginning to fray around the edges. In a few minutes I would be stepping into an unknown world, all set to find my old pal Foster and see the sights. I didn't have a passport, but there was no reason to anticipate trouble. All I had to do was let my natural identity take a back seat and allow my Vallonian background to do the talking. And yet . . .

Now Vallon spread out below us, a misty grey-green landscape, bright under the glow of the immense moonlike sister world, Cinte. I had set the landing monitor for Okk-Hamiloth, the capital city of Vallon. That was where Foster would have headed, I guessed. Maybe I could pick up the trail there.

The city was directly below: a vast network of blue-lit avenues. I hadn't been contacted by Planetary Control. That was normal enough, however. A small vessel coming in on auto could handle itself.

A little apprehensively I ran over my lines a last time: I was Drgon, citizen of the Two Worlds, back from a longer-than-average season of far-voyaging and in need of briefing rods to bring me up to date on developments at home. I also required assignment of quarters. My tailoring was impeccable, my command

of the language a little rusty from long non-use, and
the only souvenirs I had to declare were a tattered
native costume from my last port of call, a quaint
weapon from the same, and a small animal I had taken
a liking to.

The landing ring was visible on the screen now,
coming slowly up to meet us. There was a gentle shock
and then absolute stillness. I watched the port cycle
open; I went to it and looked out at the pale city
stretching away to the hills. I took a breath of the
fragrant night air spiced with a long-forgotten perfume,
and the part of me that was now Vallonian ached with
the inexpressible emotion of homecoming.

I started to buckle on my pistol and gather up a few
belongings, then decided to wait until I'd met the
welcoming committee. I whistled to Itzenca and we
stepped out and down. We crossed the clipped green,
luminous in the glow from the lights over the high-
arched gate marking the path that curved up toward
the bright-lit terraces above. There was no one in sight.
Bright Cintelight showed me the gardens and
walks and, when I reached the terraces, the avenues
beyond . . . but no people. I stood by a low wall of
polished marble and thought about it. It was about
midnight, and the nights on Vallon lasted twenty-eight
hours, but there should have been some activity here.
This was a busy port: scheduled vessels, private yachts,
official ships, all of them came and went from Okk-
Hamiloth. But not tonight.

The cat and I walked across the terrace, passed
through the open arch to a refreshment lounge. The
low tables and cushioned couches stood empty under
the rosy light from the ceiling panels. My slippered feet
whispered on the polished floor.

I stood and listened: dead silence. There wasn't even

the hum of a mosquito; all such insect pests had been killed off long ago. The lights glowed, the tables waited invitingly. How long had they waited?

I sat down at one of them and thought hard. I had made a lot of plans, but I hadn't counted on a deserted spaceport. How was I going to ask questions about Foster if there was no one to ask?

I got up and moved on through the empty lounge, past a wide arcade, out onto a terraced lawn. A row of tall poplar-like trees made a dark wall beyond a still pool, and behind them distant towers loomed, colored lights sparkled. A broad avenue swept in a wide curve between fountains, slanted away to the hills. A hundred yards from where I stood a small vehicle was parked at the curb; I headed for it.

It was an open two-seater, low-slung, cushioned, finished in violet inlays against bright chrome. I slid into the seat, looked over the controls, while Itzenca skipped to a place beside me. There was a simple lever arrangement: a steering tiller. It looked easy. I tried a few pulls and pushes; lights blinked on the panel, the car quivered, lifted a few inches, drifted slowly across the road. I moved the tiller, twiddled things; the car moved off toward the towers. I didn't like the controls; a wheel and a couple of foot pedals would have suited me better; but it beat walking.

Two hours later we had cruised the city . . . and found nothing. It hadn't changed from what my extra memory recalled—except that all the people were gone. The parks and boulevards were trimmed, the fountains and pools sparkled, the lights glowed . . . but nothing moved. The automatic dust precipitators and air filters would run forever, keeping things clean and neat; but there was no one there to appreciate it. I pulled over, sat watching the play of colored lights on a waterfall, and considered. Maybe I'd find more of a clue inside one of the buildings. I left the car and picked one at random: a tall slab of pink crystal. Inside, I looked around at a great airy cavern full of rose-colored light and listened to the purring of the cat and my own breathing. There was nothing else to hear.

I picked a random corridor, went along it, passed through empty rooms. It was all in the old Vallonian style: walls paneled in jade, brocade hangings in iridescent colors, rugs like pools of fire: in one chamber I picked up a cloak of semi-velvet and put it over my shoulders; I was getting cold in my daytime street dress. Walking among the tangible ghosts of the long past didn't warm me up any. We climbed a wide spiral stair, passed from vacant room to vacant room. I thought of the people who had once used them. Where were they now?

I found a clarinet-like musical instrument and blew a few notes on it. It had a deep mellow tone that echoed along the deserted corridor. I thought it sounded a lot like I felt: sad and forgotten. I went out onto a lofty terrace overlooking gardens, leaned on a balustrade, and looked up at the brilliant disc of Cinte. It loomed enormous, its diameter four times that of the earthly moon.

"We've come a long way to find nothing," I said to Itzenca. She pushed her way along my leg and flexed her tail in a gesture meant to console. But it didn't help. After the long wait, the tension of expectation, I felt suddenly empty as the silent halls of the building.

I sat on the balustrade and leaned back against the polished pink wall, took out the clarinet and blew some blue notes. That which once had been was no more; remembering it, I played the *Pavane for a Dead*

Princess, and felt a forlorn nostalgia for a glory I had never known . . .

I finished and looked up at a sound. Four tall men in grey cloaks and a glitter of steel came toward me from the shadows.

I had dropped the clarinet and was on my feet. I tried to back up but the balustrade stopped me. The four spread out. The man in the lead fingered a wicked-looking short club and spoke to me—in gibberish. I blinked at him and tried to think of a snappy comeback.

He snapped his fingers and two of the others came up; they reached for my arms. I started to square off, fist cocked, then relaxed; after all, I was just a tourist, Drgon by name. Unfortunately, before I could get my fist back, the man with the club swung it and caught me across the forearm. I yelled, jumped back, found myself grappled by the others. My arm felt dead to the shoulder. I tried a kick and regretted that too; there was armor under the cloaks. The club wielder said something and pointed at the cat . . .

It was time I wised up. I relaxed, tried to coax my *alter ego* into the foreground. I listened to the rhythm of the language: it was Vallonian, badly warped by time, but I could understand it:

"—musician would be an Owner!" one of them said.

Laughter.

"Whose man are you, piper? What are your colors?"

I curled my tongue, tried to shape it around the sort of syllables I heard them uttering: it seemed to me a gross debasement of the Vallonian I knew. Still I managed an answer:

"I . . . am a . . . citizen . . . of Vallon."

"A dog of a masterless renegade?" The man with the club hefted it, glowered at me. "And what wretched dialect is that you speak?"

"I have . . . been long a-voyaging," I stuttered. "I ask . . . for briefing rods . . . and for a . . . dwelling place."

"A dwelling place you'll have," the man said. "In the men's shed at Rath-Gallion." He gestured, and hand-cuffs snapped on my wrists.

He turned and stalked away, and the others hustled me after him. Over my shoulder I got a glimpse of a cat's tail disappearing over the balustrade. Outside, a long grey air-car waited on the lawn. They dumped me in the back seat, climbed aboard. I got a last look at the spires of Okk-Hamiloth as we tilted, hurtled away across the low hills.

Somewhere in the shuffle I had lost my new cloak. I shivered. I listened to the talk, and what I heard didn't make me feel any better. The chain between my wrists kept up a faint jingling. I gathered I'd be hearing a lot of that kind of music from now on. I had had an idealistic notion of wanting to fit into this new world, find a place in its society. I'd found a place all right: a job with security.

I was a slave.

Chapter Fourteen

It was banquet night at Rath-Gallion, and I gulped my soup in the kitchen and ran over in my mind the latest batch of jingles I was expected to perform. I had only been on the Estate a few weeks, but I was already Owner Gope's favorite piper. If I kept on at this rate, I would soon have a cell to myself in the slave pens.

Sime, the pastry cook, came over to me.

"Pipe us a merry tune, Drgon," he said, "and I'll reward you with a frosting pot."

"With pleasure, good Sime," I said. I finished off the soup and got out my clarinet. I had tried out half a dozen strange instruments, but I still liked this one best. "What's your pleasure?"

"One of the outland tunes you learned far-voyaging," called Cagu, the bodyguard.

I complied with the *Beer Barrel Polka*. They pounded the table and hallooed when I finished, and I got my goody pan. Sime stood watching me scrape at it.

"Why don't you claim the Chief Piper's place, Drgon?" Sime said. "You pipe rings around the lout. Then you'd have freeman status, and could sit among us in the kitchen almost as an equal."

I went after the last of the chocilla frosting, licked my fingers and laid the pot aside.

"I'd gladly be the equal of such a pastry cook as yourself, good Sime," I said. "But what can a slave-piper do?"

Sime blinked at me. "You can challenge the Chief Piper," he said. "There's none can deny you're his master in all but name. Don't fear the outcome of the Trial; you'll triumph sure." He glanced around at the kitchen staff. "Is it not so, goodmen?"

"I'll warrant it," the soup-master said. "If you lose, I'll take your stripes for you."

"You're going too fast for me, goodmen," I said. "How can I claim another's place?"

Sime waved his arms. "You have far-voyaged long indeed, Piper Drgon. Know you naught of how the world wags these days? One would take you for a Cintean heretic."

"As I've said, goodmen: in my youth all men were free; and the High King ruled at Okk-Hamiloth—"

"'Tis ill to speak of these things," said Sime in a low tone. "Only Owners know their former lives . . . though

I've heard it said that long ago no man was so mean but that he recorded his lives and kept them safe. How you came by yours, I ask not; but do not speak of it. Owner Gope is a jealous master. Though a most generous and worshipful lord," he added hastily, looking around.

"I won't speak of it then, good Sime," I said. "But I have been long away. Even the language has changed, so that I wrench my tongue in the speaking of it. Advise me, if you will."

Sime puffed out his cheeks, frowning at me. "I scarce know where to start," he said. "All things belong to the Owners . . . as is only right." He looked around for confirmation. The others nodded. "Men of low skill are likewise property; and 'tis well 'tis so; else would they starve as masterless strays . . . if the Greymen failed to find them first." He made a sign and spat. So did everybody else.

"Now men of good skill are freemen, each earning rewards as befits his ability. I am Chief Pastry Cook to the Lord Gope, with the perquisites of that station, therefore that none other equals my talents." He looked around truculently, saw no challengers. "And thus it is with us all."

"And if some varlet claims the place of any man here," put in Cagu, "then he gotta submit to the Trial."

"Then," said Sime, pulling at his apron agitatedly, "this upstart pastry cook must cook against me; and all in the Hall will judge; and he who prevails is the Chief Pastry Cook, and the other takes a dozen lashes for his impertinence."

"But fear not, Drgon," spoke Cagu. "A Chief Piper ain't but a five-stroke man. Only a tutor is lower down among freemen. And anyway, the good Soup-master had promised to take the lash for you."

There was a bellow from the door, and I grabbed my clarinet and scrambled after the page. Owner Gope didn't like to wait around for piper-slaves. I saw him looming up at his place, as I darted through to my assigned position within the huge circle of the viand-loaded table. The Chief Piper had just squeezed his bagpipe-like instrument and released a windy blast of discordant sound. He was a lean, squint-eyed creature, fond of ordering the slave-pipers about. He pranced in an intricate pattern, pumping away at his vari-colored bladders, until I winced at the screech of it. Owner Gope noticed him about the same time. He picked up a heavy brass mug and half-rose to peg it at the Chief Piper, who saw it just in time to duck. The mug hit a swollen air-bag; a yellow one with green tassels; it burst with a sour bleat.

"As sweet a note as has been played tonight," roared Owner Gope. "Begone, lest you call up the hill devils—"

His eye fell on me. "Here's Dugon, or Digen," he cried. "Now here's a true piper. Summon up a fair melody, Dogron, to clear the fumes of the last performer from the air before the wine sours."

I bowed low, wet my lips, and launched into the *One O' Clock Jump*. To judge from the roar that went up when I finished, they liked it. I followed with *Little Brown Jug* and *String of Pearls*. Gope pounded and the table quieted down.

"The rarest slave in all Rath-Gallion, I swear it," he bellowed. "Were he not a slave, I'd drink his health."

"By your leave, Owner?" I said.

Gope stared, then nodded indulgently. "Speak then, Dugong," he said.

"I claim the place of Chief Piper. I—"

Yells rang out; Gope grinned widely.

"So be it," he said. "Shall the vote be taken now, or must we submit to more of the vile bladderings ere we proclaim our good Dagron Chief Piper?"

"Proclaim him!" somebody shouted.

"There must be a Trial," another offered dubiously.

Gope slammed a huge hand against the table. "Bring Lylk, the Chief Piper, before me," he yelled. "He of the wretched air-skins."

The Piper reappeared, fingering his bladders nervously.

"The place of the Chief Piper is declared vacant," Gope said loudly. The piper pinched a pink bladder, which emitted a thin squeak.

"—since the former Chief Piper has been advanced in degree to a new office," continued Gope. A blue bladder moaned, lost amid yells and cheers.

"Let these air-bags be punctured," Gope cried. "I banish their rancid squeals forever from Rath-Gallion. Now, let all know: this former piper is now Chief Fool to this household. Let him wear the broken bladders as a sign of his office." There was a roar of laughter, glad cries, whistles. Volunteers leaped to rip the colored air-bags; they died in a final flurry of trills and flutters. A fool-slave tied the draggled instrument to the ex-piper's head.

I gave them *Mairzy Doats* and the former piper capered gingerly. Owner Gope roared with laughter. I followed with *The Dipsy Doodle* and the new fool, encouraged by success, leaped and grimaced, pirouetted, strutted, bladders bobbing; the crowd laughed until the tears flowed.

"A great day for Rath-Gallion," Gope shouted. "By the horns of the sea-god, I have gained a prince of pipers and a king of fools! I proclaim them to be ten-lash men, and both shall have places at table henceforth!"

The Fool and I followed up with three more numbers, then Gope let us squeeze into a space on a hard bench at the far side of the table. A table slave put loaded plates before us.

"Well done, good Drgon," he whispered. "Do not forget us slaves in your new honor."

"Don't worry," I said, sniffing the aroma of a big slab of roast beef. "I'll be sneaking down for a snack every night about Cinte-rise."

I looked around the barbarically decorated hall, seeing things in a new way. There's nothing like a little slavery to make a man appreciate even a modest portion of freedom. Everything I had thought I knew about Vallon had been wrong: the centuries that had passed had changed things—and not for the better. The old society that Foster knew was dead and buried. The old palaces and villas lay deserted, the spaceports unused. And the old system of memory-recording that Foster described was lost and forgotten. I didn't know what kind of a cataclysm could have plunged the seat of a galactic empire back into feudal darkness—but it had happened.

So far I hadn't found a trace of Foster. My questions had gotten me nothing but blank stares. Maybe Foster hadn't made it; there could have been an accident in space. Or perhaps he was somewhere on the opposite side of the world. Vallon was a big planet and communications were poor. Maybe Foster was dead. I could live out a long life here and never find the answers.

I remembered my own disappointment at the breakdown of my illusions that night at Okk-Hamiloth. How much more heartbreaking must have been Foster's experience when and if he had arrived back here. And now we were both in the same boat: with our memories of the old Vallon and the dreary spectacle of the new providing plenty of food for bitterness.

And Foster's memory that I had been bringing him for a keepsake: what a laugh that was! Far from being a superfluous duplicate of a master trace to which he had expected easy access, my copy of the trace was now, with the vaults at Okk-Hamiloth sealed and forbidden, of the greatest possible importance to Foster— and there wasn't a machine left on the planet to play it on.

Well, I still meant to find Foster if it took me—

Owner Gope was humming loudly and tunelessly to himself. I knew the sign. I got ready to play again. Being Chief Piper probably wasn't going to be just one big bowl of cherries, but at least I wasn't a slave now. I had a long way to go, but I was making progress.

Owner Gope and I got along well. He was a shrewd old duck and he liked having such an unusual piper on hand. He had heard from the Greymen, the freelance police force, how I had landed at the deserted port. He warned me, in an oblique way, not to let word get out that I knew anything about old times in Vallon. The whole subject was taboo—especially the old capital city and the royal palaces themselves. Small wonder that my trespassing there had brought the Greymen down on me in doublequick time.

Gope took me with him everywhere he went: by air-car, ground-car, or formal river barge. There were still a lot of vehicles around, though few people seemed to know how to use them, simple as they were to operate. The air-cars were more useful, since they required no roads, but Gope preferred the ground cars. I think he liked the sensation of speed you got barreling along at ninety or a hundred on one of the still-perfect roads that had originally been intended merely as scenic drives.

One afternoon several months after my promotion I dropped in at the kitchen. I was due to shove off with Owner Gope and his usual retinue for a visit to Bar-Ponderone, a big estate a hundred miles north of

Rath-Gallion in the direction of Okk-Hamiloth. Sime and my other old cronies fixed me up with a healthy lunch, and warned me that it would be a rough trip; the stretch of road we'd be using was a favorite hang-out of road pirates.

"What I don't understand," I said, "is why Gope doesn't mount a couple of guns on the car and blast his way through the raiders. Every time he goes off the Estate he's taking his life in his hands."

The boys were shocked. "Even piratical renegades would never dream of taking a man's life, good Drgon," Sime said. "Every Owner, far and near, would band together to hunt such miscreants down. And their own fellows would abet the hunters! Nay, none is so low as to steal all a man's lives."

"The corsairs themselves know full well that in their next life they may be simple goodmen—even slaves," the Chief Wine-Pourer put in. "For you know, good Drgon, that when a member of a pirate band suffers the Change the others lead the newman to an Estate, that he may find his place . . ."

"How often do these Changes come along?" I asked.

"It varies greatly. Some men, of great strength and moral power, have been known to go on unchanged for three or four hundred years. But the ordinary man lives a life of eighty to one hundred years." Sime paused. "Or it may be less. A life of travail and strife can age one sooner than one of peace and retirement. Or unusual vicissitudes can shorten a life remarkably. A cousin of mine, who was marooned on the Great Stony Place in the southern half-world and who wandered for three weeks without more to eat or drink than a small bag of wine, underwent the Change after only fourteen years. When he was found his face was lined and his hair had greyed, in the way that presages the Change. And it was not long before he fell in a fit, as one does, and slept for a night and a day. When he awoke he was a newman: young and knowing nothing."

"Didn't you tell him who he was?"

"Nay!" Sime lowered his voice. "You are much favored of Owner Gope, good Drgon, and rightly. Still, there are matters a man talks not of—"

"A newman takes a name and sets out to learn whatever trade he can," put in the Carver of Roasts. "By his own skills he can rise . . . as you have risen, good Drgon."

"Don't you have memory machines—or briefing rods?" I persisted. "Little black sticks: you touch them to your head and—"

Sime made a motion in the air. "I have heard of these wands: a forbidden relic of the Black Arts—"

"Nuts," I said. "You don't believe in magic, do you, Sime? The rods are nothing but a scientific development by your own people. How you've managed to lose all knowledge of your own past—"

Sime raised his hands in distress. "Good Drgon, press us not in these matters. Such things are forbidden."

"Okay, boys. I guess I'm just nosy."

I went out to the car and climbed in to wait for Owner Gope. Trying to learn anything about Vallon's history was about like questioning a village of Eskimos about the great trek over from Asia: they didn't know anything.

I had reached a few tentative conclusions on my own, however. My theory was that some sudden social cataclysm had broken down the system of personality reinforcement and memory recording that had given continuity to the culture. Vallonian society, based as it was on the techniques of memory preservation, had gradually disintegrated. Vallon was plunged into a feudal state resembling its ancient social pattern of

fifty thousand years earlier, prior to the development
of memory recording.

The people, huddled together on Estates for protection from real or imagined perils and shunning the
old villas and cities as taboo—except for those included
in Estates—knew nothing of space travel and ancient
history. Like Sime, they had no wish even to speak of
such matters.

I might have better luck with my detective work on
a big Estate like Bar-Ponderone. I was looking forward
to today's trip. I was cramped on Rath-Gallion. It was
a small, poor Estate, covering only about twenty square
miles, with half a dozen villages of farmers and crafts-
men and the big house of Owner Gope. I had seen
all of it—and it was a dead end.

Gope appeared, with Cagu and two other bodyguards, four dancing girls, and an extra-large gift hamper. They took their places and the driver started up
and wheeled the heavy car out onto the highroad. I
felt a pulse of excitement as we accelerated in the
direction of Bar-Ponderone. Maybe at the big Estate
I'd get news of Foster.

We were doing about fifty down a winding mountain road. I was in the front seat beside the driver,
fiddling with my clarinet, and watching the road from
the corner of my eye. I was wishing the driver's knuckles didn't show white on the speed control lever. He
drove like a drunken spinster, fast but nervous. It wasn't
entirely his fault: Gope insisted on plenty of speed. I
was grateful for the auto steer mechanism; at least we
couldn't drive over a cliff.

We rounded a curve, the wheels screeching from the
driver's awkward, too-fast swing into the turn, and saw
another car in the road a quarter of a mile ahead, not
moving but parked—sideways. The driver hit the
brakes.

Behind us Owner Gope yelled, "Pirates! Don't slacken your pace, driver."

"But, but, Owner Gope—" the driver gasped.

"Ram the blackguards, if you must!" Gope shouted. "But don't stop!"

The girls in the back yelped in alarm. The flunkies set up a wail. The driver rolled his eyes, almost lost control, then gritted his teeth, reached out to switch off the anti-collision circuit and slam the speed control lever against the dash. I watched for two long heartbeats as we roared straight for the blockading car, then I slid over and grabbed for the controls. The driver held on, frozen. I reared back and clipped him on the jaw. He crumpled into his corner, mouth open and eyes screwed shut, as I hit the auto-steer override and worked the tiller. It was an awkward position for steering, but I preferred it to hammering in at ninety per.

The car ahead was still sitting tight, now a hundred yards away, now fifty. I cut hard to the right, toward the rising cliff face; the car backed to block me. At the last instant I whipped to the left, barreled past with half an inch to spare, rocketed along the ragged edge with the left wheel rolling on air, then whipped back into the center of the road.

"Well done!" yelled Cagu.

"But they'll give chase!" Gope shouted. "Assassins! Masterless swine!"

The driver had his eyes open now. "Crawl over me!" I barked. He mumbled and clambered past me and I slid into his seat, still clinging to the accelerator lever and putting up the speed. Another curve was coming up. I grabbed a quick look in the rear-viewer: the pirates were swinging around to follow us.

"Press on!" commanded Gope. "We're close to Bar-Ponderone; it's no more than five miles—"

"What kind of speed have they got?" I called back.

"They'll beat us easy," said Cagu cheerfully.

"What's the road like ahead?"

"A fair road, straight and true, now that we've descended the mountain", answered Gope.

We squealed through the turn and hit a straightaway. A curving road branched off ahead. "What's that?" I snapped.

"A winding trail," gasped the driver. "It comes on Bar-Ponderone, but by a longer way."

I gauged my speed, braked minutely, and cut hard. We howled up the steep slope, into a turn between hills.

Gope shouted. "What madness is this?! Are you in league with the villains . . . ?"

"We haven't got a chance on the straightaway," I called back. "Not in a straight speed contest." I whipped the tiller over, then back the other way, following the tight S-curves. We flashed past magnificent vistas of rugged peaks and rolling plains, but I didn't have time to admire the view. There were squeals from the odalisques in the rear seats, a gabble of excited talk. I caught a glimpse of our pursuers, just heading into the side road behind us.

"Any way they can head us off?" I yelled.

"Not unless they have confederates stationed ahead," said Gope, "but these pariahs work alone."

I worked the brake and speed levers, handled the tiller. We swung right, then left, higher and higher, then down a steep grade and up again. The pirate car rounded a turn, only a few hundred yards behind now. I scanned the road ahead, followed its winding course along the mountainside, through a tunnel, then out again to swing around the shoulder of the next peak.

"Pitch something out when we go through the tunnel!" I yelled. "Anything!"

"My cloak," cried Gope. "And the gift hamper."

One of the flunkies started to moan. The girls caught the fever, joined in with shrill lamentations.

"Silence!" roared Gope. "Lend a hand here, or by the sea-devil's beard you'll be jettisoned with the rest!"

We roared into the tunnel mouth. There was a blast of air as the rear deck cover opened. Gope and Cagu hefted the heavy gift hamper, tumbled it out, followed it with a cloak, a wine jug, assorted sandals, bracelets, fruit. Then we were back in the sunlight and I was fighting the curve. In the rear-viewer I saw the pirates burst from the tunnel mouth, Gope's black and yellow cloak spread over the canopy, smashed fruit spattered over it, the remains of the hamper dragging under the chassis. The car rocked and a corner of the cloak lifted, clearing the driver's view barely in time.

"Tough luck," I said. "We've got a long straight stretch ahead, and I'm fresh out of ideas . . ."

The other car gained. I held the speed bar against the dash but we were up against a faster car; it was a hundred yards behind us, then fifty, then pulling out to go alongside. I slowed imperceptibly, let him get his front wheels past us, then cut sharply. There was a clash of wheel fairings, and I fought the tiller as we rebounded from the heavier car. He crept forward, almost alongside again; shoulder to shoulder we raced at ninety-five down the steep grade . . .

I hit the brakes and cut hard to the left, slapped his right rear wheel, slid back. He braked too; that was a mistake. The heavy car lost traction, sliding. In slow motion, off-balanced in a skid, it rose on its nose, plowing up a cloud of dust. The hamper whirled away, the cloak fluttered and was gone, then the pirate car seemed to float for an instant in air, before it dropped, wheels up, out of sight over the sheer cliff. We raced alone down the slope and out onto the wooded plain toward the towers of Bar-Ponderone.

A shout went up; Owner Gope leaned forward to pound my back. "By the nine eyes of the Hill Devil!" he bellowed, "masterfully executed! The prince of Pipers is a prince of Drivers too! This night you'll sit by my side at the ring-board at Bar-Ponderone in the rank of a hundred-lash Chief Driver, I swear it!"

"Compared with making a left turn off the Outer Drive at 5:15 on a Friday, that was nothing," I said. I held onto the tiller and tried breathing again. I'd been a fool to try to flip a heavier car—but it had worked. And now I'd gotten another promotion. I was doing okay.

"And let no man raise a charge of Assassination," Gope went on. "I'll not see so clever a Driver-Piper immured. I charge you all: say nothing of this! We'll consider that the rascals merely outdid themselves in their villainy."

That was the first I'd thought of that angle. To take a human life was still the one unthinkable crime in this world of immortals—because you took not just one, but all a man's lives. The punishment was walling up for life . . . but just one life. In my case one would be enough; I didn't have any spares. I had taken a bigger chance with Gope than I had with the pirates.

Life here was a series of gambles, but it looked like the chance-takers got ahead fast. My best bet was to stay on the make and calculate the odds when it was over.

I spent the first day at Bar-Ponderone rubber-necking the tall buildings and keeping an eye open for Foster, on the off chance that I might pass him on the street. It was about as likely as running into an old high school chum from Perth Amboy among the body servants of the Shah of Afghanistan, but I kept looking.

By sunset I was no wiser than before. Dressed in the latest in Vallonian cape and ruffles, I was sitting with my buddy Cagu, Chief Bodyguard to Owner Gope, at a small table on the first terrace at the Palace of Merrymaking, Bar-Ponderone's biggest community feasting hall. It looked like a Hollywood producer's idea of a twenty-first century night club, complete with nine dance floors on five levels, indoor pools, fountains, two thousand tables, musicians, girls, noise, colored lights, and food fit for an Owner. It was open to all fifty-lash goodmen of the Estate and to guests of equivalent rank. After the back-country life at Rath-Gallion it looked like the big time to me.

Cagu was a morose-looking old cuss, but good-hearted. His face was cut and scarred from a thousand encounters with other bodyguards and his nose had been broken so often that it was invisible in profile.

"Where do you manage to get in all the fights, Cagu?" I asked him. "I've known you for three months, and I haven't seen a blow struck in anger yet."

"Here." He grinned, showing me some broken front teeth. "Swell places, these big Estates, good Drgon; lotsa action."

"What do you do, get in street fights?"

"Nah. The boys show up down here, tank up, cruise around, you know."

"They start fights here in the dining room?"

"Sure. Good crowd here; lotsa laughs."

I picked up my drink, raised it to Cagu—and got it in my lap as somebody jostled my arm. I looked up. A battle-scarred thug stood over me.

"Who'sa punk, Cagu?" he said in a hoarse whisper. He probed at a back tooth with a silver pick, rolled his eyes from me to my partner.

Cagu stood up, and threw a punch to the other plug-ugly's paunch. He *oof!*ed, clinched, eyed me resentfully over Cagu's shoulder. Cagu pushed him away, held him at arm's length.

"Howsa boy, Mull?" he said. "Lay offa my sidekick; greatest little piper ina business, and a top driver too."

Mull rubbed his stomach, sat down beside me. "Ya losin' your punch, Cagu." He looked at me. "Sorry about that. I thought you was one of the guys." He signaled a passing waiter-slave. "Bring my friend a new suit. Make it snappy."

"Don't the customers kind of resent it when you birds stage a heavyweight bout in the aisle?" I asked. "A drink in the lap is routine. It could happen in any joint in Manhattan. But a seven-course meal would be overdoing it."

"Nah; we move down inta the Spot." He waved a thumb in the general direction of somewhere else. He looked me over. "Where ya been, Piper? Your first time ina Palace?"

"Drgon's been traveling," said Cagu. "He's okay. Lemme tell ya the time these pirates pull one, see . . ."

Cagu and Mull swapped lies while I worked on my drinking. Although I hadn't learned anything on my day's looking around at Bar-Ponderone, it was still a better spot for snooping than Rath-Gallion. There were two major cities on the Estate and scores of villages. Somewhere among the populace I might have better luck finding someone to talk history with . . . or someone who knew Foster.

"Hey!" growled Mull. "Look who's comin'."

I followed his gaze. Three thick-set thugs swaggered up to the table. One of them, a long-armed gorilla at least seven feet tall, reached out, took Cagu and Mull by the backs of their necks, and cracked their skulls together. I jumped up, ducked a hoof-like fist . . . and saw a beautiful burst of fireworks followed by soothing darkness.

❖   ❖   ❖

I fumbled in the dark with the lengths of cloth entangling my legs, sat up, cracked my head—

I groaned, freed a leg from the chair rungs, groped my way out from under the table. A Waiter-slave helped me up, dusted me off. The seven-foot lout lolling in a chair glanced my way, nodded.

"You shouldn't hang out with lugs like that Mull," he said. "Cagu told me you was just a piper, but the way you come outa that chair—" He shrugged, turned back to whatever he was watching.

I checked a few elbow and knee joints, worked my jaw, tried my neck: all okay.

"You the one that slugged me?" I asked.

"Huh? Yeah."

I stepped over to his chair, picked a spot, and cleared my throat. "Hey, you," I said. He turned, and I put everything I had behind a straight right to the point of the jaw. He went over, feet in the air, flipped a rail, and crashed down between two tables below. I leaned over the rail. A party of indignant Tally-clerks stared up at me.

"Sorry, folks," I said. "He slipped."

A shout went up from the floor some distance away. I looked. In a cleared circle two levels below a pair of heavy-shouldered men were slugging it out. One of them was Cagu. I watched, saw his opponent fall. Another man stepped in to take his place. I turned and made my way down to the ringside.

Cagu exchanged haymakers with two more opponents before he folded and was hauled from the ring. I propped him up in a chair, fitted a drink into his fist, and watched the boys pound each other. It was easy to see why the scarred face was the sign of their craft; there was no defensive fighting whatever. They stood toe-to-toe and hit as hard as they could, until one collapsed. It wasn't fancy, but the fans loved it. Cagu came to after a while and filled me in on the fighters' backgrounds.

"So they're all top boys," he said. "But it ain't like in the old days when I was in my prime. I could've took any three of these bums. The only one maybe I woulda had a little trouble with is Torbu."

"Which one is he?"

"He ain't down there yet; he'll show to take on the last boys on their feet."

More gladiators pushed their way to the Spot, pulled off gaily-patterned cloaks and weskits, and waded in. Others folded, were dragged clear, revived to down another shot and cheer on the fray.

After an hour the waiting line had dwindled away to nothing. The two battlers on the Spot slugged, clinched, breathed hard, swung and missed; the crowd booed.

"Where's Torbu?" Cagu wondered.

"Maybe he didn't come tonight," I said.

"Sure, you met him; he knocked you under the table."

"Oh, him?"

"Where'd he go?"

"The last I saw he was asleep on the floor," I said.

"Hozzat?"

"I didn't much like him slugging me. I clobbered him one."

"Hey!" yelped Cagu. His face lit up. He got to his feet.

"Hold it," I said. "What's—?"

Cagu pushed his way through to the Spot, took aim, and floored the closest fighter, turned and laid out the other. He raised both hands over his head.

"Rath-Gallion gotta Champion," he bellowed. "Rath-Gallion takes on all comers." He turned, waved to me. "Our boy, Drgon, he—"

There was a bellow behind me, even louder than Cagu's. I turned, saw Torbu, his hair mussed, his face purple, pushing through the crowd.

"Jussa crummy minute," he yelled. "I'm the Champion around here—" He aimed a haymaker at Cagu; Cagu ducked.

"Our boy, Drgon, laid you out cold, right?" he shouted. "So now he's the champion."

"I wasn't set," bawled Torbu. "A lucky punch." He turned to the fans. "I'm tying my shoelace, see? And this guy—"

"Come on down, Drgon," Cagu called, waving to me again. "We'll show—" Torbu turned and slammed a roundhouse right to the side of Cagu's jaw; the old fighter hit the floor hard, skidded, lay still. I got to my feet. They pulled him to the nearest table, hoisted him into a chair. I made my way down to the little clearing in the crowd. A man bending over Cagu straightened, face white. I pushed him aside, grabbed the bodyguard's wrist. There was no pulse. Cagu was dead.

Torbu stood in the center of the Spot, mouth open. "What . . . ?" he started. I pushed between two fans, went for him. He saw me, crouched, swung.

I ducked, uppercut him. He staggered back. I pressed him, threw lefts and rights to the body, ducked under his wild swings, then rocked his head left and right. He stood, knees together, eyes glazed, hands down. I measured him, right-crossed his jaw; he dropped like a log.

Panting, I looked across at Cagu. His scarred face, white as wax, was strangely altered now; it looked peaceful. Somebody helped Torbu to his feet, walked him to the ringside. It had been a big evening. Now all I had to do was take the body home . . .

I went over to where Cagu was laid out on the floor.

Shocked people stood staring. Torbu was beside the body. A tear ran down his nose, dripped on Cagu's face. Torbu wiped it away with a big scarred hand.

"I'm sorry, old friend," he said. "I didn't mean it."

I picked Cagu up and got him over my shoulder, and all the way to the far exit it was so quiet in the Palace of Merrymaking that I could hear my own heavy breathing and the tinkle of fountains and the squeak of my fancy yellow plastic shoes.

In the bodyguards' quarters I laid Cagu out on a bunk, then faced the dozen scowling bruisers who stared down at the still body.

"Cagu was a good man," I said. "Now he's dead. He died like an animal . . . for nothing. That ended all his lives, didn't it, boys? How do you like it?"

Mull glowered at me. "You talk like we was to blame," he said. "Cagu was my compeer too."

"Whose pal was he a thousand years ago?" I snapped. "What was he—once? What were you? Vallon wasn't always like this. There was a time when every man was his own Owner—"

"Look, you ain't of the Brotherhood—" one thug started.

"So that's what you call it? But it's just another name for an old racket. A big shot sets himself up as dictator—"

"We got our Code," Mull said. "Our job is to stick up for the Owner . . . and that don't mean standing around listening to some japester callin' names."

· "I'm not calling names," I snapped. "I'm talking rebellion. You boys have all the muscle and most of the guts in this organization. Why do you sit on your tails and let the boss live off the fat while you murder each other for the amusement of the patrons? I say let's pay him a call—right now. You had a birthright . . .

once. But it's up to you to collect it . . . before some more of you go the way Cagu did."

There was an angry mutter. Torbu came in, face swollen. I backed up to a table, ready for trouble.

"Hold it, you birds," Torbu said. "What's goin' on?"

"This guy! He's talkin' revolt and treason," somebody said.

"He wants we should pull some rough stuff—on Owner Qohey hisself."

Torbu came up to me. "You're a stranger around Bar-Ponderone. Cagu said you was okay. You worked me over pretty good . . . and I got no hard feelin's; that's the breaks. But don't try to start no trouble here. We got our Code and our Brotherhood. We look out for each other; that's good enough for us. Owner Qohey ain't no worse than any other Owner . . . and by the code, we'll stand by him!"

"Listen to me," I said. "I know the history of Vallon: I know what you were once and what you could be again. All you have to do is take over the power. I can lead you to the ship I came here in. There are briefing rods aboard, enough to show you—"

"That's enough," Torbu broke in. He made a cabalistic sign in the air. "We ain't gettin' mixed up in no taboo ghost-boats or takin' on no magicians and demons—"

"Hogwash! That taboo routine is just a gag to keep you away from the cities so you won't discover what you're missing—"

"I don't wanna hafta take you to the Greymen, Drgon," Torbu growled. "Leave it lay."

"These cities," I plowed on. "They're standing there, empty, as perfect as the day they were built. And you live in these flea-bitten quarters, jammed inside the town walls, so the Greymen and renegades won't get you."

"You wanna run things here?" Mull put in. "Go see Qohey."

"Let's all go see Qohey!" I said.

"That's something you'll have to do alone," said Torbu. "You better move on, Drgon. I ain't turnin' you in; I know how you felt about Cagu getting' killed and all—but don't push it too far."

I knew I was licked. They were as stubborn as a team of mules—and just about as smart.

Torbu motioned; I followed him outside.

"You wanna turn things upside-down, don't you? I know how it is; you ain't the first guy to get ideas. We can't help you. Sure, things ain't like they used to be here—and prob'ly they never were. But we got a legend: someday the Rthr will come back . . . and then the Good Time will come back too."

"What's the Rthr?" I said.

"Kinda like a big-shot Owner. There ain't no Rthr now. But a long time ago, back when our first lives started, there was a Rthr that was Owner of all Vallon, and everybody lived high, and had all their lives . . ." Torbu stopped, eyed me warily.

"Don't say nothing to nobody," he went on, "about what I been tellin' you. That's a secret of the Brotherhood. But it's kind of like a hope we got—that's what we're waitin' for, through all our lives. We got to do the best we can, and keep true to the Code and the Brotherhood . . . and someday the Rthr will come back . . . maybe."

"Okay," I said. "Dream on, big boy. And while you're treasuring your rosy dreams you'll get your brains kicked out, like Cagu." I turned away.

"Listen, Drgon. It's no good buckin' the system: it's too big for one guy . . . or even a bunch of guys . . . but—"

I looked up. "Yeah?"

" . . . if you gotta stick your neck out—see Owner Gope." Abruptly Torbu turned and pushed back through the door.

See Owner Gope, huh? Okay, what did I have to lose? I headed back along the corridor toward Owners' country.

I stood in the middle of the deep-pile carpet in Gope's suite, trying to keep my temper hot enough to supply the gall I needed to bust in on an Owner in the middle of the night. He sat in his ceremonial chair and stared at me impassively.

"With your help or without it," I said, "I'm going to find the answer."

"Yes, good Drgon," he said, not bellowing for once. "I understand. But there are matters you know not of—"

"Just get me back into the spaceport, noble Gope. I have enough briefing rods aboard to prove my point—and a few other little items to boot."

"It's forbidden. Do you not understand—"

"I understand too much," I snapped.

He straightened, eyed me with a touch of the old ferocity. "Mind your tone, Drgon! I'm Owner—"

I broke in. "Do you remember Cagu? Maybe you remember him as a newman, young, handsome, like a god out of some old legend. You've seen him live his life. Was it a good life? Did the promise of youth ever get paid off?"

Gope closed his eyes. "Stop," he said. "This is bad, bad . . ."

" 'And the deaths they died I have watched beside, and the lives they led were mine,' " I quoted. "Are you proud of them? And what about yourself? Don't you ever wonder what you might have been . . . back in the Good Time?"

"Who are you?" asked Gope, his eyes fixed on mine. "You speak Old Vallonian, you rake up the forbidden knowledge, and challenge the very Powers . . ." He got to his feet. "I could have you immured, Drgon. I could hand you to the Greymen, for a fate I shudder to name." He turned and walked the length of the room restlessly, then turned back to me and stopped.

"Matters stand ill with this fair world," he said. "Legend tells us that once men lived as the High Gods on Vallon. There was once a mighty Owner, Rthr of all Vallon. It is whispered that he will come again—"

"Your legends are all true. You can take my word for that! But that doesn't mean some supernatural sugar daddy is going to come along and bail you out. And don't get the idea I think I'm the fabled answer to prayers. All I mean is that once upon a time Vallon was a good place to live and it could be again. Right now, it's like a land under an enchantment—and you sleeping beauties need waking up. Your cities and roads and ships are still here, intact. But nobody knows how to run them and you're all afraid to try. Who scared you off? Who started the rumors? What broke down the memory recording system? Why can't we all go to Okk-Hamiloth and use the Archives to give everybody back what he's lost—"

"These are dread words," said Gope.

"There must be somebody behind it. Or there was once. Who is he?"

Gope thought. "There is one man pre-eminent among us: the Great Owner, Owner of Owners: Ommodurad by name. Where he dwells I know not. This is a secret possessed only by his intimates."

"What does he look like? How do I get to see him?"

Gope shook his head. "I have seen him but once, closely cowled. He is a tall man, and silent. 'Tis said—" Gope lowered his voice, "—by his black arts he possesses all his lives. An aura of dread hangs about him—"

"Never mind that jazz," I said. "He's a man, like other men. Stick a knife between his ribs and you put an end to him, aura and all."

"I do not like this talk of death. Let the doer of evil deeds be immured; it is sufficient."

"First let's find him. How can I get close to him?"

"There are those Owners who are his confidants," said Gope, "his trusted agents. It is through them that we small Owners learn of his will."

"Can we enlist one of them?"

"Never. They are bound to him by ties of darkness, spells and incantations."

"I'm a fast man with a pair of loaded dice myself. It's all done with mirrors. Let's stick to the point, noble Gope. How can I work into a spot with one of these big shots?"

"Nothing easier. A Driver and Piper of such skills as your own can claim what place he chooses."

"How about bodyguarding? Suppose I could take a heavy named Torbu; would that set me in better with a new Owner?"

"Such is no place for a man of your abilities, good Drgon," Gope exclaimed. "True, 'tis a place most close to an Owner, but there is much danger in it. The challenge to a bodyguard involves the most bloody hand-to-hand combat, second only to the rigors of a challenge to an Owner himself."

"What's that?" I snapped. "Challenge an Owner?"

"Be calm, good Drgon," said Gope, staring at me incredulously. "No common man with his wits about him will challenge an Owner."

"But I could if I wanted to?"

"In sooth . . . if you have tired of life—of all your

lives; 'tis as good a way to end them as another. But you must know, good Drgon: an Owner is a warrior trained in the skills of battle. None less than another such may hope to prevail."

I smacked my fist into my palm. "I should have thought of this sooner! The cooks cook for their places, the pipers pipe . . . and the best man wins. It figures that the Owners would use the same system. But what's the procedure, noble Gope? How do you get your chance to prove who can own the best?"

"It is a contest with naked steel. It is the measure and glory of an Owner that he alone stands ready to prove his quality against the peril of death itself." Gope drew himself up with pride.

"What about the bodyguards?" I asked. "They fight—"

"With their hands, good Drgon. And they lack skill with those. A death such as you described tonight— that is a rare and sorry accident."

"It showed up this whole grubby farce in its true colors. A civilization like that of Vallon—reduced to this."

"Still, it is sweet to live—by whatever rules—"

"I don't believe that . . . and neither do you. What Owner can I challenge? How do I go about it?"

"Give up this course, good Drgon—"

"Where's the nearest buddy of the Big Owner?"

Gope threw up his hands. "Here, at Bar-Ponderone. Owner Qohey. But—"

"And how do I call his bluff?"

Gope put a hand on my shoulder. "It is no bluff, good Drgon. It is long now since last Owner Qohey stood to his blade to protect his place, but you may be sure he has lost none of his skill. Thus it was he won his way to Bar-Ponderone, while lesser knights, such as myself, contented themselves with meaner fiefs."

"I'm not bluffing either, noble Gope," I said, stretching a point. "I was no harness-maker in the Good Time."

"It is your death—"

"Tell me how I offer the challenge . . . or I'll twist his nose in the main banqueting salon tomorrow night."

Gope sat down heavily, raised his hands, and let them fall. "If I tell you not, another will. But I will not soon find another Piper of your worth."

Chapter Fifteen

Gaudy hangings of purple cut the light of the sun to a rich gloom in the enormous, high-vaulted Audience Hall. A rustling murmur was audible in the room as uneasy courtiers and supplicants fidgeted, waiting for the appearance of the Owner.

It had been two months since Gope had explained to me how a formal challenge to an Owner was conducted, and, as he pointed out, this was the only kind of challenge that would help. If I waylaid the man and cut him down, even in a fair fight, his bodyguards would repay the favor before I could establish the claim that I was their legitimate new boss.

I had spent three hours every day in the armory at Rath-Gallion, trading buffets with Gope and a couple of the bodyguards. The thirty-pound slab of edged steel had felt right at home in my hand that first day—for about a minute. I had the borrowed knowledge to give me all the technique I needed, but the muscle power for putting the knowledge into practice was another matter. After five minutes I was slumped against the wall, gulping air, while Gope whistled his sticker around my head and talked.

"You laid on like no piper, good Drgon. Yet have you much to learn in the matter of endurance."

—And he was at me again. I spent the afternoon back-pedaling and making wild two-handed swings and finally fell down—pooped. I couldn't have moved if Gope had had at me with a hot poker.

Gope and the others laughed til they cried, then hauled me away to my room and let sleep. They rolled me out the next morning to go at it again.

As Gope said, there was no time to waste . . . and after two months of it I felt ready for anything. Gope had warned me that Owner Qohey was a big fellow, but that didn't bother me. The bigger they came, the bigger the target . . .

There was a murmur in a different key in the Audience Hall and tall gilt doors opened at the far side of the room. A couple of liveried flunkies scampered into view, then a seven-foot man-eater stalked into the hall, made his way to the dais, turned to face the crowd . . .

He was enormous: his neck was as thick as my thigh, his features chipped out of granite, the grey variety. He threw back his brilliant purple cloak from his shoulders and reached out an arm like an oak root for the ceremonial sword one of the flunkies was struggling with. He took the sword with its sheath, sat down, and stood it between his feet, his arms folded on top.

"Who has a grievance?" he spoke. The voice reverberated like the old Wurlitzer at the Rialto back home.

This was my cue. There he was, just asking for it. All I had to do was speak up. Owner Qohey would gladly oblige me. The fact that next to him Primo Carnera would look dainty shouldn't slow me down.

I cleared my throat with a thin squeak, and edged forward, not very far.

"I have one little item—" I started.

Nobody was listening. Up front a big fellow in a black toga was pushing through the crowd. Everybody turned to stare at him: there was a craning of necks. The crowd drew back from the dais leaving an opening. The man in black stepped into the clear, flung back the flapping garment from his right arm, and whipped out a long polished length of razor-edged iron. It was beginning to look like somebody had beaten me to the punch.

The newcomer stood there in front of Qohey with the naked blade making all the threat that was needed. Qohey stared at him for a long moment, then stood, gestured to a flunky. The flunky turned, cleared his throat.

"The place of Bar-Ponderone has been claimed!" he recited in a shrill voice. "Let the issue be joined!" He skittered out of the way and Qohey rose, threw aside his purple cloak and cowl, and stepped down. I pushed forward to get a better look.

The challenger in black tossed his loose garment aside, stood facing Qohey in a skin-tight jerkin and hose; heavy moccasins of soft leather were laced up the calf. He was magnificently muscled but Qohey towered over him like a tree, with a build that would have taken the Mr. Muscle Beach title any time he cared to try for it.

I didn't know whether to be glad or sad that the initiative had been taken out from under me. If the man in black won, I wondered would I then be able to step in in turn and take him on? He was a lot smaller than Qohey but there was always the chance . . .

Qohey unsheathed his fancy iron and whirled it like it was a lady's putter. I felt sorry for the smaller man, who was just standing, watching him. He really didn't have a chance.

I had got through to the fore rank by now. The challenger turned and I saw his face. I stopped dead, while fire bells clanged in my head.

The man in black was Foster.

In dead silence Qohey and Foster squared off, touched their sword points to the floor in some kind of salute . . . and Qohey's slicer whipped up in a vicious cut. Foster leaned aside, just far enough, then countered with a flick that made Qohey jump back. I let out a long breath and tried swallowing. Foster was like a terrier up against a bull, but it didn't seem to bother him—only me. I had come light years to find him, just in time to see him get his head lopped off.

Qohey's blade flashed, cutting at Foster's head. Foster hardly moved. Almost effortlessly, it seemed, he interposed his heavy weapon between the attacking steel and himself. *Clash, clang!* Qohey hacked and chopped . . . and Foster played with him. Then Foster's arm flashed out and there was blood on Qohey's wrist. A gasp went up from the crowd. Now Foster took a step forward, struck . . . and faltered! In an instant Qohey was on him and the two men were locked, chest to chest. For a moment Foster held, then Qohey's weight told, and Foster reeled back. He tried to bring up the sword, seemed to struggle, then Qohey lashed out again. Foster twisted, took the blow awkwardly just above the hand guard, stumbled . . . and fell.

Qohey leaped to him, raised the sword—

I hauled mine half way out of its sheath and pushed forward.

"Let the man be put away from my sight," rumbled Qohey. He lowered his immense sword, turned, pushed aside a flunky who had bustled up with a wad of bandages. As he strode from the room a swarm of bodyguards fanned out between the crowd and

Foster. I could see him clumsily struggling to rise, then I was shoved back, still craning for a glimpse. There was something wrong here; Foster had acted like a man suddenly half-paralyzed. Had Qohey doped him in some way?

The cordon stopped pushing, turned their backs to the crowd. I tugged at the arm of the man beside me.

"Did you see anything strange there?" I started.

He pulled free. "Strange? Yea, the mercy of our Lord Qohey! Instead of meting out death on the spot, our Owner was generous—"

"I mean about the fight." I grabbed his arm again to keep him from moving off.

"That the impudent rascal would dare to claim the place of Owner at Bar-Ponderone: there's wonder enough for any man," he snapped. "Unhand me, fellow!"

I unhanded him and tried to collect my wits. What now? I tapped a bodyguard on the shoulder. He whirled, club in hand.

"What's to be the fate of the man?" I asked.

"Like the Boss said: they're gonna immure the bum for his pains."

"You mean wall him up?"

"Yeah. Just a peep hole to pass chow in every day . . . so's he don't starve, see?" The bodyguard chuckled.

"How long—?"

"He'll last; don't worry. After the Change, Owner Qohey's got a newman—"

"Shut up," another bruiser said.

The crowd was slowly thinning. The bodyguards were relaxing, standing in pairs, talking. Two servants moved about where the fight had taken place, making mystical motions in the air above the floor. I edged forward, watching them. They seemed to be plucking imaginary flowers. Strange . . .

I moved even farther forward to take a closer look, then saw a tiny glint . . . A servant hurried across, made gestures. I pushed him aside, groped . . . and my fingers encountered a delicate filament of wire. I pulled it in, swept up more. The servants had stopped and stood watching me, muttering. The whole area of the combat was covered with invisible wires, looping up in coils two feet high.

No wonder Foster had stumbled, had trouble raising his sword. He had been netted, encased in a mesh of incredibly fine tough wire . . . and in the dim light even the crowd twenty feet away hadn't seen it. Owner Qohey was a good man with the chopper but he didn't rely on that alone to hold onto his job.

I put my hand on my sword hilt, chewed my lower lip. I had found Foster . . . but it wouldn't do me—or Vallon—much good. He was on his way to the dungeons, to be walled up until the next Change. And it would be three months before I could legally make another try for Qohey's place. After seeing him in action I was glad I hadn't tried today. He wouldn't have needed any net to handle me.

I would have to spend the next three months working on my swordplay, and hope Foster could hold out. Maybe I could sneak a message—

A heavy blow on the back sent me spinning. Four bodyguards moved to ring me in, clubs in hand. They were strangers to me, but across the room I saw Torbu looming, looking my way . . .

"I saw him; he started to pull that fancy sword," said one of the guards.

"He was asking me questions—"

"Unbuckle it and drop it," another ordered me. "Don't try anything!"

"What's this all about?" I said. "I have a right to wear a Ceremonial Sword at an Audience—"

"Move in, boys!" The four men stepped toward me, the clubs came up. I warded off a smashing blow with my left arm, took a blinding crack across the face, felt myself going down—another blow and another: killing ones . . .

Then I was aware of being dragged, endlessly, of voices barking sharp questions, of pain . . . After a long time it was dark, and silent, and I slept.

I groaned and the sound was dead, muffled. I put out a hand and touched stone on my right. My left elbow touched stone. I made an instinctive move to sit up and smacked my head against more stone. My new room was confining. Gingerly I felt my face . . . and winced at the touch. The bridge of my nose felt different: it was lower than it used to be, in spite of the swelling. I lay back and traced the pattern of pain. There was the nose—smashed flat—with secondary aches around the eyes. They'd be beautiful shiners, if I could see them. Now the left arm: it was curled close to my side and when I moved it I saw why: it wasn't broken, but the shoulder wasn't right, and there was a deep bruise above the elbow. My knees and shins, as far as I could reach, were caked with dried blood. That figured: I remembered being dragged.

I tried deep-breathing; my chest seemed to be okay. My hands worked. My teeth were in place. Maybe I wasn't as sick as I felt.

But where the hell was I? The floor was hard, cold. I needed a big soft bed and a little soft nurse and a hot meal and a cold drink . . .

Foster! I cracked my head again and flopped back, groaned some more. It still sounded pretty dead.

I swallowed, licked my lips, felt a nice split that ran well into the bristles. I had attended the Audience clean-shaven. Quite a few hours must have passed since then. They had taken Foster away to immure him, somebody said. Then the guards had tapped me, worked me over . . .

Immured! I got a third crack on the head. Suddenly it was hard to breathe. I was walled up, sealed away from the light, buried under the foundations of the giant towers of Bar-Ponderone. I felt their crushing weight . . .

I forced myself to relax, breathe deep. Being immured wasn't the same as being buried alive—not exactly. This was the method these latter-day Vallonians had figured out to end a man's life effectively . . . without ending all his lives. They figured to keep me neatly packaged here until my next Change, thus acquiring another healthy newman for the kitchen or the stables. They didn't know the only Change that would happen to me was death.

They'd have to feed me; that meant a hole. I ran my fingers along the rough stone, found an eight-inch square opening on the left wall, just under the ceiling. I reached through it, felt nothing but the solidness of its thick sides. How thick the wall was I had no way of determining.

I was feeling dizzy. I lay back and tried to think . . .

I was awake again. There had been a sound. I moved, and felt something hit my chest.

I groped for it; it was a small loaf of hard bread. I heard the sound again and a second object thumped against me.

"Hey!" I yelled, "listen to me! I'll die in here. I'm not like the rest of you; I won't go through a Change. I'll rot here till I die . . . !"

I listened. The silence was absolute.

"Answer me!" I screamed. "You're making a mistake . . . !"

I gave up when my throat got raw. The people who dropped the bread through the little holes to the prisoners had heard a lot of yelling in their time. They didn't listen any more. I felt for the other item that had been pushed in to me. It was a water bottle made of tough plastic. I fumbled the cap off, took a swallow. It wasn't good. I tried the bread; it was tough, tasteless. I lay and chewed, and wondered what I was supposed to do about toilet facilities; it was an interesting problem. I could see it was going to be a great life, while it lasted. I laughed: a weak snort of despair.

As a world-saver I was a bust. I hadn't even been able to get around to bailing out my pal Foster after Qohey had booby-trapped him. I wondered where he was now. Sealed up in the next cubby-hole probably. But he hadn't answered my yells.

Yeah, mine had been a great idea, but it hadn't worked out. I had come a long long way and now I was going to die in this reeking hole. I had a sudden vision of steaks uneaten, and life unlived. I would have been good for another few decades anyway—

And then I had another thought: if I never had them was it going to be because I hadn't tried? Abruptly I was planning. I would keep calm and use my head. I wouldn't wear myself out with screams and struggles. I'd figure the angles, use everything I had to make the best try I could.

First, to explore the tomb-like cell. It hurt to move, but that didn't matter. I felt over the walls, estimating size. My chamber was three feet wide, two feet high, and seven feet long. The walls were relatively smooth, except for a few mortar joints. The stones were big: eighteen inches or so by a couple of feet. I scratched at the mortar; it was rock hard.

I wondered how they'd gotten me in. Some of the stones must be newly placed . . . or else there was a door. I couldn't feel anything as far as my hands would reach. Maybe at the other end . . .

I tried to twist around: no go. The people who had built the cage knew just how to dimension it to keep the occupant oriented the way they wanted him. He was supposed to just lie quietly and wait for the bread and water to fall through the hole above his chest.

That was reason enough to change positions. If they wanted me to stay put I'd at least have the pleasure of defying the rules. And there just might be a reason why they didn't want me moving around.

I turned on my side, pulled my legs up, hugged them to my chest, worked my way down . . . and jammed. My skinned knees and shins didn't help any. I inched them higher, wincing at the pain, then braced my hands against the floor and roof and forced my torso toward my feet . . .

Still no go. The rough stone was shredding my back. I moved my knees apart; that eased the pressure a little. I made another inch.

I rested, tried to get some air. It wasn't easy: my chest was crushed between my thighs and the stone wall at my back. I breathed shallowly, wondering whether I should go back or try to push on. I tried to move my legs; they didn't like the idea. I might as well go on. It would be no fun either way and if I waited I'd stiffen up, while inactivity and no food and loss of blood would weaken me further every moment. I wouldn't do better next time—not even as well. This was the time. Now.

I set myself, pushed again. I didn't move. I pushed harder, scraping my palms raw against the stone. I was stuck—good. I went limp suddenly. Then I panicked, in the grip of claustrophobia. I snarled, rammed my hands hard against the floor and wall, and heaved— and felt my lacerated back slip along the stone, sliding

on a lubricating film of blood. I pushed again, my back
curved, doubled; my knees were forced up beside my
ears. I couldn't breathe at all now and my spine was
breaking. It didn't matter. I might as well break it, rip
off all the hide, bleed to death; I had nothing to lose.
I shoved again, felt the back of my head grate; my neck
bent, creaking . . . and then I was through, stretching
out to flop on my back, gasping, my head where my
feet had been. Score one for our side.

It took a long time to get my breath back and sort
out my various abrasions. My back was worst, then my
legs and hands. There was a messy spot on the back
of my head and sharp pains shot down my spine, and
I was getting tired of breathing through my mouth
instead of my smashed nose. Other than that I'd never
felt better in my life. I had plenty of room to relax
in, I could breathe. All I had to do was rest, and after
a while they'd drop some more nice bread and water
in to me . . .

I shook myself awake. There was something about
the absolute darkness and silence that made my mind
want to curl up and sleep, but there was no time for
that. If there had been a stone freshly set in mortar
to seal the chamber after I had been stuffed inside,
this was the time to find it—before it set too hard. I
ran my hands over the wall, found the joints. The
mortar was dry and hard in the first; in the next . . .
under my fingernail soft mortar crumbled away. I
traced the joint; it ran around a twelve-by-eighteen-
inch stone. I raised myself on my elbows, settled down
to scratching at it.

Half an hour later I had ten bloody tips and a half-
inch groove dug out around the stone. It was slow work
and I couldn't go much farther without a tool of some
sort. I felt for the water bottle, took off the cap, tried

to crush it. It wouldn't crush. There was nothing else in the cell.

Maybe the stone would move, mortar and all, if I shoved hard enough. I set my feet against the end wall, my hands against the block, and strained until the blood roared in my ears. No use. It was planted as solid as a mother-in-law in the spare bedroom.

I was lying there, just thinking about it, when I became aware of something. It wasn't a noise, exactly. It was more like a fourth-dimensional sound heard inside the brain . . . or the memory of one.

But my next sensation was perfectly real. I felt four little feet walking gravely up my belly toward my chin.

It was my cat, Itzenca.

Chapter Sixteen

For a while I toyed with the idea of just chalking it up as a miracle. Then I decided it would be a nice problem in probabilities. It had been seven months since we had parted company on the pink terrace at Okk-Hamiloth. Where would I have gone if I had been a cat? And how could I have found me—my old pal from earth?

Itzenca exhaled a snuffle in my ear.

"Come to think of it, the stink is pretty strong, isn't it? I guess there's nobody on Vallon with quite the same heady fragrance. And what with the close quarters here, the concentration of sweat, blood, and you-name-it must be pretty penetrating."

Itz didn't seem to care. She marched around my head and back again, now and then laid a tentative paw on my nose or chin, and kept up a steady rumbling purr. The feeling of affection I had for that cat right then was close to being one of my life's grand passions. My hands roamed over her scrawny frame, fingered again the khaffite collar I had whiled away an hour in fashioning for her aboard the lifeboat—

My head hit the stone wall with a crack I didn't even notice. In ten seconds I had released the collar clasp, pulled the collar from Itzenca's neck, thumbed the stiff khaffite out into a blade about ten inches long, and was scraping at the mortar beyond my head at fever heat.

They had fed me three times by the time the groove was nine inches deep on all sides of the block; and the mortar had hardened. But I was nearly through, I figured. I took a rest, then made another try at loosening the block. I thrust the blade into the slot, levered gently at the stone. If it was only supported on one edge now, as it would be if it were a little less than a foot thick, it should be about ready to go. I couldn't tell.

I put down my scraper, got into position, and pushed. I wasn't as strong as I had been; there wasn't much force in the push. Again I rested and again I tried. Maybe there was only a thin crust of mortar still holding; maybe one more ounce of pressure would do it. I took a deep breath, strained . . . and felt the block shift minutely.

Now! I heaved again, teeth gritted, drew back my feet, and thrust hard. The stone slid out with a grating sound, dropped half an inch. I paused to listen: all quiet. I shoved again, and the stone dropped with a heavy thud to the floor outside. With no loss of time I pushed through behind it, felt a breath of cooler air, got my shoulders free, pulled my legs through . . . and stood, for the first time in how many days . . .

I had already figured my next move. As soon as
Itzenca had stepped out I reached back in, groped for
the water bottle, the dry crusts I had been saving, and
the wad of bread paste I had made up. I reached a
second time for a handful of the powdered mortar I
had produced, then lifted the stone. I settled it in place,
using the hard bread as supports, then packed the open
joint with gummy bread. I dusted it over with dry
mortar, then carefully swept up the debris—as well as
I could in the total darkness. The bread-and-water man
would have a light and he was due in half an hour or
so—as closely as I had been able to estimate the time
of his regular round. I didn't want him to see anything
out of the ordinary. I was counting on finding Foster
filed away somewhere in the stacks, and I'd need time
to try to release him.

I moved along the corridor, counting my steps, one
hand full of breadcrumbs and stone dust, the other
feeling the wall. There were narrow side branches every
few feet: the access ways to the feeding holes. Forty-
one paces from my slot I came to a wooden door. It
wasn't locked, but I didn't open it. I wasn't ready to
use it yet.

I went back, passed my hole, continued nine paces
to a blank wall. Then I tried the side branches. They
were all seven-foot stubs, dead ends; each had the
eight-inch holes on either side. I called Foster's name
softly at each hole . . . but there was no answer. I heard
no signs of life, no yells or heavy breathing. Was I the
only one here? That wasn't what I had figured on.
Foster had to be in one of these delightful bedrooms.
I had come across the universe to see him and I wasn't
going to leave Bar-Ponderone without him.

It was time to get ready for the bread man. I had
a choice of trying to get back into my hole and replac-
ing the block, or of hiding in one of the side branches.

I thought it over for a couple of microseconds and decided against getting back in my tomb. If there were as many vacancies here as I guessed, I'd be safe in any one of the side passages but my own.

I groped my way into a convenient hidey-hole, Itzenca at my heels. With half a year's experience at dodging humans behind her, she could be trusted not to show at the crucial moment, I figured. I had just jettisoned my handful of trash in the backmost corner of the passage when there was a soft grating sound from the door. I flattened myself against the wall. I'd know in a second or two how observant the keeper was.

A light splashed on the floor; it must have been dim but seemed to my eyes like the blaze of noon. Soft footsteps sounded. I held my breath. A man in body-guard's trappings, basket in hand, moved past the entry of the branch where I stood, went on. I breathed again. Now all I had to do was keep an eye on the feeder, watch where he stopped. I stepped to the corridor, risked a glance, saw him entering a branch far down the corridor. As he disappeared I made it three branches farther along, ducked out of sight.

I heard him coming back. I flattened myself. He went by me, opened the door. It closed behind him and the darkness and silence settled down once more. I stood where I was, feeling like a guy who's just showed up for a party . . . on the wrong day.

The bread man had stopped at one cell only—mine. Foster wasn't here.

It was a long wait for the next feeding but I put the time to use. First I had a good nap; I hadn't been getting my rest while I scratched my way out of my nest. I woke up feeling better and started thinking about the next move. The bodyguard who brought the food was the first item: I had to get a set of clothes somewhere and he'd be the easiest source to tap. If my mental clock was right it was about time—

The door creaked, and I did a fast fade down a side branch. The guard shuffled into view; now was the time. I moved out—quietly, I thought, and he whirled, dropped the load and bottle, and fumbled at his club hilt. I didn't have a club to slow me down. I went at him, threw a beautiful right, square to the mouth. He went over backwards, with me on top. I heard his head hit with a sound like a length of rubber hose slapping a grapefruit. He didn't move.

I pulled the clothes off him, struggled into them. They didn't fit too well and they probably smelled gamey to anybody who hadn't spent a week where I had, but details like those didn't count anymore. I tore his sash into strips and tied him. He wasn't dead— quite, but I had reason to know that any yelling he did was unlikely to attract much attention. I hoped he'd enjoy the rest and quiet until the next feeding time. By then I expected to be long gone. I lifted the door open and stepped out into a dimly-lit corridor.

With Itzenca abreast of me I moved along in absolute stillness, passed a side corridor, came to a heavy door: locked. We retraced our steps, went down the side hall, found a flight of worn steps, followed them up two flights, and emerged in a dark room. A line of light showed around a door. I went to it, peered through the crack. Two men in stained Kitchen-slave tunics fussed over a boiling cauldron. I pushed through the door.

The two looked up, startled. I rounded a littered table, grabbed up a heavy soup ladle, and skulled the nearest cook just as he opened up to yell. The other one, a big fellow, went for a cleaver. I caught him in two jumps, laid him out cold beside his pal.

I found an apron, ripped it up, and tied and gagged

the two slaves, then hauled them into a storeroom. I was stacking Vallonians away like a squirrel storing nuts.

I came back into the kitchen. It was silent now. The room reeked of sour soup. A stack of unpleasantly familiar loaves stood by the oven. I gave them a kick that collapsed the pile as I passed to pick up a knife. I hacked tough slices from a cold haunch of Vallonian mutton, threw one to Itzenca across the table, and sat and gnawed the meat while I tried to think through my plans.

Owner Qohey was a big man to tackle but he was the one with the answers. If I could make my way to his apartment and if I wasn't stopped before I'd forced the truth out of him, then I might get to Foster and tell him that if he had the memory playback machine I had the memory, if it hadn't been filched from the bottom of a knapsack aboard a lifeboat parked at Okk-Hamiloth.

Four 'ifs' and a 'might'—but it was something to shoot at. My first move would be to locate Qohey's quarters, somewhere here in the Palace, and get inside. My bodyguard's outfit was as good a disguise as any for the attempt.

I finished off my share of the meat and got to my feet. I'd have to find a place to clean myself up, shave—

The rear door banged open and two bodyguards came through it, talking loudly, laughing.

"Hey, cook! Set out meat for—"

The heavy in the lead stopped short, gaping at me. I gaped back. It was Torbu.

"Drgon! How did you . . . ?" He trailed off.

The other bodyguard came past him, looked me over. "You're no Brother of the Guard—" he started.

I reached for the cleaver the kitchen-slave had left on the table, backed against a tall wall cupboard. The bodyguard unlimbered his club.

"Hold it, Blon," said Torbu. "Drgon's okay." He

looked at me. "I kind of figured you for done for, Drgon. The boys worked you over pretty good."

"Yeah," I returned, "and thanks for your help in stopping it."

"This is the miscreant we immured!" Blon burst out. "Take him!"

Torbu shifted. "Hold it a minute," he said. He looked uncomfortable.

"Listen, you two!" I said. "You claim to believe in the system around here. You think it's a great life, all fair play and no holds barred and plenty of goodies for the winner. I know, it was tough about Cagu, but that's life, isn't it? But what about the business I saw in that Audience Hall? You guys try not to think about that angle, is that it?"

"The noble Owner's gotta right—" Blon started.

"I didn't like the caper with the wires, Blon," said Torbu. "You didn't either; neither did most of the boys—"

"And I don't remember getting much of a show myself," I said. "There are a couple of your buddies I plan to look up when I have some free time—"

"I didn't lay a hand on you, Drgon," said Torbu. "I didn't want no part of that."

"It was the Owner's orders," said Blon. "What was I gonna do, tell him—"

"Never mind," I said. "I'll tell him myself. That's all I want: just a short interview with the Owner—minus the wire nets."

"Wow . . ." drawled Torbu, "yeah, that'd be a bout." He turned to Blon. "This guy's got a punch, Blon. He don't look so hot but he could swap buffets with the Fire Drgon he's named after. If he's that good with a long blade—"

"Just lend me one," I said, "and show me the way to his apartment."

"The noble Owner'll cut this clown to ribbons in two minutes flat," said Blon.

"Let's get the boys."

"How could we explain it afterwards to the noble Owner?" said Blon. "He ain't gonna think much of guys he thought was immured nice and safe turnin' up in his bedchamber . . . armed."

"We're Brothers of the Guard," said Torbu. "We ain't got much but we got our Code. It don't say nothing about wires. If we don't back up our oath to the Brotherhood we ain't no better than slaves." He turned to me. "Come on, Drgon. We'll take you to the Guardroom so you can clean up and put on a good blade. If you're gonna lose all your lives at once, you wanna do it right."

Torbu watched as the boys belted and strapped me into a guardsman's fighting outfit. I had made him uneasy, maybe even started him thinking. If I could last—just those 'two minutes flat'—before Owner Qohey killed me, then he'd collect his bet, I'd be out of his hair, and he could go back to being Torbu, a plain tough guy with a Code he could still believe in. And if I won . . .

I felt better in the clean trappings of tough leather and steel. Torbu led the way and fifteen bodyguards followed, like a herd of trolls. There were few palace servants out at this hour; those who saw us gaped from a safe distance and went on about their business. We crossed the empty Audience Hall, climbed a wide staircase, went along a spacious corridor hung with rich brocades and carpeted in deep-pile silk, with soft lights glowing around ornate doors.

We stopped before a great double door. Two guards in dress purple sauntered over to see what it was all about. Torbu clued them in. They hesitated, looked us over . . .

"We're goin' in, rookie," said Torbu. "Open up." They did.

I pushed past Torbu into a room whose splendor made Gope's state apartment look like a motel. Bright Cintelight streamed through tall windows, showed me a wide bed and somebody in it. I went to it, grabbed the bedclothes, and hauled them off onto the floor. Owner Qohey sat up slowly—seven feet of muscle. He looked at me, glanced past me to the foremost of my escort . . .

He was out of the bed like a tiger, coming straight for me. There was no time to fumble with the sword. I went to meet him, threw all my weight into a right haymaker and felt it connect. I plunged past, whirled.

Qohey was staggering . . . but still on his feet. I had hit him with everything I had, nearly broken my fist . . . and he was still standing. I couldn't let him rest. I was after him, slammed a hard punch to the kidneys, caught him across the jaw as he turned, drove a left and right into his stomach—

A girder fell from the top of the Golden Gate Bridge and shattered every bone in my body. There was a booming like heavy surf, and I was floating in it, dead. Then I was in Hell, being prodded by red-hot tridents . . . I blinked my eyes. The roaring was fading now. I saw Qohey, leaning against the foot of the bed, breathing heavily. I had to get him.

I got my feet under me, stood up. My chest was caved in and my left arm belonged to somebody else. Okay; I still had my right. I made it over to Qohey, maneuvered into position. He didn't look at me; he seemed to be having trouble breathing; those gut punches had gotten to him. I picked a spot just behind the right ear, reared back, and threw a trip-hammer punch with my shoulder and legs behind it. I felt the jaw go. Qohey jumped the footboard and piled onto the floor like a hundred-car freight hitting an open switch. I sat down on the edge of the bed and sucked in air and tried to ignore the whirling lights that were closing in.

After awhile I noticed Torbu standing in front of me with the cat under one arm. Both of them were grinning at me. "Any orders, Owner Drgon?"

I found my voice. "Wake him up and prop him in a chair. I want to talk to him."

Ex-Owner Qohey didn't much like the idea but after Torbu and a couple of other strong-arm lads had explained the situation to him in sign language he decided to cooperate.

"Get off his head, Mull," Torbu said. "And untwist that rope, Blon. Owner Drgon wants him in a conversational mood. You guys are gonna make him feel self-conscious."

I had been feeling over my ribs, trying to count how many were broken and how many just bent. Qohey's punch was a lot like the kick of a two-ton ostrich. He was looking at me now, eyes wild.

"Qohey, I want to ask you a few questions. If I don't like the answers, I'll see if I can't find quarters for you in the basement annex. I just left a cozy room there myself. There's no view to speak of but it's peaceful."

Qohey grunted something. He was having trouble talking around his broken jaw.

"The fellow in black," I said, "the one who claimed your place as Owner. You netted him and had your bully boys haul him off somewhere. I want to know where."

Qohey grunted again.

"Hit him, Torbu," I said. "It will help his enunciation." Torbu kicked the former Owner in the shin. Qohey jumped and glowered at him.

"Call off your dogs," he mumbled. "You'll not find the upstart you seek here."

"Why not?"

"I sent him away."

"Where?"

"To that place from which you and your turncoat crew will never fetch him back."

"Be more specific."

Qohey spat.

"Torbu didn't much like that crack about turncoats," I said. "He's eager to show you how little. I advise you to talk fast and plain, before you lose a whole raft of lives."

"Even these swine would never dare—" I took out the needle-pointed knife I was wearing as part of my get-up. I put the point against Qohey's throat and pushed gently until a trickle of crimson ran down the thick neck.

"Talk," I said quietly, "or I'll cut your throat myself."

Qohey had shrunk back as far as he could in the heavy chair.

"Seek him then, assassin," he sneered. "Seek him in the dungeons of the Owner of Owners."

"Keep talking," I prompted.

"The Great Owner commanded that the slave be brought to him . . . at the Palace of Sapphires by the Shallow Sea."

"Has this Owners' Owner got a name? How'd he hear about him?"

"Lord Ommodurad," Qohey's voice grated out. He was watching Torbu's foot. "There was that about the person of the stranger that led me to inform him."

"When did he go?"

"Yesterday."

"You know this Sapphire Palace, Torbu?"

"Sure," he answered. "But the place is taboo; it's crawlin' with demons and warlocks. The word is, there's a curse on the—"

"Then I'll go in alone," I said. I put the knife away. "But first I've got a call to make at the spaceport at Okk-Hamiloth."

"Sure, Owner Drgon. The port's easy. Some say it's kind of haunted too but that's just a gag; the Greymen hang out there."

"We can take care of the Greymen," I said. "Get fifty of your best men together and line up some air-cars. I want the outfit ready to move out in half an hour."

"What about this chiseler?" asked Torbu.

"Seal him up until I get back. If I don't make it, I know he'll understand."

Chapter Seventeen

It was not quite dawn when my task force settled down on the smooth landing pad beside the lifeboat that had brought me to Vallon. It stood as I had left it seven earth-months before: the port open, the access ladder extended, the interior lights lit. There weren't any spooks aboard but they had kept visitors away as effectively as if there had been. Even the Greymen didn't mess with ghost-boats. Somebody had done a thorough job of indoctrination on Vallon.

"You ain't gonna go inside that accursed vessel, are you, Owner Drgon?" asked Torbu, making his cabalistic sign in the air. "It's manned by goblins—"

"That's just propaganda. Where my cat can go, I can go. Look."

Itzenca scampered up the ladder, and had disappeared inside the boat by the time I took the first rung. The guards gawked from below as I stepped into the softly lit lounge. The black-and-gold cylinder that was

Foster's memory lay in the bag I had packed and left behind, months before; with it was the other, plain one: Ammaerln's memory. Somewhere in Okk-Hamiloth must be the machine that would give these meaning. Together Foster and I would find it.

I found the .38 automatic lying where I had left it. I picked up the worn belt, strapped it around me. My Vallonian career to date suggested it would be a bright idea to bring it along. The Vallonians had never developed any personal armament to equal it. In a society of immortals knives were considered lethal enough for all ordinary purposes.

"Come on, cat," I said. "There's nothing more here we need."

Back on the ramp I beckoned my platoon leaders over.

"I'm going to the Sapphire Palace," I said. "Anybody that doesn't want to go can check out now. Pass the word."

Torbu stood silent for a long moment, staring straight ahead.

"I don't like it much, Owner," he said. "But I'll go. And so will the rest of 'em."

"There'll be no backing out, once we shove off," I said. "And by the way—" I jacked a round into the chamber of the pistol, raised it, and fired the shot into the air. They all jumped. "If you ever hear that sound, come a-running."

The men nodded, turned to their cars. I picked up the cat and piled into the lead vehicle next to Torbu.

"It's a half-hour run," he said. "We might run into a little Greymen action on the way. We can handle 'em."

We lifted, swung to the east, barreled along at low altitude.

"What do we do when we get there, boss?" said Torbu.

"We play it by ear. Let's see how far we can get on pure gall before Ommodurad drops the hanky."

The palace lay below us, rearing blue towers to the twilit sky like a royal residence in the Munchkin country. Beyond it, sunset colors reflected from the silky surface of the Shallow Sea. The timeless stones and still waters looked much as they had when Foster set out to lose his identity on earth, three thousand years before. But its magnificence was lost on these people. The hulking crew around me never paused to wonder about the marvels wrought by their immortal ancestors—themselves. Stolidly, they lived their feudal lives in dismal contrast with the monuments all about them.

I turned to my cohort of hoodlums. "You boys claim it's the demons and warlocks that keep the whole of Vallon at arm's length from this place. In that case there's no protocol for a new Owner's reception at the Blue Palace. A guy with a little luck and even less of a memory than usual could skip the goblins and play it good-natured but dumb: show up at the Palace grounds, out of common politeness to the Top Dog, to pay his respects. Anything wrong with that?"

"What if they rush us first . . . before we got time to go into the act?" said somebody in the mob.

"That's where the luck comes in," I said. "Anybody else?"

Torbu looked around at his henchmen. There was some shrugging of shoulders, a few grunts. He looked at me. "You do the figurin', Owner," he said. "The boys will back your play."

We were dropping toward the wide lawns now and still no opposition showed itself. Then the towering blue spires were looming over us, and we saw men forming up behind the blue-stained steel gates of the Great Pavilion.

"A reception committee," I said. "Hold tight, fellas. Don't start anything. The further in we get peaceably, the less that leaves to do the hard way."

The cars settled down gently, well-grouped, and Torbu and I climbed out. As quickly as the other boats disgorged their men, ranks were closed, and we moved off toward the gates. Itzenca, as mascot, brought up the rear. Still no excitement, no rush by the Palace guards. Had too many centuries of calm made them lackadaisical, or did Ommodurad use a brand of visitor-repellent we couldn't see from here?

We made it to the gate . . . and it opened.

"In we go," I said, "but be ready . . ."

The uniformed men inside the compound, obviously chosen for their beef content, kept their distance, looked at us questioningly. We pulled up on a broad blue-paved drive and waited for the next move. About now somebody should stride up to us and offer the key to the city—or something. But there seemed to be a hitch. It was understandable. After all there hadn't been any callers dropping cards here for about 2900 years.

It was a long five minutes before a hard case in a beetle-backed carapace of armor and a puffy pink cape bustled down the palace steps and came up to us.

"Who comes in force to the Sapphire Palace?" he demanded, glancing past me at my team-mates.

"I'm Owner Drgon, fellow," I barked. "These are my honor guard. What provincial welcome is this, from the Great Owner to a loyal liege-man?"

That punctured his pomposity a little. He apologized—in a half-hearted way—mumbled something about arrangements, and beckoned over a couple of side-men. One of them came over and spoke to Torbu, who looked my way, hand on dagger hilt.

"What's this?" I said. "Where I go, my men go."

"There is the matter of caste," said my pink-caped greeter. "Packs of retainers are not ushered *en masse* into the presence of Lord Ommodurad, Owner of Owners."

I thought that one over and failed to come up with a plausible loophole.

"Okay, Torbu," I said. "Keep the boys together and behave yourselves. I'll see you in an hour. Oh, and see that Itzenca gets made comfy."

The beetle man snapped a few orders, then waved me toward the palace with the slightest bow I ever saw. A six-man guard kept me company up the steps and into the Great Pavilion.

I guess I expected the usual velvet-draped audience chamber or barbarically splendid Hall, complete with pipers, fools, and ceremonial guards. What I got was an office, about sixteen by eighteen, blue-carpeted and tasteful . . . but bare-looking. I stopped in front of a block of blue-veined grey marble with a couple of quill pens in a crystal holder and, underneath, leg room for a behemoth, who was sitting behind the desk.

He got to his feet with all the ponderous mass of Nero Wolfe but a lot more agility and grace. "You wish?" he rumbled.

"I'm Owner Drgon, ah . . . Great Owner," I said. I'd planned to give my host the friendly-but-dumb routine. I was going to find the second part of the act easy. There was something about this Ommodurad that made me feel like a mouse who'd just changed his mind about the cheese. Qohey had been big, but this guy could crush skulls as most men pinch peanut hulls, and in his eyes was the kind of remote look that came of three millennia of not even having to mention the power he asserted.

"You ignore superstition," observed the Big Owner.

He didn't waste many words, it seemed. Gope had said he was the silent type. It wasn't a bad lead; I decided to follow it.

"Don't believe in 'em," I said.

"To your business then," he continued. "Why?"

"Just been chosen Owner at Bar-Ponderone," I said. "Felt it was only fitting that I come and do obeisance before Your Grace."

"That expression is not used."

"Oh." This fellow had a disconcerting way of not getting sucked in. "Lord Ommodurad?"

He nodded just perceptibly, then turned to the foremost of the herd who had brought me in. "Quarters for the guest and his retinue." His eyes had already withdrawn, like the head of a Galapagos turtle into its enormous shell, in contemplation of eternal verities. I piped up again.

"Ah, pardon me . . ." The piercing stare of Ommodurad's eyes was on me again. "There was a friend of mine—" I gulped, "swell guy, but impulsive. It seems he challenged the former Owner of Bar-Ponderone . . ."

Ommodurad did no more than twitch an eyebrow but suddenly the air was electric. His stare didn't waver by a millimeter but the lazy slouch of the six guards had altered to sprung steel. They hadn't moved but I felt them now all around me and not a foot away. I had a sinking feeling that I'd gone too far.

"—so I thought maybe I'd crave Your Excellency's help, if possible, to locate my pal," I finished weakly. For an interminable minute the Owner of Owners bored into me with his eyes. Then he raised a finger a quarter of an inch. The guards relaxed.

"Quarters for the guest and his retinue," repeated Ommodurad. He withdrew then . . . without moving. I was dismissed.

I went quietly, attended by my hulking escort.

I tried hard not to let my expression show any excitement, but I was feeling plenty.

Ommodurad was close-mouthed for a reason. I was willing to bet that he had his memories of the Good Time intact.

Instead of the debased modern dialect that I'd heard everywhere since my arrival, Ommodurad spoke flawless Old Vallonian.

It was 27 o'clock and the Palace of Sapphires was silent. I was alone in the ornate bed chamber the Great Owner had assigned me. It was a nice room but I wouldn't learn anything staying in it. Nobody had said I was confined to quarters. I'd do a little scouting and see what I could pick up, if anything. I slung on the holster and the .38 and slid out of the darkened chamber into the scarcely lighter corridor beyond. I saw a guard at the far end; he ignored me. I headed in the opposite direction.

None of the rooms was locked. There was no arsenal at the Palace and no archives that lesser folk than the Great Owner could use with profit. Everything was easy of access. I guessed that Ommodurad rightly counted on indifference to keep snoopers away. Here and there guards eyed me as I passed along but they said nothing.

I saw again by Cintelight the office where Ommodurad had received me, and near it an ostentatious hall with black onyx floor and ceiling, gold hangings, and ceremonial ringboard. But the center of attraction was the familiar motif of the concentric circles of the Two Worlds, sketched in beaten gold across the broad wall of black marble behind the throne. Here the idea had been elaborated on. Outward from both the inner and outer circles flamed the waving lines of a sunburst. At dead center, a boss, like a sword hilt in form, chased in black and gold, erupted a foot from the wall. It was the first time I'd seen the symbol since I'd arrived on Vallon. I found it strangely exciting—like a footprint in the sand.

I went on, toured the laundry and inspected pantries large and small and caught a whiff of stables. The palace was asleep; few of its occupants noticed me, and those who did hung back, silent. It looked as if the Great Owner had given orders to let me roam freely. Somehow I didn't find that comforting.

Then I came into a purple-vaulted hall and saw a squad of guards, the same six who'd kept me such close company earlier in the day. They were drawn up at parade rest, three on each side of a massive ivory door. Somebody lived in safety and splendor on the other side.

Six sets of hard eyes turned my way. It was too late to duck back out of sight. I trotted up to the first of the row of guards. "Say, fella," I stage-whispered, "where's the ah—you know."

"Every bed chamber is equipped," he said gruffly, raising his sword and fingering its tip lovingly.

"Yeah? I never noticed." I moved off, looking chastened. If they thought I was a kewpie, so much the better. I was a mouse in cat country here and I wasn't ready to fake a *meow*—not yet.

On the ground floor I found Torbu and his cohort quartered in a barrack-room off the main entry hall.

"We're still in enemy territory," I reminded Torbu. "I want every man ready."

"No fear, boss," said Torbu. "All my bullies got an eye on the door and a hand on a knife-hilt."

"Have you seen or heard anything useful?"

"Naw. These local dullards fall dumb at the first query."

"Keep your ears cocked. I want at least two men awake and on the alert all night."

"You bet, noble Drgon."

I judged distances carefully as I went back up the two flights to my own room. Inside I dropped into a brocaded easy chair and tried to add up what I'd seen.

First: Ommodurad's apartment, as nearly as I could judge, was directly over my own, two floors up. That was a break—or maybe I was where I was for easier surveillance. I'd skip that angle, I decided. It tended to discourage me and I needed all the enthusiasm I could generate.

Second: I wasn't going to learn anything useful trotting around corridors. Ommodurad wasn't the kind to leave traces of skullduggery lying around where the guests would see them.

And third: I should have known better than to hit this fortress with two squads and a .38 in the first place. Foster was here; Qohey had said so and the Great Owner's reaction to my mention of him confirmed it. What was it about Foster, anyway, that made him so interesting to these Top People? I'd have to ask him that one when I found him. But to do that I'd have to leave the beaten track.

I went to the wide double window and looked up. A cloud swept from the great three-quarters face of Cinte, blue in the southern sky, and I could see an elaborately carved façade ranging up past a row of windows above my own to a railed balcony bathed in a pale light from the apartment within. If my calculations were correct that would be Ommodurad's digs. The front door was guarded like an octogenarian's harem but the back way looked like a breeze.

I pulled my head back in and thought about it. It was risky . . . but it had that element of the unexpected that just might let me get away with it. Tomorrow the Owner of Owners might have thought it through and switched me to another room . . . or to a cell in the basement. Then too, wall-scaling didn't occur to these Vallonians as readily as it did to a short-timer from earth. They had too much to lose to risk it on a chancy climb.

Too much thinking is never a good idea when your pulse is telling you it's time for action. I rolled a heavy armoire fairly soundlessly over the deep-pile carpet and lodged it against the door. That might slow down a casual caller. I slipped the magazine out of the automatic, fitted nine greasy brass cartridges into it, slammed it home, dropped the pistol back in the holster. It had a comforting weight. I buttoned the strap over it and went back to the window.

The clouds were back across Cinte's floodlight; that would help. I stepped out. The deep carving gave me easy handholds and I made it to the next windowsill without even working up a light sweat. Compared with my last climb, back in Lima, this was a cinch.

I rested a moment, then clambered around the dark window—just in case there was an insomniac on the other side of the glass—and went on up. I reached the balcony, had a hairy moment as I groped outward for a hold on the smooth floor-tiling above . . . and then I was pulling up and over the ornamental iron work.

The balcony was narrow, about twenty feet long, giving on half a dozen tall glass doors. Three showed light behind heavy draperies, three were dark. I moved close, tried to see something past the edge of the draperies. No go. I put an ear to the glass, thought maybe I heard a sound, like a distant volcano. That would be Ommodurad's bass rumble. The bear was in his cave.

I went along to the dark doors and on impulse tried a handle. It turned and the door swung in soundlessly. I felt my pulse pick up a double-time beat. I stood peering past the edge of the door into the ink-black interior. It didn't look inviting. In fact it looked repellent. Even a country boy like me could see that to step into the dragon's den without even a Zippo to spot the footstools with would be the act of a nitwit.

I swallowed hard, got a firm grip on my pistol, and went in.

A soft fold of drapery brushed my face and I had the pistol out and my back to the wall with a speed that would have made Earp faint with envy. My adrenals gave a couple of wild jumps and my nervous system followed with a variety of sensations, none pleasant.

It took me a minute to get my Adam's apple swallowed again and remind myself that I was a rough tough son-of-a-gun from the planet Earth who had parlayed one short life into more trouble than most Vallonians managed in half of eternity, and I was on my way to get my pal Foster out of a tight spot, hand him back his memory, and set the Two Worlds back on the rails they had fallen off of about six hundred years before Alexander started looking around for his first rumble.

I stopped before I got so confident I charged into the next room and challenged Ommodurad to wrestle, two falls out of three. I could hear his voice better now, muttering beyond the partition. If I could make out what he was saying . . .

I edged along the wall, found a heavy door, closed and locked. No help there. I felt my way further, found another door. Delicately I tried the handle, eased it open a crack.

A closet, half filled with racked garments. But I could hear more clearly now. Maybe it was a double closet with communicating doors both to the room I was in and to the next one where the Great Owner was still rambling on. Apparently something had overcome his aversion to talking. There were pauses that must have been filled in by the replies of somebody else who didn't have the vocal timbre Ommodurad did.

I felt my way through the hanging clothing, felt over the closet walls. I was out of luck: there was no other door. I put an ear to the wall. I could catch an occasional word:

" . . . ring . . . Okk-Hamiloth . . . vaults . . ."

It sounded like something I'd like to hear more about. How could I get closer? On impulse I reached up, touched a low ceiling . . . and felt a ridge like the trim around an access panel to a crawl space.

I crossed my fingers, stood on tiptoe to push at the panel. Nothing moved. I felt around in the dark, encountered a low shelf covered with shoes. I investigated; it was movable. I eased it aside a foot or two, piled the shoes on the floor, and stepped up.

The panel was two feet long on a side, with no discernible hinges or catch. I pushed some more, then gritted my teeth and heaved. There was a startlingly loud *crack!* and the panel lifted. I blinked away the dust that settled in my eyes, reached to feel around within the opening, touched nothing but rough floor boards.

This would be an excellent time, I reflected, to back out of here, get a few hours' sleep, and tomorrow bid Ommodurad a hearty farewell. Then in a few months, after I had had time to organize my new Estate and align a few supporting Owners I could come back in force.

I cocked my head, listening. Ommodurad had stopped talking and another voice said something. Then there was a heavy thump, the clump of feet, and a metallic sound. After a moment the Great Owner's voice came again . . . and the other voice answered.

I stretched, grabbed the edge of the opening, and pulled myself up. I leaned forward, got a leg up, and rolled silently onto the rough floor. Feeling my way, I crawled, felt a wall rising, followed it, turned a corner . . . The voices were louder, quite suddenly. I saw why: there was a ventilating register ahead, gridded light gleaming through it. I crept along to the opening, lay flat, peered through it and saw three men.

Ommodurad was standing with his back to me, a giant figure swathed to the eyes in purple robes. Beside him a lean redhead with a leg that had been broken and badly set stood round-shouldered, teeth bared in an eager grimace, clutching a rod of office. The third man was Foster.

Foster stood, legs braced apart as though to withstand an earthquake, hands manacled before him. He looked steadily at the redhead, like a man marking a tree for cutting.

"I know nothing of these crimes," he said.

Ommodurad turned, swept out of sight. The redhead motioned. Foster turned away, moving stiffly, passed from my view. I heard a door open and close. I lay where I was and tried to sort out half a dozen conflicting impulses that clamored for attention. A few were easy: it wouldn't help matters to yell "Stop, thief!" or to fall through the register and chase after Foster with loud cries of joy. It wouldn't be much better to scramble out, dash downstairs, and turn out my bodyguards to raid Ommodurad's apartment.

What might do some good was to gather more information. It had been bad luck that I had arrived at my peephole a few minutes too late to hear what the interview had been all about. But I might still make use of my advantage.

I felt over the register, found fasteners at the

corners. They lifted easily and the metal grating tilted back into my hands. I laid it aside, poked my head out. The room was empty, as far as I could see. It was time to take a few chances. I reversed my position, let my legs through the opening, and dropped softly to the floor. I reached back up and managed to prop the grating in position—just in case.

It was a fancy chamber, hung in purple and furnished for a king. I poked through the pigeonholes of a secretary, opened a few cupboards, peered under the bed. It looked like I wasn't going to find any useful clues lying around loose.

I went to the glass doors to the balcony, unlocked one and left it ajar—in case I wanted to leave in a hurry. There was another door across the room. I went over and tried it: locked.

That gave me something definite to look for: a key. I rummaged some more in the secretary, then tried the drawer in a small table beside a broad couch and came up with a nice little steel key that looked like maybe . . .

I tried it. It was. Luck was still coming my way. I pushed open the door, saw a dark room beyond. I felt for a light switch, flicked it on, pushed the door shut behind me.

The room looked like the popular idea of a necromancer's study. The windowless walls were lined with shelves packed closely with books. The high black-draped ceiling hung like a hovering bat above the ramparted floor of bare, dark-polished wood. Narrow tables choked with books and instruments stood along a side of the chamber and at the far end I saw a deep-cushioned couch with a heavy dome-shaped apparatus like a beauty shop hair-dryer mounted at one end. I recognized it: it was a memory reinforcing machine, the first I had seen on Vallon.

I crossed the room and examined it. The last one

I had seen—on the Far-Voyager in the room near the library—had been a stark utility model. This was a deluxe job, with soft upholstery and bright metal fittings and more dials and idiot lights than a late model Detroit status symbol. This solved one of the problems that had been hovering around the edge of my mind. I had fetched Foster's memory back to him, but without a machine to use it in it was just a tantalizing souvenir. Now all I had to do was sneak him away from Ommodurad, make it back here . . .

All of a sudden I felt tired, vulnerable, helpless, and all alone. I had been taking wild chances, setting my head more and more brazenly into the kind of iron noose the Big Owner would arrange for his enemies . . . and without the ghost of a plan, without even an idea of what was going on. What was Ommodurad's interest in Foster? Why did he hide away here, keeping the rest of Vallon away with rumors of magic and spells? What connection did he have with the disaster that had befallen the Two Worlds—now reduced to One, and a poor one at that.

And why was I, a plain Joe named Legion, mixed up in it right to the eyebrows, when I could be sitting safe at home in a clean federal pen?

The answer to that last one wasn't too hard to recite: I had had a pal once, a smooth character named Foster, who had pulled me back from the ragged edge just when I was about to make a bigger mistake than usual. He had been a gentleman in the best sense of the word, and he had treated me like one. Together we had shared a strange adventure that had made me rich and had showed me that it was never too late to straighten your back and take on whatever the Fates handed out.

I had come running his way when trouble got too thick back home. And I'd found him in a worse spot than I was in. He had come back, after the most agonizing exile a man had ever suffered, to find his world fallen back into savagery, and his memory still eluding him. Now he was in chains, without friends and without hope . . . but still not broken, still standing on his own two feet . . .

But he was wrong on one point: he had one little hope. Not much: just a hard-luck guy with a penchant for bad decisions, but I was here and I was free. I had my pistol on my hip and a neat back way into the Owner's bedroom, and if I played it right and watched my timing and had maybe just a little luck, say about the amount it took to hit the Irish Sweepstakes, I might bring it off yet.

Right now it was time to return to my crawlspace. Ommodurad might come back and talk some more, tip me off to a vulnerable spot in the armor of his fortress. I went to the door, flicked off the light, turned the handle . . . and went rigid.

Ommodurad was back. He pulled off the purple cloak, tossed it aside, strode to a wall bar. I clung to the crack of the door, not daring to move even to close it.

"But my lord," the voice of the redhead said, "I know he remembers—"

"Not so," Ommodurad's voice rumbled. "On the morrow I strip his mind to the bare clean jelly . . ."

"Let me, dread lord. With my steel I'll have the truth from him."

"Such a one as he your steel has never known!" the bass voice snarled.

"Great Owner, I crave but one hour . . . tomorrow, in the Ceremonial Chamber. I shall environ him with the emblems of the past—"

"Enough!" Ommodurad's fist slammed against the bar, made glasses jump. "On such starveling lackwits as you a mighty empire hangs. It is a crime before the

Gods and on his head I lay it." The Owner tossed off a glass, jerked his head at the cowering man. "Still, I grant thy boon. Now begone, babbler of folly."

The redhead ducked, grinning, disappeared. Ommodurad muttered to himself, strode up and down the room, stood staring out into the night. He noticed the open balcony door, pulled it shut with a curse. I held my breath but no general check of doors followed.

The big man threw off his clothes then. He clambered up on the wide couch, touched a switch somewhere, and the room was dark. Within five minutes I heard the heavy breathing of deep sleep.

I had found out one thing anyway: tomorrow was Foster's last day. One way or another Ommodurad and the redhead between them would destroy him. That didn't leave much time. But since the project was already hopeless it didn't make much difference.

I had a choice of moves now: I could tip-toe across to the register and try to wiggle through it without waking up the brontosaurus on the bed . . . or I could try for the balcony door a foot from where he slept . . . or I could stay put and wait him out. The last idea had the virtue of requiring no immediate daring adventures. I could just curl up on the floor, or, better still, on the padded couch . . .

A weird idea was taking shape in my mind like a genie rising from a bottle. I felt in my pocket, pulled out the two small cylinders that represented two men's memories of hundreds of years of living. One belonged to Foster, the one with the black and golden bands; but the other was the property of a stranger who had died three thousand years ago, out in space . . .

This cylinder, barely three inches long, held all the memories of a man who had been Foster's confidant when he was Qulqlan, a man who knew what had happened aboard the ship, what the purpose of the expedition had been, and what conditions they had left behind on Vallon.

I needed that knowledge. I needed any knowledge I could get, to add a feather-weight to my side of the balance when the showdown came. The cylinder would tell me plenty, including, possibly, the reason for Ommodurad's interest in Foster.

It was simple to use. I merely placed the cylinder in the receptacle in the side of the machine, took my place, lowered the helmet into position . . . and in an hour or so I would awaken with another man's memories stored in my brain, to use as I saw fit.

It would be a crime to waste the opportunity. The machine I had found here was probably the only one still in existence on Vallon. I had blundered my way into the one room in the palace that could help me in what I had to do; I had been lucky; I couldn't waste that luck.

I went across to the soft-cushioned chair, spotted the recess in its side, and thrust the plain cylinder into it; it seated with a click.

I sat on a couch, lay back, reached up to pull the head-piece down into position against my skull . . .

There was an instant of pain—like a pre-frontal lobotomy performed without anesthetic.

Then blackness.

Chapter Eighteen

I stood beside the royal couch where Qulqlan the Rthr lay and I saw that this was the hour for which I had waited long, for the Change was on him . . .

The time-scale stood at the third hour of the Death

watch; all aboard slept save myself alone. I must move swiftly and at the Dawn watch show them the deed well done.

I shook the sleeping man; him who had once been the Rthr—king no more, by the law of the Change. He wakened slowly, looked about him, with the clear eyes of the newborn.

"Rise," I commanded. And the king obeyed.

"Follow me," I said. He made to question me, after the manner of those newly awakened from their Change. I bade him be silent. Like a lamb he came and I led him through shadowed ways to the cage of the Hunters. They rose, keen in their hunger, to my coming, as I had trained them.

I took the arm of Qulqlan and thrust it into the cage. The Hunters clustered, taking the mark of their prey. He watched, innocent eyes wide.

"That which you feel is pain, mindless one," I spoke. "It is a thing of which you will learn much in the time before you." Then they had done, and I set the time catch.

In my chambers I cloaked the innocent in a plain purple robe and afterward led him to the cradle where the lifeboat lay . . .

And by virtue of the curse of the Gods which is upon me one was there before me. I waited not, but moved as the haik strikes and took him fair in the back with my dagger. I dragged the body into hiding behind the flared foot of a column. But no sooner was he hidden well away than others came from the shadows, summoned by some device I know not of. They asked of the Rthr wherefore he walked by night, robed in the colors of Ammaerln of Bros-Ilyond. And I knew black despair, that my grand design foundered thus in the shallows of their zeal.

Yet I spoke forth, with a great show of anger, that

I, Ammaerln, vizier and companion to the Rthr, did but walk and speak in confidence with my liege lord.

But they persisted, Gholad foremost among them. And then one saw the hidden corpse and in an instant they ringed me in:

Then did I draw the long blade and hold it at the throat of Qulqlan. "Press me not; or your king will surely die," I said. And they feared me and shrank back.

"Do you dream that I, Ammaerln, wisest of the wise, have come here for the love of Far-Voyaging?" I raged. "Long have I plotted against this hour, to lure the king a-voyaging in this his princely yacht, his faithful vizier at his side, that the Change might come to him far from his court. Then would the ancient wrong be redressed.

"There are those men born to rule, as the dream-tree seeks the sun—and such a one am I! Long has this one, now mindless, denied to me my destiny. But behold: I, with a stroke, shall set things aright.

"Below us lies a green world, peopled by savages. Not one am I to take blood vengeance on a man newborn from the Change. Instead I shall set him free to take up his life there below. May the Fates lead him again to royal state if that be their will—"

But there were naught but fools among them and they drew steel. I cried out to them that all, all should share!

But they heeded me not but rushed upon me. Then did I turn to Qulqlan and drive the long blade at his throat, but Gholad threw himself before him and fell in his place. Then they pressed me and I did strike out against three who hemmed me close, and though they took many wounds they persisted in their madness, one leaping in to strike and another at my back, so that I whirled and slashed at shadows who danced away.

In the end I hunted them down in those corners whither they had dragged themselves and each did I put to the sword. And I turned at last to find the Rthr gone and some few with him, and madness took me that I had been gulled like a tinker by common men.

In the chamber of the memory couch would I find them. There they would seek to give back to the mindless one that memory of past glories which I had schemed so long to deny him. Almost I wept to see such cunning wasted. Terrible in my wrath I came upon them there. There were but two and, though they stood shoulder to shoulder in the entry way, their poor dirks were no match for my long blade. I struck them dead and went to the couch, to lay my hand on the cylinder marked with the vile gold and black of Qulqlan, that I might destroy it and with it the Rthr, forever—

And I heard a sound and whirled about. A hideous figured staggered to me from the gloom and for an instant I saw the flash of steel in the bloody hand of the accursed Gholad whom I had left for dead. Then I knew cold agony between my ribs . . .

Gholad lay slumped against the wall, his face greenish above the blood-soaked tunic. When he spoke air whistled through his slashed throat.

"Have done, traitor who once was honored of the king," he whispered. "Have you no pity for him who once ruled in justice and splendor at High Okk-Hamiloth?"

"Had you not robbed me of my destiny, murderous dog," I croaked, "that splendor would have been mine."

"You came upon him helpless," gasped Gholad. "Make some amends now for your shame. Let the Rthr have his mind, which is more precious than his life."

"I but rest to gather strength. Soon will I rise and turn him from the couch. Then will I die content."

"Once you were his friend," Gholad whispered. "By his side you fought, when both of you were young. Remember that . . . and have pity. To leave him here, in this ship of death, mindless and alone . . ."

"I have loosed the Hunters!" I shrieked in triumph. "With them will the Rthr share this tomb until the end of time!"

Then I searched within me and found a last terrible strength and I rose up . . . and even as my hand reached out to pluck away the mind trace of the king I felt the bloody fingers of Gholad on my ankle, and then my strength was gone. And I was falling headlong into that dark well of death from which there is no returning . . .

I woke up and lay for a long time in the dark without moving, trying to remember the fragments of a strange dream of violence and death. I could still taste the lingering dregs of some bitter emotion. But I had more important things to think about than dreams. For just a moment I couldn't remember what it was I had to do; then with a start I remembered where I was. I had lain down on the couch and pulled the headpiece into place—

It hadn't worked.

I thought hard, tried to tap a new reservoir of memories, drew a blank. Maybe my earth-mind was too alien for the Vallonian memory trace to affect. It was another good idea that hadn't worked out. But at least I had had a good rest. Now it was time to get moving. First—to see if Ommodurad was still asleep. I started to sit up—

Nothing happened.

I had a moment of vertigo, as my inner ear tried to accommodate to having stayed in the same place after automatically adjusting to my intention of rising. I lay perfectly still and tried to think it through.

I had tried to move . . . and hadn't so much as twitched a muscle. I was paralyzed . . . or tied up . . . or maybe, if I was lucky, imagining things. I could try it again and next time—

I was afraid to try. Suppose I tried and nothing happened—again? It was better to lie here and tell myself it was all a mistake. Maybe I should go back to sleep and wake up later and try it again . . .

This was ridiculous. All I had to do was sit up. I—

Nothing. I lay in the dark and tried to will an arm to move, my head to turn. It was as though I had no arm, no head—just a mind—alone in the dark. I strained to sense the ropes that held me down: still nothing. No ropes, no arms, no body. There was no pressure against me from the couch, no vagrant itch or cramp, no physical sensation. I was a disembodied brain, lying nestled in a great bed of pitch black cotton wool.

Then, abruptly, I was aware of myself—not the gross mechanism of bone and muscle, but the neuro-electric field generated within a brain alive with flashing currents and lightning interplay of molecular forces. A sense of orientation grew. I occupied a block of cells . . . here in the left hemisphere. The mass of neural tissue loomed over me, gigantic. And "I" . . ."I" was reduced to the elemental ego, who possessed as a material appurtenance "my" arms and legs, "my" body, "my" brain . . . Relieved of outside stimuli, I was able now to conceptualize myself as I actually was: an insubstantial state existing in an immaterial continuum, created by the action of neural currents within the cerebrum, as a magnetic field is created in space by the flow of electricity.

And I knew what had happened. I had opened my mind to invasion by alien memories. The other mind had seized upon the sensory centers and driven me to this dark corner. I was a fugitive within my own skull.

For a timeless time I lay stunned, immured now as the massive stones of Bar-Ponderone had never confined me. My basic self-awareness still survived, but was shunted aside, cut off from any contact with the body itself.

With shadowy fingers of imagination I clawed at the walls surrounding me, fought for a glimpse of light, for a way out.

And found none.

Then, at last, I began again to think.

I must analyze my awareness of my surroundings, seek out channels through which impulses from sensory nerves flowed, and tap them.

I tried cautiously; an extension of my self-concept reached out with ultimate delicacy. There were the ranked infinities of cells, there the rushing torrents of gross fluid, there the taut cables of the interconnecting web, and there—

Barrier! Blank and impregnable, the wall reared up. My questing tendril of self-stuff raced over the surface like an ant over a melon, and found no tiniest fissure. It loomed alien, inscrutable: the invader who had stolen my brain.

I withdrew. To dissipate my force was senseless. I must select a point of attack, hurl against it all the power of my surviving identity . . . before it too dwindled away and the abstraction that was Legion vanished forevermore.

The last of the phantom emotions that had clung—for how long?—to the incorporeal mind field had faded now, leaving me with no more than an intellectual determination to reassert myself. Dimly I recognized this sign of my waning sense of identity but there was no surge of instinctive fear. Instead I coolly assessed my resources—and almost at once stumbled into an unused channel, here within my own self-field. For a moment I recoiled from the outré configuration of the stored patterns . . . and then I remembered.

I had been in the water, struggling, while the Russian soldier waited, rifle aimed. And then: a flood of data, flowing with cold, impersonal precision. And I had deftly marshaled the forces of my body to survive.

And once more: as I hung by numbed fingers under the cornice of the Yordano Building, the cold voice had spoken.

And I had forgotten. The miracle had been pushed back, rejected by the conscious mind. But now I knew: this was the knowledge that I had received from the background briefing device that I had used in my island strongroom before I fled. This was the survival data known to all Old Vallonians of the days of the Two Worlds. It had lain here, unused, the secrets of superhuman strength and endurance . . . buried by the imbecile of censor-self's aversion to the alien.

But the ego alone remained now, stripped of the burden of neurosis, freed from subconscious pressures. The levels of the mind were laid bare, and I saw close at hand the regions where dreams were born, the barren sources of instinctive fear-patterns, the linkages to blinding emotions; and all lay now under my overt control.

Without further hesitation I tapped the stored Vallonian knowledge, encompassed it, made it mine. Then again I approached the barrier, spread out across it, probed in vain—

" . . . *vile primitive* . . ."

The thought thundered out with crushing force. I recoiled, then renewed my attack, alert now. I knew what to do.

I sought and found a line of synaptic weakness, burrowed at it—

" . . . intolerable . . . vestigial . . . erasure . . ."

I struck instantly, slipped past the shield, laid firm hold on an optic receptor bank. The alien mind threw itself against me, but too late. I held secure and the assault faded, withdrew. Cautiously I extended my interpretive receptivity. There was a pattern of pulses, oscillations in the lambda/mu range. I turned, focused—

Abruptly I was seeing. For a moment my fragile equilibrium tottered, as I strove to integrate the flow of external stimuli into my bodiless self-concept. Then a balance was struck: I held my ground and stared through the one eye I had recaptured from the usurper.

And I reeled again!

Bright daylight blazed in the chamber of Ommodurad. The scene shifted as the body moved about, crossing the room, turning . . . I had assumed that the body still lay in the dark but instead, it walked, without my knowledge, propelled by a stranger.

The field of vision flashed across the couch. Ommodurad was gone.

I sensed that the entire left lobe, disoriented by the loss of the eye, had slipped now to secondary awareness, its defenses weakened. I retreated momentarily from my optic outpost, laid a temporary traumatic block across the access nerves to keep the intruder from reasserting possession, and concentrated my force in an attack on the auricular channels. It was an easy rout. Instantly my eye coordinated its impressions with those coming in along the aural nerves . . . and heard my voice mouth a curse.

The body was standing beside a bare wall with a hand laid upon it. In the wall a recess partly obscured by a sliding panel stood empty.

The body turned, strode to a doorway, emerged into a gloomy violet-shadowed corridor. The glance flicked from the face of one guard to another. They stared in open-mouthed surprise, brought weapons up.

"You dare to bar the path to the Lord Ammaerln?" My voice slashed at the men. "Stand aside, as you value your lives."

And the body pushed past them, striding off along the corridor. It passed through a great archway, descended a flight of marble stairs, came along a hall I had seen on my tour of the Palace of Sapphires and into the Onyx Chamber with the great golden sunburst that covered the high black wall.

In the Great Owner's chair at the ring-board Ommodurad sat scowling at the lame courtier whose red hair was hidden now under a black cowl. Between them Foster stood, the heavy manacles dragging at his wrists. Ommodurad turned; his face paled, then flushed darkly. He rose, teeth bared.

The gaze of my eye fixed on Foster. Foster stared back, a look of incredulity growing on his face.

"My Lord Rthr," I heard my voice say. The eye swept down and fixed on the manacles. The body drew back a step, as if in horror.

"You overreach yourself, Ommodurad!" my voice cried harshly.

Ommodurad stepped toward me, his immense arm raised.

"Lay not a hand on me, dog of a usurper!" my voice roared out. "By the Gods, would you take me for common clay?"

And, unbelievably, Ommodurad paused, stared in my face.

"I know you as the upstart Drgon, petty Owner," he rumbled. "But I know I see another there behind your pale eyes."

"Foul was the crime that brought me to this pass," my voice said. "But . . . know that your master,

Ammaerln, stands before you, in the body of a primitive!"

"Ammaerln . . . !" Ommodurad jerked as though he had been struck.

My body turned, dismissing him. The eye rested on Foster.

"My liege," my voice said unctuously. "I swear the dog dies for this treason—"

"It is a mindless one, intruder," Ommodurad broke in. "Seek no favor with the Rthr for he that was Rthr is no more. You deal with me now."

My body whirled on Ommodurad. "Give a thought to your tone, lest your ambitions prove your death!"

Ommodurad put a hand to his dagger. "Ammaerln of Bros-Ilyond you may be, or a changeling from dark regions I know not of. But know that this day I hold all power in Vallon."

"And what of this one who was once Qulqlan? What consort do you hold with him you say is mindless?" I saw my hand sweep out in a contemptuous gesture at Foster.

"An end to patience!" the Great Owner roared. "Shall I stand in my inner citadel and give account of myself to a madman?" He started toward my body.

"Does the fool, Ommodurad, forget the power of the great Ammaerln?" my voice said softly. And the towering figure hesitated once more, searching my face. "The Rthr's hour is past . . . and yours, bungler and fool," my voice went on. "Your months—or is it years?—of self-delusions are ended." My voice rose in a bellow: "Know that I . . . Ammaerln, the great . . . have returned to rule at High Okk-Hamiloth."

"Months?" rumbled Ommodurad. "Indeed, I believe the tales of the Greymen are true and that an evil spirit has returned to haunt me. You speak of months?" He threw back his head, laughed a choked throat laugh that was half sob.

"Know, demon, or madman, or ancient prince of evil: for thirty centuries have I brooded alone, sealed from an empire by a single key!"

I felt the shock rack through and through the invader mind. This was the opportunity I had hoped for. Quick as thought I moved, slashed at the wavering shield, and was past it—

I grappled onto the foul mind-matrix, scanned its symbolisms: a miasma of twisted concepts like great webs, asquirm with bristling nodes like crouching spiders—and through it all a yammering torrent of deformed thought-shapes.

In my eagerness I was careless. The invader mind, recovering, struck back. Too late I felt it slip into my awareness, flick over the stored information. I leaped to protect one fact . . . and lost my gains. With only a single tenuous line of rapport with the alien mind still open, I clung, shaken—but hugging precious patterns of stolen data. My raid had been no more than an irritation to the other mind . . . but I had fetched away a mass of information. I interpreted it, integrated it, matched it to known patterns. A complex structure of relationships evolved, growing into a new awareness.

Upon the mind-picture of Foster's face was now superimposed another: that of Qulqlan, Rthr of all Vallon, ruler of the Two Worlds!

And other pictures, snatched from the intruder mind, were present now in the earth-consciousness of me, Legion:

The Vaults, deep in the rock under the fabled city of Okk-Hamiloth, where the mind-trace of every citizen was stored, sealed by the Rthr and keyed to his mind alone;

Ammaerln, urging the king to embark on a

Far-Voyage, stressing the burden of government, tempting him to bring with him the royal mind-trace; Qulqlan's acquiescence and Ammaerln's secret joy at the advancement of his scheme;

The coming of the Change for the Rthr, aboard ship, far out in space—and the vizier's bold stroke;

And then the fools who found him at the lifeboat . . . and the loss of all, all . . .

There my own memories took up the tale: the awakening of Foster, unsuspecting, and his recording of the mind of the dying Ammaerln; the flight from the Hunters; the memory trace of the king that lay for three millennia among Neolithic bones until I, a primitive, plucked it from its place; and the pocket of a coarse fiber garment where the cylinder lay now—on the hip of the body I inhabited but as inaccessible to me as if it had been a million miles away.

But there was a second memory trace—Ammaerln's. I had crossed a galaxy to come to Foster, and with me, locked in an unmarked pewter cylinder, I had brought Foster's ancient nemesis.

I had given it life, and a body.

Foster, once Rthr, had survived against all logic and had come back, back from the dead: the last hope of a golden age . . .

To meet his fate at my hands.

"Three thousand years," I heard my voice saying. "Three thousand years have the men of Vallon lived mindless, with the glory that was Vallon locked away in a vault without a key."

"I, alone," said Ommodurad, "have borne the curse of knowledge. Long ago, in the days of the Rthr, I took my mind-trace from the vaults in anticipation of the day of days when he should fall. Little joy has it brought me."

"And now," my voice said, "you think to force this mind—that is no mind—to unseal the vault?"

"I know it for a hopeless task," Ommodurad said. "At first I thought—since he speaks the tongue of old Vallon—that he dissembled. But he knows nothing. This is but the dry husk of the Rthr . . . and I sicken of the sight. I would fain kill him now and let the long farce end."

"Not so!" my voice cut in. "Once I decreed exile to the mindless one. So be it!"

The face of Ommodurad twisted in its rage. "Your witless chatterings too! I tire of them."

"Wait!" my voice snarled. "Would you put aside the key?"

There was a silence as Ommodurad stared at my face. I saw my hand rise into view. Gripped in it was Foster's memory trace.

"The Two Worlds lie in my hand," my voice spoke. "Observe well the black and golden bands of the royal memory trace. Who holds this key is all-powerful. As for the mindless body yonder, let it be destroyed."

Ommodurad locked eyes with mine. Then, "Let the deed be done," he said.

The redhead drew a long stiletto from under his cloak, smiling. I could wait no longer . . .

Along the link I had kept through the intruder's barrier I poured the last of the stored energy of my mind. I felt the enemy recoil, then strike back with crushing force. But I was past the shield.

As the invader reached out to encircle me I shattered my unified forward impulse into myriad nervous streamlets that flowed on, under, over and around the opposing force; I spread myself through and through the inner all-mass, drawing new power from the trunk sources.

I caught a vicious blast of pure wrath that rocked

me and then I grappled, shield to shield, with the alien. And he was stronger.

Like a corrosive fluid the massive personality-gestalt shredded my extended self-field. I drew back, slowly, reluctantly. I caught a shadowy impression of the body, standing rigid, eyes blank, and sensed a rumbling voice that spoke: "Quick! The intruder!"

Now! I struck for the right optic center, clamped down with a death grip.

The enemy mind went mad as the darkness closed in. I heard my voice scream and I saw in vivid panto-mime the visions that threatened the invader: the redhead darting to me, the stiletto flashing—

And then the invading mind broke, swirled into chaos, and was gone . . .

I reeled, shocked and alone inside my skull. The brain loomed, dark and untenanted now. I began to move, crept along the major nerve paths, reoccupied the cortex—

Agony! I twisted, felt again with a massive return of sensation my arms, my legs, opened both eyes to see blurred figures moving. And in my chest a hideous pain . . .

I was sprawled on the floor, gasping. Sudden under-standing came: the redhead had struck . . . and the other mind, in full rapport with the pain centers, had broken under the shock, left the stricken brain to me alone.

As through a red veil I saw the giant figure of Ommodurad loom, stoop over me, rise with the royal cylinder in his hand. And beyond, Foster, strained backward, the chain between his wrists garroting the redhead. Ommodurad turned, took a step, flicked the man from Foster's grasp and hurled him aside. He drew his dagger. Quick as a hunting cat Foster leaped, struck with the manacles . . . and the knife clattered across the floor. Ommodurad backed away with a curse, while the redhead seized the stiletto he had let fall and moved in. Foster turned to meet him, staggering, and raised heavy arms.

I fought to move, got my hand as far as my side, fumbled with the leather strap. The alien mind had stolen from my brain the knowledge of the cylinder but I had kept from it the fact of the pistol. I had my hand on its butt now. Painfully I drew it, dragged my arm up, struggled to raise the weapon, centered it on the back of the mop of red hair, free now of the cowl . . . and fired.

Ommodurad had found his dagger. He turned back from the corner where Foster had sent it spinning. Spattered with the blood of the redhead, Foster retreated until his back was at the wall: a haggard figure against the gaudy golden sunburst. The flames of beaten metal shimmered and flared before my dimming vision. The great gold circles of the Two Worlds seemed to revolve, while waves of darkness rolled over me.

But there was a thought: something I had found among the patterns in the intruder's mind. At the center of the sunburst rose a boss, in black and gold, erupting a foot from the wall, like a sword-hilt . . .

The thought came from far away. The sword of the Rthr, used once, in the dawn of a world, by a warrior king—but laid away now, locked in its sheath of stone, keyed to the mind-pattern of the Rthr, that none other might ever draw it to some ignoble end.

A sword, keyed to the basic mind-pattern of the king . . .

I drew a last breath, blinked back the darkness. Ommodurad stepped past me, knife in hand, toward the unarmed man.

"Foster," I croaked. "The sword . . ."

Foster's head came up. I had spoken in English; the

syllables rang strangely in that outworld setting. Ommo-durad ignored the unknown words.

"Draw . . . the sword . . . from the stone! . . . You're . . . Qulqlan . . . Rthr . . . of Vallon."

I saw him reach out, grasp the ornate hilt. Ommo-durad, with a cry, leaped toward him—

The sword slid out smoothly, four feet of glittering steel. Ommodurad stopped, stared at the manacled hands gripping the hilt of the fabled blade. Slowly he sank to his knees, bent his neck.

"I yield, Qulqlan," he said. "I crave the mercy of the Rthr."

Behind me I heard thundering feet. Dimly I was aware of Torbu raising my head, of Foster leaning over me. They were saying something but I couldn't hear. My feet were cold, and the coldness crept higher.

I felt hands touch me and the cool smoothness of metal against my temples. I wanted to say something, tell Foster that I had found the answer, the one that had always eluded me before. I wanted to tell him that all lives are the same length when viewed from the foreshortened perspective of death, and that life, like music, requires no meaning but only a certain symmetry.

But it was too hard. I tried to cling to the thought, to carry it with me into the cold void toward which I moved, but it slipped away and there was only my self-awareness, alone in emptiness, and the winds that swept through eternity blew away the last shred of ego and I was one with darkness . . .

Epilogue

I awoke to a light like that of a morning when the world was young. Gossamer curtains fluttered at tall windows, through which I saw a squadron of trim white clouds riding in a high blue sky.

I turned my head, and Foster stood beside me, dressed in a short white tunic.

"That's a crazy set of threads, Foster," I said, "but on your build it looks good. But you've aged; you look twenty-five if you look a day."

Foster smiled. "Welcome to Vallon, my friend," he said in English. I noticed that he faltered a bit over the words, as if he hadn't used them for a long time.

"Vallon," I said. "Then it wasn't all a dream?"

"Regard it as a dream, Legion. Your life begins today."

"There was something," I said, "something I had to do. But it doesn't seem to matter. I feel relaxed inside . . ."

Someone came forward from behind Foster.

"Gope," I said. Then I hesitated. "You are Gope, aren't you?" I said in Vallonian.

He laughed. "I was known by that name once," he said. "But my true name is Gwanne."

My eyes fell on my legs. I saw that I was wearing a tunic like Foster's except that mine was pale blue.

"Who put the dress on me?" I asked. "And where's my pants?"

"This garment suits you better," said Gope. "Come. Look in the glass."

I got to my feet, stepped to a long mirror, glanced at the reflection. "It's not the real me, boys," I started— Then I stared, open-mouthed. A Hercules, black-haired and clean-limbed, stared back. I shut my mouth . . . and his mouth shut. I moved an arm and he did likewise. I whirled on Foster.

"What . . . how . . . who . . . ?"

"The mortal body that was Legion died of its wounds," he said, "but the mind that was the man was recorded. We have waited many years to give that mind life again."

I turned back to the mirror, gaped. The young giant gaped back. "I remember," I said. "I remember . . . a knife in my guts . . . and a redheaded man . . . and the Great Owner, and . . ."

"For his crimes," told Gope, "he went to a place of exile until the Change should come on him. Long have we waited."

I looked again and now I saw two faces in the mirror and both of them were young. One was low down, just above my ankles, and it belonged to a cat I had known as Itzenca. The other, higher up, was that of a man I had known as Ommodurad. But this was a clear-eyed Ommodurad, just under twenty-one.

"Onto the blank slate we traced your mind," said Gope.

"He owed you a life, Legion," Foster said. "His own was forfeit."

"I guess I ought to kick and scream and demand my original ugly puss back," I said slowly, studying my reflection, "but the fact is, I like looking like Mr. Universe."

"Your earthly body was infected with the germs of old age," said Foster. "Now you can look forward to a great span of life."

"But come," said Gope. "All Vallon waits to honor you." He led the way to the tall window.

"Your place is by my side at the great ring-board," said Foster. "And afterwards: all of the Two Worlds lie before you."

I looked past the open window and saw a carpet of velvet green that curved over foothills to the rim of a forest. Down the long sward I saw a procession of bright knights and ladies come riding on animals, some black, some golden palomino, that looked for all the world like unicorns.

My eyes traveled upward to where the light of a great white sun flashed on blue towers. And somewhere trumpets sounded.

"It looks like a pretty fair offer," I said. "I'll take it."

THE CHOICE

For a second or two, when the red ALERT light started flashing, I didn't know what it meant; then I saw the crinkly lines wiggling across the counterscope and I knew that something out there was giving off patterned radiation. Considering the fact that we were nine hundred million miles out from Earth in unexplored space, that was kind of a surprise. My first impulse was to switch on the transmitter and give whatever it was a hail—but Commander Ironblood was awake when he shouldn't have been. In two of those snappy military steps he was beside me, elbowing me out of the comm seat and pushing buttons with both hands. He was a big, thick man with quarter-inch gray stubble across his skull, and barbed wire for nerves.

"Mr. Barker," he spat me as if I wasn't there, "duty station, if you please. Power off. Observe total radiation silence." I wish I could say he yelled, but he sounded just as iceberg-cool as he had back at Sands, the day he told me the personnel computer had picked me out of the reserve files as third man on the Neptune Probe.

"I didn't ask to have an untrained, unqualified civilian aboard my command," he had told me, "but since you're assigned, you'll conduct yourself as a SpArm officer. The first thing you'll do is get a haircut—and get rid of that vacuous smile. Space is a serious business."

I stopped smiling, all right, as soon as I got my first look at the ship, all gray paint and DO and DON'T signs.

"You mean I'm going to spend a year and a half cooped up in this oversized phone booth?" I yelped.

Barker, the Number Two, had grinned at me out of the corner of his mouth. He had one of those scraped-bone faces, plastered over with freckles.

"What did you expect, Goodlark," he asked, "the Imperial suite, complete with gold doorknobs, silk sheets, and breakfast in bed?"

"Sure," I said. "Why not? Exploring the planets ought to be a groove. Why come on like a bunch of monks? Why not have a little fun while we're at it?"

He was grinning the same grin now; I guess he read my expression.

"Still looking for kicks, Goodlark?"

"Why the creep routine?" I countered. "Why don't we get excited and yell and wave or something?"

"That's not the SpArm tradition, boy. No sissy stuff for us. We mean business."

"I always thought seeing Barsoom up close would be a gas," I said. "But all we gave it was a dirty look. How did we ever get started with this by-the-numbers jazz? Where's all the music and laughter gone?"

"Are you kidding?" Barker looked shocked. "At two point seven billion bucks a shot, you better not be caught laughing."

Just then the main fore DV screen picked up something. Ironblood switched it up to high mag. The image jumped at us.

"Holy leaping Mehitable," Barker said. "Would you look at that!"

It was something to look at: like the insides of a satellite radar station, but without the station. Big— no telling how big against all that blackness—and complicated, glittering all over with lights and shiny planes and tubes, and things that moved in long, slow strokes like mechanical arms. It hung there, looking at us. It was alert, aware—but not alive. Somehow you could tell that, just looking at it. It got bigger fast.

"That's nothing *our* boys ever built," Barker said. "Ye gods, Cap'n—that thing's *alien*!"

"We're closing rapidly," Ironblood said with no visible emotion. "Recommendations, Mr. Barker?"

"Let's arm our missiles and get a look at the whites of their eyes," Barker said in clipped tones.

"Captain Ironblood," I said, "I have a better suggestion: let's turn on our nav lights and blink out a greeting. Maybe an eight-bar rhythm. They might dig that better than the pussyfoot routine—"

He gave me a look like a jab with a sharp stick.

"SpArm isn't paying our salaries to play astrohippy on NASA time," he barked. That was as far as he got before there was a sharp *bleep!* and the walls dissolved around us like a switched-off solido.

We were still strapped into our acceleration couches, but now they were sitting in the middle of a little white-walled room about the size of a dentist's surgery, and with that same feeling of something painful about to happen.

"Great galloping giraffes!" Barker said. "The ship's gone! Dissolved around our ears like . . . like—"

"Like a solido projection switching off," the captain said. "Stand fast." He unstrapped and prowled the room, feeling of the walls.

"They're real enough," he said. "It appears, gentlemen, that we've been made captive." He faced the two of us. "It's pretty plain that we're in the hands of a nonhuman intelligence of a high technical competence. I don't need to remind you that from this point on, our actions will determine their impressions of the human race. Whatever happens, we must show no signs of weakness or uncertainty. We'll present a united façade of defiance and dare them to do their worst."

"B-but what if they're friendly?" I asked.

Ironblood jerked a thumb at the walls that enclosed us. "Does this look friendly?"

"Where are they hiding?" Barker blurted. "Why don't they come out and fight like men?"

There was a loud *click!* from somewhere, and he whirled, fists cocked.

"Welcome aboard, gentlemen," a smooth voice said. "Please remain calm. You have been randomly selected for stat analysis, and are herewith designated specimens A, B, and C. If you're ready, testing can commence at once."

There were a few seconds of a silence as heavy as wet underwear. Then Ironblood spoke up:

"Who are you?" he called. "*Where* are you?"

"I'm all about you," the voice said. "Or, more simply stated, you are inside me."

"You mean we've been eaten?" Barker yapped.

"Not precisely, since I don't eat. I am a mere artifact, an information gathering device dispatched by the Galactic authorities on a routine sweep of the sector."

"Galactic authorities, eh?" Ironblood muttered. "Well, now we know who the enemy is. I suppose their espionage apparatus has been spying on us for years, monitoring our radio broadcasts, waiting for this opportunity. But they'll find SpArm personnel tough nuts to crack. Name, rank and serial number, that's all we tell them."

"Listen, Captain," I said quickly, "why don't we mention that we bruise easily, and that, although we come from a small, backward planet, we're pretty important to ourselves? Once they realize we're harmless and scared—"

"As you were, Mr. Goodlark!" Ironblood cut me off. "We'll wait for their next move without whining. I suspect they can observe our actions, overhear our talk—perhaps even read our thoughts. We'll, therefore, think positively. Keep your minds on SpArm regulations. Think of the Alamo and Pearl Harbor. Let them know we're prepared to die like men!"

"Why rush things? If we think peaceful thoughts, maybe they'll get the idea—"

"The idea we're weaklings?" Ironblood barked at me.

"That's it!" I said. "I mean, why put on an act? Just let it all hang out. We'll tell them we like to dance and sing; too bad SpArm regs didn't allow me to bring my eighty-eight stringer, I could play a few cool notes for them—"

"Dance? Sing? You're out of your mind with terror, man! Consider yourself under arrest!"

"What's the point of this kamikaze approach?" I yelled. "I have plans that involve living to a ripe old age—and there's a girl named Daisy Fields who'll be pretty broken up if I don't come back—"

"Mere individuals are expendable, Goodlark, you know that—"

"Time is of the essence, gentlemen," the voice cut in. "We'll have to hurry along now. I'll fire a standard stimulus-array at you and record your response-gestalts . . ."

"Ignore Goodlark's responses," Ironblood ordered the voice. "The man is a degenerate, a freak, not representative of his species. You may base your conclusions on my reactions, and those of Mr. Barker. Remember,

Barker," he added in a low tone, "Regulations! Discipline! CinC SpArm is counting on you!"

Suddenly the floor turned to wax. As we floundered, lights flashed, red and green and blue. I was clawing my way through a fog as thick as taffy, while sounds blared, squeaked, buzzed. There was a reek of burnt feathers, synthetic rubber, a whiff of molasses, attar of roses, old socks, new leather, dead fish. I was hot, then cold. Pictures of tigers and girls and fast cars and tidal waves and pizzas and sunsets flashed through my brain. Voices yelled, whispered, things poked, rubbed, pinched, stroked me. I mustered what control I had left for a yell, and abruptly it was all gone and the white walls were back. Barker hung in his chair, looking a little pale under the freckles. Captain Ironblood's hair was slightly rumpled and his collar was turned up on one side, but he was still holding a face like a sphinx.

"Let them have their fun," he rasped. "We'll show them they can't break us."

"Why not yell or something, Captain?" I managed to croak. "Maybe they think we like it."

"I'm warning you, Goodlark," Ironblood snarled, "you do or say anything to disgrace the uniform, and I'll personally throttle you! Clear?"

"Strange, very strange," the disembodied voice of the machine said. "They're going to have a hard time believing some of this back at Galactic Center. Still, I suppose it takes all kinds of life forms to make a Universe. Now, gentlemen, Galactic policy requires that all testees be fully compensated for any inconvenience I may have caused. Accordingly, I'm prepared to render my assistance to you in the achievement of your personal goals. My facilities are limited, of course, but I can offer you a degree of choice in the matter—"

"You mean—you've already completed your evaluation?" Ironblood took a deep breath and straightened his collar.

"Chins up, men," he murmured. "We'll soon be on our way." He cleared his throat.

"Ah, before we go," he called, "I wonder if you'd mind telling us how we measured up—just as a matter of curiosity?"

"Why, you reacted as you must, what else? But now, on to the final question: Specimen A, how would you prefer to die: by hanging, drowning, or fire?"

"It's no more than I expected from the beginning," Ironblood said, looking a little pale around the jaws but still holding his cool.

"Cap'n, tell 'em they can't do this—" Barker started.

"I'll not beg for quarter."

"I guess it figures," Barker said. "It can't complete its report until it sees one of us die. Well, I guess you'll show 'em, Cap'n—"

"Stop chattering, you fool," Ironblood said. "I have a decision to make. I'll discount hanging at once. It has a felonious connotation I don't care for."

"I don't know, Cap'n," Barker said judiciously. "They say it's pretty humane. I mean the neck snaps, *zop*, like that, and it's all over—unless the drop is too short and you choke to death," he added doubtfully.

"I've never cared much for the idea of drowning," Ironblood said. "On the other hand, death by fire is reported to be rather uncomfortable too, for that matter."

"Boy, I've really got to admire the way you're taking it, Cap'n," Barker said.

"I seem to recall that if you inhale the flames, you scorch the bronchi, bringing instant death," Ironblood said hopefully.

"Hey, neat," Barker said. "I'll remember that."

"Good luck, Mr. Barker." Ironblood thrust out his hand and they gave each other the Grip, their Academy rings glinting in the glow from the walls. Ironblood looked at me.

"You're a civilian, Goodlark," he said, "but I expect you to follow Lieutenant Commander Barker's orders as if they were my own." He looked up at the ceiling.

"All right, fire it is," he said. "I'm ready."

There was a sharp hissing sound, and suddenly there was a heap of faggots half as big as a haystack, and Ironblood strapped to a stake in the middle. Smoke whiffed up, and then red flames flickered and grew and in five seconds the whole thing was blazing away. I got a last glimpse of Ironblood standing at attention in the middle of the bonfire, and then the smoke and flames covered him.

"He went out like a man," Barker said. "He gave himself to save us, and never whimpered."

A brisk draft had carried the last of the smoke away. There wasn't even a singed spot on the floor to show where the captain had made his exit.

"All right, you've had your fun," Barker said to the room. "Now how about putting us back aboard our vessel so we can get on with the mission?"

"Unfortunately," the voice stated, "your ship has been disassociated into its component atoms, in much the same manner as has Specimen A."

"You destroyed our ship?" Barker yelled.

"It could be reconstituted, of course, if needed," the voice said. "But to what end? I have a question for you to answer, remember?"

"Huh? You mean—the captain's sacrifice was for nothing? You're going to offer me the same lousy choice he had?"

"You disapprove of the alternatives offered?"

"I sure as hell do!"

"In that case, B, you may select your preference from among the following: shooting, stabbing, or garroting."

Barker gave me his favorite crooked grin. "Well, Goodlark, it looks like the end of the trail for me. But don't feel bad. I guess your turn comes next."

"Listen, Barker," I said, feeling kind of cold-sweaty and hot at the same time. "Why take it like a bunch of zombies? Why don't we do what comes naturally and kick and scream and beg for mercy or something?"

Barker showed me a large, knuckly fist. "You let the cap'n down and I'll beat your skull in."

"What I mean is, I don't like those choices at all, frankly. Do we have to just sit here?"

Barker's grin got crookeder. "Forget it, kid. We've had it. But you're right about one thing. I'm not sitting here and taking it like a little lamb, like the cap'n did. I'm giving them a fight."

"How?" I said. "Who do you fight?"

"I dislike rushing you, but I'm a hundred and three years behind schedule already," the voice said. "Your choice, please, Specimen B."

"Shooting, stabbing, or garroting," Barker mused. "A bullet is an easy out, assuming the hit man knows his job. Stabbing: slower, unless the knife gets to just the right spot—and messy. Garroting, now—that's the lousiest way to go yet. But at least there's something to get hold of. Yeah. I'll go the rope route."

Barker clenched his fists, half crouched, and tried to watch in every direction at once. He almost made it—except that the noose dropped from straight above, whipped around his neck like a snake, and snapped tight before he could make a move. His tongue poked out, and his eyeballs, and something made a noise like stepping on a paper cup, and it was all over.

And now it was my turn.

"Specimen C, judging by B's reaction, you, too, will desire a unique demise," the voice said cheerfully. "Accordingly, I can offer you the following selection: death by poisoning—fast-acting, of course; anoxia; or simple heart failure. I'd have liked to widen the scope to include exhaustion, desiccation, and starvation, but they're too time-consuming, I'm afraid."

I heard myself swallow. I tried to speak, but my tongue didn't want to cooperate. I thought about the bitter taste of arsenic; I thought about not being able to breathe; I thought about sharp pains in the chest . . .

"Well, how about it, C?" the voice said. "Name your choice."

"N-n-n," I said. "None of them."

"Eh?" the machine said. "How's that?"

"None of them, blast you!" I yelled. "I don't like any of your shortcuts to oblivion! I prefer to get there in my own way, in my own sweet time!"

"Really?" the voice sounded shocked. "But—my study of the motivations of specimens A and B indicated that their whole lives were a pell-mell rush to destruction—theirs, and everyone else's—"

"Maybe so—but don't include me in your statistics! I'm not quite as high-minded as they were."

"Then—what *do* you want?" the machine asked.

I told it.

"Routine, Mr. Barker," Captain Ironblood said. "It was a simple matter of calling their bluff. Once they saw we weren't to be intimidated by their threats, they back-tracked in a hurry."

"I've got to admit it looks that way," Barker said.

"But I'll tell you frankly, Cap'n: when I felt that hemp cut into my neck, I never expected to wake up back here aboard ship, on course and in perfect health."

"The illusions were fairly graphic," Ironblood said. "But I was quite certain, privately, that they would never go so far as to murder SpArm personnel."

"Well, I guess all's well that ends well," Barker said. "But I'd like to see the look on Headquarters' face when they get our report."

I had an urge to speak up and tell them how surprised the Census machine had been when it found out SpArm regs didn't quite cover the whole range of human aspirations, and how accommodating it had been, once it realized its mistake.

"There's one other thing," I had told it after it had reconstituted the ship and fixed it up a little. "Kind of a minor point, I guess, but don't you think you ought to reconstitute specimens A and B, too?"

"But surely, in view of their avowed aspirational patterns, they are better off where they are."

"Probably; but CinC SpArm might not understand. And I wonder if you couldn't make a few adjustments to help them adjust to the new conditions."

So the machine had popped them back into existence, as good as new, or maybe a little better. But it wouldn't do any good to tell *them* that. They wouldn't have believed a word of it.

"There's just one thing that's a little unclear, Cap'n," Barker was saying. "Why is it that you and I have to spend the rest of the cruise cooped up in this crummy little compartment, while Mr. Goodlark has the Imperial suite to himself, complete with a staff of ten, breakfast in bed, et cetera?"

Ironblood frowned. "I can't recall at the moment just why that is," he said. "No doubt the strain of what we've been through has given us a little area of confusion there. Suffice it to say it's all in accordance with SpArm regs . . . I think."

"It must be," Barker said. "Otherwise, why would there be an Imperial suite aboard a three-man scout in the first place?"

"Logical thinking, Barker," Ironblood said.

I didn't wait around to hear the rest. I eased the gold-plated door shut and turned and walked across the ankle-deep carpet past the table where the evening banquet was spread out to where Daisy Fields waited for me.

THREE BLIND MICE

As Cameron recovered consciousness, the first thing he was aware of was pain: the sting of cuts and bruises, the searing sensation of a burn that had scorched his left forearm, a dull ache spreading from his lower back. The second datum he absorbed was that the three-man scout boat was in free fall toward the glaring surface of a planet, looming on the screen before his padded command chair.

His mind raced back over the final moments before unconsciousness. He remembered the sighting of the Yrax cruiser as it had emerged from the radar shadow of the uninhabited ice-giant planet, behind which he had stationed his tiny spy ship. The great war vessel had apparently detected the presence of the intruding Terrans at the same moment. Its instant response had been a salvo capable of blasting a battleship into its component atoms.

Which it might have done, had the target been a battleship, massive and sluggish. But even as the Yrax missiles leaped forth, Cameron had stood the tiny ship on its stern and blasted it from the line of fire at full

9-G acceleration. The scout ship had pitched and bucked in the shockwaves as massive detonations ripped the space it had occupied seconds before; but it had righted itself with a scream of overstressed gyros and streaked outward. Though its crew lay stunned by the violence of the maneuvers, its recorders whined efficiently as they abstracted precious data on Yrax firepower and cruise capability from the frantically maneuvering warship—data which had until now been an absorbing mystery to Terran Space Command.

The war—if so one-sided a conflict could be called a war—was in its third year; four Terran colonies had been attacked and wiped out to the last man. Two dozen Terran freighters had been blasted from space with no survivors. Six revenue cutters of the Terran Space Arm had been jumped and vaporized without warning. Seven mining installations had been reduced to radioactive dust. And still, absolutely nothing was known of the enemy who struck so swiftly and so ruthlessly—nothing but their name, the Yrax, gleaned from intercepted transmissions in an unknown tongue, badly garbled by star static, attenuated by the vast distances of interstellar space.

And now, Cameron realized, he and his two-man crew had encountered a Yrax warship—and were still alive to report their findings—so far.

The planet below was less than five hundred miles distant, if the mass/proximity indicator was reading accurately. The ship's velocity was over 20,000 kilometers per hour, relative, fortunately at a tangent to the planetary surface. Already the first whistlings of attenuated outer atmosphere were setting up resonant vibrations in the vessel's eternalloy hull. Cameron keyed the autopilot into action. At once the braking jets flared, filling the screens with their pale fire.

Beside him, Lucas, the engineer, leaned groggily over

the auxiliary panel, his face barely visible in the dim glow of the instruments.

"Luke—you okay?" Cameron called over the sibilant shrill of the thin gases that buffeted and tore at the hurtling boat. The engineer pulled himself upright and glanced his way; his teeth showed in a brief, encouraging grin. On Cameron's right, Navigator Wybold stirred, groaned, opened his eyes, sat up.

"We're going to hit," Cameron said. "But maybe we've got enough stuff left to cushion the crunch. How're you feeling, Wy?"

"Okay—I hope," the navigator said. "How about you, Jim?"

"Still breathing," Cameron said. He studied the instrument array, forming a mental picture of the vast planet spreading below: the great ice fields, the serrated ridges of mountain ranges thrusting up like bared teeth into the dense, turbulent atmosphere. At less than one hundred miles from the surface, the broken scout boat hurtled in a long descending arc, slicing deeper into the gases of the upper stratosphere.

"We're starting to warm up," Lucas said in a clipped emotionless tone. "Hull temperature 900° and climbing fast. But so far our refrigeration gear is holding it."

"Try to put a little axial spin on us, Luke," Cameron said.

"I've only got about 25 percent control of the steering jets," Lucas said, "but I'll see what I can do."

There was a surge, as the boat responded to the spurt of energy from the small-attitude jets mounted equatorially around its hull. The panel seemed to sink away, slide sideways, rise, fall back in a nauseous gyration.

"Not so good," Lucas said. "We're spinning, but with a bad wobble. I'd better let it go at that. Another shot might put us into a full-fledged tumble."

"Luke—switch on the stern screen, will you?" Cameron ordered. The engineer fine-focused the foot-square aft viewer. Against the blackness of space, partly obscured by whipping swirls and streamers of exhaust gases, a brilliant point of light glared. Cameron saw the muscles at the corner of the engineer's square-cut jaw knot hard.

"They're following us down," he said. "Those critters don't intend to take any chances at all, do they?"

"They can't afford to—not with what we've got on our record spools," Wybold said.

"Well, maybe we'll fool them," Cameron stated flatly. "There's a lot of real estate down there to get lost in. Let's see what we can do."

Ahead, a range of knife-edged mountains towered ten miles into the eroding millrace that was the ice giant's atmosphere. Cameron jockeyed the thrust controls with a delicate touch, holding the boat prow-first in the direction of travel, using the malfunctioning steering jets to aim for the deep-cut V, like a wedge chopped by a mighty ax in the wall of jagged stone and ice. Now the peaks to left and right were above them, ripping past, aglitter in the white glare of the distant sun. A great slope of black stone rushed toward them, directly in their path. Lucas slammed full power to the remaining starboard tubes; there was a brief flare of energy, a bone-wrenching surge—then the damaged steering engines flashed in an instant to white heat. A spray of metal vapor engulfed the boat as the automatic safety circuits blasted the explosive bolts securing them to the vessel. Light flared on the screens as the jettisoned engines detonated half a mile astern. Then a crashing, clanging impact, a long, tearing screech of tortured metal that went on and on—

And then, amazingly, silence, and the absence of all motion.

❖   ❖   ❖

A fitful wind whined over the broken hull. Escaping air hissed thinly. Hot metal *pinged!* contracting. The heaters hummed, attempting to maintain a livable temperature.

Moving slowly, painfully, Cameron looked around the compartment. His couch was half-ripped from its moorings. A tangle of wiring and fluid conduits had bulged from the shattered control console. Beside him, the bulkhead was creased out of shape.

"Where are we, Wy?" he asked the navigator.

"We're down on a continental ice mass about fifty kilometers north of the estimated equator, a couple of hundred kilometers from a big sea to the north. We're about two thousand meters above nominal sea level; my range readings as we came in were kind of confused.

"We're in a high valley; peaks on all sides. Outside temperature, 210 absolute. Gravity, 1.31 standard. Air pressure, 23 psi; composition, nitrogen 85%, oxygen 10%, some water vapor. Wind velocity, 20 m.p.h. gusting to 50. It seems to be high noon; this sun radiates strongly in the upper end of the visible spectrum and in the UV, and it's pretty bright out there. It reminds me a little of Vera Cruz in that respect." He smiled briefly at the comparison of his beloved desert world with this frozen wasteland.

"I never did understand why anybody wanted to colonize that sandbox," Lucas mused, eyeing Wybold obliquely. "I suppose some people will try anything, though."

"Right—like settling down on a high-G world like Sandow, where you have to be a champion weight lifter just to walk around," Wybold replied with a ghost of a smile.

"And it looks like we'll be walking," Lucas said

bluntly. "Hull broached, main power out, auxiliary power out, emergency power at 10 percent base capability. Communications out—super-E, infrawave, SWF—the works." He shook his head. "However, I got off an all-wave Mayday, before we broke through the troposphere," he added casually.

Cameron managed a grin. "I'm glad you weren't too busy adjusting the air conditioning to see to that detail."

"Hard to say what good it will do us," Lucas said. "We're a long way from the nearest Terran base." He turned to the dark cockpit display screens, flipped switches. There was no response.

"Try the DV's," Cameron suggested. Wybold fitted his face to the padded eyepiece and turned the dials which focused the direct vision scopes. He squinted into the dazzling light reflecting from the icefield— bright enough to be painful even to his insensitive vision, adapted to the blazing sunlight of his home- world. Steep escarpments rose to either side of the long valley; against the glaring pale blue sky, a single point of brilliance winked and flickered.

"Oh-oh," he said. "They're still with us. We'll have dropped off their radar and gamma-tracer screens— but we'll show up like a bonfire on IR. If they haven't pinpointed us yet, they will any minute."

"We'll have to get out," Cameron said. "They'll blow the boat off the map. We can hole up in the rocks, maybe."

Lucas unstrapped, rose to his feet, his muscular bulk making his thick body look short in spite of his six- foot-one height. He turned to the suit locker, lifted out Cameron's suit, tossed Wybold's to him, pulled out his own.

Cameron had swiveled the DV eyepiece around, reduced the light level, and was studying the scene.

"Broken ground up ahead," he said. "Caves. That's the spot to make for."

"Sure. Better get that suit on, Jim. It's cold out there."

Cameron shook his head. "Sorry, Luke. You and Wy get moving. I'll sit tight and give them a little surprise as they close in—"

"What are you trying to do, get a medal out of this, Jim?" Lucas said. "Come on—time's a-wasting."

Cameron shook his head.

"What's this—the old captain-goes-down-with-his-ship routine?"

"My back's sprained," Cameron said. "I can't move my legs."

"Wy, let's help Jim get into his suit," Lucas said briskly.

"You're wasting time," Cameron said as the two set to work, moving clumsily in their suits, hampered by the massive tug of the big planet.

"They won't try to land that big baby," Lucas said. "She'd break up in this G-field. That means they'll have to send a shore party down in a sideboat. That will take awhile. Wy, let's unclamp my couch for a stretcher."

"That's just more extra weight," Cameron protested.

"Pile it on," Lucas said. "That's what these piano legs are for." Working swiftly, the two men freed the couch and placed the injured man in it, strapping him in securely.

Outside, Cameron looked back at the battered hull, half sunk in the frozen snow at the end of the long trough it had scored in landing.

"Take a last look," he said. "She was a good boat, but she'll never lift again—and neither will we, if we don't get out of sight in a hurry." He glanced at Lucas and saw that the big man's eyes were tight shut. Tears trickled down his cheek and froze.

"Hey, Luke—don't take it so hard," he started, only half jokingly.

"Sorry," Lucas said, opening his eyes just far enough for the navigator to see that they were enflamed and red. "I'm afraid I can't take the light. I'm snow-blind."

Wybold hesitated only for a moment. Then he stepped forward, freed a harness strap, and clipped it to a D-ring on the engineer's belt, linking them.

"Follow the leader," he said, and started up the long slope—to his desert-conditioned eyes just pleasantly illuminated—toward the jumbled rocks and the dark cave mouths a quarter of a mile away.

They had covered three quarters of the distance, when Cameron suddenly called, "Duck!"

In total silence, the Yrax gunboat rocketed into view from behind them, streaked low overhead, trailed by a deafening sonic boom that shook snow loose from the high ridges all around. In an instant, the air was filled with the rumble of sliding ice. The ground trembled underfoot, as immense glacial fragments dislodged by the sudden shock detached themselves from the slopes and started downward, driving whirling clouds of loose snow ahead.

"Run for it," Wybold shouted over the thunder, and putting his head down, he ran, with Lucas close behind.

In a blinding fog of whirling ice crystals, the men scaled the jumble of rock, searching for a cranny big enough to conceal them. They reached the top of the first incline, found a narrow ledge leading to the left and upward between high walls—a route cut by ages of runoff water from spring thaws.

"It might be a dead end," Wybold said. "What do you think, Jim?"

"We'll try it, Wy. We don't have much choice."

Even the navigator's desert-trained vision, developed on a world where blazing sunlight and obscuring dust storms were a way of life, was of little value now. He climbed doggedly on, feeling his way up the narrow trail. There was a sharp turn, and the ravine widened into a bowl-shaped hollow—possibly an old lake basin—the walls of which were riddled with shallow, water-cut grottoes. Most of these were far too small to shelter a man, and all were choked with ice. But ahead, on the right, a single black opening showed. Wybold struggled across the drifts toward it. It was a cave, its mouth protected by a narrow passage. It seemed clear, but to Wybold the interior was only an inky blackness.

"Luke—can you make out anything in there?"

The engineer moved up beside him, blinked his light-burned eyes, grateful for the soothing gloom.

"A small opening, but it widens out inside. Goes back a good twenty feet and turns. It'll do."

Inside, Lucas deposited Cameron's improvised cot in a sheltered spot well back from the entrance.

"All the comforts of home, gentlemen," he said.

"Better check out the back of the cave," Cameron said to Lucas. "There may be another way in."

Lucas nodded and set off, moving surely in the near-darkness.

"What do you suppose their plan of attack will be, Jim?" Wybold asked, scanning the expanse of dazzling white visible beyond the opening.

"If they're smart, they'll bring up some kind of heavy gun and blast away," Cameron replied. "But if they're smarter, they'll try to come in on foot and make sure of us."

"We'll know pretty soon," Wybold said.

❖   ❖   ❖

The rearmost extension of the cave, Lucas found, though it narrowed sharply, did not pinch off entirely. Concealed in deep shadow, an opening some six feet high and barely two feet in width split the rock wall. To ordinary vision, the darkness beyond would have been impenetrable; but to the Sandovian's sensitive eyes a twisting tunnel was dimly visible, leading back into the cliff. In ages past, Lucas guessed, during a warmer age in the life of the big planet, thawing ice had eroded this route down through the stone, which in turn implied an unguarded access at the far end. For a moment, he considered reporting on his finding and requesting permission to continue; then, he squeezed his powerful bulk through the narrow aperture and, ducking slightly under low clearance, prowled along the passage into the rock.

Almost at once, the way angled sharply upward, became an almost vertical shaft through tumbled rock. Climbing was difficult; the water-worn stones were smoothly rounded, hard to grip. After a dozen feet, the narrowing tunnel leveled off, became a wide, low-ceilinged shelf. Lucas was forced to lie flat and crawl, using fingers and toes.

The ceiling shelved gradually downward, closing in. When it was apparent that no more progress could be made dead ahead, he angled to the right. At once, he found himself wedged tight between floor and ceiling. With an arm-creaking effort, he pulled himself through and the passage opened out. Through a gap in the rock ahead, watery daylight leaked.

Lucas crawled forward, shielding his eyes from the light, saw a final, irregularly-walled crevice leading out to the open. He made his way along it, emerged on a windswept slope of frozen snow, bathed in the deep blue shadow of an ice peak. Here, out of the direct sunlight, he was able to see, though painfully. He made a narrow aperture between his fingers, striving to make out the details of the scene below. He was, he determined, at a point some fifty yards above and to the left of the cave mouth—a spot inaccessible to any climber from below. At his back, a vertical ice wall rose. As he was about to turn away, there was a sound from below. Motion caught his eye, below and to the left. He went flat, watched as a sticklike creature, moving quickly on four multiple-jointed legs, rounded a shoulder of ice and poised on the narrow ledge leading along the cliff face, its flexible torso curving upward in an attitude of alert listening. Four additional limbs sprang from the alien's shoulder region, the lower pair long, tipped with paired chelae, the upper pair short, flexible as a monkey's tail. The body was the color of blued steel, with a hard, polished look. Straps crisscrossed the narrow thorax, bearing badges and pouches.

For the first time, a human being was looking at a Yrax soldier.

The alien stood for a moment, the stiff, antennalike members atop its insignificant bullet-shaped head moving restlessly. Then, it darted forward. From his vantage point above, Lucas saw the narrow cleft in the ice lying directly in the Yrax's path. The Yrax, however, scanning the slopes above, failed to notice the trap. As its forelegs went over the edge, the long arms shot out, scored the ice on the far side in a vain bid for purchase. But the weight of the massive body was too great. Ice chips flew as the rear legs clawed, resisting the inexorable slide. Then the heavy torso slid down, dropped into the crevasse. For another few seconds the creature clung, while its arms raked desperately for a grip. Then, with a final screech of iron-hard claws on ice, it was gone, clattering away into the depths to lodge with a smash far below.

At the same moment, a second Yrax appeared

around the abutment. It moved briskly forward, paused for a moment at the edge of the cleft, then raised its upper body and lunged across the yard-wide gap. For a moment it seemed as though it might be safe, then the forward pair of legs—which had gained a precarious purchase on the rim of ice—slipped back. As the creature clung by its forelimbs—it had secured a better grip than its predecessor—two more Yrax came into view along the path. One veered to the right, the other to the left. Neither took any apparent notice of their fellow, still clinging to his precarious hold on safety.

One of the newcomers edged to his left along the cleft to the edge of the narrow ledge it cut. It leaned out to examine the terrain below, but seemingly found nothing there to encourage it. Moving back a few feet, it sprang forward, cleared the cleft in a bound, landing with a metallic clatter, but safely, only its hind pair of legs kicking fragments of ice free from the lip of the pitfall as it pulled itself forward and disappeared from Lucas' view.

Meanwhile, the second newcomer had explored to its right, moving out of Lucas' line of sight. He heard the scrape of the horny limbs on ice, a clatter, the sounds of falling ice chunks, then a distant crashing. The creature did not reappear.

As a fourth Yrax advanced along the ledge, the unfortunate advance guard who had been silently dangling above the abyss slipped suddenly, dropped from view. Lucas winced at the now-familiar sound of impact far below. And now more of the aliens were appearing, some scouting along the edge, some launching themselves without hesitation, some crossing the gap, others falling to unnoticed death. A few turned aside, began exploring the wall to their right. If they found a route there, Lucas realized, the rear entrance to the cave would be quickly discovered.

He eased back silently from the edge, studied the opening in the rock. It was not large, but would be obvious at even a casual glance. It would have to be camouflaged. That meant snow and ice—the only materials available.

Lucas' eyes were burning, closing in spite of his efforts to keep them open. He clambered up above the opening, then set his feet against a large block of packed snow, and pushed.

The results exceeded his expectations. The crust broke away suddenly; a slab of ice ten feet long and a yard high toppled over the edge to thud massively down before the narrow entrance—and Lucas, deprived abruptly of his grip, slid after it. He struck hard, a jagged edge of ice smashing across his ribs with stunning force. He was dimly aware of the impact of ice fragments around him, of the whirl of loose snow driven up by the displaced air, of a distant, ominous rumble.

Then something struck his head, and all thought faded into swirling darkness.

In the cave, Wybold cocked his head, listening to the muffled rumbling that seemed to come from deep inside the mountain. A sudden gust of air puffed from the dark recesses at the rear of the deep cave, bringing with it a scattering of snow crystals. The sound died away; the fitful draft dwindled and was gone. Only a long drift of powdery snow across the floor attested to the brief flurry. Wybold turned; his eyes met Cameron's.

"Sounded like a cave-in," the injured man said.

"I'd better go have a look," the navigator said. Neither man mentioned the thought uppermost on their minds: *Lucas is back there somewhere* . . .

"You'll be as blind in the dark as Luke is in direct sunlight," Cameron said bluntly.

"I can feel my way. Don't forget my famous Vera-crucian sense of direction." He tried to make the words sound light.

"Move me over beside the front door before you go," Cameron said.

Wybold paused. "I wasn't thinking," he said. "Of course I can't leave you here alone."

"I have my suit gun," Cameron said. "Just prop me up so I can see down that passage."

"Wait a minute, Jim—"

"Luke might be needing help pretty badly, Wy," Cameron cut him off. "Better hurry up."

Five minutes later, with the crippled Cameron settled in position guarding the entrance, Wybold set off along the path Lucas had followed. At first, the route was clear enough; he slipped easily through the cleft in the rock, moving forward by feeling his way with outstretched hands, sliding his feet forward to explore for unseen pitfalls. At the point where the route angled upward, he was baffled for awhile; then he found the opening leading upward and began to climb.

In the low chamber where Lucas had almost become wedged, Wybold paused for breath. In total darkness and utter stillness, he lay on his face under the shelving rock, before starting on. Directly before him, the ceiling dipped sharply. Lucas could never have negotiated that passage, the navigator felt sure. But had he gone right, or left?

Either direction seemed equally likely. Wybold chose the left. The space widened until he could rise to all fours, then to his feet, though it was still necessary to stoop. Through his open faceplate, he felt a steady flow of cold, fresh air. Feeling his way toward its source, he saw a faint glow of daylight that widened out into a steeply angled cut leading up to a strip of vivid blue sky.

It was a difficult climb up the twenty-foot slope of icy rock; but at last he reached the top and emerged on a slope of glittering snow beneath a towering crag. A ragged edge of broken snow crust ran just below his position, as from a recent snowslide. The stretch of bare rock thus exposed ended in an abrupt dropoff. Beyond and below this edge, strange figures moved.

Wybold dropped flat, watching the Yraci scouts as they scurried back and forth, exploring the extent of a great drift of broken ice blocking the ledge along which they made their separate ways. One clambered directly up the side of the heap, slipped as he neared the top, rolled helplessly back down, and disappeared over the edge. Others climbed up at other points; some succeeded in negotiating the obstruction, and hurried away along the ledge; others tumbled back to the base, back near their starting point and immediately tried again. Still others followed the one who had fallen over the side. None appeared to be aware of the efforts of his fellows. There was no particular effort to follow in the tracks of the successful climbers or to shun the routes that led to catastrophe.

For ten minutes, Wybold watched the procession. A few stragglers arrived, picked their routes, fell or passed the blockage. One last multilegged alien hurried up, skittered upslope, clattered down safely on the far side and was gone. The navigator waited another two minutes, then cautiously rose and worked his way downslope. It was an eight-foot drop to the top of the ice heap blocking the ledge. As he debated attempting the risky descent, with the idea of following the alien scouting party, he noticed a small patch of dark blue visible through the heaped ice dust—a blue of the identical shade of a regulation Space Arm ship suit.

"Luke!" he exclaimed. In a moment Wybold had turned, lowered himself over the edge, and dropped.

He struck the ice heap near its crest, caught himself as he slipped toward the adjacent chasm, and slid down beside the place where the telltale color gleamed through the drift. Quickly, he raked away the loose ice chips, lifted a larger slab aside, and exposed the engineer's left arm.

The buried man was in no immediate danger of suffocation—provided the faceplate of his suit had been closed. And the layer of fallen ice and snow did not seem to be deep enough to have done any serious damage. But Lucas lay ominously still.

Wybold cleared his arm to the shoulder, exposed his head, and breathed a sigh of relief as he saw that Lucas' faceplate was closed. Five more minutes' work had cleared the unconscious man's torso. At that point, Lucas stirred. Wybold looked back down along the ledge; the route the Yraci had used was marked by their many-limbed tracks that wound back down toward the snowfield below. Ahead, the route curved out of sight. No aliens were in view, but they could return at any moment.

"Luke! Wake up," Wybold urged. "We've got to get out of sight!"

Two minutes later Lucas was on his feet, groggy from the blow a thirty-pound ice fragment had dealt him, but able to walk.

"They've gone on along the ledge, toward the cave mouth," Wybold told him. "Let's get going. Jim's holding the fort alone."

Lucas looked up at the ice-rimmed ledge above. "I'll boost you up," he said. He squatted and Wybold stepped up; after a brief scramble, he pulled himself to the top.

"Hard work in this G," Wy panted. Lying flat, he extended an arm to the engineer. Lucas found a small foothold, reached up as far as he was able. His hand was a foot short of Wybold's outstretched hand. He found a precarious handhold, pulled himself up a few inches, but slipped back.

"No go," he said. "You go on back, Wy. I'll trail our friends and keep an eye on them. Maybe I can create a diversion—"

"Uh-uh," Wybold shook his head. "I can't see my hand in front of my face in there. I almost got lost in that maze. I'd never find my way back. And as for you keeping a watch—you can't see any better out here than I can inside. We'll stick together and watch for a break." He slipped over the edge and dropped back down beside Lucas.

"All right," the engineer said. "Let's go see what they're up to."

Alone in the icy cave, settled as comfortably as his wrenched back would allow, Cameron had lain for the better part of an hour, sighting along the barrel of the weapon propped on the stone before him. The afternoon sun glared frosty white on the patch of snow visible beyond the opening twenty feet away. Even his Earth-normal vision was beginning to suffer from the continual strain; he blinked and turned away to rest his eyes. When he looked back, an ungainly silhouette stood poised against the light.

For a long moment, neither Cameron nor the intruder moved. The Yrax seemed to be studying the dark recess, considering its next move. Suddenly it stepped forward on its four slim legs, lowering its upraised torso to duck under the entry. Cameron waited. The Yrax advanced cautiously. When it was ten feet away, it saw him. For a moment, it halted; then, it gathered its legs and crouched. Cameron took careful aim at the point of juncture of the slim neck and the horny thorax and pressed the switch of the heat gun.

A brilliant point of light glinted on the alien's shiny blue-black exoderm. In the blue-white glare, smoke puffed outward from the point of contact. The creature leaped backward, its carapace raking the sides of the entry with a metallic clatter, and was gone. A rank odor of charred horn hung in the air.

Cameron uttered a harsh sigh and blinked at sweat that had trickled into his eyes. He resighted the gun and waited, looking out at stillness and silence. And, suddenly, another Yrax was framed in the entry.

This time Cameron didn't wait. The beam lanced out, seared a smoking blister on the chitinous thorax. As before, the victim recoiled, skittered from sight, apparently unharmed.

Two Yraci arrived simultaneously. One thrust ahead; the heat beam caught him, and he leaped back but collided with his fellow. For a frantic moment, the two aliens threshed, limbs entangled, while Cameron raked them indiscriminately. Then both tumbled away, darted from view.

After that, there was a lull that stretched on for half a minute, a full minute . . .

Abruptly, an alien was there, staggering under the burden of a massive shape of dull metal, which it deposited squarely in the entrance. It set swiftly to work, adjusting the apparatus, so that a series of what appeared to be ring sights were squarely aligned along the dim tunnel. At this range—the Yrax was some twenty-five feet distant—the diverging beam of the heat projector cast a disk of light that was barely visible in the glare of the sun, and seemed to discomfit the alien not at all as it busied itself at its task. Cameron shifted aim, directing his beam at the cluster of what he guessed to be the controls of the alien machine. In seconds the iodine-colored metal glowed red hot. Moments later—as the Yrax gunner squatted, multiple

knees beside the armored body, to sight along the firing
tube—the weapon burst with a sharp detonation that
sent its operator flying in a cloud of ice chips. As the
smoke of the explosion cleared, Cameron saw that the
body of the device had burst, exposing coils of wiring
that burned with a fierce light that suggested pure
magnesium. In the next five minutes, he fired on three
more Yraci who came forward as if to inspect the
ruined gun. Their reactions never varied from the
pattern: immediate flight.

Then a lull. Ten minutes passed. Somewhere far
away Cameron heard a low rumble, as of distant cannon fire. Then nothing. Slowly, the shadows lengthened.
Cameron waited.

From a concealed ledge a hundred yards above the
cave mouth, Lucas and Wybold had watched as the
aliens crawled over the tumbled moraine of rock and
ice, poking into one cave mouth after another. They
had seen an alien halt before the cave where they knew
Cameron waited, alone and hurt, watched as the
intruder started in, then tumbled out in obvious distress. They had observed as others made the attempt,
ignored by their fellows, who continued to poke and
probe into other dark recesses in the rock. When the
weapon-bearing Yrax came up, they had tensed to jump
to their feet, shout, anything to distract the gunner. But
the machine had suddenly winked with blue-white light,
and an instant later the sharp crack of the detonation
reached their ears.

"He's holding them off," Wybold said. "But it can't
go on forever."

"They don't know much about cooperation," Lucas
said. "Look at that one—he's going to bring that whole
ridge right down on his pals—" As he spoke, a long
rim of ice which had precariously overhung the floor

of the hollow broke away, came crashing down, raising the inevitable cloud of snow and ice crystals. At
once, Wybold saw the opportunity. He scrambled to
his feet.

"Luke—come on—while they're blinded!" He
plunged forward, half slid, half fell down the slope. He
came upright in a white mist as opaque as milk glass,
and paused for a moment, attuning his directional sense.

"This way, Luke," he called, and plunged ahead. He
dodged past the dimly-seen figure of a Yrax, groping
through the murk, and skirted a mound of fallen ice;
then the cave mouth opened before him. He floundered through a waist-deep drift, gained the entry.

"Jim! It's me!" he shouted. Then he was beside
Cameron, who reached out to grip his hand.

"I knew you clowns had something to do with that
snowstorm out there," the injured man called over the
now diminishing roar. "Where's Luke?"

Wybold whirled. "He was right behind me—"

"Wait!" Cameron's voice checked him. "You can't go
back out there, Wy! They'll spot you! The snow is
already settling!"

"But—Luke . . ."

"Luke knows where we are," Cameron said. "He'll
expect to find us here."

"I guess you're right," Wybold concurred reluctantly.

When Wybold shouted and disappeared into the
obscuring whirl of snow, Lucas lowered his head against
the blinding glare and charged after him. He fell almost
at once, regained his feet, fell again. A massive ice block
crashed down directly in his path; he veered to the left,
recoiled as the ungainly shape of a Yrax appeared
before him, in distress as obvious as his own. It ignored
him, blundered past, and Lucas went on, climbing the
drifts, falling, picking himself up . . .

The ground was rising; Lucas paused, picturing the lay of the land as he had dimly seen it from above. There was no upward slope between his point of departure and the cave mouth. And he sensed that he had gone too far. He had covered a hundred feet at least, and the distance to the entry had been no more than seventy at most.

Vaguely now, he could see a slope of craggy ice rising above him. No more ice was falling from above. He looked back. The obscuring veil was settling. Vague shapes moved in the hollow below. In another moment he would be in plain view to the aliens. He resumed his climb, pulled himself up into a shallow gully, turned to scan the back trail. He saw the cave mouth now, half buried in snow. He had missed it by fifty feet. At least twenty Yraci prowled the ledge before it. Wybold was not in sight. That was good, Lucas told himself; he would be inside with Jim now.

And he was outside.

For half an hour, Lucas watched the apparently aimless movements of the aliens. Many of them attempted to scale the slopes that enclosed the ledge on three sides. All failed—which did not deter others from attempting the same task. Along the lower trail— the single access to the hollow, now that the upper trail was blocked—more aliens arrived, to repeat the performances of their predecessors. Then they settled down in apparent patience before the cave mouth.

"Stalemate," Lucas muttered to himself. "They can't get inside, and Jim and Wy can't get out. And if they could, the escape route's blocked. The only way out leads right into the arms of the Yraci." For another quarter of an hour he studied the scene, as the sun, obscured now behind a peak, sank swiftly lower, bringing a twilight that was soothing to the man's burning eyes.

Can't stay here, he thought. Temperature's already falling. Have to do something . . .

A trickle of snow slid down from the slope above the cave to form a low mound in the open trail. A lone Yrax, a late arrival, clambered up over it, leaving a busy trail of foot and drag marks, hurried on to join the waiting group before the cave. Bunched up as they were, they offered a perfect target for a few well-aimed rounds of artillery fire, Lucas reflected. All that was lacking was the artillery.

The engineer tensed suddenly, frowning in thought. Then he rose, moved silently along the gully until he had traversed the crest of the ridge. Below, the last gleam of dusk lit the long valley. Keeping to the high ground, Lucas set off at a brisk walk directly away from the cave.

"Getting cold out there," Wybold said. "Luke can't take a night out in the open. Maybe I'd better go look for him."

"To you, it's been pitch dark for an hour, Wy," Cameron said. "You couldn't see your hand in front of your face. Anyway, Luke will expect us to sit tight. If there's anything he can do, he'll do it."

"I feel pretty useless, just sitting here."

"I know how you feel," Cameron said. "But let's not make the mistake our pals the Yraci do."

"What do you mean?"

"They don't work together. We do. And our part of the job right now is just staying put."

"Maybe, Jim. But what if Luke can't reach the back door? What if he's waiting for us to come out that way?"

"Wy—we're both blind in a dark cave. And you aren't a Sandovian like Luke. You couldn't lug me that far on your back."

"I suppose you're right."

I hope so, Cameron thought.

The diffuse starlight lit the scene comfortably for
Lucas. He made good time, coming stealthily down on
the wrecked scout boat from above after a brisk twenty-
minute hike. It was nearly buried in the snow that was
shaken down by the sonic boom of the Yraci landing
craft. There were a maze of alien footprints around it;
trails led away across the snow in the direction of the
cave. But no aliens were in sight.

Lucas set to work, digging the soft drifts away from
the hull, at a point fifteen feet from the exposed stern.
In a quarter of an hour, he had excavated a pit six feet
deep and wide enough to stand in, with a minimum
of elbow room. Against the curve of hull thus revealed,
the rounded bulge of a steering engine housing flared.
The inspection cover unsnapped easily. The engine
itself was an eighteen-inch-long torpedo shape, blunt
at both ends, attached to its gimbaled mountings by
four heavy-duty retaining clamps. They were designed
to be loosened quickly; steering engine replacement
sometimes had to be made in space, under difficult
conditions. In the tool locker inside the boat, there was
a special wrench for the purpose; but the hatch was
buried now under tons of ice. If the clamps were to
be removed, it would have to be by hand.

Lucas dug away more packed snow to give his feet
good purchase. He planted himself, gripped the big
knurled knob in one hand, closed the other hand over
it, and applied pressure. His grip slipped. He squeezed
harder, threw every ounce of power in his big frame
into the effort. With a sharp *crack!* the clamp spun
free.

The second and third clamps turned more easily.
The last was balky, but on the third try—an effort that

made tiny bright lights whirl before Lucas' eyes—it yielded. Carefully, he disconnected the control leads; if they were accidentally crossed, the engine would ignite at once, ejecting a 2 cm stream of superheated ions at a velocity of 2,000 feet per second—and incidentally pulverizing anyone in the vicinity. He lifted the massive engine down—its Earth-normal weight was 240 pounds—cradled it in his arms, and started back toward the cave.

The hike back was not so easy as the outward trip. For all his giant strength, Lucas was tiring. The bitter cold had taken its toll of his resources, too. Toiling up the last few hundred yards of the climb to the vantage point in the gully overlooking the cave mouth, he was forced to halt for rest at shorter and shorter intervals. He arrived at last and sank down, dumping his burden in the snow.

It had been two hours since Lucas had left the spot, but the scene below was unchanged. The score or more of Yraci still crouched waiting, outside the dark entrance to the cranny where the men had taken refuge. The darkness or the cold, it seemed, had the effect of reducing the activity of the aliens; there was no more nervous darting here and there, no fruitless exploration of routes up the slopes, no activity along the narrow trail. The besiegers seemed content to crouch motionless but for aimless waving of arms, and wait.

Wait for what? Lucas wondered. Maybe they're bringing up some big guns of their own. And if so, I'd better get moving . . .

He righted the steering engine, placed it in a convenient crevice in an exposed rock slab, and packed snow around it, taking care to lead the control cables out into the clear. He aligned it carefully, then heaped other stones over it, packing the interstices with ice. In use, the engine was endothermic, absorbing heat from its surroundings. Firing it would freeze the entire mass into a single unit.

And now he was ready. Lying flat behind the improvised heat cannon, he grasped a wire in each hand, bringing them together—

A tremendous weight struck him in the back, slamming him against the heaped stones and ice around the engine, in the same instant that, with a hard, racking bellow, the engine burst into life. Lucas, half-stunned by the impact, twisted onto his back, fighting against the grasping, threshing bulk that had hurled itself on him so unexpectedly. He had a confused glimpse of a weird, triangular head, the scarred, horny thoracic plates and multijointed arms of a giant of the Yrax species; then the alien sprang clear, rearing up to bring its anterior limbs to bear. But Lucas was not the man to wait for the attack. He threw himself at the ungainly, ten-foot creature, knocked its rodlike legs from under it, grappled it around the body. Its limbs flashed as it struck vainly at him, but he rose to his knees, and using the full power of his giant torso and shoulders, hurled the alien from him. It raked at the ice, sending up a shower of chips; then it was gone, to slam down the steep slope with a crash like a ground car striking an abutment.

The roar of the steering engine had continued without pause. As Lucas clawed his way back to it, he saw at once that the impact of his body under the Yrax's attack had knocked it out of its careful alignment. The jet stream—a blue-white bar of ravening energy that lit the scene like a flare—instead of raking the besieging aliens, was searing the naked ice slope above the cave, sending a vast cloud of exploding steam boiling up against the sky. Vainly, the engineer threw his weight against the emplacement; but the engine was locked in a solid frozen matrix as impervious as granite.

As Lucas stared in bitter dismay at the target point across the gorge, the entire slope seemed to stir at once. With infinite leisure, cracks opened all across the great sheet of ice. Slabs the size of skating rinks came sliding down to spill over the edge and slam down on the ledge below. In moments, the hollow was a churning cauldron of whirling snow, driven up by the stream of snow, ice, and rock arriving in an ever-increasing volume from above. Here and there, around the periphery of the bowl-shaped space, a Yrax was visible, frantically attempting to climb the encircling wall, only to fall back and disappear in the blinding flurry.

Lucas found a loose fragment of stone, pounded at the ice encasing the bellowing engine, exposed the control wires. He ripped them apart and instantly the booming echoes crashed and died. The rumble and thud of falling ice dwindled, faded out. The blizzard driven up by the avalanche settled, revealing heaped banks from which here and there struggling alien limbs projected. But where the mouth of the cave had been, great drifts of broken ice rose up, burying it at least ten feet deep.

A lone Yrax freed itself from the snow, hurried to the point at which the trail had led from the hollow. But now a wall of snow barred egress. The alien scouted back and forth, tried to find a foothold, fell back, tried again, but fell back again. Others of the buried creatures were struggling clear of their icy entombment, and each tried and failed to find a route out of the hollow.

They're trapped, Lucas thought numbly. But so are Jim and Wy. I could lead them out the back way—if I could reach it. They can't do it alone in the dark, even if Wy could carry Jim.

And even if they got clear—what then? We can't live long in this ice hell . . .

There was a sound from below and behind Lucas. He crawled to the spot where he had thrust the giant alien over the edge. Twelve feet below, the alien crouched, its oddly featureless face turned up toward him. One of its legs was broken in two places.

"You're in a bad spot too, aren't you, fellow?" Lucas said aloud. "It looks like nobody wins and everybody loses."

A ratchety sound came from the creature below. Then a rasping voice which seemed to emanate from a point on the alien's back said clearly:

"Human, I underestimated you. It was a grave fault, and for that fault I die."

For a moment, Lucas was stunned into paralysis by the astonishing speech. But only for a moment.

"Where did you learn to speak Terran?" he said.

"For nine hundred ship periods I have monitored your transmissions of pictures and voices," the alien said in its flat, unaccented tone. "It was a strange phenomenon, worth investigation though passing understanding."

"Why haven't you communicated with us before?"

"For what purpose?"

"To end this tomfool war!" Lucas burst out. "What do you want from us? Why do you raid our colonies and attack our ships?"

The creature was silent for a long moment.

"It is the way of life," it said. "Could it be otherwise?"

"We could cooperate," Lucas said. "The galaxy is big enough for everybody."

"Cooperate? I know the word. It is a concept I have been unable to analyze."

"To work together. You help us, and we help you."

"But—how can this paradox be? Your survival and

mine are mutually exclusive destiny-patterns. It is the nature of life for each being to strive to destroy all competitors."

"Is that why you've been killing men wherever you found them?"

"I have not tried to kill you," the Yrax stated. "Only your . . ." It used an incomprehensible word. Lucas asked for a translation.

"Your . . . cell bodies. Minions. Worker units. Curious—I cannot find the word in your tongue."

"You're not making sense. You were trying hard to kill us when you shot our boat down!"

"You speak as though . . . there were other men in association with you." The alien seemed deeply puzzled about something.

"It takes more than one man to operate even a scout boat. Anyway, a man would go crazy in space alone."

"You are saying that you *shared your ship with other men*?"

"Naturally."

"But—what kept you from tearing each other to pieces, as is the law of life?"

"If that's a law, it's time it was repealed," Lucas said. "Listen, Yrax—you're not making any sense. You had a crew of over twenty Yraci on your own ship—"

"Never! There was only I."

"You're talking nonsense, Yrax. A couple of dozen of them are digging themselves out of the ice not fifty yards from here!"

"Those! But they are only my cell bodies, not Yraci!"

"They look exactly like you—"

"To alien sensors, perhaps—but they are no more than extensions of myself, spored off by me as needed, mindless creatures of my will. Surely, it is the same with you? I sensed, through their preceptors, that you, as I, are larger than your workers. Surely, the two units trapped in the cave are creatures of your mind and body, responsive to your thoughts, having no volition of their own? Can it be otherwise, in all sanity?"

"It is otherwise," Lucas said. "So you never heard of cooperation, eh? Well, you claim to have all the brains in your party. I have a proposition for you . . ."

"I had to give him credit for seeing logic when it was pointed out to him," Lucas said forty-one hours later, seated before the alien control panel of the launch provided by the Yrax. "Without his crew men—or cell bodies, as he calls them—and I suppose he has a right to, his biology isn't much like ours—Without them, he was dead. When I told him I knew an escape route from the trap—and that I'd show it to him, if he'd lend us transport home—he agreed in a hurry."

"You took a chance, trusting him," Cameron said. "After you hauled him out and splinted his leg, he could have nipped you in two with those arms of his."

"He'd still have been stuck. He needed me to guide his boys out. Once he got the idea through his head that we could actually work together instead of automatically killing each other, things worked fine. It took us a few hours to melt a route to the top, and clear the cave mouth, and he did his share like a trooper."

"It's strange to think of a race of intelligent beings who never see each other, never have any contact, still developing a technology."

"With mutual telepathy, what any one of them learned, they all know. And they can create as many cell bodies as they need to do whatever they want done. I don't suppose there are more than a few hundred of the 'brain' Yraci on their planet—but there are millions of their workers."

"Not what you'd call a democracy," Wybold said.

"Their 'workers' are like our arms and legs," Lucas

said. "Parts of their bodies. You couldn't very well give your fingers and toes an equal vote."

"Right now my stomach is giving the orders," Cameron said. "It says it's time to eat."

"Have a nutrient bar—courtesy of our Yrax friend," Lucas said. "They're not bad. Taste a little like stuffed dates. You know, there might be a market for them at home."

"The Yrax was pretty impressed by the energy-cell principle of the steering engine we gave him," Wybold said. "I foresee a brisk commerce between Terra and Yrax."

"It's a tragedy that there had to be all that destruction, ships blasted, lives lost—just because it never occurred to the Yraci to sit down and talk things over."

"It's not an easy lesson," Lucas said. "We humans had a little trouble learning it, if you remember your history." He grinned at Cameron, and the captain's black face grinned back at him.

MIND OUT OF TIME

One

Strapped tight in the padded acceleration couch in the command cell of the extrasolar exploratory module, Lieutenant-Colonel Jake Vanderguerre tensed against the tell-tale bubbling sensation high in his chest, the light, tentative pin-prick of an agony that could hurl itself against him like a white-hot anvil. The damned bootleg heart pills must be losing their punch; it had been less than six hours since he'd doped himself up for the mission . . .

Beside him, Captain Lester Teal cocked a well-arched eyebrow at him. "You all right, Colonel?"

"I'm fine." Vanderguerre heard the ragged quality of his voice; to cover it, he nodded toward the ten-inch screen on which the clean-cut features of Colonel Jack Sudston of Mission Control on Luna glowed in enthusiastic color. "I wish the son-of-a-bitch would cut the chatter. He makes me nervous."

Teal grunted. "Let Soapy deliver his commercial, Jake," he said. "In a minute we'll get the line about the devoted personnel of UNSA; and there might even be time for a fast mention of Stella and Jo, the devoted little women standing by."

"*. . . report that the module is now in primary position, and in a G condition,*" Sudston was saying heartily. "*Ready for the first manned test of the magnetic torsion powered vehicle.*" He smiled out of the screen; his eyes, fixed on an off-screen cue card, did not quite meet Vanderguerre's. "*Now let's have a word from Van and Les, live from the MTE module, in Solar orbit, at four minutes and fifty-three seconds to jump.*"

Vanderguerre thumbed the *XMIT* button.

"Roj, Mission Control," he said. "Les and I are rarin' to go. She's a sweet little, uh, module, Jack. Quite a view from out here. We have Earth in sight, can just make out the crescent. As for Luna, you look mighty small from here, Jack. Not much brighter than good old Sirius. MTE module out."

"*While we wait, Van and Les's words are flashing toward us at the speed of light,*" Sudston's voice filled the transmission lag. "*And even at that fantastic velocity—capable of circling the world ten times in each second—it takes a full twenty-eight seconds for—but here's Van's carrier now . . .*"

"Roj, Mission Control," Vanderguerre listened as his own transmission was repeat-beamed to the television audience watching back on Earth.

"Damn the stage machinery," he said. "We could have flipped the switches any time in the last two hours."

"But then Soapy wouldn't have been able to air the

big spectacle live on prime time," Teal reminded him
sardonically.

"Spectacle," Vanderguerre snorted. "A fractional
percentage capability check. We're sitting on a power
plant that can tap more energy in a second than the
total consumption of the human race through all pre-
vious history. And what do we do with it? Another baby
step into space."

"Relax, Jake." Teal quirked the corner of his mouth
upward. "You wouldn't want to risk men's lives with
premature experimentation, would you?"

"Ever heard of Columbus?" Vanderguerre growled.
"Or the Wright boys, or Lindbergh?"

"Ever heard of a guy named Cocking?" Teal countered. "Back in the 1800s he built a parachute out of
wicker. Went up in a balloon and tried it. It didn't work.
I remember the line in the old newspaper I saw: *'Mr.
Cocking was found in a field at Lea, literally dashed
to bits'.*"

"I take my hat off to Mr. Cocking," Vanderguerre
said. "He tried."

"There hasn't been a fatality directly attributable to
the Program in the sixty-nine years since Lunar Station One," Teal said. "You want to be the first to louse
up a no-hitter?"

Vanderguerre snorted a laugh. "I was the first man
on Callisto, Teal. Did you know that? It's right there
in the record—along with the baseball statistics and
the mean annual rainfall at Centralia, Kansas. That was
eighteen years ago." He put out a hand, ran it over
the polished curve of the control mushroom. "So what
if she blew up in our faces?" he said as if to himself.
"Nobody lives forever."

"*. . . fifty-three seconds and counting,*" Sudston's
voice chanted into the silence that followed Vanderguerre's remark. "*The monitor board says—Yes, it's*

coming down now, it's condition G all the way, the mission is go, all systems are clocking down without a hitch, a tribute to the expertise of the devoted personnel of UNSA, at minus forty-eight seconds and counting . . ."

Teal twisted his head against the restraint of his harness to eye Vanderguerre.

"Don't mind me, kid," the older man said. "We'll take our little toad-hop, wait ten minutes for the tapes to spin, and duck back home for our pat on the head like good team men."

"Fifteen seconds and counting," Sudston's voice intoned. *"Fourteen seconds. Thirteen . . ."*

The two men's hands moved in a sure, trained sequence: READY lever down and locked. ARM lever down and locked.

". . . Four. Three. Two. One. Jump."

In unison, the men slammed home the big, paired, white-painted switches. There was a swiftly rising hum, a sense of mounting pressure . . .

Two

Teal shook off the dizziness that had swirled him like a top as the torsion drive hurled the tiny vessel outward into Deep Space; he gripped the chair arms, fighting back the nausea and anxiety that always accompanied the climactic moment of a shot.

It's all right, he told himself fiercely. *Nothing can go wrong. In three hours you'll be back aboard UNSA Nine, with half a dozen medics taping your belly growls. Relax . . .*

He forced himself to lean back in the chair; closed

his eyes, savoring the familiarity of it, the security of the enclosing titanium-foam shell.

It was OK now. He knew what to do in any conceivable emergency. Just follow the routine. It was as simple as that. That was the secret he'd learned long ago, when he had first realized that the military life was the one for him; the secret that had given him his reputation for coolness in the face of danger: courage consisted in knowing what to do.

He opened his eyes, scanned instrument faces with swift, trained precision, turned to Vanderguerre. The senior officer looked pale, ill.

"Forty-two million miles out, give or take half a million," Teal said. "Elapsed time, point oh, oh, oh seconds."

"*Mama mia,*" Vanderguerre breathed. We're sitting on a live one, boy!"

The voice issuing from the command was a whispery crackle.

"*. . . that the module is now in primary position, and in a G condition,*" Sudston's distance-distorted image was saying. "*Ready for the first manned test of the magnetic torsion powered vehicle . . .*"

"We passed up Soapy's transmission," Teal said.

"By God, Teal," Vanderguerre said. "I wonder what she'll do. What she'll *really* do!"

Teal felt his heart begin to *thump-ump, thump-ump.* He sensed what was coming as he looked at Vanderguerre. Vanderguerre looked back, eyeing him keenly. Was there a calculating look there; an assessing? Was he wondering about Teal, about his famous reputation for guts?

"What you said before about spotting the record," Vanderguerre's voice was level, casual. "Is that really the way you feel, Les?"

"You're talking about deviating from the programmed mission?" Teal kept his voice steady.

"We'd have to unlock from auto-sequencing and reprogram," Vanderguerre said. "It would be four minutes before Soapy knew anything. They couldn't stop us."

"*Roj, Lunar Control,*" Vanderguerre's voice cracked, relayed from the moon. "*Les and I are rarin' to go . . .*"

"The controls are interlocked," Vanderguerre added. "We'd have to do it together." His eyes met Teal's, held them for a moment, turned away. "Forget it," he said quickly. "You're young, you've got a career ahead, a family. It was a crazy idea—"

"I'll call your bluff," Teal cut him off harshly. "I'm game."

Say no, a voice inside him prayed. *Say no, and let me off the hook . . .*

Vanderguerre's tongue touched his lips; he nodded. "Good for you, kid. I didn't think you had it in you."

Three

"I've locked the guidance system on Andromeda," Vanderguerre said. The pain was still there, lurking— and the jump hadn't helped any. But it would hold off a little while, for this. It *had* to . . .

"How much power?" Teal asked.

"All of it," Vanderguerre said. "We'll open her up. Let's see what she'll do."

Teal punched keys, coding instructions into the panel.

"*. . . UNSA Station Nine has just confirmed the repositioning of the double-X module in Martian orbit,*" the excited voice of Colonel Sudston was suddenly louder, clearer, as the big lunar transmitter beam swung to center on the new position of the experimental craft. *"Van, let's hear from you!"*

"You'll hear from us," Vanderguerre said, "You'll hear plenty."

"Board set up," Teal said formally. "Ready for jump, sir."

"Van and Les have their hands full right now, carrying out the planned experiments aboard the MTE vehicle," the voice from the screen chattered. *"They're two lonely men at this moment, over forty million miles from home . . ."*

"Last chance to change your mind," Vanderguerre said.

"You can back out if you want to," Teal said tightly.

"Jump," Vanderguerre said. Two pairs of hands flipped the switch sequence. A whine rose to a wire-thin hum. There was a sense of pressure that grew and grew . . .

Blackout dropped over Vanderguerre like a steel door.

Four

This time, Teal realized, was worse—much worse. Under him, the seat lifted, lifted, pivoting back and endlessly over. Nausea stirred in him, brought a clammy film to his forehead. His bones seemed to vibrate in resonance to the penetrating keening of the torsion drive.

Then, abruptly, stillness. Teal drew a deep breath, opened his eyes. The command screen was blank, lit only by the darting flicker of random noise. The instruments—

Teal stared, rigid with shock. The MP scale read zero; the navigation fix indicator hunted across the grid aimlessly; the R counter registered negative. It didn't make sense. The jump must have blown every breaker in the module. Teal glanced up at the direct vision dome.

Blackness, unrelieved, immense.

Teal's hands moved in an instinctive gesture to reset the controls for the jump back to the starting point; he caught himself, turned to Vanderguerre.

"Something's fouled up. Our screens are out—" He broke off. Vanderguerre lay slack in the elaborately equipped chair, his mouth half open, his face the color of candle wax.

"Vanderguerre!" Teal slipped his harness, grabbed for the other's wrist. There was no discernible pulse.

Sweat trickled down into the corner of Teal's eye.

"Interlocked controls," he said. "Jake, you're got to wake up. I can't do it alone. You hear me, Jake? Wake up!" He shook the flaccid arm roughly. Vanderguerre's head lolled. Teal crouched to scan the life-system indicators on the unconscious man's shoulder repeater. The heartbeat was weak, irregular, the respiration shallow. He was alive—barely.

Teal half fell back into his chair. He forced himself to breathe deep, again, and again. Slowly, the panic drained away.

OK. They'd pulled a damn fool stunt, and something had gone wrong. A couple of things. But that didn't mean everything wasn't going to come out all right, if he just kept his head, followed the rules.

First, he had to do something about Vanderguerre. He unclipped the highly sophisticated medkit from its niche, forcing himself to move carefully, deliberately, remembering his training. One by one he attached the leads of the diagnostic monitor to Vanderguerre's suit system contacts.

Fourteen minutes later, Vanderguerre stirred and opened his eyes.

"You blacked out," Teal said quickly, then checked himself. "How do you feel?" He forced his tone level.

"I'm ... all right. What ... ?"

"We made the jump. Something went wrong. Screens are out; comlink too."

"How ... far?"

"I don't know, I tell you!" Teal caught the hysterical note in his voice, clamped his teeth hard. "I don't know," he repeated in a calmer tone. "We'll jump back now. All we have to do is backtrack on reverse settings—" He realized he was talking to reassure himself, cut off abruptly.

"Got to determine ... our position," Vanderguerre panted. "Otherwise—wasted."

"To hell with that," Teal snapped. "You're a sick man," he added. "You need medical attention."

Vanderguerre was struggling to raise his head far enough to see the panel.

"Instruments are acting crazy," Teal said. "We've got to—"

"You've checked out the circuits?"

"Not yet. I was busy with you." Silently Teal cursed the defensiveness of his tone.

"Check 'em."

Teal complied, tight-lipped.

"All systems G," he reported.

"All right," Vanderguerre said, his voice weak but calm. "Circuits hot, but the screens show nothing. Must be something masking 'em. Let's take a look. Deploy the direct vision scopes."

Teal's hands shook as he swung his eyepiece into position. He swore silently, adjusted the instrument. A palely-glowing rectangular grid, angled sharply outward, filled the viewfield: one of the module's outflung radiation surfaces. The lens, at least, was clear. But why the total blackness of the sky beyond? He tracked past the grid. A glaringly luminous object swam into view, oblong, misty and nebulous in outline.

"I've got something," he said. "Off the port fan."

He studied the oval smear of light—about thirty inches in width, he estimated, and perhaps a hundred feet distant.

"Take a look to starboard," Vanderguerre said. Teal shifted the scope, picked up a second object, half again as large as the first. Two smaller, irregularly shaped objects hung off to one side. Squinting against the glare, Teal adjusted the scope's filter. The bright halo obscuring the larger object dimmed. Now he could make out detail, a pattern of swirling, clotted light, curving out in two spiral arms from a central nucleus—

The realization of what he was seeing swept over Teal with a mind-numbing shock.

Five

Vanderguerre stared at the shape of light, the steel spike in his chest for the moment almost forgotten.

Andromeda—and the Greater and Lesser Magellanic Clouds. And the other, smaller one! The Milky Way, the home Galaxy.

"What the hell!" Teal's harsh voice jarred at him. "Even if we're halfway to Andromeda—a million light years—it should only subtend a second or so of arc! That thing looks like you could reach out and touch it!"

"Switch on the cameras, Les," he whispered. "Let's get a record—"

"Let's get out of here, Vanderguerre!" Teal's voice was ragged. "My God, I never thought—"

"Nobody did," Vanderguerre spoke steadily. "That's why we've got to tape it all, Les—"

"We've got enough! Let's go back! Now!"

Vanderguerre looked at Teal. The younger man was pale, wild-eyed. He was badly shaken. But you couldn't blame him. A million lights in one jump. So much for the light barrier, gone the way of the sound barrier.

"Now," Teal repeated. "Before . . ."

"Yeah," Vanderguerre managed. "Before you find yourself marooned with a corpse. You're right. OK. Set it up."

He lay slackly in the chair. His chest seemed swollen to giant size, laced across with vivid arcs of an agony that pulsed like muffled explosions. Any second now. The anvil was teetering, ready to fall. And the dual controls required two men to jump the module back along her course line. There was no time to waste.

"Board set up," Teal snapped. "Ready for jump."

Vanderguerre raised his hands to the controls; the steel spike drove into his chest.

"Jump," he gasped, and slammed the levers down—

The white-hot anvil struck him with unbearable force.

Six

Teal shook his head, blinked the fog from before his eyes; avidly, he scanned the panel.

Nothing had changed. The instruments still gave their dataless readings; the screen was blank.

"Vanderguerre—it didn't work!" Teal felt a sudden constriction like a rope around his throat as he stared at the motionless figure in the other chair.

"Jake!" he shouted. "You can't be dead! Not yet! I'd be stuck here! Jake! Wake up! Wake up!" As from a great distance, he heard his own voice screaming; but he was powerless to stop it . . .

Seven

From immense depths, Vanderguerre swam upward, to surface on a choppy sea of pain. He lay for a while, fighting for breath, his mind blanked of everything except the second-to-second struggle for survival. After a long time, the agony eased; with an effort, he turned his head.

Teal's seat was empty.

Eight

What did it mean? Vanderguerre asked himself for the twentieth time. What had happened? They'd jumped, he'd felt the drive take hold—

And Teal. Where the hell was Teal? He couldn't have left the module; it was a sealed unit. Nothing could leave it, not even wastes, until the techs at UNSA Nine cut her open . . .

But he was gone. And out there, Andromeda still

loomed, big as a washtub, and the Milky Way. It was impossible, all of it. Even the jump. Was it all a dream, a dying fancy?

No, Vanderguerre rejected the idea. *Something's happened here. Something I don't understand—not yet. But I've got data—a little data, anyway. And I've got a brain. I've got to look at the situation, make some deductions, decide on a course of action.*

From somewhere, a phrase popped into Vanderguerre's mind:

"Space is a property of matter . . ."

And where there was no matter, there would be . . . spacelessness.

"Sure," Vanderguerre whispered. "If we'd stopped to think, we'd have realized there's no theoretical limit to the MTE. We opened her up all the way—and the curve went off the graph. It threw us right out of the Galaxy, into a region where the matter density is one ion per cubic light. All the way to the end of space: Dead End. No wonder we didn't go any farther—or that we can't jump back. Zero is just a special case of infinity. And that's as far as we'd go, if we traveled on forever . . ."

His eye fell on Teal's empty seat. Yeah—so far so good. But what about Teal? How does the Vanderguerre theory of negative space explain that one?

Abruptly, fire flickered in Vanderguerre's chest. He stiffened, his breath cut off in his throat. So much for theories. This was it. No doubt about it. Three times and out. Strange that it had to end this way, so far away in space and time from everything he'd ever loved.

The vise in Vanderguerre's chest closed; the flames leaped higher, consuming the universe in raging incandescence . . .

Nine

Vanderguerre was standing on a graveled path beside a lake. It was dawn, and a chill mist lay over the water. Beyond the lazy line of trees on the far side, a hill rose, dotted with buildings. He recognized the scene at once: Lake Beryl. And the date: May first, 2007. It all came back to him as clearly as if it had been only yesterday, instead of twenty years. The little skiers' hotel, deserted now in summer, the flowers on the table, the picnic lunch, packed by the waiter, in a basket, with the bottle of vine rosé poking out under the white napkin . . .

And Mirla. He knew, before he turned, that she would be standing there, smiling as he had remembered her, down through the years . . .

Ten

The music was loud, and Teal raised his glass for a refill, glad of the noise, of the press of people, of the girl who clung close beside him, her breasts firm and demanding against him.

For a moment, a phantom memory of another place seemed to pluck at Teal's mind—an urgent vision of awful loneliness, of a fear that overwhelmed him like a breaking wave—he pushed the thought back.

Wine sloshed from the glass. It didn't matter. Teal drank deep, let the glass fall from his hand, turned, sought the girl's mouth hungrily.

Eleven

"Van—is anything wrong?" Mirla asked. Her smile had changed to a look of concern.

"No. Nothing," Vanderguerre managed. *Hallucination!* a voice inside his head said. *And yet it's real— as real as ever life was real . . .*

Mirla put her hand on his arm, looking up into his face.

"You stopped so suddenly—and you look . . . worried."

"Mirla . . . something strange has happened." Vanderguerre's eyes went to the bench beside the path. He led her to it, sank down on it. His heart was beating strongly, steadily.

"What is it, Van?"

"A dream? Or . . . is this the dream?"

"Tell me."

Vanderguerre did.

"I was there," he finished. "Just the wink of an eye ago. And now—I'm here."

"It's a strange dream, Van. But after all—it *is* just a dream. And this is real."

"Is it, Mirla? Those years of training, were they a dream? I still know how to dock a Mark IX on nine ounces of reaction mass. I know the math—the smell of the coolant when a line breaks under high G—the names of the men who put the first marker on Pluto, the first party who landed on Ceres, and—"

"Van—it was just a dream! You dreamed those things—"

"What date is this?" he cut in.

"May first—"

"May first, 2007. The date the main dome at Mars Station One blew and killed twelve tech personnel. One of them was Mayfield, the agronomist!" Vanderguerre jumped to his feet. "I haven't seen a paper, Mirla. You know that. We've been walking all night."

"You mean—you think—"

"Let's find a paper. The news should be breaking any time now!"

They went up the path, across the park, crossed an empty street; ten minutes later, from the open door of an all-night dinomat, a TV blared:

"*. . . Just received via Bellerophon relay. Among the dead are Colonel Mark Spencer, Marsbase commandant—*"

"An error," Vanderguerre put in. "He was hurt, but recovered."

"*. . . Dr. Gregor Mayfield, famed for his work in desert ecology . . .*"

"Mayfield!" Mirla gasped. "Van—you knew!"

"Yes." Vanderguerre's voice was suddenly flat. "In the absence of matter, space doesn't exist. Time is a function of space; it's the medium in which events happen. With no space, there can be no movement—and no time. All times become the same. I can be there—or here . . ."

"Van!" Mirla clung to his arm. "I'm frightened! What does it mean?"

"I've got to go back."

"Go . . . back?"

"Don't you see, Mirla? I can't desert my ship, my copilot—abandon the program I gave my life to. I can't let them chalk up the MTE as failure—a flop that killed two men! It would kill the last feeble spark that's keeping the program going!"

"I don't understand, Van. How can you—go back— to a dream?"

"I don't know, Mirla. But I've got to. Got to try." He disengaged his arm, looked down into her face.

"Forgive me, Mirla. A miracle happened here. Maybe . . ." Still looking into her face, he closed his eyes, picturing the command cell aboard the MTE, remembering the pressure of the seat harness across his body, the vertigo of weightlessness, the smell of the cramped quarters, the pain . . .

Twelve

. . . the pain thrust at him like a splintered lance. He opened his eyes, saw the empty chair, the blank screens.

"Teal," he whispered. "Where are you, Teal . . . ?"

Thirteen

Teal looked up. An old man was pushing through the crowd toward the table.

"Come with me, Teal," the old man said.

"Go to hell!" Teal snarled. "Get away from me, I don't know you and I don't want to know you!"

"Come with me, Teal—"

Teal leaped to his feet, caught up the wine bottle, smashed it down over the old man's head. He went down; the crowd drew back; a woman screamed. Teal stared down at the body . . .

. . . He was at the wheel of a car, a low-slung, hard sprung powerhouse that leaped ahead under his foot, faster, faster. The road unreeled before him, threading its way along the flank of a mountain. Ahead, tendrils of mist obscured the way. Suddenly, there was a man there, in the road, holding up his hand. Teal caught a glimpse of a stern, lined face, grey hair—

The impact threw the man fifty feet into the air. Teal saw the body plummet down among the treetops on the slope below the road in the same instant that the veering car plunged through the guardrail . . .

. . . the music from the ballroom was faint, here on deck. Teal leaned against the rail, watching the lights of Lisboa sliding away across the mirrored water.

"It's beautiful, Les," the slim, summer-gowned woman beside him said. "I'm glad I came . . ."

An old man came toward Teal, walking silently along the deck.

"Come with me, Teal," he said. "You've got to come back."

"No!" Teal recoiled. "Stay away, damn you! I'll never come back!"

"You've got to, Teal," the grim old man said. "You can't forget."

"Vanderguerre," Teal whispered hoarsely. "I left you there—in the module—sick, maybe dying. Alone."

"We've got to take her back, Teal. You and I are the only ones who know. We can't let it all go, Teal. We owe the program that much."

"To hell with the program," Teal snarled. "But you. I forgot about you, Jake. I swear I forgot."

"Let's go back now, Les."

Teal licked his lips. He looked at the slim girl, standing, her knuckles pressed against her face, staring at him. His eyes went back to Vanderguerre.

"I'm coming of my own free will, Jake," he said. "I ran—but I came back. Tell them that."

Fourteen

"Not . . . much time . . ." Vanderguerre whispered as he lay slack in the chair. "Enough . . . for one more . . . try. Out here . . . the MTE can't do it . . . alone. We . . . have to help."

Teal nodded. "I know. I couldn't put it in words, but I know."

"Solar orbit," Vanderguerre whispered. "One microsecond after jump."

"Jake—it just hit me! The jump will kill you!"

"Prepare for jump," Vanderguerre's voice was barely audible. "Jump!"

Their hands went out; levers slammed home. Mighty forces gripped the Universe, twisted it inside out.

Fifteen

". . . *that the module is now in primary position, and in G condition,*" the faint voice of Colonel Sudston crackled from the screen.

Teal looked across at Vanderguerre. The body lay at peace, the features smiling faintly.

Teal depressed the XMIT button. "MTE to Mission Control," he said. "Jump completed. And I have the tragic honor to report the death of Lieutenant Colonel Jacob Vanderguerre in the line of duty . . ."

Sixteen

. . . He knew, before he turned, that she would be standing there, smiling as he had remembered her, down through the years.

"Van—is anything wrong?" Mirla asked.

"Nothing," Vanderguerre said. "Nothing in this Universe."

MESSAGE TO AN ALIEN

I

Dalton tossed the scorched, plastic encased diagram on the Territorial Governor's wide, not recently polished desk. The man seated there prodded the document with a stylus as if to see if there were any life left in it. He was a plump little man with a wide, brown, soft-leather face finely subdivided by a maze of hairline wrinkles.

"Well, what's this supposed to be?" He had a brisk, no-nonsense voice, a voice that said it had places to go and things to do. He pushed out his lips and blinked up at the tall man leaning on his desk. Dalton swung a chair around and sat down.

"I closed up shop early today, Governor," he said, "and took a little run out past Dropoff and the Washboard. Just taking the air, not headed anywhere. About fifty miles west I picked up a radac pulse, a high one, coming in fast from off-planet."

The Governor frowned. "There's been no off-world traffic cleared into the port since the Three-Planet shuttle last Wednesday, Dalton. You must have been mistaken. You—"

"This one didn't bother with a clearance. He was headed for the desert, well away from any of the settlements."

"How do you know?"

"I tracked him. He saw me and tried some evasive maneuvers, too close to the ground. He hit pretty hard."

"Good God, man! How many people were aboard? Were they killed?"

"No people were killed, Governor."

"I understood you to say—"

"Just the pilot," Dalton went on. "It was a Hukk scout-boat."

Several expressions hovered over the Governor's mobile face; he picked amused disbelief.

"I see: you've been drinking. Or possibly this is your idea of hearty frontier humor."

"I took that off him." Dalton nodded at the plastic covered paper on which a looping pattern of pale blue lines was drawn. "It's a chart of the Island. Being amphibious, the Hukk don't place quite the same importance on the interface between land and water as we do; they trace the contour lines right down past the shore line, map sea bottoms and all. Still, you can pick out the outline easily enough."

"So?"

"The spot marked with the pink circle was what he was interested in. He crumped in about ten miles short of it."

"What the devil would a Hukk be looking for out

there?" the Governor said in a voice from which all the snap had drained.

"He was making a last-minute confirmation check on a landing site."

"A landing site—for what?"

"Maybe I should have said beachhead."

"What kind of nonsense is this, Dalton? A *beachhead*?"

"Nothing elaborate. Just a small Commando-type operation, about a hundred troops, light armor, hand weapons, limited objectives—"

"Dalton, what is this?" the official exploded. "It's only been seven years since we beat the Hukk into the ground! They know better than to start anything now!"

Dalton turned the chart over. There were complex characters scrawled in columns across it.

"What am I supposed to make of this—this Chinese laundry list?" the Governor snapped.

"It's a brief of a Hukk Order of Battle. Handwritten notes, probably jotted down by the pilot, against regulations."

"Are you suggesting the Hukk are planning an invasion?"

"The advance party is due in about nine hours," Dalton said. "The main force—about five thousand troops, heavy equipment—is standing by off-planet, waiting to see how it goes."

"This is fantastic! Invasions don't happen like this! Just . . . just out of a clear sky!"

"You expect them to wait for a formal invitation?"

"How—how do you pretend to know all this?"

"It's all there. The scout was a fairly high-ranking intelligence officer. He may even have planned the operation."

The Governor gave an indignant grunt, then pursed

his lips, pushing his brows together. "See here, if this fellow you intercepted doesn't report back—"

"His report went out right on schedule."

"You said he was killed!"

"I used his comm gear to send the prearranged signal. Just a minimike pulse on the Hukk LOS freke."

"You warned them off?"

Dalton shook his head. "I gave them the all-clear. They're on the way here now, full gate and warheads primed."

The Governor grabbed up his stylus and threw it at the desk. It bounced high and clattered across the floor.

"Get out of here, Dalton! You've had your fun! I could have you thrown into prison for this! If you imagine I have nothing better to do than listen to the psychotic imaginings of a broken-down social misfit—"

"If you'd like to send someone out to check," Dalton cut in, "they'll find the Hukk scout-boat right where I left it."

The Governor sat with his mouth open, eyes glued to Dalton.

"You're out of your mind. Even if you did find a wrecked boat—and I'm not conceding you did—how would *you* know how to make sense of their pothooks?"

"I learned quite a bit about the Hukk at the Command and Staff school."

"At the Com—" the Governor barked a laugh. "Oh, certainly, the Admiralty opens up the Utter Top Secret C&S school to tourists on alternate Thursdays. You took two weeks off from your junk business to drop over and absorb what it takes a trained expert two years to learn."

"Three years," Dalton said. "And that was before I was in the junk business."

The Governor looked Dalton up and down with sudden uncertainty. "Are you hinting that you're a . . . a retired admiral, or something of the sort?"

"Not exactly an admiral," Dalton said. "And not exactly retired."

"Eh?"

"I was invited to resign—during the Hukk treaty debates."

The Governor looked blank, then startled.

"You're not . . . *that* Dalton?"

"If I am—you'll concede I might know the Hukk hand-script?"

The Governor rammed himself bolt upright.

"Why, I have a good mind to—" he broke off. "Dalton, as soon as word gets around who you are, you're finished here! There's not a man on Grassroots who'd do business with a convicted traitor!"

"The charge was insubordination, Governor."

"I remember the scandal well enough! You fought the treaty, went around making speeches undermining public confidence in the Admiralty that had just saved their necks from a Hukk takeover! Oh, I remember you, all right! Hard-line Dalton! Going to grind the beaten foe down under the booted heel! One of those ex-soldier-turned-rabble-rousers!"

"Which leaves us with the matter of a Hukk force nine hours out of Grassroots."

"Bah, I . . ." The Governor paused, twisting in his chair. "My God, man, are you sure of this?" He muttered the words from the corner of his mouth, as if trying to avoid hearing them.

Dalton nodded.

"All right," the Governor said, reaching for the screen. "Subject to a check, of course, I'll accept your story. I'll notify CDT HQ at Croanie. If this is what you say it is, it's a gross breach of the treaty—"

"What can Croanie do? The official Love Thine Enemy line ties their hands. A public acknowledgment of a treaty violation by the Hukk would discredit the whole Softline party—including some of the top Admiralty brass and half the major candidates in the upcoming elections. They won't move—even if they had anything to move with, and could get it here in time."

"What are you getting at?"

"It's up to us to stop them, Governor."

"Us—stop an armed force of trained soldiers? That's Admiralty business, Dalton!"

"Maybe—but it's our planet. We have guns and men who know how to use them."

"There are other methods than armed force for handling such matters, Dalton! A few words in the right quarter—"

"The Hukk deal in actions. Seven years ago they tried and missed. Now they're moving a new pawn out onto the board. That makes it our move."

"Well—suppose they do land a small party in the desert, perhaps they're carrying out some sort of scientific mission, perhaps they don't even realize the world is occupied. After all, there are less than half a million colonists here . . ."

Dalton was smiling a little. "Do you believe that, Governor?"

"No, damn it! But it *could* be that way!"

"You're playing with words, Marston. The Hukk aren't wasting time talking."

"And your idea is . . . is to confront them—"

"Confront, Hell," Dalton growled. "I want a hundred militiamen who know how to handle a gun: the blast rifles locked up in the local armory will do. We'll pick our spots and be waiting for them when they land."

"You mean—ambush them?"

"You could call it that," Dalton said indifferently.

"Well . . ." The Governor looked grave. "I could point out to the council that in view of the nature of this provocative and illegal act on the part of—"

"Sure." Dalton cut off the speech. "I'll supply transport from my yard, there's an old ore tug that will do the job. You can make it legal later. Right now I need an authorization to inspect the armory."

"Well . . ." Frowning, the Governor spoke a few words into the dictypen, snatched the slip of paper as it popped from the slot, signed it with a slash of the stylus.

"Have the men alerted to report to the arms depot at twenty-two hundred hours," Dalton said as he tucked the chit away. "In field uniform, ready to move out."

"Don't start getting too big for your breeches yet, Dalton!" the Governor barked. "None of this is official, you're still just the local junk man as far as I'm concerned."

"While you're at it, you'd better sign a commission for me as a lieutenant of militia, Governor. We may have a guardhouse lawyer in the bunch."

"Rather a comedown for a former commodore, isn't it?" Marston said with a slight lift of the lip. "I think we'll skip that. You'd better just sit tight until the council acts."

"Twenty-two hundred, Governor," Dalton said. "That's cutting it fine. And tell them to eat a good dinner. It may be a long wait for breakfast."

II

The Federation Post Office was a blank gray five story front of local granite, the biggest and ugliest building in the territorial capital. Dalton went in along a well-lit corridor lined with half glass doors, went through the one lettered *Terran Space Arm*, and below, in smaller letters, *GSgt Brunt—Recruiting Officer*. Behind the immaculate counter decorated with colorful posters of clear-eyed young models in smart uniforms, a thick-necked man of medium height and age, with a tanned face and close-cropped sandy hair looked up from the bare desk with an expression of cheerful determination that underwent an invisible change to wary alertness as his eyes flicked over his caller.

"Good morning, Sergeant," Dalton said. "I understand you hold the keys to the weapons storage shack north of town."

Brunt thought that over, nodded once. His khakis were starched and creased to a knife-edge. A Combat Crew badge glinted red and gold over his left shirt pocket.

Dalton handed over the slip of paper the Governor had signed. Brunt read it, frowned faintly, read it again, folded it and tapped it on the desk.

"What's it all about, Dalton?" He had a rough-edged voice.

"For now that has to be between the Governor and me, Brunt."

Brunt snapped a finger at the note. "I'd like to oblige the Governor," he said. "But the weapons storage facility is a security area. No civilians allowed in, Dalton." He tossed the note across the desk.

Dalton nodded. "I should have thought of that," he said. "Excuse the interruption."

"Just a minute," Brunt said sharply as Dalton turned away. "If you'd like to tell me what's behind this . . ."

"Then you might stretch a regulation, eh? No thanks, Sergeant. I couldn't ask you to do that."

As Dalton left, Brunt was reaching for his desk screen.

III

Dalton lived a mile from town in a small pre-fab at the side of a twenty-acre tract covered with surplus military equipment, used mining rigs, salvaged transport units from crawlers to pogos. He parked his car behind the house and walked back between the looming hulks of gutted lighters, stripped shuttle craft ten years obsolete, wrecked private haulers, to a big, use-scarred cargo carrier. He started it up, maneuvered it around to the service ramp at the back, spent ten minutes checking it over. In the house, he ate a hasty meal, packed more food in a carton, changed clothes. He strapped on a well-worn service pistol, pulled on a deck jacket. He cranked up the cargo hauler, steered it out to the highway. It was a ten minute drive past the two-factory heavy industry belt, past scattered truck-gardens, on another three miles into the pink chalk, ravine-sliced countryside. The weapons depot was a ribbed-metal Quonset perched on a rise of ground to the left of the road. Dalton turned off, pulled to a stop and waited for the dust to settle before stepping down from the high cab.

There was a heavy combination lock on the front door. It took Dalton ten minutes with a heavy-duty cutter to open it. Inside the long, narrow building, he switched on an unshielded overhead light. There was a patina of dust over the weapons racked in lock-frames along the walls.

Another three minutes with the cutter had the lock-bars off the racks. The weapons were 2mm Norges, wartime issue, in fair shape. The charge indicators registered *nil*.

There was a charging unit against the end wall, minus the energy coil. Dalton went out to the big vehicle, opened the access hatch, lifted out the heavy power unit, lugged it inside, used cables to jump it to the charger.

It took him an hour and thirty-eight minutes to put a full charge on each of one hundred and two weapons. It was twenty-one thirty when he put through a call on the vehicle's talker to the Office of the Governor. The answering circuit informed him that the office was closed. He tried the Gubernatorial residence, was advised that the Governor was away on official business. As he switched off, a small blue-painted copter with an Admiralty eagle and the letters FRS on the side settled in beside him. The hatch popped open and Brunt emerged, crisp in his khakis. He stood, fists on hips, looking up at the hauler's cab.

"All right, Dalton," he called. "Game's over. You can haul that clanker back to the yard. Nobody's coming—and you're not going anywhere."

"I take it that's a message from his Excellency the Governor?" Dalton said.

Brunt's eye strayed past the big vehicle to the shed door, marred by a gaping hole where the lock had been.

"What the—" Brunt's hand went to his hip, came up gripping a palm-gun.

"Drop it," Dalton said.

Brunt froze. "Dalton, you're already in plenty of trouble—"

"The gun, Brunt."

Brunt tossed the small gun to the ground. Dalton climbed down, his pistol in his hand.

"The Council said no, eh?"

"What did you expect, you damned fool? You want to start a war?"

"No—I want to finish one." Dalton jerked his head. "Inside." Brunt preceded him into the hut, at Dalton's direction gathered up half a dozen weapons, touching only the short, thick barrels. He carried them out and stowed them in the rear of the hauler.

Dalton ordered Brunt into the cab, climbed up beside him. As he did, Brunt aimed a punch at his head; Dalton blocked it and caught his wrist.

"I've got thirty pounds and the reach on you, Sergeant," he said. "Just sit quietly. Under the circumstances I'm glad you happened along." He punched the door-lock key, started up, lifted onto the air-cushion and headed west into the desert.

IV

Dusk was trailing purple veils across the sky when Dalton pulled the carrier in under a wind-carved wing of violet chalk at the base of a jagged rock-wall and cut power. Brunt grumbled but complied when Dalton ordered him out of his seat.

"You've got a little scramble ahead, Sergeant." Dalton glanced up the craggy slope looming above.

"You could have picked an easier way to go off your rails," the recruiter said. "Suppose I say I won't go?"

Dalton smiled faintly, doubled his right fist and rotated it against his left palm. Brunt spat.

"If I hadn't been two years in a lousy desk job, I'd take you, Dalton, reach or no reach."

"Pick up the guns, Brunt."

It took Dalton most of an hour to place the five extra blast rifles in widely-spaced positions around the crater's half mile rim, propping them firmly, aimed at the center of the rock-strewn natural arena below. Brunt laughed at him.

"The old Fort Zinderneuf game, eh? But you don't have any corpses to man the ramparts."

"Over there, Brunt—where I can keep an eye on you." Dalton settled himself behind a shielding growth of salt weed, sighting along the barrel of the blast rifle. Brunt watched with a sour smile.

"You really hate these fellows, don't you, Dalton? You were out to get them with the treaty, and failed, and now you're going to even it all up, single-handed."

"Not quite single-handed. There are two of us."

"You can kidnap me at gun-point, Dalton, and you can bring me out here. But you can't make me fight."

"That's right."

Brunt made a disgusted sound. "You crazy fool! You'll get us both killed!"

"I'm glad you concede the possibility that this isn't just a party of picnickers we're here to meet."

"What do you expect, if you open fire on them?"

"I expect them to shoot back."

"Can you blame them?" Brunt retorted.

Dalton shook his head. "That doesn't mean I have to let them get away with it."

"You know, Dalton, at the time of your court-martial, I wondered about a few things. Maybe I even had a few doubts about the treaty myself. But this . . ." He waved a hand that took in the black desert, the luminous horizon, the sky. "This confirms everything they threw at you. You're a paranoiac—"

"But I can still read Hukk cursive," Dalton said. He pointed overhead. A flickering point of pink light was barely visible against the violet sky.

"I think you know a Hukk drive when you see one," Dalton said. "Now let's watch and see whether it's stuffed eggs or blast cannon they brought along."

V

"It doesn't make sense," Brunt growled. "We've shown them we can whip them in war, we gave them generous peace terms, let them keep their space capability almost intact, even offered them economic aid—"

"While we scrapped the fighting ships that we didn't build until ten years of Hukk raids forced us to."

"I know the Hardline, Dalton. OK, you told 'em so. Maybe there was something in it. But what good is this caper supposed to do? You want to be a martyr, is that it? And I'm the witness . . ."

"Not quite. The Hukk picked this spot because it's well-shielded from casual observation, close enough to Grassport and Bedrock to launch a quick strike, but not so close as to be stumbled over. That's sound, as far as it goes, but as a defensive position, it couldn't be worse. Of course, they didn't expect to have to defend it."

"Look, Dalton, OK, you were right, the Hukk are making an unauthorized landing on Grassroots' soil. Maybe they're even an armed party, as you said. Swell. I came out here with you, I've seen the ship, and I'll so testify. So why louse it up? We'll hand the file to the CDT and let them handle it! It's their baby, not yours! Not mine! We've got no call to get ourselves blasted to Kingdom Come playing One-Man Task Force!"

"You think Croanie will move in fast and slap 'em down?"

"Well—it might take some time—"

"Meanwhile the Hukk will have brought in their heavy stuff. They'll entrench half a mile under the surface and then start spreading out. By the time the

Admiralty gets into the act, they'll hold half the planet."

"All right! Is that fatal? We'll negotiate, arrange for the release of Terry nationals, the return of Terry property—"

"Compromise, in other words."

"All right, you give a little, you get a little!"

"And the next time?"

"What next time?"

"The Hukk will take half of Grassroots with no more expense than a little time at a conference table. That will look pretty good to them. A lot better than an all-fronts war. Why gulp, when you can nibble?"

"If they keep pushing, we'd slap them down, you know that."

"Sure we will—in time. Why not do it now?"

"Don't talk like a damned fool, Dalton! What can one man do?"

The Hukk ship was visibly lower now, drifting down silently on the stuttering column of light that was its lift-beam. It was dull black, bottle-shaped, with a long ogee curve to the truncated prow.

"If I had any heavy stuff up here, I'd go for her landing jacks," Dalton said. "But a 2mm Norge doesn't pack enough wallop to be sure of crippling her. And if I miss, they're warned: they can lift and cook us with an ion bath. So we'll wait until they're off-loaded, then pour it into the port. That's a weak spot on a Hukk ship. The iris is fragile, and any malfunction there means no seal, ergo no lift. Then we settle down to picking them off, officers first. With fast footwork, we should have them trimmed down to manageable size before they can organize a counterattack."

"What if I don't go along with this harebrained suicide scheme?"

"Then I'll have to wire your wrists and ankles."

"And if you're killed, where does that leave me?"

"Better make up your mind."

"Suppose I shoot at you instead of them?"

"In that case I'd have to kill you."

"You're pretty sure of yourself, Dalton." When Dalton didn't answer Brunt licked his lips and said: "I'll go this far: I'll help you burn the port, because if you foul it up it's my neck too. But as for shooting fish in a barrel—negative, Dalton."

"I'll settle for that."

"But afterward, once she's grounded—all bets are off."

"Tell that to the Hukk," Dalton said.

VI

"Lousy light for this work," Brunt said over his gunsights. Dalton, watching the Hukk ship settle in almost soundlessly in a roil of dust, didn't answer. Suddenly, floodlights flared around the base of the ship, bathing it in a reflected violet glow as, with a grating of rock, the Hukk vessel came to rest.

"Looks like a stage all set up for *Swan Lake*," Brunt muttered.

For five minutes, nothing happened. Then the circular exit valve dilated, spilling a widening shaft of green light out in a long path across the crater floor, casting black shadows behind the thickly scattered boulders. A tiny silhouette moved in the aperture, jumped down, a long-legged shadow matching its movement as it stepped aside. Another followed, and more, until seven Hukk stood outside the ship. They were slope-backed quadrupeds, hunched, neckless, long faced, knob jointed, pendulous bellied, leathery hided. A cluster of sheathed digital members lay on either side of the slab-like cheeks.

"Ugly bastards," Brunt said. "But that's got nothing to do with it, of course."

Now more troops were emerging, falling in in orderly rows. At a command faintly audible to Dalton as a squeaky bark, the first squad of ten Hukk about-faced and marched fifty feet from the ship, halted, opened ranks.

"Real parade ground types," Brunt said. "Kit inspection, no less."

"What's the matter, Sergeant? Annoyed they didn't hit the beach with all guns blazing?"

"Dalton, it's not too late to change your mind."

"I'm afraid it is—by about six years."

The disembarkation proceeded with promptness and dispatch. It was less than ten minutes before nine groups of ten Hukk had formed up, each with an officer in charge. At a sharp command, they wheeled smartly, executed a complicated maneuver which produced a single hollow square two Hukk deep around the baggage stacked at the center.

"All right, Brunt, off-loading complete," Dalton said. "Commence firing on the port."

The deep *chuff! chuff!* of the blast rifles echoed back from the far side of the crater as the two guns opened up. Brilliant flashes winked against the ship. The Hukk stood fast, with the exception of two of the officers who whirled and ran for the ship. Dalton switched sights momentarily, dropped the first one, then the second, returned to the primary target.

Now the square broke suddenly, but not in random fashion; each side peeled away as a unit, spread out, hit the dirt, each Hukk scrambling for shelter, while the four remaining officers took up their positions in the centers of their respective companies. In seconds, the dispersed troops were virtually invisible. Here and there the blink and *pop!* of return fire crackled from behind a boulder or a gully.

The port was glowing cherry red; the iris seemed to be jammed half closed. Dalton shifted targets, settled the cross hairs on an officer, fired, switched to another as the first fell. He killed three before the remaining Hukk brasshat scuttled for the protection of a ridge of rock. Without a pause, Dalton turned his fire on the soldiers scattered across the open ground.

"Stop, you bloodthirsty fool!" Brunt was yelling. "The ship's crippled, the officers are dead! The poor devils are helpless down there—"

There was a violet flash from near the ship, a deep-toned *warhoom!*, a crashing fall of rock twenty feet to their left. A second flash, a second report, more rock exploded, closer.

"Time to go," Dalton snapped and, without waiting to see Brunt's reaction, slid down the backslope, scrambled along it while rock chips burst from the ridge above him amid the smashing impacts of the Hukk power cannon. He surfaced two hundreds yards to the left of his original position, found the rifle emplacement. He aimed the weapon, depressed the trigger and set the hold-down for automatic rapid fire, paused long enough to fire half a dozen aimed bolts at the enemy, then moved on to the next gun to repeat the operation.

VII

Twenty minutes later Dalton, halfway around the crater from his original location, paused for a breather, listening to the steady crackle of the Hukk return fire, badly aimed but intense enough to encourage him to keep his head down. As well as he could judge, he had so far accounted for eight Hukk in addition to the five officers. Of the five blast rifles he had left firing on automatic, two had been knocked out or had exhausted their charges. The other three were still firing steadily, kicking pits in the bare rock below.

A few of the ship's ground-lights were still on; the rest had been shot out by the Hukk soldiery. By their glow Dalton picked an exposed target near the ship, brought his rifle to bear on him. He was about to pull the trigger when he saw Brunt sliding downslope thirty degrees around the perimeter of the ringwall from him, waving an improvised white flag.

VIII

The words from the Hukk PA system were loud and clear if somewhat echoic, and were delivered in excellent Terran, marred only by the characteristic Hukk difficulty with nasals:

"Terran warrior." The deep, booming voice rolled across the crater. " . . . orrior, rier. Hwe hno hnow that you are alone. You have fought hwell. Hnow you must surrender or be destroyed."

The lone Hukk officer stood in an exposed position near the center of the semicircular dispersement of soldiers, holding the end of a rope which was attached to Brunt's neck.

"Unless you show yourself at once," the amplified voice boomed out, "you hwill be hunted out and killed."

The Hukk officer turned to Brunt. A moment later Brunt's hoarse voice echoed across the crater:

"For God's sake, Dalton, they're giving you a chance! Throw down your gun and surrender!"

Sweat trickled down across Dalton's face. He wiped it away, cupped his hands beside his mouth and shouted in the Hukk language:

"Release the prisoner first."

There was a pause. "You offer an exchange, himself for yourself?"

"That's right."

Another pause. "Very well, I accept," the Hukk called. "Come forward now. I assure you safe-conduct."

Dalton lifted his pistol from its holster, tucked it inside his belt, under the jacket. He studied the ground below, then worked his way fifty feet to the right before he stood, the blast gun in his hands, and started down the slope along the route he had selected, amid a rattle of dislodged rock fragments.

"Throw down your weapon!" the PA ordered as he reached the crater floor. Dalton hesitated, then tossed the gun aside. Empty-handed, he advanced among the boulders toward the waiting Hukk. The captain— Dalton was close enough to see his rank badges now— had pulled Brunt in front of him. The latter, aware of his role as a human shield, looked pale and damp. His mouth twitched as though there were things it wanted to say, but was having trouble finding words equal to the occasion.

When Dalton was twenty feet from the officer, passing between two six-foot-high splinters of upended rock, he halted abruptly. At once, the captain barked an order. There was a flicker of motion to Dalton's left. He darted a hand under his jacket, came out with the pistol, fired, and was facing the officer again as a yapping wail came from the target.

"Tell your troops to down guns and pull back," Dalton said crisply.

"You call on *me* to surrender?" The officer was carefully keeping his members in Brunt's shadow.

"You've been had, Captain. Only three of your soldiers can bear on me here—and they have to expose themselves to fire. My reaction time is somewhat quicker than theirs; you see the result."

"You bluff—"

"The gun in my hand will penetrate two inches of flint steel," Dalton said. "The man in front of you is a lot softer than armor."

"You would kill the man for whose freedom you offered your life?"

"What do you think?"

"My men will surely kill you!"

"Probably. But you won't be here to transmit the all-clear to the boys standing by off-planet."

"Then what do you hope to gain, Man?"

"Dalton's the name, Captain."

"That name is known to me. I am Ch'oova. I was with the Grand Armada at Van Doom's world."

"The Grand Armada fought well—but not quite well enough."

"True, Commodore. Perhaps our strategy has been at fault." The captain raised his head, barked an order. Hukk soldiers began rising from concealment, gun muzzles pointing at the ground; they cantered away toward the ship by twos and threes, their small hooves raising cottony puffs of dust.

When they were alone, Captain Ch'oova tossed the rope aside.

"I think," he said, with a small, formal curtsey, "that we had best negotiate."

IX

"That fellow Ch'oova told me something funny," Brunt said as the cargo carrier plowed toward the dawn. "Seven years ago, at Van Doom's world, you were left in command of the Fleet after Admiral Hayle was hit. You were the one who fought the Grand Armada to a standstill."

"I took over from Hayle, yes."

"And won the battle. Funny, that part didn't get in the papers. But not so funny, maybe, at that. According to Ch'oova, after the fighting was over, you refused a direct Admiralty order."

"Garbled transmission," Dalton said.

"Tempers run high in wartime," Brunt said. "The Hukk had made a lot of enemies before we finally faced up to going to war. The High Command wanted a permanent solution. They gave you secret orders to accept the Hukk surrender, and then blow them out of space. You said no."

"Not really; I just didn't get around to carrying out the order."

"And in a few days, cooler heads prevailed. But not before you were relieved and posted to the boondocks, and your part in the victory covered up."

"Just a routine transfer," Dalton said.

"And then, by God, you turn around—you, the white-haired boy who'd saved the brass from making a blunder that would have ruined them when it got known—and went after the treaty hammer and tongs, to toughen it up! First you save the Hukks' necks— and then you break yourself trying to tighten the screws on them!"

Dalton shook his head. "Nope; I just didn't want to mislead them."

"You wanted their Armada broken up, occupation of their principal worlds, arms limitations with inspections—"

"Brunt, this night's work cost the lives of fourteen Hukk soldiers, most of them probably ordinary citizens who were drafted and sent out here all full of patriotic fervor. That was a dirty trick."

"What's that got to do—"

"We beat them once. Then we picked 'em up, dusted 'em off, and gave them back their boys. That wasn't fair to a straightforward bunch of opportunists like the Hukk. It was an open invitation to blunder again. And unless they were slapped down quick, they'd keep on blundering in deeper—until they goaded us into building another fleet. And this time, there might not be enough pieces left to pick up."

Brunt sat staring thoughtfully out at the paling sky ahead; he laughed shortly. "When you went steaming out there with fire in your eye, I thought you were out for revenge on the Hukk for losing you your fat career. But you were just delivering a message."

"In simple terms that they could understand," Dalton said.

"You're a strange man, Commodore. For the second time, single-handed, you've stopped a war. And because you agreed with Ch'oova to keep the whole thing confidential, no one will ever know. Result: You'll be a laughingstock for your false alarm. And with your identity known, you're washed up in the junk business. Hell, Marston will have the police waiting to pick you up for everything from arms theft to spitting on the sidewalk! And you can't say a word in your own defense."

"It'll blow over."

"I could whisper a word in Marston's ear—"

"No you won't, Brunt. And if you do, I'll call you

a liar. I gave Ch'oova my word; if this caper became public knowledge, it would kick the Hukk out of every Terran market they've built up in the past six years."

"Looks like you've boxed yourself into a corner, Commodore," Brunt said softly.

"That's twice you've called me Commodore—Major."

Brunt made a surprised sound. Dalton gave him a one-sided smile.

"I can spot a hotshot Intelligence type at half a mile. I used to wonder why they posted you out here."

"To keep an eye on you, Commodore, what else?"

"Me?"

"A man like you is an enigma. You had the brass worried. You didn't hew to any party line. But I think you've gotten the message across now—and not just to the Hukk."

Dalton grunted.

"So I think I can assure you that you won't need to look for a new place to start up your junk yard. I think the Navy needs you. It'll take some string pulling, but it can be swung. Maybe not as a commodore—not for a while—but at least you'll have a deck under your feet. How does it sound?"

"I'll think about it," Dalton said.

PLANET RUN

(with Gordon R. Dickson)

Chapter One

The sun was warm on his face. Through his closed
eyelids, it gleamed a hot orange—like a sunrise fog on
a world called Flamme, long ago. And Dulcia, the first
Dulcia, came toward him, smiling through the wreaths
of mist . . .

Something tickled his cheek; he brushed at it.
Damned flowerflies! He'd have to start up the repellor
field; didn't like the damned thing. Made a man's bones
itch, like a couple of hours under high R, de-leading
tube linings . . . The glory of his memory dimmed. A
grim little note of uneasiness struck discordantly
through the dream. There had been something he had
been trying to put out of his mind, lately . . .

The tickle came again, and the dream vanished. His eyes flew open and he squinted up at a slim, blond, long-legged young girl in a brief pink sunsuit, leaning over his garden chair with a long, feathery grass stem in her hand.

"Dammit, Dulcie, you're getting too old to go around like that," he growled.

"No, I'm not, Grandpa! I'm just getting old enough. You should have seen Senator Bartholomew's face when I went to the door—"

"Is that fool back again?" Captain Henry closed his eyes. But the feeling of uneasiness was stronger, suddenly. Fat Bartholomew—*Senator* Bartholomew now—was not quite a fool. Or at least he had not been a fool forty years ago as a young man. Henry, already aging at that time, had almost liked him then—sometimes.

Now of course he had become a "Senator"—and taken up the prissy modern manners of movement and speech that went with the political image. Still . . . the uneasiness moved stronger than ever in Henry.

"Send him on his way, girl," Henry said. "You know better than to interrupt my nap—"

"He says it's awfully important, Grandpa."

"Important to him, not me! I've already told him what I think of his politics, his business methods, his brains, and his taste in liquor . . ."

There was a sound of affected throat-clearing. Henry looked around. A tall, broad-bellied man with a now-flaccid face, but with the same angry black eyebrows Henry remembered from forty years ago, had come up behind the girl.

"I thought I'd better make my presence known, Captain," the Senator said.

"You wouldn't have heard anything I haven't told you to your face, Bartholomew," Henry snapped. "What's it this time? Not the same old proposition?"

Bartholomew grunted, took the chair Dulcie offered him. For a moment the girl moved between Henry and the sun—and for a second he was back in the dream of her great-grandmother and the lambent mists of Flamme. Then she moved out of the light and he was back in the present of hard reality—and Senator Bartholomew.

Henry looked at the middle-aged man with harsh distaste. Bartholomew was perspiring in a fashionable narrow-shouldered jacket of shiny green material with short sleeves showing elaborate cuffs with large, jeweled links. A three-inch campaign button lettered ELECT THE STATISTICAL AVERAGE was pinned prominently to his breast pocket. His lower lip was thrust out aggressively, frowning at the old man.

"I was hoping you'd reconsidered, Captain Henry. Since you didn't answer my call—"

"If I'd had anything new to say I'd have managed to dodder to the phone. I'm not bedridden—yet!"

Bartholomew pulled off his maroon beret, fanned at himself with it. "This is a matter of planetary importance, Captain! Corazon is a promising world. Surely you're not going to allow personal considerations—"

"Like hell I'm not!" Henry growled. "I've put in my time on the Frontier Worlds, one hundred and fifteen years of it! I've had ten good years of retirement—up until you started pestering me . . ."

"Pestering is hardly the word, Captain Henry! I'm offering you a magnificent opportunity! You'll have the finest of equipment—"

"I prefer the sunshine—I know, you've put a roof over your town to keep the fresh air out, but I like it—"

"All I'm asking is that you take the Rejuve Treatment just once more—at *my* expense—"

Henry looked across at the plump citizen.

"Your expense, eh? Hah! I've had the treatment

three times. I'm a hundred and thirty-five years old—
and I feel every month of it. You know what a fourth
Rejuve would do to me."

"But I've seen your last medical report. You're in
excellent condition, for your age! The treatment
wouldn't make you an adolescent again—but it would
restore you to full vigor . . ."

"I'd look young—for a few months. I'd fade like
yesterday's gardenia after the first year, and I'd be senile
in three. After that, it wouldn't matter whether I made
the fourth year or not." He leaned back and closed his
eyes. "That's it, Senator. You'll have to find another
errand boy."

"You're not considering this matter in depth, Captain! A new world to be opened for homesteading—
the first in sixty years! This errand, as you call it, would
require only a few months of your time, after which
you'd not only have the satisfaction of having made a
valuable contribution to the development of the frontier, but you'd bank a tidy fortune as well!"

Henry opened one eye. "Why not send that Statistical Average candidate of yours? If he's good enough
to be a Planetary Delegate to the council, he ought
to be able to handle a little assignment like this."

"You're speaking frivolously of grave matters. Our
candidate, as representative of the median of Aldoradon
society, is an eminently suitable choice, embodying the
highest concepts of democratic government."

"You can skip the campaign speech. I don't vote the
Average Man ticket . . ."

Bartholomew's veined nose darkened. He drew in a
breath through flared nostrils. "As to the venture we're
discussing," he said harshly, "your . . . ah . . . specialized
knowledge will outweigh other considerations." Bartholomew's shifting gaze fixed meaningfully on Henry.

Henry looked at him through narrowed eyes; for a

second he caught sight of his own face reflected in a polished metal chair-back. It was like a battered carving in ancient oak. "Just what specialized knowledge do you have in mind?"

Bartholomew twisted his mouth in a smile-like grimace, spread his hands. "Why, Captain, you're an old-timer, you know the space lanes, the curious mores of distant worlds. You could face up to the ruffians one would encounter out on Corazon, brazen it out, and take what you wanted. And I think you'd know what to go after," he added, eyeing the toe of his sandal.

"You do, eh?" Henry studied the other's face. "I've got twenty good years left to sniff the flowers; what would make me leave that to get my neck broken in a Run?"

"Are you interested in aluminum oxide, Captain?" Bartholomew asked casually.

The uneasiness was suddenly back—but not just uneasiness any longer. It was like an ice-cold cramp in his stomach.

"—In the form known as corundum," Bartholomew was adding.

"Just what're you getting at, Senator?" Henry said harshly.

It was Bartholomew's turn to sit silent. His glance went to the girl sunning herself by the poolside a few yards distant. Henry grunted softly.

"It's time for my lunch, Dulcie," he called. She looked up, glanced at Bartholomew's face, then rose and went off across the lawn.

"All right," said Henry, without inflection.

Bartholomew hitched his chair forward, got out a dope stick, and—as an afterthought—offered one to Henry. Henry waved it grimly aside.

"Ever since its discovery over a century ago, Corazon's been a closed world, Captain." The visitor puffed perfumed smoke past Henry. "Under close quarantine. But you were there once . . ."

"Sure. On a free-lance prospecting trip—before the Quarantine Service ever heard of the world. What about it?"

"Why . . ." Bartholomew's eyes fixed on the glowing tip of his dope stick, "just that your trip may or may not have been legal. You spent several months on the planet."

"So?"

"And you found something."

"You asking me or telling me?"

"Telling you, Captain," Bartholomew said flatly. "And I'll tell you something more. Corundum takes many forms. It makes an excellent commercial abrasive; it also appears in more attractive guises—known as ruby—emerald—sapphire, oriental topaz, amethyst, and others." Bartholomew's voice was a purr now. "There's an excellent market for natural gemstones, Captain; stones like the ones I saw your great-granddaughter wearing last month when my boy Larry took her to the graduation ball . . ."

He paused. Henry looked back at him expressionlessly, waiting. Bartholomew's voice held a rasping note now. "I know a great deal about your career, Captain—everything, in fact. I've made it my business to find out, these last few weeks." He puffed out smoke, enjoying the moment. Henry watched him, waiting.

"You've always lived modestly here—" Bartholomew waved a hand at the garden, the pool, the old fashioned glass-walled house—"But you were a wealthy man once. And 'once' is the word."

"Is it?" asked Henry, completely without inflection.

"That's right," said Bartholomew briskly. "You lived off your principal instead of your interest, Captain. Any businessman can tell you what a mistake that is. Now what you've got left is this property, barely enough income for an old man sitting in the sun, and the credit backed by the assessed valuation of those gemstones you were incautious enough to let the girl wear. I know to the penny what that assessed valuation is."

"What's this got to do with the price of wamba-pears?" growled Henry.

"Just—that those gemstones represent your great-granddaughter's inheritance," said Bartholomew.

"What's it to you? I won them free and clear."

"Did you?" said Bartholomew. "I agree you don't owe a cent—if you did I'd know about it. But *own* them—" His eyes narrowed in their folds of fat. "I happen to know you went back to Corazon at least twice—after the planet was placed under quarantine."

Henry did not move. He smiled a wintry smile.

"That was quite a while ago—if I did. Over a hundred years."

"There's no statute of limitations where possession of contraband is concerned. Your later Navy service won't affect it, either. And that last visit's essentially a matter of record. A hundred and four years ago, wasn't it, to be precise? And you got back just one week too late to be here when your wife died—"

Henry sat suddenly forward in his chair. His eyes locked with the Senator's.

"Never mind my wife, Bartholomew," he growled.

"What's the matter, Captain?" Bartholomew spread his white, slablike hands. "You couldn't have known she needed you. Or could you? Of course it was a pity, your getting back with the gemstones that would have paid for the operation that might have saved her—just one week too late. But there's no need to let your conscience bother you . . . though I suppose it's hard, having a great-granddaughter around who's the image of the wife you let die—"

Henry moved. It was a small move—simply a little
shifting forward of his weight onto the left elbow and
the right fist as they rested on the arms of his chair.
But Bartholomew shut up suddenly. His sagging face
had tightened.

"Easy, Captain . . ." he muttered.

"Never mind my wife," repeated Henry, tonelessly.

"Of course . . ." Bartholomew wet his lips. Henry sat
slowly back in his chair. Bartholomew breathed deeply
once more and his voice strengthened.

"It doesn't matter, anyway," he said, "—about your—
about anything that happened after you came back. It's
Corazon, and your illegal trip there I'm talking about.
You're still a hero, Captain, still the first and greatest
of the old star-frontiersmen. The Quarantine Service
wouldn't do anything to you, personally. But those
gemstones would be confiscated, if someone whispered
in their ears to run lattice comparison tests between
them and other, sample minerals from Corazon itself."

He stopped speaking, flicked his eyes at Henry.
Henry stared back; his upper lip twisted.

"And you'd do the whispering, is that it?" Henry
said. The other man did not answer, letting silence
speak for him. "I don't get it. You could hire an army
of hard cases, if you wanted to back somebody in the
Run on Corazon next month."

Bartholomew nodded, shortly.

"In spite of the fact that every slum in the Eastern arm has its quota of gun handlers, you want me—
a worn-out old space-hulk—because you think I know
something!"

"I know damned well you know something!" said
Bartholomew suddenly and viciously. "My God, man,
there's a fortune to be made! I'll supply everything you
need. With my financing your entry, you'd be able to
stake your claim successfully—and you'd legally own

those deposits of stones you found more than a hundred years ago!"

Henry laughed suddenly, a mirthless, barking laugh that made the other stare at him.

"I see," Henry said. "What kind of split did you have in mind?"

"In view of the risk—and the heavy initial expense—"

"*How much?*"

" . . . And under the circumstances of my knowledge of your past—90 percent for me, and a full 10 percent for yourself." Bartholomew smiled ingratiatingly, puffed at his dope stick.

Henry gripped the arms of his chair with gnarled hands, shoved himself to his feet.

"Get out!" he said.

Bartholomew's heavy jowls paled. He dropped the dope stick, scrambled hastily to his feet.

"You don't talk to me that way—" he began.

Henry took a step forward. His throat felt as if it was on fire, and there was a gathering haze, a blurring before his eyes. The pulse of his blood pounded like a tom-tom in his skull.

Bartholomew stumbled backward. Two . . . three steps, but then he stopped. The soft fat of his face hardened. He had been a tall man in his younger years—although even then he had lacked half a head of Henry's massive height and a full third of Henry's fighting weight.

"You'd kill me if you thought you needed to, wouldn't you, Captain?" he said thinly, his eyes narrowing in their cushions of fat. Close to him, Henry checked himself, fought down the rage that burned in him.

"Don't try me on that, Bartholomew," he said hoarsely.

"Oh, I believe you." The Senator laughed harshly. "But since there's just the two of us here, let me tell you something. I'm capable of killing, too, if it comes to that. —I'll go!" he added hastily, as Henry took another step forward. "But think it over," he went on, talking rapidly as he backed away. "I still know what I know about you, the gemstones, and Corazon; and the time for you to enter the Run is getting shorter every day. Think about that great-granddaughter of yours—and what it would be like for her to be just another penniless young girl, with no hope of what she's grown up to expect—except possibly a wealthy marriage—"

"Like your young whelp Larry, I suppose!" roared Henry, rolling forward.

Bartholomew turned and fled. For a few steps Henry pursued him; then he stopped, and breathing hard, let the other man go. He turned and stumped back toward the pool, stared down through the clear water at the multicolored grotto of the mineral spring that fed it.

"Gemstones," he muttered; and then—*"Dulcie!"*

. . . And not even he could have said for sure if it was the girl who had left them a few moments earlier, or his long-dead love, of whom he thought as he spoke.

"You should have seen the Senator, Uncle Amos!" Dulcia said. She poured coffee into Henry's cup, passed the decanter of brandy to the small, turkey-necked man who drained his glass, exhaled noisily, refilled it.

"Huh! Wish I'd been there!" He winked at the girl, tugged at one end of a stained white moustache. "The Senator's used to getting what he goes after. Guess it's the first time anybody's ever turned him down flat."

Captain Henry grunted, took an old-fashioned cigar from the heavy silver box on the table. The girl held a lighter to it. The odor of tobacco mingled with the scent of wood smoke from the fireplace.

"The man's a damned fool," he muttered uneasily. "Rubs me the wrong way; chatters like a haki bird in molting season—and says all the wrong things."

She filled her cup and sat down. "Why does Mr. Bartholomew want you to go to Corazon, Grandpa?"

The small man cackled. "'Cause he knows damn well he's the only man on Aldorado that can walk into that Corazon free-for-all and come out with the back of his head still on—to say nothing about grabbing off a nice chunk of real estate."

Henry blew out a cloud of smoke, leaned back in his chair, his long legs propped on a footstool carved from the wood of the Yanda tree and upholstered with the knobbed gray hide of a dire-beast. It was a relaxed pose, but the tension shouted in the narrowing of his eyes, the set of his shoulders.

"The frontier's finished," he said. "Corazon's its last dying gasp. It's a hard world—rock and ice and tundra. No fit place for a man to live."

"But like you said, it's the last chance for a man with a yen for a gamble."

"Sure—if it had been halfway habitable, it'd have been settled a long time ago—"

"I don't know—I've heard the Quarantine Service run into some funny stuff out there—that's why they set on it for a hundred years." The small man's dark, birdlike eyes were suddenly diamond sharp on Henry.

Henry met their stare, his own eyes as flat as a command.

"I remember," he said, "when there were fresh green worlds for the asking right here in the Sector. That's what's wrong with people today—all this Statistical Average horsefeathers. A man's got no new frontier to go out and fight for."

"Unless," said Amos, softly, "you want to count Corazon."

"There'll be plenty that'll be after it—but not any Average Man party Nancies . . ."

"There it is—a world for the taking." The small man put a log on the fire, resumed his seat, dusting his hands. "With the new Terraforming techniques, they'll transform her. Thirty million square miles of real estate: farms, mines, ports; land that'll have cities growing on it in a few years; open tundras where a man could run a million head of snow cattle; mountains and waterfalls, and rivers, and sea beaches—free to anybody that can grab and hold onto it. For a stake like that, every gambler, pirate, soldier of fortune, and con man in forty parsecs would sell his hope of a ringside seat in hell . . ."

"And Mr. Bartholomew wants Grandpa to go *there*?"

"Sure. I remember the first Run we was on together—out on Adobe, that was." Amos turned to the girl. "We staked our claim to our legal hundred square miles—a burned-out slab of desert tilted up on one side to where a Bolo couldn't climb it. I went into a nine-day crap game with it at Square-deal Mac's place on Petreac, and ran it up to half a continent . . ." he cackled softly. "Before I lost it all on a deck cut with Mac."

Dulcia's eyes shone. "That sounds like you. Was Grandpa ever on another Run?"

Amos nodded his bald, freckled head. "Yep—last one was right here on Aldorado. He was a little shrewder by then; grabbed off a nice piece of land backed up to a mountain range, with forests and minerals—and facing the sea, with a natural harbor that could handle any surface liner ever built."

"Why, Amos—that sounds like right here—Tivoli Harbor, and the Mall . . ."

He nodded. "That's right, girl."

She turned to her great-grandfather. "But—then you must have owned the whole town . . ."

Amos shook his head. "Nope. He was just a young fella then. It was just before his second Rejuve. There were a lot of homesteaders who lost out—left on the beach, with no money, no land, kids crying for home— all that kind of thing. He didn't want the land; to Henry, it was a game. He gave it to 'em. All he asked for was this little piece—and a house and a garden— whenever he got ready for it."

"You mean all those people—Senator Bartholomew, all of them—owe their whole old Mall, and everything, to you, Grandpa? And then they—" she broke off.

"It was mostly their great-grandpas, girl," Henry said. "These people don't owe me anything. I got what I wanted."

"And they're all working so hard to elect their stupid old Statistical Average as Delegate! Why don't they send you, Grandpa? You've done more for them than anybody!"

"Now, why would I want to be Delegate, Dulcie-girl? I just want to sit in the sun and rest my old bones . . ."

"You know," Dulcia said. Her eyes went to him and fell.

He glanced sideways at her. Her eyes were large and dark; how much she resembled her great-grandmother, now, sitting there in the firelight . . .

"You're thinking about the Aeterna treatment," he said. "Forget it—"

"Why should I forget it! You could be young again— and stay young for years and years—nobody knows how long! If they'd only had the treatment back when you were opening up the Frontier, you'd have gotten it anyway for Unusual Service to the Race—the way explorers and scientists get it now!"

"Well," said Henry, smiling, "I missed my chance then—"

"But you can still get it! All Planetary Delegates get the treatment. And you could get elected just by lifting your finger if you wanted. People around here remember—"

"I'm no politician, Dulcie. Don't want to be. And I don't want to live forever. I've had my life—more than enough. I've seen my friends go—all but Amos here—killed or dead of old age, or just drifted away. It's not the same universe any more I knew when I was young. It's the day of the Statistical Average—"

"Oh, stop it, Grandpa!"

"I mean it, girl. They want the man I was, not the old buzzard I am now."

"Old buzzard!" said Dulcia, fiercely. "You're still twice the man any of them is!"

"That's putting it mild, honey," Amos put in. "And in the old days he was the meanest, wildest, hardest-hitting young devil in the space service. Many's the time I tried to whip him myself. Never could though—he had too much reach on me."

"That was a long time ago," Captain Henry said. "We had our time, Amos—and we lived it to the hilt—with no regrets. Now we've got a chair by the fire. Let's leave it that way."

Amos poured again, tossed the drink back with a practiced gesture, sat staring into the fire.

"Then the war came along. Your great-grandpa'd just paid for the prettiest little fifty-ton fast-cargo cutter that ever outran a Customs Patrol; he signed it up for the duration. They made him a Reserve Battle Ensign; two years later he was a Battle Captain—Regular—and his boat was a burned-out wreck."

"Grandpa—you never told me you were in the war . . . !"

"Ask Amos to show you his medals some day. He forgot to mention that I was in the wreck when it was hit; he got me out."

"Oh, Grandpa—wouldn't it be exciting if you did— I mean if you took the Rejuve, and showed them all . . ."

He looked at the glowing end of the cigar. "You mean you want me to go along with Bartholomew's idea?"

"No—of course I don't! I want you to stay here— and live a long, long time. I just meant . . ."

"Oh, well; I was exaggerating a little. If I took another Rejuve, I'd still have maybe as much as five good years—" He broke off, glanced at the radium clock on the wall, a relic of Old Mars. "Say, it's getting late. What about that big dance you're going to with young Bartholomew?"

"I'm not going," she said shortly.

"Eh? Why this afternoon, it was all you could do to eat your lunch before you dashed down to the Mall to buy a dress . . ."

"I don't want to go."

"Now, wait a minute, honey. Just because old Bartholomew's Average Man party doesn't want me as a Delegate's no reason to miss your party—"

"It isn't that . . ."

"Hmm. How much of my talk with the old man did you 'overhear' today, girl?"

"I heard him say—you stole something! He ought to be ashamed of himself."

Amos cackled. "He called Henry a thief and got away with it? Say, I'd like to back the Senator in a crap game, with *his* luck . . ."

"So you think seeing the boy would be disloyal to the old man?" Henry shook his head, smiling at the girl. "Don't visit the sins of the old on their offspring.

You go put that fancy dress on and go on to the dance; have a good time—"

"That Bartholomew boy's not good enough for a gal like Dulcie, Cap'n," Amos cut in. "Always got his hair combed and not a scar on his knuckles—"

"Shut up, Amos. Larry's no worse than any other young fellow with a delicate upbringing—" Henry frowned. "And what other kind is there these days?"

"A ribbon counter boy—" jeered Amos, "and a girl like Dulcie? Why you ought to—"

"You go ahead, Dulcie-girl. Amos and I want to talk a while." Captain Henry paused to bite down on a fresh cigar and puff it alight. He blew out smoke, winked grimly at the girl. "Leave the fighting for the older generation; I think I can handle Bartholomew Senior."

The sound of Dulcie's Turbocad faded in the distance. Captain Henry looked into the fire, drawing on his cigar. Abruptly, he took the cigar out of his mouth, scowled at it, tossed it into the fire.

Amos looked sideways at him.

"What kind of bribe's the Senator offering, Henry?"

Henry snorted. "Ten percent of a jewel mine—that I've got hidden up my sleeve."

Amos whistled. "Who's he been talking to?"

"I've been wondering about that."

"So the Senator thinks you know something, hey?" Amos cackled again. "Say, now, that's an idea, Henry . . ."

"You're too damned old to be getting ideas, Amos. Fill your glass and prop your feet up in front of the fire—that's our speed."

"Is it, Henry? There might be something in what the Senator was peddling. These young squirts nowadays— they ain't got what it takes. Look at that boy of his—a tennis-playing, baby-faced greenhorn. He wouldn't last a week on a Run. But you and me, Henry . . ." Amos leaned forward, his eyes sharp in his gnome-like face. "We could walk in there and skim the gravy off Corazon like a barman cutting suds."

"How old are you, Amos?" Henry asked abruptly.

"Huh? I'm lesee, a hundred and fifty-two."

"How long since your last Rejuve?"

"Forty-five, forty-six years." He leaned forward, his old eyes bright.

"What do you say, Henry? We never were the kind to go to bed while the party was still on. This setting around counting down to a funeral—that's no fun. I want to go one more time, Henry! Sure I won't last— but I want to be hungry again, and kiss a girl again, and pick one more fight in one more bar—"

"Forget it, Amos. You're too old. The Rejuve would kill you."

"Forget it, huh? Too old—!" Amos came out of his chair like a jack-in-the-box. He tossed the cigar over his shoulder. "I ain't too old to have one more try—"

"Calm down, Amos. If guts were all you needed, you'd live forever. But it's a little more complicated than that. Rejuve won't work at your age. You can't change that."

"So you're just going to sit here and let a bunch of fuzz-cheeked Johnnies walk off with Corazon?"

"Talk sense, Amos. I don't need a piece of Corazon; I've got enough to last me."

"Yeah—but what about the girl? How's she going to be fixed?"

"Dulcie'll be all right. She's a smart girl—"

"Sure, she's smart—and purty. Purty enough to marry some lightweight like Master Bartholomew and spend the rest of her days hand-washing his silk socks while he's out campaigning for the Territorial Statistical Average. That what you want?"

"I was wondering what brought you over here today, Amos." Henry glanced across at him; their eyes caught and held level, and a near-forgotten current of danger seemed to wake the drowsy air of the garden.

"Cap'n, I get around." Amos's voice was different, suddenly, harder and more deliberate. "I pick up all kinds of conversation. I heard the Senator had a bug in his bonnet to talk you into Rejuve so he could hire you on for the run."

"So?" Henry's voice was equally flat and deliberate.

"So, Old Man Bartholomew's got some kind of a Nancy working for him—a private secretary. He likes to drink. I bought him a few, and he got to talking—"

"You wouldn't have put a few drops of something pink in his glass, would you, Amos?" The irony in Henry's voice was heavy.

"That ain't the point, Cap'n," the little man said grimly. "I told you—the Nancy talked."

"Whatever he said," Henry's voice marked the words like the slow beat of a hammer on a forge, "it doesn't change anything."

Their eyes met and locked again. Amos drew a deep breath. "Henry," he said, "what's on Corazon?"

Henry did not answer for a long moment. Then he picked up another cigar and savagely bit off the end of it.

"Go to hell!" he said.

"All right," answered the little man, still steely-voiced and undismayed, "I'm headed there anyway. Meanwhile I won't go away—and neither will whatever the Senator's holding over you, Cap'n. Now if it was just you, I'd say damn your worthless old hide and Bartholomew's welcome to it. But according to that Nancy, it's something to do with Dulcie—"

Henry jerked the cigar from his teeth and hurled it into the fire.

"That's a lot of good imported smoking you're making kindling out of tonight," said Amos. "All right, I won't say any more. Only as I remember, you used to be able to dicker and deal a bit. But I don't recall it ever doing you any good until you started to talk trade."

Henry glared across at him.

"Bartholomew's not invulnerable, you know," said Amos, mildly. "If he's got a hook on Dulcie, maybe I could cook up something about that lace-britches son of his—"

Henry sat up suddenly. Amos abruptly stopped talking, watching him with bright, old eyes.

"Corazon's a hell of a place, Amos," Henry said thoughtfully.

"Sure," said Amos, "all raw worlds are hell—but we could have ourselves some fun, you and me, taming her down a little . . ." For a moment the small man's eyes softened and became wistful. " . . . One last go-around before the Big Dark. Remember, Cap'n, how it feels to have a deck under your feet—going for broke against all the odds there are . . ."

"Damn your hide, Amos," Henry said softly. There was a new light in his eyes. He got to his feet, grunting a little as he straightened his back. "Maybe I've got things to say to old man Bartholomew at that!"

Amos jumped to his feet and laughed aloud, slapping Henry's shoulder.

"That's the idea, Cap'n! He can hum the tune—but we'll put the words to it!"

Henry scribbled a brief note to Dulcia, propped it on the table; then the two went out through the kitchen entrance to the garage of the antique-style villa. Captain Henry slid behind the wheel of a low-slung black Monojag, started up, gunned it out along the drive. It was a clear night with Hope, the bigger moon, riding high in the sky, and the pale disk of Dream just peeping above the tops of the imported poplars.

He took the shore road toward the lighted towers of the Mall, driving fast on the empty tarmac.

Senator Bartholomew stood in the doorway in his sequined dressing gown, blinking from Captain Henry to Amos.

"What's this all about?" he blurted, staring at the tall old man with the leathery face and the white bristle of cropped hair. "Why, it's the middle of the night—"

"You were out at my place today, Senator, asking me to do a job for you. I'm here to call your bet."

"You'll . . . you'll go?" The Senator stepped back, inviting the callers inside. He ran his fingers through his thin hair. "Why, that's wonderful! Marvelous! But why in the name of order didn't you say so today . . . ?"

Henry glanced around the dim-lit, luxuriously furnished lounge room. "I'm not doing this in the name of order. I'm doing it for the hell of it. I guess maybe I've had enough naps in the sun to last me for a while—or maybe the prospect of seeing your long face every time I came down to the Mall for supplies was too much for me. What difference does it make? I'm here."

"Yes . . . ." Bartholomew was nodding his head. He rubbed his hands together. "Wonderful news, Captain. I was sure you'd come to your senses—that is, I knew you had a sense of community spirit—"

"Community bath water! Now, before we go any further, let's get a couple of things straight. First—the split will be fifty-fifty."

Bartholomew jumped as though poked by a sharp instrument.

"Here—that wasn't the understanding—"

"Half to my great-granddaughter," Henry went on, "and half to your son."

Bartholomew's heavy eyebrows went up. "To Larry?" He looked dumbfounded.

"I don't like the idea of working for you, Senator—and your bank balance is top-heavy already."

Bartholomew breathed heavily through clamped jaws. "It's the boy's future I had in mind from the beginning—but why *your* interest . . ." he broke off, eyed Henry sharply, then nodded wisely. "Aha, I think I understand. Your great-granddaughter—and—Larry—"

"Maybe you'd better drop that line right there," Henry said in a steely tone.

Bartholomew tugged at the lapels of his dressing gown, "Very well; far be it from me to quibble—but the profits will be calculated after expenses, mind you!"

"All right; that's agreed then."

Bartholomew pulled at his lip. "You surprise me, Captain; I never knew you to be partial to my boy . . ."

"He deserves his share, Senator; he'll earn it."

"Hey, Henry!" Amos started.

"Shut up, Amos; I'll handle this."

Bartholomew gaped at Henry. "Look here," he blurted. "You don't mean—"

Captain Henry nodded. "Sure I do, Senator. You don't think I'm going out there alone, do you?"

"What is this—some—some sort of elaborate and reprehensible joke . . . ?"

Henry's eyes were sharp under white brows. "You want me to go to Corazon. Sure, I'll go—but not unless your Statistically Average son goes with me."

Bartholomew was mopping at his face with a large flower-embossed tissue. He flung it to the floor, faced Captain Henry.

"No! I've told you ten times! You can have any other man you want—but not my boy . . . !"

Captain Henry turned to the door. "Come on, Amos. I'm going home to bed, where I belong—"

Senator Bartholomew pushed before him. His face was red. He raised a finger and wagged it.

"Do you mean, with the wealth of a planet at stake, you'd make a game of setting up fantastic conditions? What kind of insane prankster are you, you . . . you . . ."

"A minute ago it was a noble undertaking—now you're calling it a crazy prank."

"I didn't mean that! You're twisting my words!"

"Well, don't twist mine, Senator. Let's get it straight and clear. You're risking your capital; I'm risking my neck. I'll come back—and so will the boy—with a slice of Corazon that will make us all too rich to talk to."

"I think I see; you want a hostage! You don't trust me!"

"That might be a point—in case you were thinking of cutting any corners."

Bartholomew took out another tissue, wiped at his face, patted behind his ears.

"My boy's not prepared for this sort of thing," he said. "He's not strong; he's overworked himself on behalf of his Territory—"

"I know: a politician never sleeps; he also never breathes fresh air, feels the unfiltered sunlight on his skin, eats raw meat, or sleeps in his socks. He'll do all those things on a Run."

"Captain Henry, you're jeopardizing a golden opportunity for a vindictive whim! There'll never be another Run in this Sector! The nearest uncolonized worlds are a hundred years away—!"

Captain Henry looked at Senator Bartholomew, the long, pale, soft face, the extra chins, the damp, pudgy hands, the paunch straining under the tightly buttoned weskit.

"Your son, Senator," he said flatly. "Or it's no go . . ."

Bartholomew stared at Henry, his jaw muscles jumping.

"Very well, Captain," he said in a whisper. "My son will go."

"Now," Henry said briskly. "I want a brand-new scout boat—a Gendye, *Enamorata* Class; and I want it trajectoried in here as hold cargo, regardless of expense."

"But—that will cost thousands—" Bartholomew swallowed. "Agreed," he said.

"The same goes for her outfitting; I'll supply the list—no questions to be asked."

The Senator nodded.

"No need to look like an old maid agreeing to lose her virginity," Henry said. "It's for the good of the mission. Call your lawyers in and we'll get the papers signed now. And you can call the Rejuve Clinic and tell 'em I'm on the way over."

"Oh, yes, certainly. First thing in the morning. I'll call Dr. Spangler as soon as his office opens—"

"Tomorrow be damned! I'm here now—ready. Tomorrow I may be dead."

"Dead? You're not feeling ill . . . ?"

"Don't worry—I'll last out the night."

"But—it's after midnight—"

"Sure," Amos put in. "And in Antipode it's quarter after nine tomorrow morning. When the Cap'n wants to do something, he wants to do it *now!*"

"Very well . . ." Bartholomew tugged at the violet lapels of his dressing gown. "You enjoy an advantage, but that's no reason to bully."

"Sure it is," Amos barked. "We've got to maintain our reputations as a couple of ornery old buzzards. It's one of the few pleasures we got left."

Back in the car, Henry swung out onto the third-level interchange, gunned toward the glittering spire of the Med-center.

"All right, Henry," Amos demanded. "What's all this Young Bart business? What do we want with that pantywaist?"

"Simple, Amos—I need a crewman—"

"What do you mean?" Amos's voice was hoarse with indignation. "Ain't I—"

"No. You know damned well you can't go through another Rejuve; I'm not too damned sure I can."

"Now, wait a dad-blamed minute, Henry! I was in this all the way—"

"Sorry, Amos," Henry said more gently. "You know I want you—but facts are facts . . . And maybe the trip will do the boy good," he added.

"Hummph!" Amos sat silent for a moment. "So that's why you was so easy to convince all of a sudden," he said. "You figure you can make a man out of a boy."

"Maybe; it won't hurt for a handpicked sample of Aldorado's ideal average manhood to find out what it's like outside a climate-conditioned city."

"You're making a mistake, Henry. Young Bartholomew spends all his time playing tennis and reading statistics; he'll cave in on you the first time the going gets rough."

"I hope not, Amos—for a lot of reasons." The image of the first Dulcia rose to shimmer before him. She seemed to be weighing his motives in the balance with her clear, gray eyes.

Under the blue-white lights of the Rejuve Clinic, Captain Henry watched as the doctor nervously laid out equipment.

"This is the most ridiculous thing I've ever heard of," he snapped. He was a tiny, birdlike man with overlarge eyes behind tinted contact lenses. "A man of your age—and at this time of night. Why, there are dozens of tests, measurements, biochemical analyses; you need at least three weeks on a special diet—and I haven't so much as checked your pulse, Captain Henry! And you expect me to put you in a regeneration tank and subject your metabolism to seventy-two hours of profound shock—"

"I have three months to get ready and get to that staging area, doctor," Henry said. "I'll need all my horsepower to make it; I don't have three weeks to waste."

"I have a good mind to refuse . . ." Spangler winked owl eyes defiantly at Henry. "There is the matter of professional ethics to consider . . ."

"I've signed the release," Henry said. "It's my neck."

The medic picked up a hypospray angrily, took Henry's arm. "Very well—but I wash my hands of responsibility; I won't guarantee an L.P. of even twelve months . . ." He pressed the plunger, tossed the instrument on the table, wiped his hands nervously.

"Kindly stretch out on the table here, Captain," he said. "You'll feel the effects of the shot in a moment now. You're committed; it's too late to turn back . . ." His voice seemed to come from far away. " . . . I hope you know what you're doing . . ."

There were sounds that approached and receded, the booming of cannon, cries, voices out of the past . . . There were moments of sharp pain, and he fought, striking out at an enemy that fled always before him. Light glared, blindingly; then there was darkness through which he swam alone, suitless, in the emptiness of space, and in his body a terrible sickness flooded in relentless waves . . .

Later, he seemed to float, drugged, aware of an ache all through his body like a gigantic throbbing tooth.

*Under him, hardness pressed; his arms and legs tingled
now. He tried to remember the accident, but there was
nothing; only the irritating voice that probed, prodded,
forcing itself into his awareness . . .*

" . . . up! Wake up! Wake up!"

He opened his eyes. A vague face floated over him.
It was not a pleasing face, like some of those he had
seen—or dreamed about . . . He closed his eyes to the
grateful darkness . . .

"He's coming out of it!" The voices were sharp now;
they rasped his nerves like files.

"Go 'way," he muttered. He was abruptly aware of
his tongue in his mouth, a vile taste, dryness . . .

"Water . . ." he croaked.

Arms lifted him, hands fumbled over him. He felt
straps being released, the cold touch of a hypospray.
He was sitting up now, dizzy, but awake, looking around
a small, bright room.

"You had us worried, Captain," a thin voice was saying. Captain Henry concentrated. He knew the man . . .

"One hundred and eight hours," the voice went on.
"For a while there it was touch and go."

He was remembering now. Amos had been with
him—

"Where's Amos?" Henry's voice boomed loud in his
ears. He took a deep breath, felt sharp pains that faded
quickly. He shook his head. "I want Amos . . ."

"He . . . ah . . . isn't here, Captain."

"He didn't wait . . . ?" Henry asked.

"Mr. Able . . . didn't make it . . ."

"Make what?" A feeling of immense irritability rose
up in Captain Henry. "What kind of a pal is he? Get
him—now!"

"You don't understand, Captain. His system wasn't
able to endure the strain . . ."

"Where is he—" Captain Henry got to his feet, weaving. "Strain, my elbow!"

"He's dead, Captain," the thin-faced man said. "The Rejuve treatment—it was too much for him. He died four hours ago. I did all I could . . ."

"You gave Amos a Rejuve? Why, you damned fool!"

"But—he said those were your orders—" Spangler gestured to a sheet-covered table. "I haven't even had time—"

Henry stepped to the table, reaching out a hand for support, flipped back the sheet. A waxy face, thin-nosed, sunken-cheeked, stared up at him with eyes as remote as a statue of Pharaoh.

"Amos . . ." Captain Henry looked around blankly at the other two. "He was my partner . . . ever since the beginning . . ."

"He . . . left this for you." The medic offered a white envelope. Henry tore it open.

> If it works, I'll make you a better partner than six green kids. If it's a no go—then happy landings, Henry. I wish I could of been with you.
>
> *Amos Able.*

Henry put a hand on Amos's shoulder, felt the bones through the skin and the sheet.

"You didn't wait," Henry said. "You went ahead without me . . ."

An hour later, Captain Henry stood in the UV filtered light of the Mall, flanked on one side by Dulcia, trim in a close-fitting suit of pale green that accented the gold of her hair, and on the other by Dr. Spangler, his hand under Henry's arm, chatting nervously.

"A fine recovery after all, Captain. Frankly, I'm surprised at the outcome; I think I'm safe in saying we've achieved a Senility Index of around .40—"

"Grandpa, I've been so worried," the girl almost wailed. "You're so weak . . ."

"He'll recover his strength quickly," Spangler bobbed his head reassuringly. "In a week he'll be his old self again. That is—his *new* self." He beamed at his jest.

A wide low car, gleaming with pale gray porcelain and bright chromalloy, swung up to the entry. A tall, slender young man with short curly dark hair, clad in stylishly cut sport togs, jumped out. He came forward, took Henry's elbow.

"Certainly fine to see you looking so chipper, sir," he said. "Dulcia's been beside herself . . ."

"That was mean, Grandpa, to go off and just leave me a note!" the girl put in.

The lad went through a gesture of assisting Henry into the car, went around and took a seat in front; he turned, a polite smile on his regular features.

"I was certainly pleased when I heard you'd agreed to let me go along on the cruise, Captain; I'm sure I'm going to enjoy it immensely. I'm quite looking forward to it."

Henry leaned back, feeling the sweat of exertion trickling down behind his ear. He stared hard at the youth.

"I doubt that all to hell, son," he said. "A better man than either of us has already died in the name of this caper. Maybe before it's over you'll wish you had, too."

The smile dropped from the young man's face.

"Grandpa!" Dulcia said. "What a terrible thing to say to Larry."

"I know," Captain Henry said. "This is not the time for a pep talk about how teamwork pays off. I'm not in the mood. I'm going home and sleep for forty-eight hours—and then we're starting to work."

"Very well, Captain," young Bartholomew said. "I fully expect—"

"It's what you don't expect that hurts," Henry cut him off. "Pull in your belt, youngster. You've got a tough sixty days ahead—and after that it'll get tougher."

Chapter Two

Senator Bartholomew hurled the machine listing to the table before Captain Henry, waved his dope stick wildly.

"This equipment list is fantastic!" he stormed. "You're spending thousands—thousands, do you hear! For what?" He slapped the paper with a damp palm. "A battery of three-centimeter infinite repeaters; a demi-total all-wave detector screen; a fire control board designed for a ship of the line! Have you lost your mind? This is a peaceful homesteading venture you're outfitting for—not a commando raid—"

"Uh-huh . . ." Henry grinned cheerfully at the paunchy financier. "I intend to keep it peaceful, Senator—if I have to gun my way through an army to do it. By the way, I've got a new list of stores for you somewhere . . ." He slapped pockets, went to the desk, tried drawers.

"Dulcie!" he called out. "Where's that list we made up this morning?"

The girl put her head in the door. "Larry took it down a few minutes ago— Oh, good morning, Senator Bartholomew."

Bartholomew grunted. "Now you're employing my boy as a common messenger, eh? I suppose this is your idea of getting back at me for some fancied slight."

"Why, Senator," Dulcia said. "Larry volunteered to go; he was going over to the Mall anyway—"

"Never mind the Senator's cracks," Henry said. "His indigestion's probably bothering him. Let's go over and take a look at the ship; I want to show you something."

"Look here, I came out here to talk to you!" Bartholomew barked.

"Come around when you feel better." Henry took the girl's arm, escorted her out to the Monojag.

"Really, Grandpa, you shouldn't goad him that way—"

"To hell with him. It's too nice a day to breathe second-hand dope." He wheeled the car out across the ramp toward the silver lance-head of the ship.

"She's really beautiful," Dulcia said. "Have you decided what to call her yet?"

Henry pulled the car up in the shadow of the fifty-foot vessel, poised on four slim vanes among stacked crates and boxes. Men in coveralls paused in their work to eye the girl appreciatively. Henry reached in the back of the car, brought out a tissue-wrapped bottle.

"In answer to that last question," he said, "I have." He stripped the paper from the heavy bottle, held it up. The label read "Piper Hiedsieck—extra brut." "So, if you'll kindly do the honors . . ."

"Oh, Grandpa . . ." Dulcia took the champagne. She giggled. "It seems funny to go on calling you Grandpa; you look so dashing . . ."

"Don't get flustered, girl. Smash it over her stern pipes and give her her name."

"Do you really want me to? Now? With just us here? Can't I call Larry?"

"Sure; go ahead."

The girl went excitedly to the field screen, located the youth at an office across the field. A minute later his scarlet sportster headed across from the Admin building, squealed to a halt beside the Monojag. Larry

Bartholomew stepped out, greeted Henry, beamed at Dulcia.

"Well, this is quite an occasion; real champagne, too . . ." He frowned slightly.

"Don't worry," Henry said. "I paid for it myself. Go ahead, girl, let her have it."

Dulcia took up a position by the stern tubes. "Grandpa," she said. "You haven't told me her name yet."

"*Degüello*," Henry said.

"*Degüello*?" Dulcia repeated.

"Ah, a charming choice," Larry commented, nodding. "An old Spanish word, isn't it?"

"That's right."

Dulcia took a breath, gripped the bottle by its neck. "I christen thee *Degüello*!" she cried, and swung the bottle. Wine foamed as the glass shattered; a splash of gold ran down across the bright hull plates. The workmen raised a cheer in which Henry's bellow joined. Larry clapped.

"Well, Captain, I suppose I'd better be getting back to my ah . . . duties," he said, when the broken glass had been swept up.

"Not a bad idea, Larry. You're due at the gym now."

"Yes," his smile was a trifle strained. As he turned away, he waved at Dulcia almost as if signaling her, and Henry, turning aside, later thought he had caught sight of a small lifting of her hand in return. But when he turned back to her, there was no sign of it in her face or manner.

"Larry looks so much better, Grandpa, since you've had him working out," she said, "and getting out in the unfiltered sunlight. I really think the trip is going to be good for him." She looked at her great-grandfather with a sudden, unusual seriousness. "—It isn't really going to be as . . . dangerous as Amos made out? Is it?"

"It'll be a picnic," Henry said breezily; he ran a

finger under her chin. "A couple more weeks and we'll be out of your hair."

"I keep telling myself . . . the sooner you go, the sooner you'll be back."

"That's the spirit; now, what do you say to dinner at the Fire Palace and a swim under Castle Reef afterward?"

Dulcia hugged his arm. "Wonderful! And I've got something to talk to you about, anyway."

"Something?" He stared at her. "What, girl?"

"Oh . . . something. I'll tell you later." She let go of his arm, danced away. Wondering a little, he followed her to the Monojag.

The dinner at the Fire Palace was all that anyone could have expected of it. They sat on the terrace afterward, watching the twilight deepen over the sea, then changed and went down on the beach.

There, as the night closed down, they swam—and then, afterward, Henry, out of sheer high spirits, built a roaring fire of driftwood. His strength was back on him and it felt good to lay arms once more around some log two ordinary men could barely lift, and heave it, crashing, in among the crackling flames and glowing sparks. He was half drunk with his return to an age of vigor; and in his exuberance, he did not notice Dulcia's quietness until he dropped down once more on the sand beside her and saw her sitting silent, hugging her knees, pensively.

He looked at her sharply; and she turned her face away from him, but not before he had seen the sparkle of tears on her lashes.

"Dulcie-girl . . ." he put out a hand to her, but she shook her head.

"No, Grandpa," she said, "I'm all right. Really, I'm all right . . . It's just that you look so happy. Grandpa . . . tell me about her . . ."

"Her?" He scowled at the girl.

"You know . . . my great-grandmother. Was she really so much like me?"

In spite of himself his voice thickened in his throat as he answered.

"Haven't I told you a thousand times, she was?"

"It must . . ." still she would not look at him, "have been terrible for her. Having you go off that way . . ."

A sudden deadly coldness moved in him. All the guilt that had lain hidden in him all these years leaped snarling from the dark parts of his mind to tear at him. But Dulcie—this Dulcia, the young girl of now—was talking on.

"Grandpa, I told you I wanted to tell you something." She turned finally to look at him. "It's . . . about Larry. I love him."

The coldness moved out to encase him complete, like a block of ice.

"Love?"

She nodded. "So now you see . . . There are only two people I love anywhere—now that Amos is dead— and the two of you are going off on this Run."

"Dulcia . . ." his tongue felt clumsy in his mouth, "I told you there's nothing to worry about. Nothing . . ."

"Isn't there? Really, isn't there?" She searched his face with her gray eyes. "You've always told me the truth, Grandpa. But you tell me there's nothing to worry about; and then you tell Larry something different. Do you know why he's going on this trip, Grandpa? *Do* you?"

"Why, his dad's sending him—"

"Oh Grandpa, stop and think for a moment!" Her tone was almost exasperated. "Larry may be just a boy to you, but to himself and the Senator and everyone on this planet, he's a man—man enough to run for high political office. Larry's father can't send him any place he doesn't want to go! Larry's going because he *wants* to go—and you don't even know the reason!"

Suspicion stiffened Henry.

"What reason?" he said, sharply.

"What do you think? *You!*" She stared at him with an expression caught between affection and frustration. "You don't know—you've never known how people think of you. Don't you know you're a living hero, a living *legend* to the people my age and Larry's, on this planet? To their folks, you may still be just a man— but to my generation you're a walking, breathing piece of a history book. Now, do you understand why Larry never even thought of hesitating when his father told him you wanted him to go with you to Corazon and the Run?"

Henry grunted, off-guard.

"But you scare him half to death!" said Dulcia. "According to you, he can't do anything right, and all you have to do is look at him, to make him so self-conscious that he trips over his own feet and starts talking twice as foolish-stilted fashionable as he would ordinarily. But he'd give his right arm to please you. Grandpa, *I know!*"

Henry stared fiercely at her. A small door somewhere in the back of his mind where the memory of her great-grandmother lived, wavered half-open, wanting to believe what she had just told him.

But then, unbidden, an image of the Senator rose in his mind's eye. The fat, flabby man with the ruthless core. The boy was blood and bone of his father. If there was something worthwhile in him, it would show itself when the Run had ground the fancy manners and nonsense off him. Until then— the small, half-open door in the back of his mind slammed shut.

"All right, honey, I'll bear it in mind," he said, patting

her shoulder gently. He rose to his feet like a spring uncoiled. "Now, we better be getting home. Tomorrow's a large day."

They picked up their towels and climbed the beach back to the Monojag. Driving home, Dulcia suddenly broke the silence.

"*Degüello . . .*" she said, unexpectedly. "Larry said when I christened the ship that the name was an old Spanish word. What does it mean, Grandpa?"

Henry was suddenly conscious of her staring across at him, her face white in the moonlight coming through the windscreen of the car climbing the steep and winding road.

—And even as he spoke, he realized how his lips thinned at the word, and he heard, like an echo, the grim, harsh note of hungry violence in his voice as he answered: "Cutthroat."

From the window, Henry's eyes followed the white strip of beach that curved along under the cliff-face, widening to the distant glistening bubble of the Mall and the rectangle of the port, where the ship threw back a blinding glint of reflected sun. Tiny figures swarmed around its base; by now, Senator Bartholomew and his committee of Averages would be getting impatient at the delay.

He turned, looked into the long mirror. The narrow-cut, silver-corded black trousers fitted without a wrinkle into the well-worn but brightly polished ship boots. He plucked the short tunic from the bed, slipped it over the white silk shirt; the silver buttons, the swirl of braid on the cuffs gleamed against royal blue polyon. He buckled on the broad woven-silver belt with the ebony-gripped bright-plated ceremonial side arm; he smiled, and a lean, bronzed face with blue-green eyes and short blond hair touched with gray smiled back. He opened

the door and walked along the hall, down three steps
to the lounge room.

Dulcia turned; her eyes widened. "Oh, Grandpa . . . !"

He grinned. "Come on, honey; takeoff in forty
minutes. Let's go give the natives a treat."

They took the Monojag, howled down the winding
cliff road, along the beach, cut across the Port Authority
ramp, screeched to a halt beside the ship. A crowd of
stylishly dressed citizens waited behind a red plush
guard rope. On a platform beside the service gantry,
a cluster of officials stood.

"Everybody's here," Dulcia said breathlessly. "Look,
there's the Council Monitor . . . and—"

"Uh-huh; they'll have speeches planned, but I'm
afraid I won't be able to wait around for 'em." Henry
stepped out, offered Dulcia a hand. The babble of the
crowd rose higher. Fingers pointed; strobe lights flashed.

"You were late on purpose," she whispered. "That's
mean, Grandpa; I wanted to see everybody cheering
you."

"Where's young Bartholomew?" They crossed the
open space, mounted the steps to the platform. A short,
narrow-shouldered man stepped forward, offered a
hand, adjusted a microphone.

"Mr. Mayor," he began, his amplified voice echoing,
"honorable guests, citizens of Aldorado—"

Captain Henry gently plucked the microphone from
his hand.

"We're lifting off in twenty-one minutes," he said
briskly. "Everybody back behind the yellow safety line.
Where's Mr. Bartholomew?"

There was a surprised stir in the crowd. Larry
pushed through, mounted the platform. He was
strapped and buckled into an expensive ship suit hung
with bright-colored emergency gear.

"Ah, Captain, I was just saying good-by to—"

Captain Henry put his hand over the mike.

"Get aboard, Larry. Start the countdown clock. You know how to do that—"

"Of course, I do," Larry said urgently. His eyes went past Henry to Dulcia. "But I don't see—"

"That's an order, Mister!" Captain Henry said softly.

Bartholomew reddened, turned abruptly, and stepped into the entry port. Captain Henry faced the open-mouthed officials beside him.

"All right, gentlemen; everybody clear. The killing radius of the drive is a hundred yards." He turned to his great-granddaughter, put an arm around her, kissed her casually on the forehead.

"Better beat it, Dulcie-girl. Drive up to the cliff-head and watch from there. You'll get a better view."

She threw her arms around his neck. "Be careful, Grandpa—and come back safe . . ."

"Nothing to it," he said. He chucked her under the chin, steered her to the stair, waved cheerfully to the assembled crowd, then keyed the mike:

"All right, you gantry crews; pull back there; disconnect all and make secure . . ."

Inside the vessel, Henry climbed a short companionway in a smell of new paint and insulation, emerged into a handsomely appointed control center. Larry lay strapped into the right-hand cradle, watching the blink of red, green, amber, and blue lights on a console that rimmed half the chamber. He turned a resentful glance at Henry.

"Captain, I didn't have an opportunity even to wave to Dulcia—"

Standing in the winking multicolored glow of the panel lights, Henry stripped off the braid-encrusted tunic, dropped the heavy belt with its decorative weapon into a wall locker.

"Let's get a couple of things straight, Larry," he said evenly. "Up to now it's been fun and games . . ." He took a plain black ship suit from the locker, began pulling it on. "But the games are over. You're signed on for the cruise—and maybe, if we're very careful, and very lucky, we'll get home again some day. Meanwhile, we'll concentrate on the job ahead with every ounce of brains and guts we've got—and hope it'll be enough."

Bartholomew looked at Henry doubtfully.

"Surely you're exaggerating, Captain. This is merely a matter of selecting a suitable area and establishing our claim . . ."

"There's more to it than that. There's money at work in this Run. From what I've been able to find out, some of the toughest operators in the Sector are staking outfits. New land's hard to come by these days; we won't get ours without a fight." He took a second suit from the locker, tossed it across to Bartholomew. "Better get that Mickey Mouse outfit off and get into this. You've got about five minutes till blast-off."

Bartholomew climbed out of the couch, began changing suits. "This is a very expensive suit," he said, folding it carefully. "A gift from the Sector Council—"

"The shoes, too," Henry said. "Save those fancy ones for cocktail parties after we get back."

Larry looked indignant. "Now, Captain; my father had these boots specially made for me; they're the finest that money can buy. He particularly insisted that I wear them—"

"All right; they're your feet, Larry; and they'll be going into some pretty strange places."

"You make this sound like—like some sort of crazy suicide mission!"

"Sure . . ." Captain Henry settled himself in his

couch, clamped in, snapped his lifeline connection in place. "All suicides are crazy. Buckle in now and get set for blast-off."

The ground-control screen glowed. "Zero minus one minute," a voice said. "Ramp clear, final count." There was a loud click.

"Minus fifty seconds," the voice said. Henry adjusted the clock, watched the sweep hand.

"Forty seconds. Thirty seconds. Twenty seconds. Ten seconds . . ."

Bartholomew cleared his throat. "Captain—"

"Too late now for second thoughts, Larry."

" . . . eight . . . seven . . . six . . ." the voice droned.

"I have an important primary in the fall," Bartholomew said. "I just wanted to ask when we'd be returning."

A whine started up deep in the ship. Relays clicked.

"If we're lucky—three months," Henry said.

" . . . three . . . two . . . one—"

Pink light winked in the rear visiscreen. A deep rumble sounded. Captain Henry felt the pressure, gentle at first, then insistent, then fierce, crushing him back as the roar mounted to a mighty torrent which went on and on. The weight was like an iron mold now pressing over his body.

"What if . . . we're not lucky . . . ?" Bartholomew croaked.

Captain Henry smiled tightly. "In that case," he said with difficulty, "the question won't arise."

"I'm going to be sick again," Bartholomew gasped.

"Sure," Captain Henry said absently, studying instrument readings. "Just be sure you clean it up afterward."

"That's what makes me sick . . ."

"Your stomach ought to be empty by now. Why didn't you take the Null-G shot?"

"I heard—they made one . . . ill."

Henry tossed a white capsule over. "Swallow this. You'll be all right in a few minutes. I'll put a spin on the ship in another hour or so, as soon as I've finished the final tower check." He spoke softly into his lip-mike, jotted notes on a clipboard.

An hour passed. Captain Henry made adjustments to the controls; a whining started up. Under the two men, the cradles pressed faintly, then more firmly.

"That's a standard G," Henry said cheerfully. He unstrapped and swung out of the cradle. "You'll feel better in a few minutes."

"The pressure was bad enough," Bartholomew said weakly. "It seemed like a week—"

"Only nine hours. I didn't want to put you under more than 2G—or myself either." He took equipment from a locker, set about erecting a small unit like a twelve-inch tri-D tank at one side of the twelve-foot room. He buckled on a plain gun belt, fitted a pistol into the holster, took up a stance, then drew suddenly, aimed, and pressed the firing stud. A bright flash showed at the edge of the screen, faded slowly. He holstered the gun, drew, and fired another silent bolt.

"What are you doing?" Bartholomew craned from his cradle.

"Target practice. Two hours in every twelve—for both of us—until we're scoring ten out of ten. Better get out of that cradle now and get your space legs. I'm upping the spin one rev per hour. It's a twenty-nine-day run to Corazon. By the time we get there, we'll be working under a G and a half."

"Whatever for?"

"Good for the muscles. Now hop to it. When you finish cleaning up in here, we're going down to the engine compartment and I'll show you your duties there."

"Good Lord, Captain! I'm not a . . . a grease monkey!"

"That's all right; you will be."

"Captain, I'm a trained Administrator. I thought that on this venture my executive abilities—"

Henry turned on him. "Start swabbing that deck, Mister. And when you're finished, there'll be other duties—none of 'em easy and none of 'em pleasant!"

"Is that my part of the mission?" Bartholomew's cheeks were pink. "To do all the menial work?"

"I'll navigate this tub. I'll be on the board twelve hours out of every twenty-four, and I'll spend another four getting my reflexes back in shape. If I have any time left over, I'll do my share of the shipboard routine. If not, you'll do it all."

Bartholomew looked at Henry. "I see," he said. He got out of the cradle and silently set about cleaning up the compartment.

Coming up the companionway, Captain Henry paused, hearing a voice above. He came up quietly, saw Bartholomew, tall and thin in the black ship suit, standing across the room, his gun belt slung low on his narrow hips.

"Very well, you scoundrel," the youth murmured. He whipped out the training pistol, fired; a flash of greenish light winked in the gloom of the control chamber.

He holstered the gun, half-turned, then spun back. "Aha!" he muttered. "Thought you'd slip up on me unawares, I see . . ." He yanked the gun up, fired—

There was no answering flash.

"Drat it!" Bartholomew adjusted the gun belt, took a turn up and down the room, spun suddenly and fired, was rewarded with a flash.

"Ha!" he said. He blew on the gun barrel, jammed it in the holster.

"Not bad," Henry said, stepping up into the room. "You may make a shooter yet, Larry."

Bartholomew jumped. "I was . . . ah . . . just practicing . . ." He unbuckled the belt, tossed it in the locker. "Though I confess I can't imagine any occasion for the exercise of such a skill."

"Oh, it's handy," Henry said, "when scoundrels sneak up on you."

Bartholomew blushed. "One must have *some* amusement to while away the hours."

"Call it an amusement if you want to—but keep practicing. Your neck may depend on it in the very near future."

"Surely you're exaggerating the danger, Captain. All that talk of hired killers and opportunists was all very well back on Aldorado, when you were dramatizing the perils of the undertaking—"

"If you've got the idea a Run is something like bobbing for apples, forget it. We're going to be in competition with men that are used to taking what they want and worrying about the consequences later—much later."

Larry smiled patiently. "Oh, perhaps in the old days, a century ago, lawless characters perpetrated some of the atrocities one hears of; but not today, Captain. These are modern times; Council regulations—"

"Council regulations are dandy—to start a fire with when your permatch goes dry." Henry settled himself in his couch, swung it around to face Bartholomew.

"Corazon is a holdover from an earlier era. She was held under quarantine for an extra seventy-five years, because of some funny business with disappearing viruses combined with bureaucratic inertia. The day of frontiering in the Sector is past; this is a freak, a one-time opportunity—and every last-chance Charlie in this end of the Galaxy who can beg, borrow, or steal a ship will be at that staging area, ready to get his slice of Corazon. It'll be every man for himself, and the devil take the slow gun . . ."

"But the Council Representatives—the referees—"

"How many? A hundred men? And no fonder of getting killed than any other salaried employee. Sure, they'll be there to take your claim registrations, hand out the official map, run a scintillometer over you to make sure you aren't packing a fission weapon in your hip pocket—but out of sight of the Q. S. Tower at Pango-Ri, it will be up to you and your handgun and your bare knuckles and your brain."

"But, Captain, a few sane-minded claimants could easily band together, form a common defense, and set about organizing matters as reasonable men."

"You won't find any sane-minded claimants; the sane people stay home and buy their minerals from the developers after the gunsmoke has blown away."

Bartholomew pursed his lips. In the past two weeks aboard ship his black hair had grown; it curled around his ears, along his neck.

"Then—how are we going to invade this hotbed of criminal activity and establish our claims?"

"That's a fair question. I'm glad to see you taking an interest in these little matters. It gives me hope you may wake up at some point before it's too late and start taking this thing seriously." Henry crossed to the chart table, flipped the switch. A map appeared on the screen.

"The big thing is to know what you want. Now, the official throwaway charts give you continental outlines, and mark a few hot spots such as deserts, active volcanoes, and so on. The rest is up to the customer—"

"Why, that's ridiculous! Surely the officials have detailed knowledge of the terrain—"

"Yeah—but that would take all the romance out of it. The idea is for all parties to have the same handicap: ignorance. But the result is that line-jumpers have been going into Corazon for the last thirty years, making up aerial surveys, taking harbor soundings, doing minerals exploration—"

"Impossible! The Quarantine Service—"

"—is made up of people. Funny, fallible—corruptible—human beings. Not all of them, of course. Not even most of them. But it only takes one bought Quarantine Warden to let a man in—and out again, with the dope."

"But—we won't have a chance against anyone armed with that kind of data—"

"No, we wouldn't—if we didn't have a good bootleg map of our own."

Bartholomew looked at the map on the screen. Henry twisted the magnification control; details leaped out; mountain ranges, contour lines, notations of temperature, humidity, air pressure readings.

"You mean—" Bartholomew gasped, "this is an illegal instrument? We're smuggling contraband?"

"Uh-huh. You remember the special appropriation of twenty thousand credits I asked for—for navigational equipment?"

"You're saying that—this map—"

"That's right. It's the best there is. I've spent a lot of hours studying it. I've picked out initial target point—and you can count on it that the same spot will have been pinpointed by others."

"You paid twenty thousand credits of my father's money for this—this stolen information?"

Henry nodded.

"Why—we don't even know if it's accurate! It could be some sort of counterfeit, constructed out of whole cloth—"

"Nope. I got it from a friend of mine—an old space hand—too old to make the Run himself."

"But how could he be sure it was authentic—even if he believed in it?"

"Easy; he made it. He always intended to use it himself, but the Q. S. held off a little too long for him. So he let it go to me."

"This is—unheard of! Good Lord, Captain Henry, do you realize what the penalty for possession of this document is?"

"Nope—but I know the penalty for *not* having it."

"You talk as though this were some sort of military campaign!"

"Right. Now, the ground rules of the Run are simple. All entrants report in to the staging area—that's a ten-mile radius around Pango-Ri—and register. Then we wait for zero hour and hit the trail. There's no restriction on the kind of equipment you use. We've got a nice converted Bolo Minor in the hold. There'll be heavier equipment than that up against us, but not much. There'll even be a few old-time hill runners going in on foot; men who've spent their last credit on a space lift in to Corazon. Believe me, there'll be dirty work in the underbrush when they start to clash over who grabs what."

"Surely there's enough for all—"

"You tell that to a man who's walked day and night for a week to stake out a mining claim that some tipster's sold him on—and finds three other customers on the same spot. Now, all entrants depart at dawn—that's oh-six hours, Pango-Ri mean time—from the staging area. They're allowed to carry all the food they want, four issue markers—a special self-embedding electronic model—communications gear, and light hand-weapons—for hunting, it says in the Prospectus."

Bartholomew shook his head. "This is a pathetically ineptly organized affair. Why, it would have been simplicity itself to survey the planet, set out markers on a grid, and assign areas by lot to qualified entrants."

"Face it, Larry. New land on virgin worlds isn't doled out like slices of cake at a church social. They can make all the rules they want, back at Galaxy Central—but on Corazon, it'll be nature's old law. It's not the Statistical Average that survives—it's the son-of-a-bitch that's tougher than the hard case that's hunting him. Maybe the Survey Authorities don't know that—or maybe they're smarter than we give them credit for. You don't tame alien worlds with busloads of bureaucrats."

"But this arrangement is an open invitation to lawlessness."

Henry nodded. "And you can count on it there'll be plenty of takers."

"But—what can we do against men of that sort?"

"Easy," Henry said. "We'll do the same thing—only we'll do it first."

It was the seventeenth day in space. Captain Henry sat at the plotting table. He lifted his head, sniffed the air, then rose, went to the companionway, sniffed again. He grabbed the handrail, leaped down, dived for the power compartment. Dense fumes boiled out from a massive grilled housing. Coughing, Henry fought through to the emergency console, hauled down on a heavy circuit breaker. A sharp whining descended the scale. The smoke churned, trailing toward wall registers. Henry retreated to the corridor, coughing violently.

"Are you all right, Captain?" Bartholomew's strained voice sounded behind him.

"I don't know yet; we've got gyro trouble," Henry snapped, and plunged back into the smoke. The haze was thinning quickly. The whine had fallen to a growl, dropped lower, clicked to a stop.

"Bearings gone," Henry snapped. "Maybe we can replace 'em, and maybe we can't. Let's jump, Mister. Every minute counts! Grab that torquer—get that housing off!" Henry sprang for the parts index, punched keys. A green light winked. A clattering came from behind the panel. He lifted out two heavy, plastic-cocooned disks, eight inches in diameter and three inches thick. The *ping!* of cooling metal sounded in the room. Bartholomew's wrench clattered against metal.

"It's awfully quiet, suddenly," the boy called.

"I've shut down the air pumps." Henry ripped at the plastic covering; polished metal emerged from the dull brown casing.

"We'll choke," Bartholomew said. "The room's still full of smoke."

"Feel that faint surge underfoot, every five seconds or so . . . ?" Henry snapped.

"Yes, but—"

"Keep working!" Henry ripped into the second bearing. "This ship isn't a statically balanced unit. It's spinning a little over one revolution per second. The axis of spin and the centroid of mass don't coincide. There's also a matter of fluid inertia; the air, the water in the tanks, lubricant reservoirs. I shut the pumps down to minimize the eccentric thrusts as much as possible—but it won't help much. The wobble will increase—and the worse it gets, the faster it will build. It's a logarithmic curve; we'll go into a tumble in a few minutes, then she'll start to break up. Got the picture? Now fumble that damned housing out of the way, and I'll find out if we're going to live another hour . . ."

Bartholomew, white-faced, worked frantically at the fasteners; Henry cleared the second bearing, leaped to help the younger man lift the housing aside. A cloud of smog churned out from the uncovered gyro chassis. Henry fanned it, peering down at the blackened shafts.

"No wonder she burned," he said harshly. "The bearings were running dry . . . !" He turned to Bartholomew. The younger man swallowed, stared back wide-eyed.

"When's the last time you made your maintenance check, Larry?"

"I . . . ah . . . this morning—"

"Don't lie to me! There's been no lubricant on these bearings for at least thirty-six hours!"

"How was I to know this would happen?"

"Your orders were to take your readings at four-hour intervals and maintain one hundred and twenty pounds oil pressure! I said orders, Mister—not suggestions! Sometime in the past day or so a blockage developed in the feed line; the pressure dropped. And where were you, Mister?"

"I thought it was just a—a drill!" Bartholomew burst out. "I got tired of dragging up and down those stairs! I didn't know—"

"That's right. You didn't know . . ." Henry slapped the blackened shaft of the main gyro. "Let's get this bearing changed!"

The floor lifted, tilted to the right, fell, slanted to the left . . .

"Brace your feet, and when I give the word, guide that end out." Henry grasped the control of the cable hoist, waited while Bartholomew fumbled for a grip.

"Up—and over—" Henry grunted. His biceps bulged; his straining shoulders straightened. The shaft cleared the edge of the casing, teetered, then swung over the side. Henry lowered it to the deck.

"It's getting worse—rapidly . . ." Bartholomew said.

"Yeah."

One of the old bearings, loose on the floor, bounded past, crashed against the bulkhead. Henry hauled at the cable hoist; the servomotor groaned under the unaccustomed load as the swing of the ship pulled at the heavy shaft. At the other end of the shaft, Bartholomew clung, green-faced.

"Steady as she goes, boy . . ." The walls seemed to tilt crazily now, whirling. The loose bearing slid, bounced off a heaving casting, clattered across the room.

"We should have tied that son-of-a-bitch down," Henry grated. "Don't let her swing!"

The surge of the floor threw Henry sideways. He grabbed, raised an arm to fend off the swinging shaft. The bearing, bounding across the room, cannoned against Captain Henry's hand, where it gripped the housing.

Bartholomew straightened, breathing noisily. His eye fell on Henry's hand. He yelped at the glimpse of bloody flesh, exposed knuckle bones; he started toward him.

"Belay that, Mister," Henry ground out between clenched teeth. "It's now or never . . ." He hauled at the cable; the wounded hand slipped; he cursed, fought the hoist savagely. Bartholomew hung on the free end of the shaft; his feet swung free of the deck for a moment. He oofed as he slammed against the housing. Then the shaft dropped a foot, another, clanged as it seated. Henry held on for a moment, breathing hard.

"All right, Larry. Cast off and button her up . . ."

Two hours later, stretched in his cradle, Captain Henry laughed shortly, holding up his bandage-encased hand.

"Nice," he said. "We don't happen to have a depot

handy to calibrate the gyros again, so I'll be on the board, manually balancing her, watch on and watch off, for the next six days."

"Are you in much pain, Captain?" The young man's face was white.

Henry shook his head.

Larry swallowed. He took a deep breath and stiffened, seeming to brace himself. His face became, if possible, even a bit whiter.

"It's my fault, Captain," he said stiffly. "My fault entirely."

Henry looked at him grimly and a little curiously. By the boy's standards, at least, it had taken a certain amount of guts to say that. For a moment Dulcia's words about Larry on the beach the night before they had lifted ship, came back to him. But he shoved them aside once more. Larry might be showing something— it was too early to tell.

"Ever hear of shipboard responsibility?" said Henry harshly. "It's the Captain's fault if he trusts a man who can't be trusted. Only a damn fool would go on to Corazon now. You know that, don't you? We're asking for trouble, going in like this."

"I'll not let you down again, Captain. The young man's jaw muscles were knotted at the angle of his sharp face on each side. The sweat stood in little beads on his pale forehead. "You'll see. When we get there, you'll see that my knowledge of administrative routine will be a help to you. As an official—"

"I don't know about that part," Henry cut him off roughly, looking at his bandaged hand. "But you stitch a nice seam, I'll say that for you."

Larry flushed, opened his mouth as if to say something, then clamped it determinedly shut again and turned away. He went out without a word.

All right, boy, thought Henry, looking after him.

One swallow doesn't make a summer. You've got a lot to learn yet—even if it turns out you're capable of learning, after all.

Chapter Three

The last murmur of the pumps died away. In the ground-view screen, Henry studied the massive concrete block of the Pango-Ri Port Authority building stretching to the barrier wall lining the ramp edge; beyond, a mushroom-town of flimsy prefabs, inflated domes, and low wooden shacks sprawled across the dusty plain. Farther away, clumsy structures, garish with colored plastic, loomed up into the hazy afternoon sky of Corazon.

Henry shifted the field of view; a line of space vessels appeared, parked in an irregular rank that stretched away toward the purplish line of distant hills.

"All these ships are here for the Run?" Larry stared. "There must be hundreds of them—thousands . . ."

"Yep; and every one of those tubs will be hauling anywhere from a couple of men to a platoon. I'd say we've got upwards of a quarter of a million competitors in this little rummage sale."

"All for this wasteland? I had rather pictured our wandering through unpeopled forests, surveying vast, deserted tracts, selecting our claim . . ."

"We'd better get over to Run HQ and get on the log or we'll be wandering around an unpeopled port— after the rest of the Run has left."

Bartholomew frowned thoughtfully. "I think my informal official blazer with the Statav pocket watch will be correct; I've no desire to overawe the registration personnel." He glanced at Captain Henry. "I think I should be the one to deal with the Quarantine authorities."

"We'll both deal with 'em—at the tail end of a long line. Wear warm clothes you don't mind sleeping in— something with pockets; we'll pack some hard rations. We'll be lined up for a good twelve hours."

Bartholomew raised an eyebrow. "I don't think that will be necessary, Captain. A word from me to the appropriate individual, and we'll be whisked through the formalities."

"Try bucking the line and they'll be whisking you off the deck with a ramp broom. Let's go." Henry started past Bartholomew.

"Captain, surely you're not thinking of making your appearance in a soiled ship suit? I'd suggest the outfit you wore when you came aboard; it was quite impressive—to a layman, I mean."

Henry smiled. "You might have an idea there, Larry. It could cut down on the competition. They'd die laughing."

Bartholomew shrugged, looked at Henry's bandaged hand. "How is your hand? Perhaps I'd better call for a doctor."

Henry carefully pulled on a pair of soft leather gloves; he flexed his fingers. "The hand's not too bad. Remembering not to bang it will be the problem."

"It should be in a sling . . ."

Henry laughed. "Don't let's tip off the opposition, Larry. My little infirmities will be our secret." He took a small box from the wall locker, handed Bartholomew a palm-sized slug gun. "Keep this where you can get a hand on it in a hurry."

Bartholomew looked at the weapon, a dull gray lozenge shaped like a water-worn stone. "A gun? Whatever for?"

Henry pocketed the twin to Bartholomew's gun. "That's it," he said. "Whatever . . ."

A heavy-faced man with a crooked jaw and a scar-furrowed cheek slammed a huge rubber stamp against a blue form and flipped it into the hopper. He jerked his head at Captain Henry. "Let's go, bud. Shake a leg." His voice was a blurred growl. Henry dropped the sheaf of forms before the official; he leafed through them, snapped one out, shot Henry a look.

"Where you been, *Degüello*? This is the old PC Master's ticket; they been invalidated over nine years."

Henry took a folder from an inner pocket, dropped a plastic-covered card before the man. "Maybe this will do."

The crooked-faced man squinted at the card, looked up quickly.

"Why didn't you say you were Navy, pal?" He leaned forward. "Welcome to the psych ward, brother," he said in a changed tone. "What brings you out in the hot sun with this bunch of hull-scrapings?" He jerked his head toward the crowd milling in the vast rotunda.

"Land," Henry said. He took the card, tucked it away.

The registration official nodded. "O.K., so I asked a stupid question. Say . . ." he looked past Henry's ear. "You weren't at Leadpipe with Hayle's squadron, I guess . . . ?"

"Second echelon. We hit Stapp's flank element just before the old *Belshazzar* blew."

"Whatta you know? I was in Culberson's Irregulars, covering off Amory IV. We never got close enough to pick up a ping on the IFF, but we mixed in nine days later, when Stapp pulled his Bogan reserves out of his sleeve. Let's see now . . . what was the name of his flagship . . ." The man rolled an eye toward the distant ceiling.

"*Annihilator.* A hundred and forty thousand tons, mounting six hellbores and a stern battery of ten centimeter infinite repeaters; crew of ninety-seven, Coblentz commanding . . ." Henry leaned heavily on the table with his unbandaged hand. "Do I pass the quiz . . . ?"

"You got me wrong, brother . . ." the man looked at Henry reproachfully.

Bartholomew pushed up beside Henry. "Captain, I think this fellow's hinting for a bribe," he said sharply.

The registrar's heavy brows drew down. His face folded in a pained frown.

"Back in line, buster—"

"Just a minute." Larry looked severe. "I happen to be a Designated Territorial Statistical Average; I've been standing in this line for over fourteen hours, and I have no intention of submitting to any sort of shakedown!"

"You don't, hey?" the slurred voice cut in. "I wonder if you know that guys get disqualified from registration for jumping the line—"

"You're drunk!" Bartholomew snapped. "You can hardly speak coherently!"

"Uh-huh." The official nodded. "You're right; I don't talk so good. But I'm a whiz at blackballing lightweights that talk themselves out of the Run—"

"Mr. Bartholomew would like to apologize to you, Registrar," Henry cut in. "He had a hard trip out and he's not responsible. I'll see that he keeps his chin dry from now on."

"This kewpie is with you?" The registrar aimed a finger at Bartholomew, staring at Henry.

Henry nodded.

The registrar motioned; "Let's have the papers."

Bartholomew fumbled the documents out, thrust them toward the man, opened his mouth—Henry's elbow stuck him under the ribs. He oofed, grabbed at his side with both hands.

"A guy's got to have a sidekick," the registrar banged the stamp down on the two sets of papers, shoved them across to Captain Henry. "But if I was you, brother, I'd sell this one and buy a poodle."

"Thanks, pardner." Henry took a firm grip on Bartholomew's arm and led him away.

The younger man caught his breath. "I'll . . . report him . . . Drinking on duty—"

"Uh-uh," Henry shook his head. "War wound. Notice the scars? On his jaw and throat? Blaster burns always leave a bluish edge."

"Eh?" Bartholomew pulled free. "You mean . . . the way he talked . . ."

"He had half his face shot off. They did a nice job of putting it back—the tongue is tough to rebuild."

"Oh . . . I . . ."

"Forget it. We're registered. We've got a full day before the gun goes off. Let's get a meal and then take a walk around Tent Town and find out who's here. After that we'll have a better idea of what to expect—guns or knives."

They sat in a booth in a low-ceilinged, dirt-floored shack, squat finger-marked glasses before them on a rough plank table. Henry lit up a dope stick, looked over the crowd. At the bar, a small man in undersized sailing togs and a soiled white yachting cap with bristly blond hair showing under its edge lifted a glass to him in a sardonic toast. Beside Henry, Bartholomew nodded, waved. The small man rose, said something to the man beside him, slipped off into the crowd.

"I see you've made a friend," Henry said.

"I met him while you were buying supplies," Larry said.

"What's he selling?"

"Selling? Nothing. He's retired, actually. His name

is Mr. Columbia. He owns a fleet of freighters. He's just here as a sort of relaxation. He agrees that if we work together—"

"His name's Johnny Zaragamosa. He's put on weight since I saw him last, but he's still wearing the same hat."

Larry opened his mouth; then he shut it with a snap. "Oh? Just because I was the one who met him—"

Henry cocked a sardonic eye at the younger man. Larry was beginning to feel his oats and answer back, was he?

"He was a dope runner when I knew him," Henry said. "Of course, he may have quit and bought a freight line since then."

"Just—" said Larry, stiffly, "because it was my suggestion—"

"Why did he leave so suddenly, Larry?"

"How should I know?"

"Maybe he left the water running in one of those freighters of his."

"Captain, if there's an opportunity to work out a peaceable partnership arrangement, surely you're not going to spurn it?"

"The only arrangements you could work out with Johnny would be for a quiet funeral. Now keep your eyes open and let's see how many other chiselers we can spot."

They were in another dive—the tenth—or was it eleventh—of the evening. Larry leaned across the table, his eyes squinted against the layered smoke.

"It's almost three in the morning," he stated. "We've done nothing but visit unsavory bars and drink unlicensed spirits with unshaven roughnecks."

"And so far we're still unshot, unknifed, and unpoisoned. We're doing all right."

Larry gulped half his drink, made a face. "This time could have been put to good use, working out a *modus operandi* with other gentlemanly entrants."

"I agree the booze is bad," Henry went on. "And some of the boys haven't seen their barbers lately; but we might pick up something valuable talking to the old hands at the game—"

"Drunken derelicts!" Bartholomew snapped. "They look like the sweepings of prisons for incorrigibles—"

"Some of them are—and I wouldn't count on it they left by the front gate. You'll also find ex-military men, cashiered cops, former bouncers, bodyguards, and prize fighters, not to mention stickup artists, needle-men, pickpockets—"

A small, slim man with an empty glass in his hand slipped into the seat beside Henry.

"Twenty years no see, Cap," he said, bright eyes darting to Bartholomew and back to Henry. "Did I hear you mention my name?" He had a hooked nose and dense black brows, a thin-lipped mouth with a nervous smile.

"No, but I was getting to it. Mr. Bartholomew, this is Mr. Minot—sometimes known as Back Fence Louie."

"Around here, they call me Lou the Shoe; it's like old times, Cap. I heard you was here . . ." His eyes went to Henry's gloved hands. "And that you had a little trouble on the way out . . ."

"Have a drink, Lou." Henry pushed the bottle across. "What else do you know that's free?"

Minot poured, drank, sighed, refilled his glass. "You been here twelve hours. You're riding fast iron; there's a roll behind you, so the small operators are staking you out. They figure you're tracked. You're hauling green freight—" Lou glanced at Bartholomew. "But the wise money says there's an angle . . ."

Henry laughed. "You're slipping, Lou. Your curiosity's showing."

The little man leaned close, glanced around. "The word is," he said in a low voice, "you went for the big Four, you must have a wire."

"I'm afraid I'm not following the conversation," Bartholomew interrupted. "I confess this specialist's jargon is beyond me."

Lou the Shoe looked Bartholomew over.

"Your first time out, bud?"

"And my last!"

Lou nodded. "Could be," he agreed. He turned back to Henry. "They're all aboard, this cruise, Cap; mop-up boys, dozers, kangaroos. There's three backbone squads working Tent Town right now. Don't shop around, is my advice: plant your markers and get out before the tombstone lawyers dope your pattern."

Bartholomew shook his head sadly, leaned in his corner, his arms folded. Lou blinked at him, gulped down the rest of his drink, wiped his lips with a limber forefinger.

"Lou's just warming up," Henry said. "He's tossing out all the common gossip on the off-chance I might look interested—"

"Gossip nothing," Louie countered, looking indignant.

"And meanwhile, he's trying to pick up salable information from us." Henry refilled Minot's glass.

"Oh, yeah?" The small man's lips pulled taut, showing a gap in a rank of ocher teeth. He leaned close. "Get this: Heavy Joe Saggio's in town . . ."

Henry paused in the act of pouring, then he topped off his glass, lifted it in salute, drank half. His eyes seemed brighter suddenly.

"You wouldn't kid an old pal, Lou . . . ?"

Lou's face twitched. "He's holed up in the private

room at the Solar Corona right now, talking business with a sandbag squad from Croanie."

"Don't tell me you leaned over Heavy Joe's shoulder and heard him mention me by name . . . ?"

Lou grinned nervously. "Could be, Cap. The way I remember it, you and him had a couple of run-ins."

"That was a long time ago."

Lou nodded. He emptied the glass again. "Look, Cap," he lowered his voice, talking behind a hand with which he seemed to be rubbing the side of his nose casually. "There's dough behind Heavy Joe this trip; a syndicate, out of Aldo Cerise. The word is, it's a split-and-snatch deal, a kid-glove caper. That's all I could get. And stay away from a joint named Stella's."

Henry put his hand in a knee pocket of his ship suit.

"Never mind that," Lou said. "It's on the house. Thanks for the drink." He rose. Henry raised an eyebrow inquiringly. Lou leaned over the table.

"You got a lousy memory, Cap; I owe you a couple of favors. And take it from me—keep your screens open tonight . . ." He slipped away in the crowd.

Bartholomew shook his head. "A childishly transparent effort," he said. "I suppose later he'll be back, offering late bulletins for a price."

"Maybe—but I think maybe we'd better drift on now and see what jumps out at us . . ."

Captain Henry and Bartholomew went in under a glare sign reading STELLA'S, climbed the rickety stairs, emerged into a wide, crowded room with an uneven ceiling half-hidden by a layered smoke. A short, burly waiter with a black jacket and soiled ruffles came up, offered an edge-curled menu badly printed on cheap wine-colored paper.

"What'll it be, gents?" he yelled over the blare of taped music, the surf-roar of boisterous conversation.

"How about a nice algisteak with a side order of recon spuds?"

"We want steak off a cow," Henry said. "At a corner table."

"Sure—but it'll cost you . . ."

Henry fished a hundred credit token from a pocket, flipped it to him.

"Make it good," he said.

Bartholomew trailed Henry and the waiter to a table. Henry ordered; the waiter slapped at the table with a damp cloth, moved off with the gliding gait of an old Null-G hand. Two girls with dyed lips and eyelids, swirling hairdos in silver and violet, multiple necklaces, and bare breasts squeezed above dresses like sequined corsets, appeared out of the crowd, dropped into the empty chairs.

"Hi, fellas. I'm Rennie; she's Nicki," the taller of the two said cheerfully. "Got a smoke? Brother, what a day!"

"Yeah," Nicki agreed. "Did you see the big slob I was with? For ten cees he wanted me to stand behind him all night while he shot dice; he said I'd bring him luck. Boy . . . !"

Henry offered dope sticks. "Have you ladies dined? If not, please be our guests."

"Hey!" Rennie smiled. "A nice guy for a change."

The waiter reappeared, hovering. Henry signaled. He grinned and went away.

"What's your name, Dreamboat?" Nicki smiled warmly at Bartholomew.

He cleared his throat. "Lawrence H. Bartholomew."

"Wow! That's a lot of moniker. I'll call you Bart. What's your friend's name?"

"Why, ah Cap—"

"Call me Henry. You girls work here?"

Rennie lit up, blew out smoke, shook her head. "Not

exactly; we're free-lance. Stella's O.K., though. We get along. How about a dance?" She stood and tugged at Henry's hand. He glanced over the crowd, then rose and followed the girl out onto the floor. She moved into his arms—a strong, slender, young body with a faint fragrance of exotic blossoms.

"I don't think I've seen you around, handsome," she said. "Just get in?"

"Uh-huh." The band changed its tempo, took up a rhythmic triple-beat flamencito. The girl moved with a smooth, sure rhythm, following Henry's lead.

"Say, you're good," she said. She glanced toward the table. "Your partner's pretty young, isn't he?"

"You've got to start some time."

"Sure."

The beat changed again. "My God, it's great to find a real dancer, after these cargo-sled operators that have been trampling me." Rennie executed an intricate maneuver, looked at Henry with shining eyes. He grinned back, made a sudden graceful move, twirled her to the left, then to the right, let her fall almost to the floor, caught her up on the beat. She laughed aloud. "Hey, Henry, you're the greatest! How about this one . . . ?"

The band played; the crowd milled and chattered. Against the backdrop of people, the girl's face floated, a disembodied smile, her eyes on Henry's.

A heavy body slammed against Henry. He caught himself, turned to look into a wide, broad-nosed face with scarred lips and a half-closed eye.

"Blow a whistle next time and I'll get out of your way," Henry said. He half-turned away, turned back quickly and knocked aside a hand that had reached for his shoulder. Rennie pushed in front of him, facing the intruder.

"Get going, you big ape!" she spat. "Fade. Take the air!"

The scarred lips pulled back to show a chipped tooth; a square hand with hair on the back reached for the girl. Henry eased her aside, stepped close, grabbed the thick wrist. Over the man's shoulder, Henry caught a glimpse of Bartholomew, nodding across the table at a man in a too-tight uniform blouse; it was the man he had called Mr. Columbia and he leaned toward him, talking earnestly. Nicki was gone. Then the crowd closed in, shutting off the view.

The scar-faced man struggled to free his arm. Henry smiled tightly, face to face with the other.

"Go play some other place, stranger," he said easily. "This spot's taken."

The wide face grew dusty red. "Don't get in my way, Mister." His voice was a bass wheeze. "The doll is with me."

"Anybody can make a mistake," Henry said. "But only a damned fool insists on it." He pushed the man from him; he staggered back a step, then growled and moved in. Henry blocked a low punch with his left forearm, set himself and slammed a short right that smacked home just below the ribs. The man oofed and leaned on Henry as the waiter appeared, fumbling at his hip pocket. Henry passed the man to him.

"He got hold of some bad lobster; help him outside." He turned; the girl was gone. He pushed through to the table where he had left Bartholomew. It was empty.

The waiter came up with a tray; he dumped it on the table, slid two plates off. He looked past Henry's left ear.

"The ladies ah . . . run into a old customer," he said. His tongue touched his upper lip. He reached over, dropped a used napkin in front of Henry, tossed another before Bartholomew's empty chair. He stared at Henry's napkin, then picked up the tray and slid into the crowd.

Henry prodded the napkin, palmed a slip of paper from under it.

DON'T EAT ANYTHING. WATCH YOUR-
SELF. SORRY TO CUT OUT, BUT I'VE
GOT MY OWN PROBLEMS. RENNIE.

Henry turned away from the table. The headwaiter appeared, blocking his way.

"Anything wrong, fella?" His thick lips twitched in a sick smile.

"I just got a good offer from a Mr. Columbia, and I'm hurrying to take him up on it," Henry said. "Which way did he go?"

The man's hand strayed toward his pocket. "How about the bill?" His voice was thin and high now. There was a scar down the side of his face like a seam in a football.

"There was a mistake on the order," Henry said. He looked into the man's small gray eyes, set deep under meaty brow ridges. "The wrong kind of sauce." There was a sudden shout outside. Henry turned, looking down the stairs. He pushed past the headwaiter, went down into a rising clamor of voices.

The crowd on the boardwalk was a dense-packed, pushing, bottle-waving, curse-shouting mass of glassy-eyed, open-mouthed men in use-worn ship suits, odds and ends of uniforms, patched weatheralls. Heavy guns were strapped to swaggering hips; massive boots clumped; hoarse voices bellowed greetings, snarled threats, blasphemed the gods of a hundred worlds under the flashing, multicolored glare signs on bars, joy houses, game rooms. Across the narrow strip of mud that served as a street, massed backs formed a dense ring. Henry shouldered his way through, reached the front rank. Half in a narrow alleyway between two shacks built of packing case boards stamped KAKA, a body lay sprawled, face down.

"... turned around and there he was," another voice said plaintively. "I always gotta miss the action ..."

Henry stepped to the body, turned it over. The big-nosed face was a mask of mud. A six-inch length of fine-gauge steel wire projected from just below the left collarbone. It was Louie Minot, dead.

Henry looked across at a heavy-featured man who plied a toothpick on large square teeth, looking down on the body.

"Did you see it?" Henry asked.

"Naw." The man smiled. "I'm ankling along, minding my own business, and a guy shoves me. I damn near swallow my toothpick. I turn around and there he is."

"Who shoved you?"

"What's it to you?"

Henry moved close. "You sure you didn't see it?" he said softly.

The bland expression changed. "Listen, you—" A fist started up in a short, vicious jab; Henry's hand shot out, grabbed the other's wrist, wrenched it behind him. The wide mouth opened; the toothpick fell. Henry drew the man close.

"What's your name?"

"Pore Scandy. What's it to you?" the man blustered.

"Give, Pore," Henry said.

"Hey, that hurts," the wide-faced man was on tiptoes. All around, the crowd watched, suddenly quiet.

"It was a guy with a mustache," the man blurted. "He had a pot belly, and warts, and lessee—yeah, he had a game leg."

"You forgot the long red beard." Henry reached across, lifted a small handgun from the man's side pocket. He put the muzzle against the straining chest beside him.

"Your gun?" he inquired conversationally.

"Somebody planted it on me."

"A wire-gun. A torturer's rod. I ought to feed you one through the knee."

"Look, what's the beef—" the thick man grimaced.

"Where's the kid, Pore?" Henry asked softly, his face close to the other's. The man's mouth went slack.

"Gimme a break," he hissed. "I don't know nothing."

Henry twisted the arm; the joint creaked. "Where's the kid?" he repeated tonelessly.

"Look, it's all my neck is worth—"

Henry gave the arm another half turn. "Don't let's waste time; talk it up, fast."

"Look, if I knew, I'd spill—but who tells me anything?" Sweat was running down the heavy cheeks. "All I know is, it was a fifty-credit caper. An old guy with a bad hand, Joe said—"

"Joe won't like you with a broken arm. Funerals are cheaper than doctors."

"O.K., O.K.," the man whispered hoarsely. "Go to the Solar Corona. That's where the stakeout was—I swear that's all I know . . ."

Henry shoved him away; he turned and dived into the crowd, which was breaking up and moving off now. A moment later, Minot's body was alone in a ring of trampled mud. Henry looked down at the crumpled corpse.

"I should have listened closer, Lou," he said softly. "And so should you."

The Solar Corona was a blaze of garish light from the writhing lines of neon radiating from the wide door cut in the corrugated metal front. Inside, Captain Henry bought a drink at the bar, looked over the crowd.

"You have somebody special in mind, or will I do?"

a voice rasped at his side. A woman's face, haggard under uneven paint, looked up at him. A thin hand tucked back a wisp of dead hair.

"Brother, what a night," she focused with difficulty on a jeweled finger watch taped to a bony finger. "Two hours to go; three weeks I been here—and I hardly make expenses . . ." She leaned on the bar, hitched onto the stool.

"Seen Johnny Zaragamosa around?" Henry asked idly.

The woman leaned closer. Henry caught a whiff of stale face powder.

"Friend of yours?" Her voice was scratchy, like a cheap tri-D.

"A friend of a friend."

"Then your friend better keep his hand in his pocket, or Johnny'll be in there ahead of him . . ." She showed her false teeth, swallowing half the contents of the glass the barman had thrust in front of her. Henry glanced sideways at her.

"My friend's got a strange sense of humor," he said. "But sometimes he carries a joke too far."

The woman fumbled out a dope stick, drew on it, puffed out violet smoke.

"As far as Heavy Joe Saggio's rooms at the Dead Dog?"

"Maybe," Henry said. "He's a pretty funny guy."

The woman turned toward him, opened dry, crimson lips to speak—

She stared at him for a long moment. The dope stick dropped to the bar, rolled off on the floor. She stooped swiftly, came up with it, leaned on her elbows, staring at the ranked bottles on the back bar.

"I got a message for you from a girl named Rennie," she said rapidly. "Your pigeon's in deep. Johnny used the pink stuff—too much. The kid folded like a pair of deuces to a ten-cee raise. They're trying to bring him out now. After they milk him—" She finished the drink in a gulp. "If he's a friend . . . well, you'd better hurry . . ."

"Where's this Dead Dog?" Henry snapped out.

"A flop, a couple blocks from here—but some rooms fixed up in back."

"Show me." Henry slid a hundred-credit token along the bar. The woman's thin hand went over it, whisked it out of sight.

"Listen to me," the woman said urgently. Her fingers dug into Henry's arm. "The run starts in less than two hours. Leave the poor crut—there's nothing you can do."

"Just a call on an old associate," Henry said. "I wouldn't want to leave town without dropping a card."

"Don't be a fool! What can one man do—" she broke off. "Hey—your boat; is it a Gendye fifty-tonner, a new job, plush . . . ?"

Henry nodded.

Her clutch on his arm tightened. "My God, listen! They're pulling a hijack on you! Get back to your boat—fast! But watch it; there's a stakeout on the gate . . ."

Henry peered at her in the darkness. "Who are you? Why are you helping me?"

"They call me Stella. Rennie said you were a right guy; let's let it go at that." She plucked at his sleeve. "If you go in there alone, you'll only get yourself killed. Play it smart! You've got a boat to save."

Henry took her hand from his arm gently. "I'd have to give it a try, Stella—wouldn't I?"

She was a shadow against the faint glow from the crosswalk.

"Yeah, you would, wouldn't you?" Her voice caught. "Come on. I'll show you . . ."

✧   ✧   ✧

Captain Henry stood in the dark courtyard, scanning the barely visible alleyway which ran along the left side of the ramshackle two-story building. A cold rain was falling steadily now; Henry's left hand ached inside the tight glove; he cradled it in his right, listening. The silence rang in his ears. Far away, a drunken voice called; faint footsteps hurried, faded. A night lizard scuttled in the shadows. Somewhere behind the sagging façade of the Dead Dog, Bartholomew would be coming out of the drug now, blinking at hard faces, feeling the smash of heavy fists. Henry smiled tightly, hefted the wire-gun, then started forward, hugging the wall. Skirting the yard, he moved quietly to the back of the building. The alley ended against a sheet of perforated metal. Above, he could see a glassless window opening overhung by a crude awning. He listened for a moment, then tucked the wire-gun into the thigh pocket of the ship suit, started up.

The reach from the metal wall to the window was a long one. He pulled himself up and in, ducked under the header, stood in an unlighted room. From somewhere, a murmur of voices sounded. A damp odor of moldy wood hung in the air. He crossed the room, brushed aside a coarse hanging, felt his way along an uneven floor to the wall against which two vertical rails ran up, with heavy cross members spiked against them at eighteen-inch intervals; the grand staircase of the Dead Dog.

The voices came from the other side of the partition. Henry felt along the wall to the left, reached a blank corner. There was no door.

He went to the ladder, tested the rungs, then climbed carefully. His outstretched hand touched the ceiling. He pushed; the cover lifted. Cold, wet air blew in. He went up, emerged on a sloping roof. Rain drummed against plastic roof panels; through wide gaps, lines of light glared. He moved softly to the nearest aperture, knelt, looked down into an empty room with a sagging cot, a rough pallet with a snarl of dirty blankets, a table with glasses, an empty bottle. The voices were louder now.

He went on across the roof, following the line of the bearing wall. Before him, a thin, translucent roof panel glowed softly; below, a thick voice was talking in a monotone, not quite loudly enough to be understood. Henry crouched, brought his face close to a quarter-inch crack.

A tall, heavily built man with a bald head fringed by curly black hair paced under him, turned, waved a hand on which four rings winked against sallow skin. A small man with bushy hair followed nervously, staying at the bald man's side. Beyond, Larry Bartholomew leaned forward in a chair, his hands tied behind him. The square-toothed face of Pore Scandy was visible behind the captive. A pair of feet showed on the right.

Henry put an ear to the crack.

" . . . only got an hour; this punk's dry. We got to cut for it—now!" The voice was Scandy's.

"When I need your mouth, I tell you, O.K.?" Heavy Joe Saggio's voice was the growl of an old and ill-tempered grizzly.

"Maybe he got a point, *capo*—"

There was a sound like a dead fish hitting a sidewalk.

Saggio was standing, feet apart, a gun in his hand. The bushy-haired man was dabbing at his cheek where a line of red showed. Scandy shrugged; his mouth twisted. He came around Bartholomew, reached out. Saggio threw the gun toward him; his hands curled lovingly around it.

Henry took the wire-gun from his pocket, flipped

the safety off; he rose to a kneeling position, aimed carefully through the crack, centered the sights on Scandy's neck just below the hairline, squeezed the trigger. As the gun barked, he shifted to the bushy-haired man, fired again. A gun fell from the small man's hand. Scandy leaned, fell against Bartholomew, slammed the floor. The small man was bent over, clutching his side. Henry swung the sights to Saggio as the big man ducked back, out of sight. The fourth man crossed Henry's field of vision in a jump. The lights died.

Henry pocketed the gun, moved back quickly, got to his feet. He took three running steps, crossed his arms over his face, jumped, landed squarely on the thin panel that had glowed on the roof; sharp edges raked the tough ship suit as he slammed through, hit the floor in a shower of broken plastics. He rolled, came to his knees with the gun in his hand. There was a tinkle as a final fragment dropped from the smashed panel; then silence.

Across the room, Henry could see a thin line of light around the door in the opposite wall. Against it, something moved, down low, coming between Henry and the light—a man on all fours.

There was a sound of movement near the middle of the room. A groaning sigh came from Bartholomew.

"One more move and the pigeon gets it," Saggio's deep voice rumbled. Henry crouched motionless, silent. The crawling man came closer. Henry could see his hands now, feeling over the floor. It was the fourth man, searching for one of the dropped guns.

"I'm covering the pigeon," Saggio said from the darkness. "I know where he is, O.K. I'm going out now—I leave him to you, nobody shoots. Deal?"

Henry breathed slowly, with his mouth open, not moving.

"I'm making my move now," Saggio said. "Hang loose . . ."

The crawling man turned suddenly, moved across the room, careless of noise now. His breathing was fast and shallow. A board creaked; a doorknob rattled, hinges squeaked.

"It's all yours—su—" Henry fired at the same instant that Saggio's needler spat, heard Saggio's words break off into a snarl of pain. A door slammed back against the wall. Henry fired again, dropped and rolled, fired, heard a shrill ahh! that choked off. He fired again as running feet pounded, receded into silence.

He got to his feet, flicked a permatch alight. Scandy lay crumpled by Bartholomew's chair, a length of wire bright against the pale, coarse skin of his neck. The small man lay against the baseboard, his toes in neat shoes pointed like a diver in free-fall, his arms hugging his chest, his mouth open, the cut on his cheek purple against green-white skin. In the wood frame of the door an eight-inch length of wire stood, still quivering.

Henry wedged the match in a crack in the wall; by its feeble light took out a pocketknife, cut Bartholomew free, hauled him to his feet. The younger man sagged, babbling. Blood dribbled from his cut mouth. Henry shook him, then slapped his face with his open hand. A dim light seemed to focus in the vacant eyes.

"Let's go, Larry. Make your feet work."

Larry groaned, tried to pull free.

"Before Mr. Columbia gets back," Henry said. Bartholomew's eyes steadied; his feet groped, found balance.

"Come on . . ." Henry helped him to the door, plucked the match from the wall. The narrow, unevenly floored hallway was empty, dark. They went along it to a well with a ladder. At its foot, a man lay, face down. A length of wire protruded from his back under the right shoulder blade. Bartholomew shied when he saw the body.

"Don't worry about the dead ones," Henry said softly. "Heavy Joe's down there somewhere—and he's alive, with a piece of wire in him. He'll be in a bad mood about that. We'll take the back way. Can you stand now?"

Bartholomew nodded vaguely. "Mr. Columbia," he said thickly. "He took something out of his pocket . . ."

"Sure, we'll chew over that later. Now let's see you work those legs."

In the alley, Henry helped Bartholomew to his feet. There was a sound from the darkness. An unseen door creaked. A tall, wide figure eased out awkwardly, one hand clamped to his shoulder, throwing a long shadow across the muddy yard. He paused, reached for the light switch on the wall—

"Hold it right there, Joe," Henry said softly.

Saggio bared his teeth in a mirthless grin. He had large, dark eyes, a shapeless nose, a square jaw, blue-stubbled. His hand was clamped to his shoulder.

"Enrico, baby," he growled. "Someplace I heard you was old, you lost your steam, got a bum hand. Ha! I should have knowed better . . ."

"Rumors get around, Joe—don't feel too bad. Turn around now, and head back inside. Do it real nice."

Saggio started into the shadows. A thick tongue moved over his lips that were black in the dim light.

"What you waiting for, Enrico? Maybe you never get me under your iron again, eh?" He straightened. Some of the tension went out of him. "You don't like to kill me, and maybe a couple of my boys mark you—"

Henry squeezed the trigger of the gun in his hand. A length of wire spanged into wood. Saggio's head jerked convulsively; his eyes widened. He stood very still.

"Better move, Joe," Henry said.

Saggio grinned suddenly, nodded. "O.K., Enrico baby." He turned away, then paused, looked back.

"It's like old times, hey, Enrico? I see you again sometime, hah?" He moved off, walking briskly like a man who had suddenly remembered an errand.

Chapter Four

Inside the wide rotunda of the Port Authority Building, Henry walked Bartholomew to the processing line. A familiar scarred face frowned up at him from behind a desk, glanced at Bartholomew.

"Hi, *Degüello*. What happened to Junior?"

"He had a fall," Henry said. "He'll be O.K."

The scarred man leaned forward, sniffed. He cocked an eye at Henry.

"The pink stuff, hey? He spill his guts?"

"They overdid it. He slept through the proceedings."

"Some smart guys outsmart themselves." The scarred man stamped papers, waved toward the far side of the hall.

"You cut it close, bud. You got about thirty minutes before the red rocket goes up. You played it smart, getting the extra crewman. He went aboard the car half an hour back."

Henry looked at him. "Was he alone?"

"You ain't expecting to get a whole platoon into that Bolo Minor, I hope. You'll be squeezed with three."

"Yeah. Thanks for everything."

"Good luck, bud—I'd still ditch dreaming-boy, if I was you."

"I can't. He owns the outfit."

Henry pushed through the turnstile, walked Bartholomew across toward the high glass wall, with the sweep of flood-lit ramp beyond where the massive armored ground vehicle unloaded from *Degüello* squatted, dwarfed by the looming silhouettes of converted freighters, ancient destroyer escorts, battered short-run liners. Bartholomew staggered, breathing noisily.

"How's your head now, Bart?" Henry asked.

"Ghastly. My legs—like lead. I don't remember—"

"Forget it. Try to stay on your feet long enough to get aboard. Then you can go to sleep."

"I guess I made a fool of myself . . ."

"You had lots of help."

Faint gray tinged the eastern sky now. A power unit started up, stuttering. An odor of ozone and exhaust gases floated across from the ships. Men hurried to and fro, throwing triple shadows across the tarmac. The dawn air was tense with expectancy.

A line cart puttered into view, rounding the flank of a space-pitted vessel. Henry hailed it; it slowed in a descending whine of worn turbos.

"I need a Decon; how about it?"

A tired-faced man in a white coverall stared at him from the cart.

"You birds; you drink all night, and all of a sudden you remember you got no clearance papers. If it was left up to me, I'd say to hell with you—"

"Sure." Henry handed him a ten-credit chip. "Sorry to bother you. I've had a couple of things on my mind."

He pointed toward the Bolo, parked a hundred feet away.

"O.K.; seein' it's just a car, I guess I got time . . ." The driver maneuvered his cart into position, attached hoses. Henry lowered Bartholomew to the ground, went to the panel set in the flank of the heavy machine. There were tool marks around it; it opened at a touch. Fragments of the broken lock lay inside. The button marked PORT—UNLOCK was depressed. Henry pressed the LOCK button, heard the snick of the mechanism above.

The Decon man started up the blower. Its hum built up to a sharp whine. Minutes passed. Bartholomew had stretched on his back, snoring. Henry lifted him to his feet, walked him until he could stand alone.

The driver shut down the blower, disconnected the hoses, reeled them in. He revved up his turbos, wheeled off.

Henry helped Bartholomew to the car.

"Going to be ill . . ." the younger man said.

"Let's get aboard; then you can tell me all about it." Henry cycled the hatch open; the two men climbed inside. A faint odor of Cyanon still hung in the air. Bartholomew gagged.

"Why. . .another Decon. . . ? We did that. . .before. . ." He broke off, staring at the body of a man, lying head-down in the short companionway. The eyes of the inverted face were open; the mouth gaped, showing a thick tongue. The thin features were a leaden purple.

"G-good Lord . . . !" Bartholomew groped for support. "There was . . . man inside . . . when—"

"Yeah; let's get moving."

Henry hauled his sagging shipmate past the corpse, settled him in his cradle, buckled him in. He flipped the count-down switch, set the clock.

"You knew . . . that man . . . was aboard," Bartholomew gasped out.

"Go to sleep, Larry," Henry said. He strapped himself into his gimbaled seat before the Bolo's panel, punched buttons. A ready-light glowed on the panel. The count-down clock ticked loudly.

"Attention!" the ground-control screen said. "Zero minus two minutes . . ."

There was a sudden loud snore from Bartholomew.

Henry started the engine, glanced over instruments, flipped on the specially installed wide-vision screens.

"Ten . . . nine . . . eight . . ." the screen said. Henry slipped the clutches, revved the mighty Bolo engines.

" . . . three . . . two . . . one . . ." The Bolo moved out of the shadow of *Degüello*.

"It's all yours," the speaker said. "Go and get it!"

They were ten miles into the rough country east of the port, slamming ahead, over and through obstructions like a charging bull-devil. On the screens, the clustered blips of other vehicles had fanned out now, spreading to all points of the compass from the starting point. The port IRAD showed a massive vehicle—a ten-tonner—pacing the Bolo at one mile. To the right, two smaller vehicles raced, on courses converging from two miles. Henry's glance went over the fire-control panel. Green GO lights glowed cheerfully at him. He smiled to himself, added another five hundred meters per minute to his speed. It was time to thin out the opposition.

Beside him, Larry slept, strapped in his padded couch.

At twenty miles out, the ten-tonner—a Gendye Supreme, Henry guessed—still held position at half a mile, matching his speed. The two smaller shadowers had fallen back, were mere bright specks on the screen astern. Henry flicked a switch; a pink light winked on the panel—the BATTERY ARMED telltale from a salvaged destroyer. He boosted his speed another half kilometer per minute. The Bolo bucked, slamming through tangled desert scrub.

Forty-six minutes and forty miles from Pango-Ri, Henry adjusted course to the south, punched a random evasive pattern into the course-control monitor. The couch rocked under him as the Bolo curveted in a spiral reverse. The escorting vehicle tracked him, holding interval. Henry whistled. The boy was good— and riding good iron.

Abruptly the alarm bell clanged. Henry read dials. A forty-kilo mass, closing at a thousand feet per second; a light missile. He keyed the intercept-response circuit, felt the Bolo buck as his missiles launched. Lights flashed as new missiles slid into position in the magazines. On the screen, the two tiny rockets curved out, minute flecks of yellow-white against the blackness, converging on the attacking missile.

The screens dimmed to near-opacity as the incoming weapon detonated in a blaze of hard radiation.

Bartholomew stirred, opened his eyes. "What's . . . going on?" he managed.

"Some lawless character just took a shot at us," Henry said tightly. "Go back to sleep."

"A shot—?" Bartholomew was wide awake now. "Did you report it?"

"Too busy—"

"But that's illegal! Can't we do something—?"

"Sure; we can fire back with our own illegal battery."

"Captain, my father—"

"Shut up! I'm busy . . . !"

Ten minutes passed while the two war-cars

raced northward side by side, their courses steadily converging.

"A little closer," Henry muttered. "Just come in a little closer, baby . . ."

"What are you doing?" Larry demanded.

"I'm letting him get his head well into the noose," Henry said. "If I close with him, he might spook—but since he's playing the heavy . . ."

"Perhaps he just wants to—to negotiate!" Larry said.

"We'll fool him by opening the conversation first," Henry said, and thumbed the FIRE button. A flickering glare sprang up around the Bolo. The screens flickered uncertainly as excited ions struck in uneven waves. The speeding Supreme veered away, suddenly wary too late. As it turned, its image flicked into incandescence. The screen went from white to yellow to red, faded to show long streamers trailing out to all sides in a blaze of hard radiation. Dark pinpoints of solid wreckage fanned out; a vast smoke ring shot through with bright flashes formed, grew.

The ground-control screen crackled.

"*Degüello*—what's going on out there? A while ago, I read two blasts near you—just now I picked up a two K-T flash less'n a mile abeam of you. Plenty of the hard stuff, too! It'll be raining hot iron around here for a week! Are you in trouble?"

"*Degüello* to tower," Henry grated against the slam of the speeding machine. "No, I'm having myself a time. I guess some of the boys are sloppy drivers . . ."

"If I didn't know a Minor didn't pack an armory, I might get an idea you carted some contraband in here, *Degüello*! You wouldn't pull one like that, would you?"

"Goodness, that would be illegal, tower."

"It would at that. Maybe you better call a misdeal, *Degüello* . . ."

"I hate lawsuits, tower. I'll take my chance."

"It's your play. But watch somebody moving in at two-seven-oh. Tower over and out."

A bell clanged. The IRAD showed a small car emerging from the dust cloud that was all that remained of the heavy Gendye. It swung toward the Bolo.

"Looks like he carried a spare," Henry muttered; he waited, frowning, his finger poised over the firing key. The car flashed past a hundred yards distant, close enough for Henry to read *ISV MANTA-II* lettered on the side.

At the last instant, a bright flash winked from it. Henry's finger went down on the key. The Bolo lurched. The vision screens blacked. Henry fought the controls while Bartholomew clung to his cradle, his eyes and mouth wide.

"Tricky," Henry grated. "A gyrob—a remote job. But I think we outgunned them."

"Who are they?" Bartholomew demanded. "What does it mean?"

Henry was studying the terrain map. A long peninsula stretched north from Pango-Ri, curving to the horizon and beyond—fifteen hundred miles of mountain, desert, and ice.

"It means we're in the clear for the moment," he said. "We're IRAD-negative, so maybe we've lost them for good—if we can stay ahead of them. But hold on to your hat, Larry, the next few days are going to be a little hectic."

Three days and nights had passed, Henry and Larry alternating at the controls as they raced northward. Now massive ice crags loomed on the forward direct view panel; a wilderness of broken ice was visible beyond. Strangling voices were coming from the Bolo's power compartment. Henry wrestled the wheel, attempting to brake the speeding machine to a halt.

"We can't stop here," Bartholomew yelled above the tumult. "Nothing but ice and broken rock . . . !"

"Left track's locking!" Henry shouted. "We'll settle for what we can get!"

Low, scrub-like trees hurtled past the Bolo. There was a rending crash, a shock, and the car skidded wildly. The emergency retrorockets fired a brief burst; then the car was careening sideways, throwing a spray of pulverized ice a hundred feet in the air. It shot over the crest of a rise, dropped into deep snow, plowed on another hundred yards, and came to rest with a final bone-jarring impact in a jumble of fallen rock and ice.

Bartholomew fumbled his way from his couch, bleeding from a cut on the side of his head. Choking, black smoke still wafted from the panel. Bartholomew coughed, groped his way to the view screen.

"Where are we?" he gasped, staring out at the bleak, white wilderness visible beyond the prow, half-buried in snow.

"About twelve hundred miles north of Pango-Ri, I'd estimate." Henry tossed a smashed ration box aside, got to his feet, cradling his left hand. There was blood on the tight black glove. "And lucky to be talking about it. That last shot must have gotten to us."

"You've hurt your hand," Bartholomew said. There were dark circles under his eyes, and his face was greenish pale.

"I'm all right." Henry looked him over. "How do you feel?"

"I ache all over," Bartholomew said. "And my mouth is cut . . ." He explored the raw marks on his lip with his tongue.

Henry scattered gear aside, examining the panel. "Let's see how bad off we are—"

He broke off as his eye fell on an instrument on the still-smoldering panel. He swore with feeling.

"What is it?"

"Right on our tail—so much for forty thousand credits' worth of radar-negative gear. A heavy job— a fifteen-tonner, anyway—about fifty miles out."

"You mean there's a vehicle nearby?" Bartholomew babbled. "Thank heaven! Signal them! Try the communicator—!"

"Calm down, Bart. Could be it's a far-out coincidence; wouldn't bet my second-best brass cufflinks on it."

"But, Captain—it's an incredible stroke of luck—"

"The worst luck you could have would be for that car to pay us a call. We've got to get clear of here— fast. Come on; get your pack ready!"

"Leave the car? But this is our only shelter!" Henry ignored him, shoving food into his pack, checking the charge in his power gun.

"We don't need shelter, Larry," he said. "We need distance between us and them."

"But they're our only hope of getting help!"

"Don't bitch about a little thing like a twelve-hundred-mile hike back to port. We have more immediate worries. Get the first-aid kit!" Henry picked up the folding marker frame and the plastic carton containing the four official markers that had been issued to them at Pango-Ri, then cycled the hatch open, looked out at blowing snow. Icy air cut at him like a saw.

"Captain . . ." Bartholomew stood beside him, shivering in the arctic wind. "You actually think they might *attack* us?"

"Uh-huh."

"But—they can't do this! There must be a law—!"

"Sure; the Survival of the Fittest, they call it. It may not be democratic, but it still works."

"It's madness!" Larry shivered. "This violence, lawlessness. Those are civilized men—"

"Not these boys; they intend to kill us. I don't plan to let 'em, if I can help it." Henry jumped down into the soft snow.

Bartholomew followed, then looked back at the warm cabin.

"But to leave this—to go out into a blizzard—how do we know we can even survive?"

"We don't," Henry said. "That's what makes it fun."

An hour later, Henry and Larry came down off the broken rock-slopes to a gravel-spit at the edge of a frozen river.

Larry dumped his fifty-pound pack with a groan of relief.

"Troubles?" demanded Henry, sardonically.

Larry looked over at him.

"My feet hurt," he answered. He looked at his hands. "I've already worn blisters on my palms from trying to lift the straps free of my shoulders." He stared at Henry. "How about you?"

"All right. You'll be all right, too. It's a matter of getting used to the idea a little discomfort won't kill you."

Larry bit his lower lip.

"You're in command," he said. "But it's only fair to warn you I'm not convinced of the need for abandoning the car and all the expensive equipment in it. It'll be my duty to report that fact to my father, as backer, when we return."

"Don't bother; he wouldn't appreciate the humor of it." Henry broke off, looking back in the direction from which they had come. A low rumble sounded; a flickering light winked against the lead-colored sky.

"Oh-oh; company's here." He got to his feet. "I hope this dissipates any last, lingering doubts you may have had that we're the object of someone's attentions," Henry said.

"But—if they're really after us—why aren't they following our trail? We've only come two or three miles."

"Maybe they're a little extracautious. I did what I could to discourage 'em back at Pango-Ri."

"What *did* happen there? Was there . . . violence?" Larry trailed as Henry headed upslope against a driving wind.

"I guess you could call it that."

"Was anyone . . . injured?"

"Well, you got a split lip."

"I mean, seriously?"

"I don't think so. I left a couple of lads in an alley, nursing headaches, and Heavy Joe has a piece of Pore Scandy's wire in his arm, but they'll recover."

"Well, then, why are you so sure—"

"Of course, I killed four of them," Henry added.

Bartholomew stopped dead. "You k-k-killed four m-men?"

"Remember the chap we found when we came aboard? He got an overdose of rat poison—"

"I-I seem to remember—something—a face, upside down . . ."

"That's the guy. You were coming out of the gas by then."

"But—you'll be tried for murder—"

Henry started off. "Who by?"

Bartholomew trailed him, still struggling into his pack harness. "By the planetary law-enforcement agencies . . ."

"Not here; there's no law, no cops, no murder trials."

"Then the Quarantine Service—"

"They're busy managing the Run. They don't bother much with unsuccessful entrants."

"But when we return to civilization—"

"We're outside the jurisdiction of Aldorado. The only law here is what you make up as you go along. Heavy Joe sent his boys up against me, and I outgunned 'em. It could have been the other way around."

"But—how could you do it, Captain—kill a man, a fellow human?"

"Before you see home again you may know the answer to that one."

They tramped on in silence for an hour; the probing wind bit at the exposed skin of their faces and wrists; dry snow particles stung like flying sand.

"What will we do when night falls?" Bartholomew called suddenly. "The temperature is well below freezing now; it will drop even lower—"

A bright flash glared briefly against the snow, throwing long shadows for an instant ahead of the men. Underfoot, the ground quivered. A dull *boom!* sounded, rolled, faded.

"There went the Bolo," Henry said. He stood, staring back along the trail. Across the icy rock, a few footprints showed, filling rapidly with brown snow. "She deserved better than that."

"They blew up our car?" Bartholomew's face was haggard in the fading light.

"Still think it's a detachment of the Travelers' Aid?"

Bartholomew stared around at the broken landscape of gray rock, white ice. "What if they follow us—attack us here . . . ?"

"We're dead meat if they follow up close. My idea is to reach the hills; maybe we'll find a spot to hole up."

"What then? Our suit power packs won't last forever; we'll freeze—even if they don't kill us . . ."

"We're not dead yet. Let's stay alive and wait for the opposition to make a mistake."

✧ ✧ ✧

"Listen," Larry cupped an ear. "Isn't that the sound of engines?"

"Could be. I guess the boys plan to make sure of us."

"How—how many of them—" panted Larry, leaning against the slope and the wind, "did you say you killed?"

Henry smiled grimly. "You like the revenge motive, eh?" He shook his head. "It doesn't figure; they're spending a lot of money chasing us; sentiment isn't in it."

"Captain—do you notice anything . . . ?" Larry stopped, stood with his head up, sniffing the air. "I detect—a sort of fresh, green odor—very faint . . ." He nodded forward, toward the next line of hills. "From up ahead there . . ."

"That so?" said Henry. He turned to look oddly at the younger man. "Well, the unexpected always demands an explanation. Let's shove ahead and take a look."

Ten minutes later they topped a rise to look down across a sheltered valley that stretched to a distant, hazy line of high white hills. A dark clump of foliage showed starkly a quarter of a mile distant.

"Good Lord, Captain," Bartholomew stared at the scene. "Those are trees down there . . ."

"That's right. We'll have cover—and they'll stand out like flies on a wedding cake in all this nice smooth snow."

They tramped down across the snowy field. Ahead, the clump of trees loomed up, tapered, pale-barked tree ferns, fifty feet high. The two men circled cautiously, then came close. A breath of warm air seemed to flow upward from the shadowed grove. They went in under the trees. A gentle breeze stirred the feathery leaves on low-hanging branches.

"Captain—this is grass underfoot! And that wind! It's warm! It's coming from there . . ." Bartholomew went toward the mound at the center of the copse, almost buried under creeping vines. Henry stood watching the younger man. Larry stopped, came up with a tiny, pale yellow flower of intricate shape.

"It's incredible! This oasis—"

He broke off. There was a sudden motion; a tiny winged creature whirred from the dark mound, darted past Bartholomew's head as he ducked. It fluttered on, then fell to the snow at the outer edge of the ring of trees. It lay, beating gossamer wings, then fell still.

"Captain!" Larry looked from the vine-grown mound. "There's a light shining from here . . ." Henry came up beside him. Through the blanketing tangle of fluttering leaves, a greenish glow filtered from below.

"There's sort of a crack down there—a slot in the face of the mound!" said Larry, excitedly. "The air is coming from there!"

Henry shoved past him, pulled aside finger-thick creepers, revealing a smooth, rock-like surface. It was geometrically flat, dull grayish-black in color, with a five-foot-wide, three-inch-high opening.

"Why, it's man-made," Larry said. Henry nodded. He had drawn his gun, almost absently. There was no sound but the steady sigh of air flowing from the opening.

"It looks old," Bartholomew whispered. "But the light . . . Do you suppose . . . ?"

"Nobody home—for a long time now." Henry holstered the gun, worked his way behind the screen of vegetation; his feet sank into a soft mulch of decayed vegetation. "Let's get this stuff cleared away and take a look inside."

❖   ❖   ❖

Half an hour later, Henry's knife sawed through the last of the interwoven network of twisted vines; a mass of heavy foliage fell away from the opening. A warm draft gushed out, blowing fallen leaves, whipping at dangling tendrils of greenery. Henry looked down into a rectangular chamber fifteen feet on a side, bare, unadorned, its floor drifted deep with blown dust and dead leaves, dotted over with tiny green plants and the white knobs of fungus. At the far side, a slab door stood ajar; soft green light came from beyond it.

"If we pull a little more of this debris away, we can climb down in there," Henry said. "Then if we can douse the light, we'll have a first-class defensive position."

"Is that wise, Captain?" The green light cast shadows on Bartholomew's face. "It may be some sort of trap."

Henry shook his head. His eyes glittered in the eerie light. "The boys are tricky, all right; they trailed us a hundred miles off the beaten track. But I'm pretty sure they didn't rush ahead and set up a booby trap at the end of the line. Nobody's that good."

He dug into the loose-packed rubbish, cleared a trough, then turned and lowered himself down the sloping heap to the floor of the buried room. The light glowed from an open doorway. Beyond it was another room, much like the first, but longer, bright-lit by the glare from still another door. In the middle of the floor lay a pattern of small objects like scattered sticks.

Bartholomew dropped down, came up behind Henry.

"What do you suppose it is?"

Henry stooped, picked up a curiously shaped object of reddish metal. A shred of grayish fabric clung to it. He stirred the stick-like remains with his finger.

"It's a skeleton," he said.

"A skeleton? Of what?"

"Something that wore clothes."

"Clothes . . . ? But those don't look like anything human . . ."

"Who said it was human?" Henry's voice was rough; it tore at his throat. He turned toward the bright doorway, twenty feet away at the end of the long chamber. A haze like hot air rising from a blast pad shimmered in the rectangular archway. Beyond stretched a view of rolling green hills, dotted with groves of thin-stemmed trees with celery-like tops. Far away, wooded mountains reared up under a sky as deep and clear as green glass.

"What . . ." Larry's voice stumbled. "What is it? How . . ."

But Henry scarcely heard him. He was already walking toward the mirage-like scene. A steady flow of warm air pushed into his face, bringing an odor of spring.

There was a moment of pressure as he passed through the door, like the surface of a pond breaking; and he was standing among nodding wild flowers. He filled his lungs with the warm air; like a man who has at last come home, and something that had been locked inside him for so long that he had all but forgotten it was there, released.

Then he came back to the present. He made himself turn and step back into the chamber. Larry was staring at him.

"Good Lord!" said the young man, softly. His face was pale. "What is it, Captain? What does it mean? Why didn't you toss something through there before you tried stepping through yourself? Anything could have happened to you, when you stepped through that—that *hole* in the world."

"Let's get back topside and camouflage the opening," Henry said brusquely. "Then we'll come back down and you can take a look for yourself."

❖   ❖   ❖

The distant mutter of turbos rose and fell. "They're coming up fast," Henry said. "We left a pretty good trail that last half mile or so. When they hit that, they'll be here in minutes."

"We've done all we can," Larry panted. "After we slide down, I'll pull the mat in place. Then if we close the inner door to shut the light away—"

"Yes," Henry said. His mind was only half on the defensive preparations they were making. He added, absently, ". . . and if they find us, they'll still have to come through the door one at a time . . ."

The two men re-entered the chamber, settled the mass of bundled vines firmly in the opening. Inside the inner room, they pushed the heavy door to. It sealed smoothly. Henry turned to the entrance.

"—That skeleton, Captain," said Larry following him. "It must be from some non-human creature—but on all the worlds we've found yet, there was nothing higher than the insect level—"

"Martian pyramids," said Henry, briefly.

"But those were natural formations—"

"Maybe." Henry was almost to the entrance. "And on the other hand, maybe whoever built this visited a few other places, too."

Larry caught at his arm, stopping him.

"Captain! You aren't just going to walk through that doorway again without checking—" Henry shook off the younger man's grasp.

"Stay behind if you want to," he growled, and walked toward the light, toward sunshine and flowers and grass. A tingling sensation washed over his face as he went through and then the feel of yielding sod under his feet. The warm, moist odor of clean earth rose up around him. Behind him he heard the last half of a spoken word.

"—air!"

He turned; beyond the delicately carved stone of the doorframe, Larry stood in the shadows, staring at him.

"Come on along, Larry," Henry said. "We've got some claim markers to plant."

"Captain . . ." Larry was staring at him strangely. "I have the impression you know this place; that you've been here before."

"Do you?" Henry said, and turned and started away across the springy turf.

Chapter Five

On the bank of a stream half a mile from the low, stone-faced building that housed the portal, Henry set up the marker frame.

"O.K.," he said, "let's have the marker, Larry."

Larry opened a light case, took out a six-inch cylinder pointed at one end, passed it over.

"These markers are the cat's meow, Larry," Henry said. "They blast their way down about forty feet into solid rock, and fuse the hole closed behind them; and a thousand years from now, they'll still be putting out a trickle signal."

"Very interesting, I'm sure," Bartholomew muttered. He looked pale, sick. Every few seconds he glanced toward the portal as if expecting to see the enemy charging through, guns blazing. Henry ignored the boy's worried look. He fitted the marker into the slide on the light frame erected on the sod, clamped the cover tight.

"Let's get back of something; there'll be vaporized granite around for a few seconds . . ." He moved off thirty feet to the shelter of a fallen log. Bartholomew followed, limping on both feet.

Henry keyed the detonator. There was a spurt of white fire from the frame, a deep-toned *whoomp!* White light glared for a moment across the sunny meadow, outlining the trees in vivid relief. An odor of hot rock whipped past as the ground underfoot trembled. Dirt pattered down all around.

Henry handed Bartholomew the bright red disk of plastic he had removed from the marker before placing it.

"She's planted—but it won't do us any good unless we can produce the tabs on demand—so take care of it."

"Why me?"

"Just in case the opposition catches me. I can't give 'em what I haven't got."

"What if they catch *me?*"

"You stay out of it—don't try to help me if I'm caught. Hide; lie low until you can get clear—then try to make it back to Pango-Ri—"

"Captain, look—I've been thinking. That other car; Ground Control at Pango-Ri must have known we were in trouble, and sent out—"

"Mighty fast work; they were there within minutes. And what about that blast we heard?"

"A signal—"

"Some signal; a flare would have been more to the point."

"But things like you're talking about just don't happen. My father—"

"Look around you, Larry . . ." said Henry, heavily, "and tell me that 'things just don't happen . . .'"

Larry glanced around at the turf, the distant trees, and the green sky. He shivered, slightly.

"I . . . don't know . . ."

"It's pretty country, Larry. Go ahead and admit it."

"Yes . . . I'll agree with you there . . ." The young man's back straightened, and a faint note of an enthusiasm Henry had never before heard in Larry's voice sounded in it now. Then his gaze came sharply back to Henry. "But we can't stay here indefinitely with the crew you say are hunting for us up there and winter coming. We could be stranded here . . . maybe we could come to terms with whoever's supposed to be after us . . ."

"You're a forgiving soul, Larry—and a forgetful one. Relax. We'll get our other markers planted; then we'll wait twenty-four hours before we have a peek outside."

A blaze of stars lit the wide summer meadow like a full moon.

"That's Iota Orionis, all right," Henry said. He lay on his back, spooning omelet from a ration can. "But I'm damned if I can find any of the rest of the Orion stars from this angle."

"It's incredible," Larry said. "Why, with that much displacement of the constellation we could be over a thousand light years from the Terran Sector—but that's impossible."

"We're here," said Henry. "You'd better pretend to believe it." He was watching the younger man. With the light of the fire on his face, Larry's features showed a wonder and a kindling of excitement, an *aliveness* that was new to him. *I never meant to bring him here, Dulcia . . .* Henry thought to his long-dead wife. *I never even meant to bring myself again—or thought I didn't . . .*

Then, suddenly, he was thinking of a duty left undone for more than a hundred years. He got up unobtrusively and left the fire. When he came back, some little while later, Larry stared at him.

"What is it, Captain?"

Henry shook his head and sat down by the fire again, dusting his hands.

"Burial detail," he said, shortly. "That's all—those bones we saw, coming in."

"You buried that alien skeleton? But—" Larry broke off abruptly, his brows narrowing thoughtfully as he stared across the flames at Henry. " . . . Of course, Captain," he wound up softly. "You know best."

He turned to look at the star-filled sky again.

"I've been watching the stars move," he went on, in a strangely quiet voice. "I've been watching the whole sky of them move as this world turns . . . and I've been thinking. You know what this means, Captain— what we've found here? We've got a universe to explore again! We've been stagnating for a hundred years now; without FTL travel, there'd never be another frontier, where a man could test himself against the odds; we'd settled down to the day of the Statistical Average—and I thought that was the millennium. But now I see it all differently! Now—we'll study this thing, learn how it works. And when we do—Captain, the whole Galaxy will be open to us!"

He swung about to face across the fire to Henry. "Do you know what I mean?"

Henry was staring into the fire. There was a look on his face that made Larry fall silent . . .

Looking into the red embers, Henry felt the old words stirring in his mind. He had thought he had forgotten them, a century before; but now they came back as they had rung in his head when he had first walked this alien earth, seen this other sky—rung in his head until he was drunk with them and the new universe before him, until he had forgotten his home, his race, even the first Dulcia, waiting for him on Flamme, alone, with the baby due and no one to whom she could turn.

Oh, Dulcia. If only I'd come back to you when I promised you I would. But it was a whole new world— a whole new Universe. I *had* to see. You understand how it was with me, don't you, girl . . . ?

—They came creakily, strangely from his tongue at first, but they rang out, gaining strength as he recited . . .

> There's no sense in going further—it's the
>   edge of cultivation,
> So they said, and I believed it—broke my
>   land and sowed my crop—
> Built my barns and strung my fences in the
>   little border station
> Tucked away below the foothills where the
>   trails run out and stop.
>
> Till a voice, as bad as Conscience, rang
>   interminable changes
> On one everlasting whisper day and night
>   repeated—so:
> Something hidden. Go and find it. Go and
>   look behind the Ranges—
> Something lost behind the Ranges. Lost and
>   waiting for you. Go!
>
> So I went, worn out of patience; never told
>   my nearest neighbors—
> Stole away with pack and ponies—left 'em
>   drinking in the town;
> And the faith that moveth mountains didn't
>   seem to help my labors
> As I faced the sheer main-ranges, whipping
>   up and leading down.
>
> March by march I puzzled through 'em,
>   turning flanks and dodging shoulders,

> *Hurried on in hope of water, headed back*
> *for lack of grass;*
> *Till I camped above the tree-line—drifted*
> *snow and naked boulders—*
> *Felt free air astir to windward—knew I'd*
> *stumbled on the Pass . . .*

He chanted on, the fire of the old poem filling his veins with its light and lifting him up, up and out toward the unknown stars as he talked. He had forgotten the past and a hundred years of penitence and sorrow. He had forgotten even the presence of Larry, staring silent across the leaping flames at him. The old call—the call that had sung him out to the worlds untrod by men ever since his strength had first come on him, was singing to him now. The last verse of the poem rolled like an anthem from his tongue . . .

> *. . . Yes, your "Never-never country"—yes*
> *your "edge of cultivation"*
> *And "no sense in going further"—till I*
> *crossed the range to see.*
> *God forgive me! No, I didn't. It's God's*
> *present to our nation.*
> *Anybody might have found it but—His*
> *Whisper came to Me!*

Slowly Henry came back from the wild cataract of feeling and memory on which the ancient words had swung him, and now he was seeing himself clearly: for the first time in a hundred years he stood face to face with himself—and saw that the flame had never left him. It had been in him, all this time, the fire that had beckoned him onward, ever onward, always onward into new worlds. A noble fire, he'd always thought it—but crimes had been committed in its name.

"Dulcie," he murmured aloud. "Oh, Dulcie . . ." He shook his head like someone coming out of a dream; and looked across the fire.

On the other side of it, Larry still sat transfixed, staring at him, the lean young face as still as if the boy had been magicked into stone.

"It's a poem," Henry said. "—*The Explorer*. An old Terran named Rudyard Kipling wrote it back in A.D. 1600 or thereabouts."

"I think—I almost understand, Captain," Larry said.

Henry laughed harshly. "Who ever understands anything, kid?" he growled and the spell that had bound both men together for a moment was broken. But not completely broken, for Larry still looked at Henry with eyes like those on someone who has seen a legend put on flesh and walk.

"Captain . . ." whispered Larry. "You . . . you'll never die . . ."

"Roll over and get some sleep," muttered Henry, lying down. "We'll leave at dawn."

He rolled over himself, turning his back on the younger man and what had just passed between them.

They climbed up at dawn through the blocked doorway, emerging into the sub-zero cold under an icy blue sky.

"That was a long night," Larry said. "It looks like late afternoon here."

Henry led the way across to the edge of the clearing, looked out across the snow.

"Footprints and tread tracks, but no signs of life now. It looks like they gave up and went away."

"What will we do now?"

"First, we'll reconnoiter the area; there may be a useful piece or two of the Bolo left lying around. Then we'll start walking."

"Walking?" Larry looked at him. "To Pango-Ri? Twelve hundred miles?"

"You have a better idea?"

"No. I . . ." the younger man hesitated. "I thought maybe we could signal for help. Build some sort of communicator. It wouldn't have to be a screen—even a spark-gap transmitter would do."

"No can do, boy," said Henry. "Not without the wrong people picking up the transmission and homing in on us. No," he shook his head, "that's out. We walk. Let's scout the remains of the car before full dark, and then hit the trail. We'll be less conspicuous by night."

They started across the churned snow, reached the surrounding line of hills, entered the area of broken rock.

Henry stopped, listening, looking into the early evening gloom with narrowed eyes.

"Maybe I was a little too optimistic," he said.

"Optimistic?" Larry stared at him, his thin face tense.

"Turbos!" Henry snapped. "Hear them? This is where we split up, Larry. Use your compass; head due south; I'll rejoin you as soon as I throw the hounds off the trail . . ."

"You mean I'm to go—alone—" there was a faint ring of panic in the young man's voice.

Henry nodded. "I'm sorry now I got you into this, Larry—but you're here. Take the blaster . . ." He handed it over. " . . . And remember what I said about letting me handle my own troubles. Good luck."

"Wait! I can't—"

"You'd better, Larry. Now split!" He turned, started toward the high ground at a trot. Behind him Bartholomew stood, the blaster in his hand, looking after him.

❖   ❖   ❖

There was a sound from the direction of the slab-tilted crest ahead, a stark and ragged silhouette against the red sky of evening. Henry dropped flat. The low outline of a tracked carryall moved into view. There was a sudden crackling sound, then an amplified voice:

"Play it smart and easy, and nobody loses nothing. I'm giving you fair warning! I got twenty men. There's only the two of you. Now, you make it easy on us, we'll make it easy on you. Put your guns down and stand up with both hands in sight . . ."

Henry groped in a flapped pocket, took out a green capsule. He swallowed it, then took the slug gun from his pocket, moved off, keeping in the shelter of massive stone fragments. Harsh voices shouted. Off to Henry's left a light winked on, a dusty blue-white lance stabbing into the twilight. It reversed, playing over the rocky ground, swept up the slope, throwing red-black shadows across the ice. Henry dropped, worked his way back as the light glared just above his head. There were more yells. A second light blinked on. Men crashed down the slope, fanning out to surround his position. The light moved on; Henry rose to a crouch, his feet dashed for a dense shadow.

Lying flat among tumbled boulders heaped at the foot of an exposed rock face rising among the trees, Henry listened to the shouts behind him. If he could make it to the top of the outcropping, he might get clear . . .

Henry moved forward, keeping low; a cleft split the wall before him. He wound his way into it, braced his back, got a grip above, pulled himself up. The injured hand gave a stab of pain; blood trickled down his wrist, hot as melted lead. Henry swore, reached again . . . the blood-wet hand slipped. Henry lunged, missed, fell with a clatter. Someone yelled nearby. Feet pounded, a man burst into view.

"Hold it right there!" The voice was like a knife grating on bone. A whistle shrilled. Men closed in on either side; Henry saw the glint of guns. Around him, the scene held a curiously remote quality; the capsule he had swallowed was taking effect. There was a whine of turbos; the carryall came up, light glared on its side. It halted; a big man jumped down and came up to Henry. He was a looming black outline against the blinding light.

"This him, Tasker?" somebody said.

"Sure, who was you expecting, the fat lady in the circus?" The silhouette had a meaty voice. A hand prodded Henry.

"Where's the kid, Rube? You boys had me worried there for a while; you dropped right off the scope. Where were you?"

Henry said nothing; silently, he repeated the auto-suggestion which the hypnotic drug would reinforce. *I can't talk, I can't talk . . .*

"I'm talking to you, hotshot!" the big man said. He took a step closer. "I ast you where the kid was."

Henry watched; a heavy fist doubled, drew back—

Henry shifted, and swung a hearty kick that caught the big man solidly under the ribs; as he doubled, Henry uppercut him. The impact against his fist seemed as insubstantial as smoke. Someone yelled. A blow across the neck sent Henry to his knees. He saw a knee coming, turned his face in time to take it on the side of the jaw. The cold rock hurt his knees—but distantly the drug was working.

Hands were hauling him upright. The big man stood before him, holding one hand against his stomach, dabbing at his mouth with the other.

"I left myself open for that one," he said between clenched teeth. "Now let's get down to business. You got some marker tabs; hand 'em over."

Henry shook his head silently. There were men holding his arms. The big man swung a casual back-handed blow, rocked Henry's head. "Shake him down, boys," he growled.

Heavy hands slapped at Henry, turning out his pockets. His head rang from the drug and the blows he had taken. Blood trickled down his cheek from a cut on his scalp.

"Not on him, Tasker."

"Give, hotshot," Tasker said. "You think we got all night?"

"What's with this guy?" a small voice asked. "He ain't said a word."

"Yeah; that's what they call psychology. Guys that think they're tough, they figure it's easier that way; if they don't start talking they don't have to try to remember when to quit." He hit Henry again. "Of course, hotshot here knows better than that. He knows we got the stuff that will make a brass monkey deliver a lecture. He just likes to play hard to get." He swung another open-handed blow.

"That's O.K. by me," he added. "I kind of like it; takes my mind off my bellyache."

"Look, we're wasting time, Tasker. Where's the kid at?" someone called.

"Probably hiding back of a daisy someplace. He won't get far in the dark. After we work hotshot over, we'll have plenty time to collect the kid. Meantime, why not have a little fun?"

"Yeah; this is the punk that drilled Pore with his own iron—"

"To hell with Scandy; he was a skunk. This crut clubbed *me* down . . ." A thick-set man with a droop-ing eyelid pushed to the fore, set himself, slammed a left and right to Henry's stomach . . .

To Henry, the pain of the blows seemed as blurred

as a badly recorded sense tape. His tongue was thick, heavy, responding to the autohypnotic suggestion. Something as soft as down tugged his arms over his head. The throbbing in his skull and chest was no more than a drumbeat now. He blinked, saw Tasker's heavy-jawed face before him—like a slab of bacon with a frown.

"This son of a bitch don't act right, Gus," he growled. A small man with dark lips and white hair came close, stared at Henry. He thumbed his eyelid back, then leaned close and sniffed.

"Ha! A wise jasper! He's coked to the eyebrows, boss. Some kind of a CNS damper and paraben hypno, I'd guess." He looked sharply at Henry. "That right, bud?"

Henry looked at the man. His vision was clear enough. He moved his fingers; he still had motor control. If he got a chance, it would be pleasant to kick Tasker again . . .

A pillow struck him in the face. "There's no use hitting him; he can't feel it," the small man said.

"Slip him some of your stuff, Gus," Tasker snapped. "He's clammed up; O.K.; I know how to open clams."

"I haven't got anything that will kill this effect. We'll have to wait until it wears off—"

"Wait, hell!" Tasker barked. "I want action—now!"

"Of course, he can hear everything we say." The little man's deep-set eyes studied Henry's face. "Tell him you're going to break his legs, cut him up. He won't feel it, of course—but he'll know what you're doing—and if he tries hard enough, he can throw off the hypnotic inhibition on talking . . ."

Tasker's face came close. "You heard that, didn't you, hotshot? How do you feel about a little knifework? Or a busted bone or two? Like this—" He bared his teeth, brought his arm up, chopped down with terrific force.

Henry heard the collarbone snap, and even through the anesthetic, pain stabbed.

"Careful—the shock to the system can knock him out . . ." The small man fingered Henry's wrist.

"Pulse is good," he commented. "He has a very rugged constitution—but exercise a little restraint."

Tasker wiped the back of his hand across his mouth. His eyes were unnaturally bright. "Restraint, yeah," he said. "You got one of them scalpels, ain't you, Gus?"

"Umm. Good idea." The little man went away.

Tasker came close. His eyes were slits, like stab wounds in a corpse.

"To hell with the kid," he said softly. "Where's the mine at?" He waited, his lips parted. His breath smelled of raw alcohol.

"I been over this ground like ants on a picnic; I'll be frank with you, hotshot. I didn't see no mine—and my plans don't call for waiting around . . ."

If he'd come just a little closer . . .

"Better give, sweetheart. Last chance to deal . . ."

Henry swung his foot. Tasker danced back. Gus came up, handed over a short knife with a glittering razor edge. Tasker moved it so that it caught the light, reflected into Henry's eyes.

"O.K., hotshot," he said in a crooning tone. "That's the way you want it. So now let's you and me have a talk . . ."

Henry hung in the ropes, his body laced in a net of pain like white-hot wires. His heart slammed against his ribs like a broken thing.

"You'll have to slack off," Gus said. "He's coming out of it; he's lost a great deal of blood."

"It's getting daylight," someone growled. "Look, Tasker, we got to round up the kid . . ."

"You think I don't know that?" the big man roared. "What kind of a guy is this? I done everything but gut him alive, and not a squeak out of him. Where's them tabs, you son of a one-legged joy-girl?" He shook the black-crusted scalpel in a blood-stained fist before Henry's eyes. "Listen to me, you! I got a pain-killer; it works fast. As soon as you tell us where the tabs are, I'll give it to you . . ."

Henry heard the voice, but it seemed no more than a small annoyance. His thoughts were far away, wandering by a jeweled pond in the sunlight . . .

"All right, hotshot—" Tasker was close, his eyes wild. "I been saving the big one . . ." He brought the scalpel close. "I'm tired of playing around. Talk—now—or I'll gouge that eyeball out there like a spoonful of mushmelon—"

"You'd better let me close up a few of these cuts," Gus said. "And I need a blood donor; type O plus, alpha three. Otherwise he's going to die on you."

"All right; but hurry it up." Tasker turned to the men lounging around the clearing in the dim light of predawn. "You guys scatter and find the punk. Slim, take your car and run east; Grease, you cover west. The rest of you fan out south . . ."

Fingers fumbled over Henry; the net of wires drew tighter. His teeth seemed to be linked by an electric circuit which pulsed in time to the jolting in his chest.

Turbos whined into life; the high-wheeled carryalls moved off among the rock. A tinge of pink touched the sky now. Henry drew a breath, felt steel clamps cut into his side as broken ribs grated.

The small man whistled tunelessly, setting clamps with a bright-metal tool like a dentist's extractor. The sharp points cut into Henry's skin with a sensation like the touch of a feather. A grumbling man stood by, watching his blood drain into a canister hung from a low branch. Gus finished his clamping, turned to the blood donor, swabbed the long needle, plunged it into Henry's arm, smiling crookedly up at him past brown teeth.

"He felt that, Tasker. He's about ready . . ."

It was quiet in the clearing now. An early-rising song lizard burbled tentatively. The trees were visible as black shapes against a pearl-gray sky. Suddenly it was very cold. Henry shivered. A blunted steel spike seemed to hammer its way up his spine and into the base of his skull, driven by the violent blows of his heart.

"Where'd you hide the tab?" Tasker brought the scalpel up; Henry felt it against his eyelid. The pressure increased.

"Last chance, hotshot," Tasker's face was close to Henry's. "Where's that kid?"

Henry dried to draw back from the knife, but his head was cast in lead. There was a snarl from Tasker. Light exploded in Henry's left eye, a fountain of fire that burned, burned . . .

"Watch it! He's passing out . . ." Voices faded, swelled, mingled with a roaring in which Henry floated like a ship in a stormy sea, spinning, sinking, down, down into blackness.

A veil of red-black hung before the left side of Henry's face. Dim shapes moved in a pearly fog. Strident voices nagged, penetrating the cotton-wool dream.

" . . . I found him," Gus was saying. His voice was urgent. "Right over there . . . hunkered down back of your carryall."

Another voice said something, too faint to hear.

"You don't need to worry. We're your friends," Gus said.

"I've got my guys running all over the country, looking for you," Tasker said heartily. "I guess you was hiding out right here all the time, hey?"

"Where's the Captain?" Bartholomew's voice almost squeaked.

"Don't worry about him none. Say, by the way, you haven't got the tabs on you—?"

"Where is he, damn you?" Bartholomew's voice burst out.

Henry hung slackly in the ropes that bound his wrists to the side of the carryall. By moving his remaining eye, he was able to make out the figure of Tasker, standing, feet planted wide, hands on hips, facing away from him. Bartholomew was not in sight. Beside Tasker, Gus sidled off to the left.

"Hey, youngster, let's watch yer language," Tasker growled. "We're here to help you, like I told you . . ." He moved forward, out of range of Henry's vision.

"Leave me alone . . ." Bartholomew ordered. There was a quiver in his voice.

"Looky here, sport, I guess maybe you don't get the picture," Tasker chuckled. "Hell, we come out here to help you. We're going to get you back to Pango-Ri, where you can get that claim filed—"

"I want to see Captain Henry. What have you done with him?"

"Sure," Tasker said agreeably. "He's right over there . . ."

There was a sound of steps in the brittle snow crest underfoot. Bartholomew stepped into view, a tall figure wading through the ground mist under the tilted rocks. He stopped abruptly as he saw Henry. His mouth opened. He covered it with his hand.

"Hey, take it easy," Tasker said genially. "Ain't you ever seen blood before?"

"You . . . you . . . incredible monster . . ." Bartholomew got out.

"Say, I told you once about talking so damn smart. What the hell you think we're out here for, the fun of it? This boy's kind of stubborn; didn't want to cooperate. I done what I had to do. You can tell that to your old man; we went all the way. Now let's have those tabs and get the hell out of here."

"My God . . ." Bartholomew's eyes held on Henry, sick eyes in a pale face.

"Weak stummick, hey? Don't look at him, then. I'll call the boys in and—"

"You filthy hound—" Bartholomew turned away, stumbling.

"Hey, you crummy little cushion-pup!" Tasker's voice rose to a bellow. "I got orders to safe-conduct you back to your pa—but that don't mean I can't give you a damned good hiding first—"

The little man came into view, moving quickly after Bartholomew. A gun barked; he stumbled, fell on his face, bucked once, clawing at himself, then lay still.

There was a moment of total silence. Then Tasker roared.

"Why, you flea-brained mamma's boy, you went and shot the best damned surgeon that ever sold dope out of a Navy sick bay! You gone nuts or something . . . ?"

"Cut him down," Henry heard Bartholomew's voice. "I'm going to take him to your car. There'll be a med cabinet there—"

"Look here, buster," Tasker grated, "this bird alive is one little item I don't want around, get me? You must be outa your mind. Your old man—"

"Leave my father out of your filthy conversation! He wouldn't wipe his feet on scum like you . . ."

"He wouldn't, hey? Listen, you half-witted little milk-sucker, who do you think sent us out here?"

"What do you mean . . . ?"

"I mean our boy here got a little too sharp for his own good. He held your old man up for half a cut—and high-pressured him into sending his pup along, just for insurance. The old man don't take kindly to anybody twisting his arm. He give orders to let hotshot here stake out his claim. Once he done that, we get the tabs and take 'em back—and you along with 'em . . . And I'll tell you, buddy-boy, you're damn lucky your old man's who he is, or I'd string you up alongside this jasper!"

"You're saying—my father sent you here?"

"That's it, junior. Your old man's quite a operator."

"You're lying! He couldn't have told you where to come; I didn't even know myself . . ."

"There's a lot you don't know, sonny. Like that beacon you got built into them trick boots you're wearing. The hotshot fooled the boys back at Pango-Ri, all right—but it didn't make no difference. I had a fix on the left heel of yours ever since you hit atmosphere." He chuckled. "What do you think of that, boy?"

"I'll show you," Bartholomew said. He moved into Henry's field of vision, a tall, slender figure with a gun in his hand.

"Hey—hold on—" Tasker started. Bartholomew brought the gun up and shot Tasker in the face.

Henry lay on the ground, looking up at the pale light that illuminated the eastern sky. A turbo started up, whined up to speed. Bartholomew jumped down, bent over him.

"Captain—can you hear me?"

Henry drew a breath, tried to move his tongue; it was five pounds of dead meat. Over his body, fire ants crawled, devouring. Deep inside, an ache swelled and throbbed. He tried again, managed a grunt.

"You're horribly injured, Captain. I'm going to try to get you into the car." Henry felt Bartholomew's hands under his. Red-hot knives plunged into his body.

Then his feet were dragging. Bartholomew's heavy breathing rasped in his ear.

"I've got to try to get you up over the side now, Captain . . ." He felt the other's shoulder under his chest, lifting. The pain swelled, burst in a cloud of incandescent dust that filled the Universe . . .

He was on his back again, feeling the bed of the carryall under him, jolting, jolting. The sky was a watery gray now, heavy with snow.

"We'll be there soon, Captain," Bartholomew was saying. "Not much farther now. We'll be there soon . . ." The turbos snarled, driving the heavy wagon at high speed, changing tone as the ground sloped upward.

"Only a little farther, Captain," Bartholomew said. "Then you'll be all right . . ."

The car was crawling now, wallowing along in deep snow. The turbos slowed to a petulant growling. The jolting which had filled the Universe since the remote beginning of time ceased suddenly, like a vast crystal soundlessly shattering. Pain poured into the sudden silence. Henry was aware of snow blowing against his face.

A voice dug at him like a knife. "I'll be back in just a minute, I have to clear the entry."

Cold seared his face, like frost on an ax blade. How the ax cut as it struck! But the blows were somehow less now, fading, like a pendulum on an ancient clock, running down . . .

Henry blinked. His left eye was glued shut. A heavy weight seemed to press into his brain. Far away a drumming sound started up, rose to a steady roaring. It reminded Henry of a waterfall he had seen once on a low-gravity world, far out toward the galactic rim. Galatea, that was it. A wide river had wound across a plain and spilled into a gorge, fanning out into a rainbowed curtain, and the scattered droplets fell around you, soft and warm . . .

But the drops were cold snow, and they struck hard, hammering at him like hailstones . . .

Bartholomew was standing over him. Snowflakes clung to his cheeks, melting, running down to drip from his chin. His ship suit glistened wetly, its shoulders frosted.

"I'm going to lift you again, Captain . . ." Then there was movement, and pain, and a scent of growing things.

" . . . be all right, Captain . . ." Bartholomew was saying. "All right . . ."

Chapter Six

The dream beckoned, but first there was something that had to be done. He tried to remember; his mind seemed to slip away so easily, back into the soft, distant dream . . .

He tried again, rousing himself to urgency. *The carryall—it would betray them. Get rid of it . . . to the east, about three miles, there were high sea cliffs . . .*

And the birds would soar there, floating effortlessly on wide wings, white and silent under the high sun . . .

"—operating off broadcast power from their ship," Bartholomew was saying. "They'll follow us—find our hideaway . . ."

Henry could see Bartholomew's face, hollow-cheeked, colorless, unshaven, his lips black against the pale skin. Poor kid. He hadn't understood what he was up against . . .

"Captain—I've got to get rid of the carryall. I'm

going to head east. The map showed the coast—it's only a few miles. Maybe I can run it into the water . . ."

Henry felt muscles twisting in his face. Good boy, he said clearly—then realized, with a sudden pang of dismay, that his lips hadn't moved. He tried to draw a breath—

The jaws of some ravening bird of prey clamped down on him, hurled him into a red-shot blackness. A rotten log made of fire burst open, and the grubs writhed there, deep inside him, while time passed like flowing wax . . .

" . . . Captain . . . it went over. It hit an outcropping on the way down, and bounced out. It hit in deep water and sank. I don't think there'll be any signal from it. But they can follow the trail. The snow . . ."

The voice echoed on in the great hall. The lecture was dull. Henry tried to settle himself comfortably and sleep. But the chair was hard. It cut into his neck. And someone was shaking him. Morning already. And cold. He didn't want any breakfast, he was sick. Tell them . . . too sick . . .

"I salvaged a handgun and some cable, and a med kit, a small box of rations—and the tarp. I'm going to have to leave you here a few minutes while I try to find a spot . . ."

. . . Something moved in the blackness between the stars. It was a strange, arrowhead-shaped ship. Light winked from it—and his own ship leaped and shook. It fled. But the path of its flight was clear in his tracer tank.

He limped after it. It had homed for the desert world marked on the charts as Corazon. In the hills he located it—and a lance of light reached across to touch his ship and the metal flared and burned.

On foot, he moved through darkness, firing a handgun at a strange, long-legged shape in glittering black silks. He drove it back to its own ship, to the portal it had landed to build. The door was barred and locked, but he blasted it in. Then he was inside and it was hand-to-hand.

It was larger, but he was stronger. Finally, it lay still. He looked down at the strange, peaceful face in the metal room. Face and body, clothing the bones he had buried . . . when? Yesterday? Then when had they fought?

But he bore it no ill will. They were both forerunners—outliers of their people, breakers of new ground, claimers of new worlds. It had beaten him in space, ship-to-ship, but body-to-body on the ground, he had beaten and killed it. That was how the chips fell.

. . . It had completed the receiving end of its portal before he found it. Wondering, he put his hand through, then stepped past the door into a new world, with the green sky . . .

And he had almost forgotten to come back . . .

The music was gay. Dulcia, the young Dulcia, was dancing with him at the Fire Palace . . . There was no need to worry, Dulcie-girl, he was telling her . . .

No need . . . He would not leave her defenseless to the wolves, that much he could still do for her. If young Bartholomew was salvageable . . . if there was enough in him to make a man . . . the Run would show it up; and Henry would bring him back. If he was not, if he was not fit to take care of Dulcia after Henry was gone, then he would not come back. Henry would see to that. She didn't know. God willing, she would never know . . .

The boy was flesh and blood of his father. If he was headed the way his father had gone, he would

never see Aldorado again. Time would tell. Time . . .
and the Run . . .

The music was gay. Dulcia smiled at him small and
golden-haired, slim in a silvery dress with a long skirt,
cut in the style of long ago. The cloth rustled, whispering. It was cold to the touch. Dulcia's face was cold.
How still she lay, under the glaring lights. There was
no smile on the dead lips.

"We tried to reach you, Captain. I didn't know if
you'd want to authorize the surgery; fifty thousand
credits—after all, this is not a charity—"

Blood ran out of the pale, fat face. The hands on
his arms were like paper. He crushed the stones in
his hand until blood ran out between his fingers, and
for a moment it seemed the rubies themselves were
bleeding . . .

He threw them against the antiseptic white floor; they
bounded, sparkling red and green and blue. Stones . . .

"There's your damned fifty thousand credits! Why
didn't you save her life!"

Under the harsh light, the jewels winked against
dead tiles. How cold her face was . . . They pulled at
him, and he struck out, but someone had tied his
arms now, and someone had broken his bones, and
the pain was an awful reality that raked at him,
roaring in fury . . .

Eons passed. Mountains rose up from the sea,
streaming mud and innumerable corpses of the
microscopic dead. Storms beat about the peaks;
rivers sparkled, carving gorges. The surf rolled across
low beaches, flat in the white sunlight. Ice formed,
broke with a booming as of distant cannon.

He lay in the icy surf, stirred by the breakers that
tugged, tugged, unceasingly.

" . . . have to wake up, Captain. Don't die . . ."

His eye was open. He saw Bartholomew's face quite clearly. *If only he could explain that he was encased in ice; the boy would understand that it mustn't be broken, or the pain would flood back in . . .*

Henry blinked. He saw Bartholomew's expression brighten. The kid was having a tough time of it. Henry drew a breath; he wanted to tell him . . . But no voice came.

His tongue—my God, had Tasker cut his tongue out . . . ? With an agonizing effort, Henry pushed, bit down—

There was a stab of pain like a candle flame against charred wood. He felt a hot tingle of reaction. His chest moved in a ghost of a laugh. What did it matter whether a corpse had a tongue . . . ?

Something fumbled at his arm.

"I have the med kit here. This is supposed to kill pain. I hope it helps, Captain."

It's all right, Larry. I don't feel a thing, as long as I lie still. You see, I'm inside this cake of warm ice . . .

No, dammit. Keep your thoughts clear. This is that last lucid spell before the end; . . . don't louse it up with fantasies. Poor kid. How the hell will he get back? It's a long walk; twelve hundred miles, mountains, deserts, bogs—and winter coming on. He's got a year—a short Corazonian year—to file his claim . . .

Bartholomew's face was strained. "I'm going to try to set the bones, Captain. I can do it, all right, I think. I took a course at the State Institute . . ."

Don't waste time on me, Larry. Tasker's men will be showing up, up above, any time now. They'll see the tracks, all right. Maybe they'll come in after us, maybe not. A shame for those bastards to get their hands on this . . .

You'd be safe here—if you ran, hid in the woods—but what will you eat? Maybe, if you start back now, before the snow fills the passes . . . But it's cold out there; the storm's just starting. It might last a week—or two weeks. There's nothing to eat here—but if you leave, the wind and snow will get you. Don't worry about the tabs, they don't matter anymore. Too bad. Dulcia will be O.K., she's a smart girl—

But Old Man Bartholomew; I should have figured that angle . . . a tough old pirate . . . fooled me . . .

"All right, Captain. I'm going to start now."

The real pain began then. It went on and on. After a while Henry forgot it. He forgot the broken bones and the new world, found and lost again so soon, and the storm that howled beyond the portal, and the men above who hunted them and the endless wilderness that stretched to Pango-Ri. He forgot all these things, and many more, and it was as though they had never been; and he was alone in the darkness that is between the stars.

And then he was remembering. First the pain, of course; then the reason for the pain . . .

That was a little more difficult. There had been the order to disengage and pull back to Leadpipe. His boat had been hit . . . a rough landing, and then the fire. Amos—

Amos was changed. His face—all wrinkled, and his red hair gone—

Amos was dead. Something about a garden, and jewels—and a girl! Dulcia—but not Dulcia. Only something in her smile, and the curve of her cheek as she sat by the fire.

Old Man Bartholomew. Don't trust him. He wants—

The Run. Young Bartholomew was with him; smoke, and burned bearings . . .

No. That was O.K. Just the hand. But maybe they'd piled in—

He opened his eyes . . .

Just one eye. A knife had done that. But it was a dream. My God, what a dream. Let it fade, lose itself in the shadows of the night . . . It was good to be back in his own bed; but the mattress was hard. Where was Dulcia?

"Captain . . . ?"

Henry made out a vague form bending over him. It was a boy—Larry . . . the name came from somewhere. What was he doing here . . . ?

"I've got some soup for you . . ." Larry's voice shook. He went away. The light was brighter now. Larry was back. His face was like a skull with skin stretched over it. He was wearing a false beard half an inch long. It was ridiculous; Henry wanted to laugh. The false face had fooled him for a moment.

Something warm touched his lips; an indescribably delicious flavor flooded his mouth. He felt his throat contract painfully. More of the warm fluid came. It burned its way down. Henry ate eagerly, lost in the ecstasy of hunger appeased . . .

Later, Bartholomew was back.

"I rigged a sort of bunk out of the tarp, to get you up off the ground. I was worried, Captain. Almost a week. I was afraid you'd starve. I saved the canned rations for you . . ."

Larry talked. It was a long story he was telling. Henry wondered why he talked so much. What was it about, anyway . . . ?

" . . . I went up again, three times. I didn't see any signs of them . . . I saw a few animal tracks. I'm going to try to hunt . . ."

Sometimes he wondered who Larry was, and he would rouse himself to ask, but always it was too hard, too hard, and he would sink back, and Larry would lean over him, with anxious eyes, and then the room would fade and he would roam again through great deserted valleys where icy winds blew without surcease, toil up lonely hills whose tops were hidden in mist, following lost voices which called always from beyond the next divide.

He was looking at a hand—a broken claw, twisted, marked across by purplish scars, vivid against the pale skin.

Gray light gleamed wanly through a narrow cleft in a wall of rock. Snowflakes blew in, swirling, to settle melting, in a long puddle. Shaggy animal hides lay scattered on the floor. A wisp of smoke rose from a heap of embers against a blackened wall. There was a stack of blackish firewood, two crude clay dishes and a large pot, a heap of shredded greens, and a joint of purplish-black meat. It was a strange dream— almost real.

Henry moved to push himself up to a sitting position. There was a weight against his chest, pressing him back. He gritted his teeth, raised himself to one elbow. An odor of wood smoke and burned meat hunt in the air, and a thick, cloying reek of uncured hides. A coarse-haired fur lay across his lap. He reached to throw it back—

His head rang from the blow it took as he fell. What the hell was wrong with him? Drugged, maybe?

His eye fell on the butt of a Mark IX pistol. Beside it was a pair of boots, caked with mud—and with a darker stain.

His boots. Quite suddenly, he remembered.

Tasker, and the little man, Gus. He had supplied the scalpel. They had strung him up, and carved him into strips. And he had died, and gone to hell.

And now he was here, alive.

Strange.

A pulse thudded like the beat of a hammer in Henry's temples. Larry Bartholomew had killed Tasker—and Gus. Some kid! Well, life was full of surprises. And he had brought him here—somehow—and kept him alive.

Henry moved then, pushed him over, face down, got his hands under him, pushed himself up to a sitting position. His left hand—it was useless, a frozen tangle of broken fingers. But the right—it would hold a gun . . .

No telling how long the boy had wasted here, nursing him back to a dim half life. Feeding soup to a broken body that should have died . . .

He could reach the blaster; one quick squeeze, and the agony would be over. And Larry could make a start for Pango-Ri. Henry dragged himself, feeling the cold of the rough wet floor against his body. He rested, with his face against the stone. He had a beard, he noticed. He touched it with his left hand; over half an inch; a month's growth, anyway. Damn! A wasted month, with winter setting in. If the boy had started back as soon as he had killed Tasker . . .

He reached the plastic case by the pallet of furs, fumbled the blaster out. He set it on narrow beam, dragged it up until the cold muzzle pressed against the thudding pulse above his ear—pressed the firing stud.

Nothing happened. The blaster fell with a clatter. He lay, limp, breathing in wracking, shallow gasps.

He'd never committed suicide before. It was quite an experience. Even when it didn't work.

Larry had used the blaster for hunting, exhausted the charge. So much for the easy way. Now, he would have to crawl outside—as soon as the faintness passed.

Bartholomew was squatting beside him. "Easy, Captain. Easy. You're better! You crawled all that way—

but what in the name of sanity were you doing? It's cold over here . . ."

Henry looked at Bartholomew leaning over him, draped in a long-haired animal hide. His face had aged; the skin was rough, scored red by the wind and snow, with a network of tiny red veins across the cheekbones, from frostbite. His beard was thick, black, curling around his mouth, meeting the tangle of overlong hair about his ears. There were lines beside the mouth. He was holding up two bedraggled creatures, half rabbit, half bird.

"I'll broil these, Captain! They ought to be good! You should be able to take a little solid food now!"

Bartholomew bustled over the crude pots. "You'll feel even better after you eat, Captain. I've got some plant hearts here—ice bushes, I call them—they're not bad. I've tried just about everything. We need some sort of fresh vegetable along with the meat. And hunting's getting harder up above, Captain. There seems to be no wildlife—out there . . ." He nodded toward the shimmering wall.

He talked, building up the fire, setting out pots, cutting up the small carcasses with a short-bladed pocketknife. He roasted the animals whole, then cut off choice bits, fed them to Henry with his fingers. Henry's mouth gulped them down like an automatic disposer, as though his appetite were a thing apart from the rest of his body.

"Captain, soon you'll be strong enough to talk; we have so many things to discuss—so many plans to make."

With a mighty effort, Henry pushed the food away, shook his head. Bartholomew stared at him, then at the bit of meat in his fingers.

"You must eat, Captain—"

Henry shook his head again, fell back, breathing hard, his eyes fixed on Bartholomew's.

"What is it, Captain?" Bartholomew put the clay pot

of meat aside, crouched over Henry. "What's wrong?" His expression changed abruptly.

"Captain, you CAN hear me . . . ?"

Henry managed a nod.

"And you're strong enough—you eat easily enough. Captain—why don't you speak?"

Henry felt the pulse throb in his temples. He drew a breath, concentrated every ounce of energy on forming a word . . .

A grunt . . .

"You *know* me, don't you, Captain? I'm Larry—"

Henry nodded.

"You were injured. But you're safe here now. You understand that, don't you?"

Henry nodded.

"Then—why don't you speak?"

Henry's chest rose and fell, rose and fell. Perspiration trickled down the side of his face.

Bartholomew's face stiffened. His hand dropped from Henry's shoulder.

"Good Lord, Captain . . ." His voice broke. "You haven't spoken—because you can't! Your voice is gone; you're a mute . . . !"

"It's all right," Bartholomew was saying. "It must have been the shock; I've heard of such things. You'll get your voice back eventually. Meanwhile, I'll just ask you questions—and you can nod, or shake your head. All right?"

Henry nodded. Bartholomew settled himself, pulled his fur about his shoulders, adjusted Henry's malodorous coverlet.

"Are you comfortable? Warm enough?"

Henry nodded impatiently, watching Bartholomew's face. *To hell with that! Ask me about the weather, the mountains, the winter setting in . . .*

"Do you remember . . . what happened?" Bartholomew looked anxious. Henry nodded. Bartholomew swallowed. "You . . . were right, of course, Captain. I . . . I never dreamed such men really existed—"

Henry raised his head. *Why didn't the boy get on with it—get to the important things?*

"I've concentrated on hunting and gathering firewood. In the evening, I've been skinning animals, and trying to scrape the hides and sew them together . . ." He tugged at his cape; the green hide crackled. "I'm afraid I'm not very good at it. And I made the pots from clay—there are great slabs of it along the river—" He broke off.

"But, of course, that's not important. Captain, do you suppose they'll send out search parties from Pango-Ri?"

Henry shook his head.

"They won't find us . . . ?" Bartholomew's voice trailed off. Henry opened his eye. *Now they would be getting to the point . . .*

"I suppose I knew that . . . with a whole world to be lost in. But we're running out of food. Game is getting scarcer—the cold, I suppose. And I haven't dared try anything from—the other side . . ."

Bartholomew was getting to his feet. "You're tired, Captain. You'd better sleep now. We'll talk again tomorrow—"

Henry tried to sit up, shaking his head, watching Larry's face.

"But I'll bring you food, Captain—and I'll keep the fire up. You'll see! We'll be fine, Captain. And you'll get better—soon . . ."

There were tears on Bartholomew's face. He wiped at his eyes with the back of his hand. "You have to be all right, Captain!"

Yeah. Otherwise little Larry Bartholomew would be on his own. So that was what was bothering him . . .

"I think I understand, Captain. You think that you might slow me down—be a, well, burden. Nonsense! We'll wait here until the worst of the cold weather has passed, and by then you'll be—"

Henry was shaking his head.

"You're thinking of the claim? The time limit?"

Henry shook his head.

"Then you think—we won't manage through the winter?"

Henry nodded, waiting for the next question . . .

Bartholomew chewed his lip. "Then you'll just have to hurry up and get well, Captain."

Henry shook his head wearily.

"Oh, yes you will, Captain. I'm not leaving without you."

Henry nodded angrily.

"You feel we'll have to go soon—before the weather gets even worse. Very well; I understand. We'll go as soon as you're ready—and don't bother shaking your head—I'm not going without you. So if you want me to get back and file the claim, you'll have to try very hard to get well, Captain. You see that, don't you?"

Henry looked at Bartholomew. There were fine lines around his eyes—the weeks of no sleep, overwork, and cold had left their marks. His eyes held steady on Henry's.

Henry opened his mouth; Bartholomew fed him a charred lump. He sighed and lay with closed eyes, chewing the rank, tough meat.

Chapter Seven

"You're sitting up very nicely, Captain," Bartholomew nodded and smiled. "Perhaps tomorrow you can try standing."

Henry shook his head. He laid the bowl aside, fumbled with his hands for a grip on the wall beside him.

"I don't think you ought to try it yet . . ." Bartholomew fluttered, then took Henry's arm. "But I suppose you're determined . . ."

Henry gripped Bartholomew's shoulder. It felt solid under his hand; hunting and hauling wood and rope-climbing were filling out the boy's lean frame. Then he let go, leaned against the wall.

It was a strange feeling to be standing again—or almost standing—after—how long? Six weeks now? His legs were like rotten sticks.

"Captain, that's marvelous; now you'd better lie down again—"

Henry held on, straining to move the left leg; it hung limp and dead. He clamped his teeth, heaved; the leg twitched. O.K.; at least it wasn't paralyzed. Now the right . . .

"Really, Captain . . ."

Henry struggled, concentrating on the leg. It was the bad one; the broken knee hadn't turned out too well. He leaned his weight on the left leg, the toes of the crooked right leg just touching the floor. He was already dizzy—and all he'd done so far was get to his feet and lean on the wall.

Bartholomew moved to help him. "Careful, Captain, you can't afford a fall—"

He shook his head, elbowed himself from the wall, stood teetering. *God, how the hell did a kid ever learn this balancing act!* He put the short leg forward, then hopped. His leg was like a stick of soft clay. Bartholomew was chewing his lip, getting ready to jump for him . . .

The right leg again; another hop. *Watch it; almost went over that time.*

"Wonderful, Captain! That's enough for this time. Let me help you back now." He came across, reached for Henry's arm. Henry motioned him back. *One more step first.* He took a breath, felt his heart thud. *To hell with the pain; that's nothing. Getting across the room—it just takes one more step. And another. And another . . .*

"I don't like that wind, Captain. You shouldn't try it today. Probably tomorrow it will have died down. After two months, another day won't matter." Bartholomew looked at him anxiously.

Wrapped in his stiff fur clothing, Henry pushed at the cape with the twisted left hand, gripped the stick with the right. It was amazing how much you could do with a hand, even with three fingers broken and stiff, as long as the tendons hadn't been cut.

He moved across to the entry with his hopping gait, his left elbow pressed to the side where badly mended ribs ached under their tight binding. The scars on his face itched under the two-inch beard— a tangle of gray and white. He staggered as the icy wind whipped through the opening; Bartholomew boosted and hauled him up, out into the stinging mist of blown snow. He squinted his eye against the cold that cut at him like a great knife; the cape lifted, slapping at his back. His breath seemed to choke off in his throat. He took a step; Bartholomew was beside him, his arm under Henry's. "Watch out, Captain! That breeze is pretty strong."

Bartholomew tightened Henry's pack straps. He

moved his shoulders, felt the dull pang from his left side. The coat Bartholomew had stitched up for him felt better now; and his boots fitted better, too, with the fur linings stuffed inside.

"Captain, are you sure it wouldn't be better to wait until tomorrow, just on the off-chance—"

Henry shook his head, started unsteadily across toward the edge of the grove.

The prints of Larry's shaggy homemade mukluks were bare patches of black rock through the powdery snow. They led up a sharp incline among tumbled boulders. Henry fought his way up, scrabbling with one hand and an elbow, groping with feet that were like old boots filled with ice water.

There was Larry's face, Larry's hand reaching out to help, Larry's voice: " . . . we've made a start! We're on our way!"

Uh-huh. We've gone fifty feet. Only twelve hundred miles to go.

Henry ducked his head against the wind, started off down the blizzard-swept slope. Forget about the pain. *Walk as if you knew how. What's pain, anyway? Nature's little warning. O.K. I've been warned. Just make the legs work, one after the other, and don't think about anything else.*

It was hard, counting the paces. Ten; and then fifteen. Then twenty. Five times that, and it would be a hundred. *Nine more hundred and it would be a thousand. Another couple of thousand, and I'll have walked a mile.*

Where was I? Twenty-five? Four times twenty-five is a hundred . . .

To hell with that. All right so far. Thirty paces. Thirty-one steps from the room; thirty-two crab steps away from the next by the fire . . . God how it hurts . . .

Bartholomew's hand was under his arm. "You're doing fine, Captain." He had to yell to make himself heard over the shrilling of the wind, through the muffling fur turned up about Henry's ears. The boy hadn't done a bad job, making the parkas. And he'd killed the animals and skinned them out, too. Not bad, for a lad who'd never chased anything livelier than a statistic in his life. Larry might make it; stranger things had happened. If he didn't panic. If he had luck with the hunting, before he tackled the passes. If he didn't get lost. If—

If he had a magic carpet, he could fly back to Pango-Ri. Never mind the ifs.

Damn! He'd lost count again. *Call it fifty. Still on my feet. Getting a little numb, but that's O.K.; I can't feel the wind now. Frostbite is the least of my worries. Fifty-five. Thank God the ground's level here, no gullies to scramble through. Just put the foot, hop, put the foot, hop. It's easy. Just do it enough, then you can rest. Lie down in this nice white, clean stuff, and dream off into wherever it is that memories go when they're forgotten, and let Larry get on with the business of surviving . . .*

He was aware of Bartholomew's hand on his arm. "Half a mile, Captain. The going gets a little rough ahead, I'm afraid. Broken ground, and rock fragments—"

Henry's foot caught on an upjutting projection; he stumbled, tried to stiffen his legs; they folded like paper. He went down, sagging in Bartholomew's arms.

"I'm sorry, Captain! I should have stopped for a break before now, but you were moving along so well . . ." Henry slumped in the snow. His chest burned; the right knee pulsed like a great boil, ready for lancing. His side—the damned ribs felt as though they hadn't even started to knit; the raw ends were grating together . . .

"A few minutes' rest . . . you'll feel better . . ." Bartholomew fumbled in his monstrous pack, brought out something. He worked over it . . .

An odor of hot stew struck Henry's nostrils with an almost painful intensity; his salivary glands leaped into action with a stab like a hot needle behind his jaws.

"I saved this, Captain . . . for the march."

Then he was chewing, swallowing. Food. It was better than rest, better than warmth, better than the most elaborate pleasures devised in the harems of kings. He finished, pushing himself to a sitting position, got his feet under him. Larry was helping him up. He stood, still tasting the wonderful stew.

"Watch your footing now, Captain." Bartholomew's hand was under his arm; he leaned on it, tried a step. It worked. Ahead, the gray landscape stretched off into the mist of blown snow. It was a little like life—a foggy vista into which you pressed on, and on. And when you had gone as far as you could—and you fell and the snow covered you—the unknown goal was as far ahead, as unattainable as ever . . .

The knee was the worst part; his face was nicely anesthetized by the cold, and the side had settled down to a dull explosion that pulsed in counterpoint to the fire in his lungs, and the drag-hop, drag-hop was a routine, like breathing, that seemed to carry itself along by its own momentum. But the knee . . . Surely, there were bone chips grinding the flesh to shreds. The pain ran up to his hips, down to his ankle.

They had stopped. Henry looked around, saw nothing but endless snow.

"We've done a mile and a half, Captain. Shall we take a short rest now?" Bartholomew's voice was an irritation, penetrating the simple equation of agony and endurance. Henry shook his head; he took a step, faltered for a moment, then caught up the rhythm again.

He drew a deep breath; that was a mistake—the fire leaped up, chokingly, died slowly back to the cozy bed of red-hot embers. That was fine; it was keeping him warm. But the knee . . . How long could a man walk on a broken leg? There was only one way to find out.

Later, he was sitting with his back against a drift of snow, the bad knee propped before him, the pain only a remote thump, like a doctor's rubber mallet against a wooden leg. Bartholomew had his arm, doing something to it. He felt a brief pang of a hypospray.

The snow was red, cut by the black shadows of tall trees.

"We'll camp here, where we have a little shelter," Bartholomew said. He was roasting a curiously scaled and beaked creature with a meaty tail, over a tiny fire.

"This is some sort of relative of the rabbity things I shot, back at the portal. I'm sure it will be edible. A pity it smells so much like burning butadiene."

Henry stared into the small, bluish flames. It had been memorable day. Walking, falling, getting up, walking . . .

"I think it's done, Captain." Bartholomew took the roast from the spit, sawed off a joint, passed it over to Henry. "I think we're going to be all right for game from now on; there are a lot of these fellows around. I shot three; I'm letting them freeze as reserve supplies."

Good boy. Hang on to the food. Twenty thousand feet; that's four miles, straight up. Figure an average thirty-degree slope . . . A squared plus B squared . . . call it a nine-mile trek to the summit of the pass. It might be possible. It depended on things like snow depths, winds, unseen crevasses, avalanches, snow blindness, or little unscalable rock faces a few inches higher than a man could jump . . .

Better tell him to rig some grapple hooks—out of what? And how to tell him? Tramp out letters in the snow?

The meat was good—a little like turtle flesh, but tenderer. There was no salt, no melted butter, no silver and linen and thin glass and fragile porcelain, no candles and wine . . . but by God, it was as rare a feast as had ever been laid before a hungry man.

"More, Captain? It's rather good, isn't it? I wonder if the animals would be easy to raise, commercially? It's a mystery what they live on; nothing here but rock and ice . . ."

Bart rambled on. Henry half-listened, his mind drifting off on side trails. Old Man Bartholomew; would he live up to his agreement—if Larry did get back with the claim? Too bad Amos wasn't there, to look out for Dulcie's interests. He'd wanted to come pretty bad. Poor Amos. But maybe he was lucky at that. His death hadn't been an easy one, but then these last few weeks were a memory a man could do without, too . . .

"We'd better tuck in now, Captain. A long day ahead tomorrow."

Henry nodded, managed to move, crawl the three feet to the tiny tent. Bartholomew helped him inside; God, how it stank! But it broke the force of the wind, and kept the snow out of his face. He pulled his blanket of fur over him, settled himself. *So this was the way it ends; you eat dinner, and go to bed . . .* Henry closed his eyes. *And that was that . . .*

There was a smell of vulcanizing rubber, and for an instant, Henry was back in a town on a small, backward world called Northroyal, standing in the tree-shaded courtyard of an inn, watching the stableman weld a new set of retreads to the worn wheels of the little red two-seater that he and Dulcia had driven down from the port . . .

"Breakfast is about ready, Captain," Bartholomew was silhouetted against the pale light that filtered through the tent flap. The cold bit at Henry's nose like pliers. He moved, felt stabs from every joint.

Doctor prescribes long, invigorating walks in the open air for the patient; this is guaranteed to give him an understanding of how a mummy would feel, if you unwrapped him in a cold-storage vault . . .

He lay, listening to the thump of his heart, the rasp of breath in his throat. So he was still alive! He moved his right leg tentatively. Fresh, vivid pain flooded up from it. Oh yes, he was alive, all right! That wasn't what the program had called for. When a man—sick unto death, with more half-healed wounds than the average accident ward, undernourished and poorly clad—spent a long day overexerting in sub-freezing weather—and then went to sleep in the snow—he was expected to die of exposure, if nothing else.

But instead, he was alive—awake—still a dead weight on young Bartholomew's back—and time was running out even for a healthy man, alone, to have a chance of making it.

Henry drew a deep breath; his chest gave a dutiful stab of agony. He got his hands under him, sat up. There was a moment of vertigo; the ribs complained a little more. He rolled over, worked his way out of the tent, feeling the icy fingers of the fitful morning breeze nipping at him. The food smelled better now; he was getting used to the stink. Knowing how it tasted helped; it was like cheese in that respect. He took a mouthful of snow, let it melt and trickle down. Bartholomew handed across a slab of meat. Henry bit into it. It was burned on the outside, chilled in the center. He ate it hungrily.

"I slept on the breakfast steaks, Captain," Bartholomew said cheerfully. "Didn't want them to freeze. We're getting an early start; sun won't be up for another half hour."

Life was a perverse damned phenomenon; if there were a prize waiting for him just across the next rise, a pretty girl, a bank account, a vacation, all expenses paid—

He'd have dropped dead a hundred yards from the cave.

But all there was was twelve hundred miles of wilderness or maybe eleven hundred and ninety-five, now. And he was good for another hour, or two, three, of dragging himself on, spinning out the declining threads . . .

"The wind's behind us now," Bartholomew said. "That will help some, of course, but I imagine it will bring colder weather. I'd say it's down close to thirty degrees of frost now. I suppose a little more won't make much difference."

No, not much; it would just freeze you, standing up, between one step and the next; it would kill a patch of exposed skin quicker than a dozen unshielded megacuries. But that might make it easier; a fast death was more fun any day than this teasing along . . .

Bartholomew folded the tent, strapped up his pack, hoisted it onto his back. He stood before Henry.

The damned fool was actually grinning.

"We're going to make good time today, Captain. I have a feeling." He took Henry's arm; Henry shrugged him off, got to his feet unassisted. Why the hell had he been letting the boy waste strength, supporting him, saving his own waning vitality? It was almost as though dying wasn't what he wanted at all . . .

✧   ✧   ✧

Later, he was sure it was. It wasn't as though there were any hope of surcease, ever; the supply of miles was limitless; the depths of cold only skimmed so far. And if some weatherproof St. Bernard came along now, with a keg of miracles hung around his neck—

He'd still be a mute, one-eyed cripple, pitifully maimed, horribly scarred, lacking all sorts of useful parts. A man wouldn't want to live in that condition, even if he weren't a drag on the living. That was simple enough. Why, then, did he go on, head down, parka hood pulled close about his face, lurching grotesquely onward, teeth clenched against the pain, while thoughts of food, and warm beds, and blessed rest tormented him like jeering imps?

Time lost its meaning. There are an infinity of infinities within infinity; and an infinity of eternities within eternity. Forever passed, while he endured; then there was a time of lying in the snow, mindless with exhaustion, and then the brief, sharp sensation of food, and then again, eternity . . .

The sun was high, a pale disk in a glaring sky; later it hung in the west, shedding its cold light without the faintest hint of heat, smaller than it should be, subtly the wrong color. Bartholomew was moving about, making a fire, chattering.

" . . . a good twelve miles, I'd estimate. And the mountains are closer than we thought. It's the misty air; it makes things look far away. We're almost into the foothills now; the ground was rising for the last hour's hike today . . ."

The voice tuned in and out.

" . . . do you agree, Captain?"

Was the boy still asking questions of the oracle— the halt, the lame, the half-blind oracle, dying before his eyes?

Sure. Anything you say. It doesn't matter. Let's get

going. Henry swallowed, got to his feet, pulled away angrily as Bartholomew attempted to help him with his pack. The younger man started off, stamping away through foot-deep snow; and Henry followed.

The peak loomed over them, dominating the sky. The wind had shifted again, blowing across the slope from the west now, bringing a stinging hail of snow particles. The drifts were deeper here—dry, powdery drifts, that flowed underfoot like desert dust, each footprint sending down a minor avalanche. Henry's eye burned from the white glare. Ahead, Bartholomew stamped on, long-legged, tall, bounding up the slope like a deer, then waiting while Henry dragged his way up behind him.

"I don't like the look of the clouds, Captain," he called. "They have a sort of yellowish tinge; I'm afraid that means more snow . . . And it's getting dark fast . . ."

Henry came up, kept going; the long slope stretched ahead, white, smooth, blue-shadowed, rising in an unbroken sweep to the far heights of the pass. Why waste time talking about the weather? Just keep going, up, up, into the cold, into the thin air, thinking about nothing except the fact that it was reach the summit—or die here.

He had fallen, and Bartholomew was pulling at his arm. Henry groped, got his feet under him, struggled up. Couldn't let the boy waste his strength. Had to go on . . . as far as he could . . . walk on until the plunging heart burst. Maybe someday their bodies would be found, frozen deep inside a glacier of blue ice, preserved intact, a silent memento of the old days, long ago, when men had come, barehanded, to tame the alien world . . .

He was down again. Bartholomew's hands hauled at

him. The wind howled, drowning the boy's words. He
shook his head; heavy, wet snow was caked against his
lips, his eye. He thrust with his feet, found a purchase,
crawled forward another foot. It was easier this way.
The ground sloped steeply up here. He reached, with
one hand and one crippled claw; his feet groped.
Another foot. Where was Larry now? Good boy; not
wasting his strength any more. Gone on ahead . . . He
could rest now . . .

Bartholomew was back, pulling at him. Still at
it . . . still determined to coax a dead man over a
mountain. Couldn't let the boy wear himself out that
way . . . Go on, a little farther. Die, body . . . Die, and
let both of us rest . . .

He couldn't remember why the operation was necessary. It had been going on for such a long time. The
anesthetic was wearing off; he could feel the scalpel
cutting in—cutting into his eye—

No, it was his knee. They had cut it off, and now
they were welding a steel joint in place. The fools.
You couldn't weld steel to flesh! And the gas he was
breathing; the welding torch had started a fire; the
gas was burning, and he was breathing in the pale
flames, the blue fire that was burning his chest
out . . .

It was a hell of a funeral. The pallbearers were
carrying him, head down—without even a coffin. A
man needed a coffin. It was cold, when you were
dead, without a box to keep off the icy wind. And
they had stripped the body, too. And someone had
cut off his hands, and his feet—

The stumps ached—but not as badly as the knee.
They had tried to cut that off, too, but it had been
too hard. That was because it was made of steel . . .

The explosion jarred Henry alive. The end of the

world. In a moment the other bodies which had been blown out of the graveyard would come raining down . . .

" . . . sorry . . . Captain . . ."

There was one of them now. Not a body, though. It had spoken.

What were the words? Sorry . . .

Oh, how sorry a man was, once it was all over—sorry for all the lost opportunities, all the cruel words, all the joys untasted, all the little trusts betrayed . . .

"Couldn't be . . . much farther . . ." Henry heard. *Much farther. Much farther . . .*

" . . . a minute . . . try again . . ."

Try again. If only a man could. The awful thing about death was the barrier that stood between you and all the things that you should have done, once, long ago, when you were still alive.

But if you could push through the barrier . . .

Perhaps if you tried . . .

There had been something that someone had wanted. It had been a simple thing, if he could only remember . . .

"Please, Captain. Wake up. Wake up . . ."

That was it. He had to wake up. That meant to open his eye . . .

No, that was too hard. It was easier just to pretend he was awake—and who would know the difference? It was a clever idea. Henry wanted to laugh aloud. He would pretend to be awake. He would move his legs—that was important, he seemed to know, somehow—and his arms . . .

One arm was gone. Yes, someone had cut it off once—But the other was there. It had a steel hand at the end of it, and he would reach out, catch it on something, pull, then reach out again . . .

✧   ✧   ✧

The shout rang, loud and clear—cut off quickly. Henry waited, listening. He heard the screech of wind, the beat of blood inside his skull; nothing more.

He was on a mountain—he remembered that. He remembered the funeral clearly . . .

But someone had shouted. He was alone, here, on the mountain that dead men climbed—and yet a shout had sounded just ahead . . .

His arm was a grappling hook. He threw it out, caught it, pulled himself forward. It was not an easy way to travel, but it seemed correct, somehow. He pulled, reached again, touched nothing. Strange. He pushed with his feet, stretching . . .

The world was tilting under him. He poised for a dizzy moment, hanging in air—and then he was falling—and then a shock, an instant of wrenching pain—and a vast softness that enveloped him in silence through which, far away, a voice called.

There was an odor of wood smoke and hot food. Henry pried an eye open. He was half sitting, half lying against a fur-padded wall of rock. Overhead, a ledge slanted down to a curtain of animal hides. Beside him, Bartholomew squatted by a small fire, feeding twigs to the flames.

"Just in time for dinner," Bartholomew croaked. His eyes were bright, set deep in a weather-ravaged face above an ice-matted black beard. "I dug you out of the snowbank; it broke your fall."

Henry's hands ached. He lifted one, stared at flushed, dusky-red fingers.

"Your hands were pretty cold, Captain, but I massaged them by the fire; I think they'll be all right. My feet were a bit chilled, too."

Henry looked, saw bloody rags of fur wrapped

around Bartholomew's lower legs. He leaned back, closed his eyes.

"You understand, don't you, Captain?" Bartholomew said hoarsely. "We've made it across the mountains; we're over the pass and a couple of hundred feet down the south slope. We're going to make it, Captain! We're going to make it . . ."

Chapter Eight

Standing in the autumnal clearing, Captain Henry pressed the stiff fingers of his right hand against his thigh; pain shot up to his elbow. He pressed harder. The knuckle joints yelled reluctantly; the fingers bent a quarter of an inch.

There was a sound of footsteps tramping through underbrush. Bartholomew came into view, black-bearded, wide-shouldered; there were half a dozen bug-eyed, thin-bodied animals looped to his belt. He tossed them down, unslung his bow and quiver, crouched in the snow by the fire with the short-bladed knife he used for skinning.

"Spider rats," he said. "No other game."

Henry picked up the bow clumsily with his stiff-fingered right hand, looked at it critically, then pointed to the game and nodded.

"I'm getting quite accurate," Bartholomew said. "I picked off that last fellow at over thirty yards."

Henry drew the blaster clumsily from the holster at his hip, closed his thumb and little finger around it, tried to fit his forefinger around the firing stud. The gun dropped to the ground. Henry shook his head angrily, bent stiffly to pick up the weapon, holstered it, and resumed his pacing, working at the stiff fingers.

"I saw traces of another camp fire," Bartholomew said. "Not over a week old."

Henry picked up a stick, smoothed a muddy patch with his boot, scratched words. Bartholomew craned to read them:

WE'LL SET WATCH TONIGHT

Bartholomew nodded. He reached up, caught a three-inch branch, with a pull brought it crashing down. He stripped off the twigs and broke it over his knees. His leather jerkin had split up the side, days before; through the tear, Henry could see the play of heavy lateral muscles under the shirt. His face was burned dark by the weather; the powerful lines of his neck rose from wide, solid shoulders. His forearm, wrist, hand were tanned, sinewy. He had changed, these last months on the trail.

There was a flicker of motion among the trees; Bartholomew dropped, whipped his bow clear, and nocked an arrow in one motion. Henry hauled the blaster from the holster at his side. His fingers closed clumsily on the grip. A long-legged, long-necked creature bounded from a coppice, scrambled up the slope, kicking up a scatter of rotted vegetation. Henry brought the blaster up, fumbled at the firing stud. A brief glare winked against the nearby tree trunks—

Bartholomew's bow twanged; an arrow flashed. The beast stumbled, struck, and rolled, kicking, coming to rest with oddly joined legs atangle.

The two men moved up; Bartholomew's bolt projected from behind the left shoulder blade, the bare-scraped wood white against the smooth gray pelt. Beyond, a wisp of smoke curled up from a tree trunk, scorched by Henry's miss.

Bartholomew took out the skinning knife, set to

work. Henry picked up the empty water bottle in his better hand, set off downslope. A hundred feet from the clearing he halted abruptly, peering through underbrush at a hut among the trees.

It was a flimsy construction of prefab plastic panels. Around it, nothing stirred. There were two small windows on the side facing him; dark, empty squares of translucent plastic. Dead leaves were drifted against the side of the shack; wild spring flowers clustered about a weathered refuse heap.

He moved back softly, retraced his steps to the clearing where Bartholomew was turning steaks over the fire. As the young man looked up, Henry motioned. Bartholomew's bow leaped into his hand.

Henry turned, led the way back through the deep forest trail. They circled the hut, moved closer. A quarter of an hour later they stood by the front of the deserted structure. There was a blaster burn on the curled plastic panel. The door hung open, its lock broken. Henry stepped through into an odor of mold and decay. A badly rotted corpse was curled in a corner. Behind Henry, Bartholomew peered at the shriveled face. Henry went across to a weather-stained chest, pulled open a drawer; a twelve-legged spider leaped out, scuttled away.

"They deliberately smashed everything before they abandoned the place . . ." Bartholomew opened a wall locker. Dusty garments dangled from hooks. He pulled out a musty ship suit, tried the control; the fabric warmed to the touch.

"Here, Captain—you'll sleep warm from now on."

Henry's scarred face twitched in a crooked smile. He began stripping away his rotted furs.

Bartholomew took a box from the shelf, opened it. "They left us a few amenities! God, won't it be wonderful to wash—and get rid of these ghastly whiskers?"

❖   ❖   ❖

Henry looked into the mirror; under grizzled brows, a single bright eye set in a gray-whiskered face carved of scarred and ancient leather stared back at him. Lank white hair fell in tangles to his shoulders. Behind him, Bartholomew's scissors snicked. He caught Henry's eye in the mirror.

"Captain, I wonder—the scars . . . What I mean is, your beard—I think it's quite distinguished-looking . . ."

Henry's mouth twisted in amusement. He nodded.

"I'll just trim it up a little . . ." Bartholomew snipped carefully at Henry's tangled mane, then shaped the three-inch beard before starting on his own snarled black curls.

He trimmed his hair short, clipped the beard away, then lathered and shaved with the old-fashioned blade razor.

"That's a bit better . . ." He stared at himself in the cracked mirror. "I've changed, Captain," he said. "I don't think I'd know myself . . ."

Henry watched as Larry pulled on the ship suit, zipped it up; it was a snug fit over his solid chest and filled-out shoulders.

"Clothes make a difference," Larry said. "Suddenly I remember some of the comforts we've done without for a hundred and ninety days."

He threw a sharp look Captain Henry's way. "We've come over eleven hundred miles, by my reckoning. We can't have much farther to go."

Henry nodded briefly. He went outside, picked a spot where soft ferns padded the ground, stretched out. Bartholomew followed.

"That's the idea, Captain; get some rest." Larry took a spot beside Henry.

"It's been over six standard months since we left Pango-Ri," he said thoughtfully. "They'll have forgotten all about us by now. When we reach the port, suppose you go along to arrange for our passage out, and I'll register the tabs . . ."

Henry glanced at him.

"It's in both our names, of course," Larry added. "Either of us can file it. If one of us is killed, the survivor gets it all."

Henry's eyes narrowed. His glance held on Larry's face as the sunlight struck across it, highlighting the new muscle of the jaw, the squareness of the features. Henry frowned. Larry frowned in response.

"What's the matter? You think there'll be trouble?"

Henry smiled faintly. The eyes of the young man were seasoned now, and wary. As Henry watched, they grimmed and harshened. For the first time Henry noticed how the black eyebrows above those eyes had thickened and begun to resemble the dark and angry eyebrows of Bartholomew senior.

The Run would toughen a man—but a toughened man could go either to the good or the bad. Larry had yet to show which way events here on Corazon had turned him—toward someone who would be good for Dulcia—or toward being his father's son. If he was his father's son, it would be the worth of their claim that would be filling his mind now . . .

"Well, never mind now," said Larry abruptly. "Let's get a good night's sleep. We'll talk about it in the morning."

The sun woke Henry, shining in his eyes. A piece of paper was pegged to the ground beside him with a rusted kitchen knife from the cabin. He unfolded it.

I'M GOING ON AHEAD TO PANGO-RI. ALONE, I CAN TRAVEL FASTER. IF THERE'S TROUBLE, I'M IN BETTER SHAPE TO HANDLE IT THAN YOU. BY

THE TIME YOU GET TO PANGO-RI
THE CLAIM WILL BE FILED. AND A
WORD TO THE WISE—WATCH YOUR-
SELF COMING INTO TOWN.

LARRY

Henry crumpled the paper savagely, hurled it from
him. He caught up his pack, stuffed it hastily with what
provisions Larry had left him, pulled it onto his back,
glanced at the sun, and set out southward.

Two days later, he struck a raw, unpaved road, rutted
and potholed, slashing through the dense timber like
a wound.

After an hour, a heavy truck came into view from
the north, its air-cushion jets spattering wide sheets of
mud. It halted, settled into the muck; a red-faced man
opened the cab, leaned out.

"You got a long walk ahead of you, pal, if you're
headed for Pango; it's a hundred and thirty miles. You
better hop aboard." He looked at Henry, lowered his
voice. "What happened to you, brother?"

Henry swung aboard, flashed the driver a quick
smile.

"Cautious, too, hey? Well, can't say as I blame you."
He let in the clutch and the truck heaved itself up,
moved off in a howl of worn turbos.

Five hours later, Henry dropped from the truck at
the edge of the sprawling new city that had sprung up
around the booming port of Pango-Ri. The driver
waved.

"Good luck, pal. You ain't much company, but I'll
say this fer ya—you don't talk a guy's ear off . . ." He
gunned the truck. Henry watched him out of sight, then

set off as quickly as his crippled knee would allow toward the shabby towers that had risen where Tent Town had been.

The crowd at the Solar Corona had changed. The bustling women were gone; the loudmouthed hopefuls had disappeared; the hard-drinking adventurers had sought cheerier surroundings for their dissipations.

Now half a dozen stony-faced teamsters hunched over the shabby bar where a dyed slattern poured undersized drinks from a finger-stained bottle. At a back table, a group of sullen-eyed men nursed thick glasses. The late evening street noises seemed remote, far away.

Henry took a seat in a booth halfway down the room, signaled for a sealed bottle, poured an inch of thin yellowish fluid into his glass, sat waiting. One of the men from the table rose, walked past Henry's table, darted a sharp look at him, went out through a side door.

Henry finished his drink, poured a second. The man who had gone out returned, glanced at Henry again. Henry stared into his glass.

Three slow hours passed. The street door swung open abruptly; a narrow-shouldered, gray-haired man with close-set eyes and a puckered mouth slipped in, walked quickly back to the man at the table. He leaned close to a thick-necked coarse-skinned redhead, muttered something. The redhead barked a question. Henry caught a scrap of the conversation: " . . . he look like . . . ?"

Under the table, Henry gripped the butt of the blaster, eased it from its holster, fitting his clumsy fingers to its curve with his thumb resting lightly on the firing stud.

The small man stepped back from the table; the

redhead rose, headed for the door, followed by the other three men; heavy power guns bobbed at their hips. They moved up the aisle.

As they reached Henry's table, he brought the gun up into view, leveled it at the square buckle on the belt that cinched in the redhead's ample midriff. The man jerked to a halt; his freckled hand went toward his hip, paused, dropped to his side. Behind him, the third man in line dropped into a half crouch, reaching for his gun—

Henry moved the blaster half an inch, stared into the other's eyes; the man straightened slowly, raised his hands clear of his sides.

Henry motioned toward the table; his glance darted aside to take in the men at the bar; they hunched over their drinks, unaware of the byplay.

"What's the game, grandpa?" the redhead grated softly.

Henry motioned again, his eyes on the redhead's face. The other's pale eyes narrowed under bushy auburn brows.

"You tired of being alive—" he started. His expression flickered suddenly.

"Hoad!" he snapped. The man behind him moved up cautiously, stared into Henry's face.

"Ever seen him before?"

"Naw, I—" Hoad stopped. He gaped at Henry. "Jee-zus . . ."

"Uh-huh," the redhead said. "O.K., pop; I guess maybe you might use the iron after all . . ." He backed slowly, his men behind him. Carefully, they resumed their seats. Henry watched them, the gun resting on the table, aimed steadily at the redhead's chest.

From his table, Henry had a good view of both the front door and the four men at the table. Slow minutes ticked past. The men muttered together. The man called Hoad rose, came carefully up to Henry, his eyes on the blaster. His tongue darted out, touched his upper lip.

"Listen," he said. He had a small, hoarse voice, like a man who had been choked too hard once. "Rusty says—he wants to make a deal . . ."

Henry looked at him with his one eye.

Hoad went on. "The deal is—a trade. You got something we want, see? And we got something you want . . ."

Henry sat in the shadowy booth, the gun butt against the table, the sights centered on Hoad's chest. Silently he waited.

"You give Rusty the tabs—and you get her back— all in one piece."

Henry's eye seemed to glitter under his shaggy gray brows.

"We got her, all right," Hoad said. He edged back from the table, eyes on Henry. "Look, I'm just delivering the message, see? I ain't the one . . ." He fumbled in his pocket, brought out a small object folded in a twist of grimy paper. He peeled the paper away, held up a large violet stone in a cage of gold wire, swinging from a delicate golden chain.

"Rusty says you'll know when you see this."

Light glinted from the swinging stone. It was a forty-karat amethyst, flawless, polished in its natural shape. Henry had seen it last on Dulcia's throat.

He stood, pushed out from the booth. Hoad licked his lip again. "So you don't want to try nothing, or—"

Henry slammed the gun barrel down across the man's collarbone; he stumbled back with a shrill yelp, fell on his back. Henry swung his foot, booted him hard in the ribs. Hoad rolled to hands and knees, scuttled under a table. The men at the bar were turning now, mouths open. Henry walked toward the table where Rusty and his two men waited. The big redhead rose, took a step toward Henry, hooked his thumbs in his belt, waiting boldly. The other two crouched back, watching the gun.

"Easy now, pop," Rusty growled softly. He took a step back as the gun moved up to within five feet of him. "We got the girl—you know that. You better play ball, hah?"

Henry stepped around the table, stood covering the door and the men at the bar.

"Put the gun up," Rusty said. "You ain't going to use it now, pop. Just lay it on the table over there, and come on with me; I'll take you to the girl." He watched Henry, his eyes narrowed. Henry stood unmoving, the gun trained on the other.

"For Chrissake, say something," Rusty grated. "You ain't going to get the kid killed, just for those lousy tabs . . ."

Henry moved suddenly; Rusty started, jerked his hands high. "Hold on, damn you—"

Henry threw the gun on the floor, turned and walked toward the door. There were quick muttered words behind him. Rusty pushed past him. The blaster was in Rusty's hand now. He was grinning as he pulled the door open; he motioned with the gun.

"For a minute there, grandpa, I thought you'd popped your hatch. Now let's go see a man that's got things to say to you . . ." Rusty's glance went to the men at the bar, watching, open-mouthed.

"You boobs didn't see nothing," Rusty grated. "That makes you lucky, get me?"

Henry followed the redhead out into the street, into a dusty old-model Turbocad. It started up and wheeled off toward the lights of the tall towers beyond the port.

As it rounded the corner, Henry caught a glimpse of Bartholomew's tall figure standing on the curb, staring after it.

It was a dowdy copter hotel, with rooms strung like cardboard beads on the undersized trusswork of the open-bar frame. They went in by a side door between overflowing refuse bins, rode a noisy lift to the tenth level, walked along a slanting floor to a door before which two undesirables in loud clothes of cheap cut lounged, busy with toothpicks. Their eyes darted over Henry. Rusty pushed between them, shouldered the door open. His hand was near his hip.

"I got my eye on you, pops," he said softly. "So don't get any ideas!" It was a floridly decorated room. Polarized panels let purplish light in on high-gloss woven plastic rugs which stretched to walls hung with hand-painted color-reversal scenes of night life on exotic worlds. Shaded lamps glowed in each corner. In a high-backed contour chair done in yellow plush, Senator Bartholomew sat, buttoned into a tight business suit of conservative cut.

He glanced briefly at Henry; his mouth went down at the corners, opened—

His glance went back to Henry; his eyes widened. Behind Henry Rusty chuckled. "I told you Tasker didn't sell out—he was cut out," he said. "Some time I'd like to hear pops here tell me how he pulled it off."

"Where . . ." Bartholomew's eyes went past Henry. He clamped his mouth, gripped the arms of the chair. His jowls were pale. "Where's my boy . . . ?" he said hoarsely.

"Pops was alone," Rusty said.

Bartholomew looked at Henry, reluctantly.

"Where is he . . . ?" His voice was thin, stretched.

"Pops don't talk much," Rusty said. "Maybe he needs some encouragement . . ." He moved to Henry's side.

"No!" Bartholomew put up his hands.

"He'll talk." His eyes held on Henry's face now. "Where's Larry? He's done you no harm. Give me my boy and . . ." he swallowed. "I'll see that you're well repaid for your efforts."

"I told him we got the girl," Rusty put in. Bartholomew's face dropped into a slack mask of dismay—then tightened into fury.

"You . . . blundering idiot!"

Rusty swaggered over to the chair, looked down on the red-faced Senator.

"You may be Mr. Big back on Elderberry or wherever it is—but here, I'm the one that draws the water. Sure, I mentioned the kid. I had to." He barked a short laugh. "The old man had a blaster on me."

Bartholomew came out of his chair. "Where's my boy?" he demanded. He took out a scented tissue, wiped at his forehead. He looked from Henry to the redhead. "I have to know! Where is he?"

"Cool it, Senator. I can find out—but not by giving him lollipops."

"All right. Do—whatever you have to do." Bartholomew sank bank into the chair, his eyes on Henry.

"You heard him, granddad . . ." Rusty's eyes were narrowed. "I don't like to pick on cripples, but business is business . . ."

"If you want to see the girl again—alive—you'd better speak up," Bartholomew blurted.

"Shut up, Senator," Rusty snarled. "Sometimes you give me the feeling I'm in a dirty racket." He faced Henry, scowling. "The Senator knows all about your corundum mine; you've been feeding a few nice stones into the market every year, just enough to get by on. He checked you out, found out where you'd been; he narrowed the mine down to Corazon. Then he foxed you into making the Run. He's put time and money into this deal—and he wants his payoff. You can see that, pops. So give. Where's your tabs—"

"Never mind the tabs—for now," Bartholomew cut in. "My boy—"

"You sent a guy to the Registry Office," the redhead went on. "He didn't make it—"

"He sent a man? That might be Larry—"

"Naw—this guy was a bruiser. He caught wise and smeared two of the boys and got clear—but he didn't register no tabs. Probably some timber bum that pops here met up with and worked out a split."

"Split? I'll split him—" Bartholomew pushed up to Henry. "I see it now—why you demanded that the proceeds be divided between you and—Larry. You killed him—and now you think you can steal it all—"

Rusty elbowed the Senator aside. "You get too excited, Senator. Go sit down. This is business." He sighed, looking at Henry. "Better give, old-timer. Where do you and your sidekick meet? Where's the mine located at? And just by the way, where's the Senator's kid?"

"Why doesn't he talk?" Bartholomew screeched. "Why doesn't he say anything . . . ?"

"Maybe you make him nervous," Rusty snapped.

"I'll kill the girl!" Bartholomew snarled. "I swear I'll kill her—"

"Hold onto your hairpiece, Senator! Maybe this guy didn't kill your kid; maybe he's just got a natural yen to hold on to the marbles; after all, he found 'em—"

"If Larry's dead, I'll kill her!" Bartholomew pointed to a thin man standing quietly near the wall. "Bring her in; I'll show him I mean what I say—"

The thin man went through a connecting door; half

a minute later he pushed Dulcia into the room. Her hands were trussed together with a wide strap; her mouth was gagged. She stared at Bartholomew, then at Henry. Tears started, ran down her face.

There was a sound beyond the hall door. A brief *whap! whap!* Then a heavy fall. Rusty's hand darted to his hip, whipped out a 2mm needler. He plunged for the door—

Henry took a quick step, thrust out a foot, hooked the redhead's ankle, chopped hard at the back of his neck as he went down. Across the room, the thin man yelled, jumped clear of Dulcia, reaching—

She spiked his foot with a heel, threw herself at him; they went down together. As Henry turned, Bartholomew dived for a desk, snatched up a gun, whirled—

The door slammed wide. Larry Bartholomew stood in the entry, a power gun in his hand. The thin man flung clear of Dulcia, brought up a gun—

Larry fired, knocked the thin man flat; he whirled on the Senator—and stood, frozen, staring at his father.

The gun in the Senator's hand jumped, a flat bark echoing in the room. Larry spun sideways, fell against the wall, blood spattering behind him. He went down on his face; his breath went out in a long sigh.

"Stand where you are," the Senator said in a high, thin voice. "You saw how I shot that man. I'll kill both of you if I have to. Now answer when I speak, or—"

A gun cracked beyond the door. Bartholomew tossed the gun from him, looking startled. His expression changed, became blank. He leaned forward, fell over the yellow chair, slammed the floor.

Heavy Joe Saggio eased his bulk through the doorway, stood, smiling gently around the room. His eyes

fell on Henry; he stared. The smile faded. The thick
tongue came out, touched his lips.

"Enrico, baby. I heard you had a tough time." From
behind him, a small man in a tight jacket and a yachting
cap sidled into the room, looked around.

"This is the kind of hotel I like," he said in a thin
nasal. "Nobody sticks their nose in, just because maybe
they hear guns working."

Henry went past him, knelt at Larry's side, turned
him over. There was a scorched furrow across the side
of his chest. His breathing was shallow, noisy. Unseen,
Henry slipped a hand into Larry's breast pocket,
removed the red marker tabs.

"The kid bad?" Saggio stood behind Henry, looking
down at young Bartholomew. Henry rose, shook his
head, went to Dulcia, raised her, pulled the gag from
her mouth.

"Oh, Grandpa . . ." She smiled, crying. He fumbled
out a knife with his stiff fingers, cut the strap from
her hands. She threw her arms around him.

"We . . . thought you were dead . . . It was so long . . .
and then Mr. Bartholomew invited me to come with
him . . . to try to find you . . ."

On the floor, the thin man sat up, whining. Saggio
jerked his head at the man in the cap.

"Take care of these bums, Johnny—and get a medic
up here for the kid."

"Listen," the thin man gasped. "I know plenty, see?
You want to get me a doc, treat me right. This old guy's
got this mine—the Senator knew about it—"

Saggio stood by Henry. "I din't have nothing to do
with it, Enrico—you know I don't play them games . . ."

"Listen . . . !" The thin man was babbling, fighting
as the small man tugged at him. "It's a corundum mine,
you got to listen! Stones like pigeon eggs! He knows
where it is, I swear—"

"What's he talking?" Saggio stepped to the thin man, slammed a blow to the side of his head. The man went limp.

"Dump him in the alley. He's delirious. Then get that medic up here quick." Saggio looked at Dulcia, showed a gold-toothed smile, bowed.

"I heard about the young lady, Enrico—but I don't know she's your grandbaby. Otherwise, I fix these bums a long time ago."

"Grandpa—is Larry—did he . . . die out there . . ."

Henry nodded toward the tall, solidly built man lying on the floor. Dulcia's eyes went to him. She gasped, darted to his side.

"Larry! Oh, Larry . . . Grandpa—will he be all right?"

Henry nodded. Saggio caught his eye. "The little lady's all right now, Enrico. I get the doc here in a minute for the boy. I guess maybe you got business now, hey?" His eye went to the empty holster at Henry's side. He stooped, picked up the gun Larry had dropped, handed it to Henry.

"Maybe you need this, hah?"

Henry holstered the gun. Dulcia looked up.

"Grandpa—where are you going . . . ?"

"It's O.K.—your grandpapa, he's got a problem to settle," Saggio nodded to Henry. "I'll see she's O K."

Henry nodded. Saggio smiled, his eyes cool.

"I see you in a little while, Enrico baby . . ."

Henry stepped out into early-evening light, looked up and down the gaudy street, spotted a glare panel indicating a bar. Inside, he nodded toward a bottle on the back bar, took it and a glass to the table.

He poured a drink, swallowed it, then looked at the half-stiff fingers of his right hand. He flexed them; they were like rusted metal. He gripped the pistol butt, straining to fit his fingers to the contours. It was like picking up an ice block with paper tongs.

He shoved the pistol back into the holster, had a second drink. Then he rose, went out into the light-strung street, walked slowly west along the plastic boardwalk toward the square.

The wide plaza was empty, bleak under the polyarcs of the port, an arena ringed by the dark mouths of deserted streets. The harsh squares of light that were the windows of the Registry Office threw pale rectangles across the oily pavement. A block away, music thumped and screeched, voices rang; here in the deserted square it was silent.

Henry moved out from the wall. Across the square, a large shadow stirred. Heavy Joe Saggio stepped into view, a wide pistol belt strapped across his chest, sagging with the weight of the heavy blaster under his arm.

"I guess we're square now, hey Enrico?" he called softly. "You let me go one time; I help you out just now . . . It's nice like this: Just you and me—like the old days . . ."

Henry walked steadily toward the lighted door, halfway down the side of the plaza.

"That kid, your compadre; he's O.K.; he was talking soft words with the little lady when I go; it's a nice couple, Enrico; you should be proud."

It was a hundred feet to the office door. Henry walked slowly, not favoring the knee.

"It was a kick, seeing you here last fall, Enrico; I'm getting dumb in my old age, I didn't figure you had an angle. Corundum hey, Enrico? Nice, those gem-stones. I got a real fondness for them. They're nice to look at, hah? Not like dirty money . . ."

Saggio came toward him, moving heavily—a big, thick-set, powerful man, getting old now, but never soft . . .

He stopped, fifty feet away, facing Henry. Henry saw his tongue touch his lower lip, the glint of the gold tooth.

"You put up a good fight, Enrico. You make a monkey out of Tasker, I hear. That's good. I never like that guy. And you make a great hike back. It's a story I tell my grandchildren—only someplace I forget to have some . . ."

Henry came on; somewhere a night lizard called monotonously.

"Look, Enrico—you make a split, now, hey? It's plenty for all, I hear. You got a right—but what about me? I win a share on points, hey?"

They were thirty feet apart now. Saggio's eyes narrowed. His shoulders tightened.

"That's far enough now, Enrico," he growled. "You don't talk much, baby—that's O.K. But you don't go through that door before you give me an answer. And I tell you, Enrico; the next word I speak will be the big one, and the last one . . ." Saggio's hand edged toward the shoulder holster, fingers curled—

Henry stopped and spread his legs, braced to draw—

"Captain!"

Henry whirled. Behind him, coming at him from the opposite side of the square, was Larry Bartholomew, a white gleaming swathe of bandage under his open jacket, his hands held out from his sides. Light glinted from the polished butt of a power pistol at his hip.

"Back off, Captain!" he shouted at Henry. "Back off the way you came—"

Henry glanced over his shoulder at Saggio. Saggio's hand darted toward his gun. Henry was caught between them. He drove his stiff hand for his own gun, glancing back at Larry. Drawing as he ran, Larry was running to his right. Saggio's gun coughed and the shot went

wide of Henry, toward Larry. Larry stopped; his gun
was out; he stood, a hand on his hip, sighting down
the barrel at seventy yards. Saggio's gun snarled again.
Larry's pistol jumped, racketed. Saggio leaped back,
tumbled down, his gun clattering away; he coiled,
grinding his face into the pavement; then the big body
went slack.

Chapter Nine

The sun was warm on Henry's face. Dulcia sat
beside him on the pool edge, brushing her long pale
gold hair. Behind her, the sunlight sparkled in the
varicolored spray of the fountain.

"I'm so pleased about your hand, Grandpa," she said.
"Dr. Spangler said it's almost well now. Please let him
do your knee . . ."

Henry shook his head. Dulcia laughed.

"You don't have to make signs, Grandpa! Your voice
is as good as new."

"Waste of money," Henry said gruffly. "Wants to graft
an eye, too. What for? I can see all the foolishness I
want to with this one."

"Please don't be that way, Grandpa. You should be
so proud! No one else could have done what you did—
a whole new universe opened up! Admiral Hayle said
in his letter it was the greatest discovery of the millennium. They promoted you to Commodore—"

"Posthumous promotion," Henry growled. "And I
didn't do it. Larry—"

"I'd rather we didn't talk about Larry," Dulcia said
shortly. She tossed the brush aside, picked up a colored pebble from the poolside, stared into it.

"Where the devil is the boy?" Henry said. "Hardly seen him since we got back."

"Making more deals, I suppose! You should have seen him when we landed. Some of those terrible men who worked for his father were there; the big ones—Councilman Hogger—came up and started to say something about how they'd been the Senator's best friends. I wanted to tell him he ought to be ashamed to admit it. I thought Larry would tell them to stay away from him, that he wanted nothing to do with all that crooked political dealing—but do you know what he did?" Dulcia stared at Henry indignantly. "He started shaking hands and telling them how glad he was to be back in time for the big campaign, and that he had ideas for the Galactic Council nominee . . ."

"Can't blame the boy; politics is all he knows . . ."

"He ought to know a lot more now! He spent nearly a year with you on Corazon, Grandpa. And he saw what his father was really like . . ."

"Can't ask a man to turn against his father—no matter what, Dulcie-girl."

Across the lawn, the porter chimed. Dulcia looked up. Larry Bartholomew stood in the doorway, tall, solid, his hair neatly trimmed, a smile on his regular features; he was dressed in the latest mode, and the tiny broken veins just under the skin over his cheekbones from frostbite gave him a look of ruddy health. He carried a box in his hand.

He came across the lawn, shook Henry's hand, turned to the girl.

"Dulcia, I want to apologize for my neglect these last few weeks; I've been tied up—"

"I know. Politics," Dulcia said shortly.

Larry extended the legs of a small portable Tri-D, set it up in front of Henry. "The election results are coming in," he said. "I wanted to be sure you—"

Dulcia jumped up. "You know what Grandpa thinks of your Statistical Average! No, Larry! I've kept all that away from him! I don't want him upset!"

"But the delegates are on the final roll call now, Dulcia! This is an important moment; Aldorado's first Galactic Delegate—"

"I don't care about that! It's peaceful here—"

"It's all right," Henry cut in, almost gently. "We can't stay shut away forever, girl. Turn it on, Larry."

"Thank you, Captain." Bartholomew twiddled the control. A voice boomed:

" . . . candidate of the new Statistical Excellence party which Lawrence Bartholomew, son of the late Senator . . ." Larry tuned it down.

"It's been a hectic seven weeks, Captain," Larry said. "I arrived in the nick of time. My father's organization had been holding off their big push, waiting for his return. I jumped in and started spending money where it would do the most good the quickest."

Dulcia stared at Bartholomew. "You ought to be ashamed to admit you used your money to influence the voting!"

"Why? That's the system, after all. I learned that from your great-granddad; there's no point in waving flags; if you believe in something, go get it—any way you have to."

Dulcia threw the bright stone down, walked away.

"Dulcia—" Larry started after her.

"Let her go," Henry said. "Let's hear what's going on."

Bartholomew turned the volume up. On the small screen, a wide-mouthed man in an artificial-looking hairdo blared on:

" . . . slate of pledged delegates from their sector. And now the weight of the entire northern tier will be thrown behind the Statex candidate! It's an

astonishing last-minute upset, a tribute to the orga-
nizational powers and crusading zeal of young Bartholomew! Now here's the vote from the Seaboard
delegate, and yes! It's a bolt to the Statex standard!
The delegates are crowding down now, all eager to
get on the Statex bandwagon . . ."

Music blared up, drowning the shouting voice.
Bartholomew tuned to another channel:

" . . . and it is now conceded by all dopesters that
the Statex slate has taken the election by a rapidly
widening margin, as delegation after delegation goes
over to make this a landslide victory for the dark-horse
candidate . . ."

"And yes, here it is! Provincial Chairman Crodfoller
has conceded to Lawrence Bartholomew, the Statex
candidate, and the crowd here at election headquarters is going mad with enthusiasm. Aldorado has a
Delegate to the Galactic Council! And—hold everything, folks!"

There was a new tumult off-microphone.

"Listen, everyone!" the announcer's voice came back,
babbling with excitement. "A flash, just in—Mark
Hanforth, Chairman of the Galactic Council, now
meeting on Terra, has just proposed a further honor
for Aldorado. Speaking before the Council, just this past
hour, he said, in part, '. . . it is fitting that we take this
moment in which a new world is represented on this
Council to repay a debt long owed by the whole human
race to a resident of that new world. I refer, Council
Members, to Commodore Henry of Aldorado, who in
my opinion earned the title and honors of Citizen of
the Race, several generations ago—but who found it
necessary to discover even newer worlds for the
human race to conquer, before we laggards were
reminded of the need to honor him.

" '. . . I propose, therefore, that without delay, and

at the same time as the new Delegate from Aldorado is invested with his rank and accorded the Aeterna treatment—the prerequisite of that rank—that the treatment also be accorded to Commodore Henry, as his long-overdue wages for a long lifetime already devoted to the future of the human race . . .' "

The announcer babbled on. But the door of the house burst open and Dulcia came running, her face alight with joy, sparkling with tears. She threw herself at the old man.

"Grandpa! Did you hear? Now you'll get the Aeterna treatment and . . . and . . ." She looked toward Larry. "Larry! Why didn't you say something? You must have known something like this was in the wind! The Council President's an Expansionist, just like your new Statex party is—"

"Knew!" grunted Henry, staring over her head at Larry. "He must have been the one to arrange it—weren't you, boy? Hanforth wouldn't make a move like this just at this moment without some reason!"

Dulcia turned to stare at Larry, who laughed with a rough touch of embarrassment.

"Politics, Dulcie," he admitted. "The Expansionist and Conservative sides of the Council table are tied even. The new delegate from Aldorado was bound to break the tie. I just mentioned something about the Captain—"

"As the price of your party's alignment!" grunted Henry. "Very neat. Did you ever think of asking me if I wanted to be one of their Citizens of the Race?"

Larry looked squarely at him.

"Captain," he said, "I don't give a damn if you wanted it or not. I wasn't much good for anything until you took me on the Run; and the Run made a man out of me. But being with you on Corazon did more than just that. It shook me up and let me see things squarely for the first time in my life—and not just things about myself, but about you as well."

"Me?" growled Henry, shoving himself up from his chair.

"Sit down," said Larry, levelly. "And listen to me for a change. You can cut a rough, whitish stone into a diamond that will knock your eye out—but it has to have been a diamond to start off with. All right, I needed to be cut to shine the way I should—but I never was a diamond, Captain. Maybe a passable emerald, but that's it. I'm a politician—maybe, with luck and Dulcie's help a great one, one day—but I never was a Captain Henry!"

"What makes you think—" snapped Henry.

"I said, shut up and listen," Larry said evenly. "When I'm through you can say anything you want. I'm telling you—there's only one Captain Henry. I didn't get you the Aeterna treatment for yourself! I did it for me—for Dulcie—for all of us. You remember that poem of Kipling's about the explorer? The one you quoted, that night we went through the portal on Corazon? Well, do you remember one of the verses to it—one that goes:

> . . . *Well I know who'll take the credit—all*
> *the clever chaps that followed—*
> *Came, a dozen men together—never knew*
> *my desert fears;*
> *Tracked me by the camps I'd quitted, used*
> *the waterholes I'd hollowed.*
> *They'll go back and do the talking. They'll*
> *be called the Pioneers! . . .*

" . . . that's you, Captain!" said Larry. "There's hundreds and thousands of good men who can come . . . 'a dozen men together' . . . and follow up where you've blazed the trail. But there's only one man who can blaze that trail. That's you—and by God, the human race needs you!"

Larry took a deep breath.

"I told you once, Captain, that you'd never die," he said. "And you never will, if I have anything to say about it. If you don't want to take the Aeterna treatment, I'll help hold you down myself while they stick the first needle in. Because we're not going to lose you while I have anything to say about it—and that's final!"

He swung about to the girl.

"Come on, Dulcie!" he said. "Let's leave him a while and give him time to let some common sense soak into that diamond-hard head of his!"

He turned on his heel and left. Dulcie jumped up and ran after him.

"Dulcie!" roared Henry, in outrage at her abandonment of him at the command of this brash young man. Still roaring, he heaved himself heavily to his feet— but they were already disappearing into the house. He was alone by the pool.

Snorting, he fell back into his chair.

"Hold *me* down!" he growled in white-hot fury. "Why . . ."

He stopped. Slowly, the picture he must have made blowing and roaring in protest like an overage walrus, began to grow inside him. Gradually the humor of it kindled in him, and after a long moment he threw his head back and began to laugh.

The laughter washed him clean inside. He sobered at last. Of course the young squirt was right. He'd be the worst possible sort of pouting idiot to turn down a chance at unlimited life and all the exploration that a man could dream of doing. Henry laughed—softly this time.

Hayle had made him a Commodore. Well, he'd take him up on that. He'd have a deep-space scout carted through the portal, piece by piece—and reassembled— and he'd see what lay beyond those farther stars.

He stooped, picked up the bit of colored stone Dulcia had tossed aside. It was twelve-karat amethyst of a flawless pale violet. He dropped it into the pool, watched it sink down to nestle among its brilliant fellows, stirring and sparkling in the natural spring which had washed them up from the corundum deposit far below.

Colored stones. Men had died for them, too. And on the far worlds, what unknown treasures might not be waiting . . .

If only Dulcia could have been here. But a man couldn't have everything. Life was compounded of equal parts of joy and sorrow; the trick was to savor the one while you had it—and not let the other make you forget that once life had been good—and could be good again.

Henry stood, looking down into the water, while the setting sun painted the sky in the colors of jewels.